AN
EROTIC
ADVENTURE
NOVEL

BOOK THREE IN THE BLACK WIDOW TRAINER SERIES

HANGING
BY A
THREAD

CRAIG
ODANOVICH

LIVE OAK
BOOK COMPANY

Published by Live Oak Book Company
Austin, TX
www.liveoakbookcompany.com

Distributed by Live Oak Book Company

For ordering information or special discounts for bulk purchases, please contact Live Oak Book Company at PO Box 91869, Austin, TX 78709, 512.891.6100.

Design and composition by Greenleaf Book Group LLC
Cover design by Greenleaf Book Group LLC

Cataloging-in-Publication data
(Prepared by The Donohue Group, Inc.)
Odanovich, Craig.
  Hanging by a thread / Craig Odanovich. -- 1st ed.
   p. ; cm. -- (Black Widow Trainer series ; bk. 3)
  "An erotic adventure novel."
  Issued also as an ebook.
  ISBN: 978-1-936909-36-0

  1. Women personal trainers--Fiction. 2. Escort services--Fiction. 3. Sex customs--Fiction. 4. Erotic stories, American. I. Title.
PS3615.D36 H26 2012
813/.6   2012932044

Print ISBN: 978-1-936909-36-0
eBook ISBN: 978-1-936909-37-7

First Edition

1

HUNT FOR THE *DIRTY PIRATES*

Misty peered out the back window of the limo as Thor frantically zoomed down the narrow, winding coastal road. "There's an opening, Thor," she yelled. "Pull in over there!"

Thor turned onto the bumpy, dirt road, the thick underbrush scraping the bottom of their vehicle. When the car came to a sliding stop, Misty flung her door open and fought her way through the dust cloud to the water's edge. She climbed to the top of a rocky outcrop and peered out. The Rio de la Plata was the widest river known to man and the causeway to Buenos Aires from the Atlantic Ocean. Misty motioned for Thor to kill the engine so she could use both sight and sound to help her locate her Alaskan companions.

"Who or what are we looking for?" Thor asked when he reached her.

"Ghosts for all I know," Misty said. "I could swear I saw a familiar boat from the balcony of the cottage. A boat I last saw leaving Resurrection Bay."

"Where's Resurrection Bay?"

"Sorry, it's in Alaska."

"What's the name of the boat, just in case I spot it later?"

She grinned. "'Dirty Pirates,' appropriately named after its captain and his running mate."

Thor looked puzzled, so Misty explained. "Captain Kev and Miniature Mike are two of the more colorful characters I've met on my adventures, and I'm sure they're not the last. Are you sure you still want to be my bodyguard?"

"I'm your man!" Thor said. "I'm up for anything."

The old diesel engine strained as it navigated up the river toward Buenos Aires. As the boat came into view, Misty could tell that it was, indeed, the *Dirty Pirates*.

"Let's go!" she said. "I want to be there when they find a place to dock."

For over an hour they followed along as the boat made its way up the river. Finally, it set course for shore. Misty and Thor waited for them in an old, abandoned marina. Misty smiled when she first heard Captain Kev barking out instructions. "What's taking you so long, Mikey? Get over here and grab some rope. I told you not to stay up all night."

Mikey slammed his left hand over his bicep as he raised his right arm, giving the captain the "up yours" sign. Captain Kev broke out laughing. Mikey secured a ramp to the dock below and walked away.

"Permission to come aboard, Captain!" Misty shouted.

Mikey jerked his head around and stared at Misty as if he couldn't believe his eyes.

"Well, I'll be damned!" bellowed the captain. What in the hell are you doing in Buenos Aires, Sweetie?"

"I live here, Capitan," Misty said as she and Thor walked up the ramp. The question is, what are you doing in Buenos Aires?"

The captain scratched his chin with his prosthetic right forearm as he always did when trying not to tell the entire truth. "Oh, we're only here for a short stay, and then we'll be on our way." Then something occurred to him. "Hey, when we left Seward, Alaska, in the early dawn, didn't you say we should think about coming to Buenos Aires, since that's where the old Nazis hid out after World War II?"

Mikey interrupted the conversation by running up and giving Misty a big hug. At only four foot eight inches, he was eye level with her breast, which is where he planted his face. Misty was so happy to see him that she ignored his brashness. After the hug, he looked up at her with puppy dog eyes, and she patted his head.

She pinched Mikey's cheek. "You're a weird one, little fella." Mikey grinned profusely.

"Who's that good-looking young man standing behind you?" the captain asked.

"Oh, where are my manners?" Misty gestured toward Thor. "This is Thor, my new bodyguard in training."

"What happened to Migs? I really liked that guy."

"Long story, Captain. Miguel was stabbed while we were in New York."

She could see the look of concern in Mikey's eyes. Miguel had been like a big brother to him in Alaska.

Misty placed her hands on the sides of his face. "Not to worry, Mikey. Miguel came through it fine and is well on his way to recovery. But if he hasn't healed by the time I hire my next client, Thor might be taking his place."

Mikey walked over to Thor, raised his arms, and flexed his biceps. Thor looked at Misty dumbfounded.

"Show him your biceps, Thor."

Thor gave her a funny look but did as she requested. Unbuttoning his shirtsleeve, Thor pulled it back, exposing his full arm, and then flexed. Mikey's eyes opened at the sight of Thor's cantaloupe-sized biceps. Misty reevaluated her stance on bringing Thor with her on her next adventure.

Mikey patted his other bicep, so Thor pulled back the other sleeve and then raised both arms. Mikey reached up, placed a hand on each bicep, and began doing chin-ups. Thor stood there like a rock and shook his head.

Someone behind them said, "My, my, my. What a strapping young man!"

Misty turned around to see a woman emerging from the deck below. She had gorgeous, silky, jet-black hair that hung all the way down to the middle of her back. She glanced confidently at Misty. Lush eyebrows that seemed even darker than her hair framed her catlike greenish-blue eyes. The woman turned her head and set course for Thor. From her firm, protruding butt anchored by muscled thighs to her powerfully built arms, her body was exquisite in every way. Although she was clearly strong, she looked more like a finely honed athlete than a female weight lifter. Her movements were as smooth and agile as a gazelle. Her breasts lay heavy on her chest, an overflowing D cup, Misty presumed. Misty looked down at her own body and then back at the woman's. *Surely I can't be jealous!* she thought.

What troubled Misty more was that Mikey intercepted the woman and gave her a hug every bit as tight as the hug he had just given her.

"Hey there, Mikey. You've been doing some chin-ups, I see."

Mikey grinned when the woman patted his head, just as Misty had. The woman continued over to Thor until her face was inches from his. Her captivating eyes held him hostage.

"My, aren't you the strong one," she said.

Misty walked over to Thor's side and tapped the woman on the shoulder. When the woman whipped her head around, the two stood face-to-face.

The captain gulped and hurried over to the women. Mikey took a seat on a large crate and settled in for the show. "Uh, Misty. I would like to introduce you to Monique," said the captain. When neither responded, he added, "Monique, this is Misty." Misty extended her hand and Monique gripped it firmly. Each made the other aware of her full strength.

"What brings you to Buenos Aires?" Misty asked.

Captain Kev spoke up. "We met Monique in the Virgin Islands. She introduced us to a friend of hers who has a bar for sale. When we buy the bar, Monique is going to be our partner."

"I see," said Misty. "So you have money to invest, Monique?"

Monique moved next to Captain Kev and placed her arm on his shoulder.

"Well, no, she doesn't," said the captain. "But we're giving Monique a share of the bar, and in return we will get a share of the treasure.

Monique pinched Captain Kev in his side.

"It's okay, Misty is like family. It's not like I showed her the treasure map!"

"I'll go get the map so we can show Misty!" yelled Mikey.

"Why don't we just put it on the Internet for everyone to see, while we're at it?" Monique said. She walked over to Thor and patted him on his chest. "Of course, we could always use a strapping young man like Thor. I'll bet you would make a great digger."

Misty took Thor by the arm and pulled him away. Looking directly at Monique, she said, "If there's a gold digger on this boat, it's not Thor!"

They all turned to Mikey as he came back, waving a folded, wrinkled piece of paper.

"Put the map up, Mikey. Now is not the time," yelled Captain Kev.

Mikey gave Captain Kev a stare and then stormed off.

The treasure map had piqued Misty's interest, but she didn't want to give Monique the satisfaction of knowing. Instead she said, "So what are your plans, Captain?"

"Well, we need to find someplace to moor old *Dirty Pirates* while we're here."

"For how long?" Misty asked.

"Not sure. We need to find someone, but we don't know exactly where he lives. Could take some time, but if we get lucky, we'll be leaving soon."

Realizing how matter-of-fact that probably sounded to Misty, he walked over and put his arm around her. "Of course, I hope it takes a while, because I've missed you. We have a lot of catching up to do."

Misty smiled. "Hey," she said, "why don't you take your boat back down the river? My friend has an estate on a cliff overlooking the Atlantic. Not too far offshore is a tiny island. Actually, it's pretty much just a bunch of rocks, but you could moor your boat there and then row to shore."

The captain scratched his chin and said, "I like that idea. We won't draw much attention way out there."

Misty gave him a sly look. "So you're still running from the law?"

"Yep, and we're doing a pretty good job of staying a step ahead."

"Aren't you afraid they will find you if you buy a bar?"

"You're still smart as a whip, Misty. That's why we're here. Monique knows someone she thinks will agree to put the bar in his name for a piece of the action. He's a quiet guy. Likes to keep to himself."

"Probably why he's so hard to find," Misty said. "Well, that's your business anyway. Listen, why don't you head back out to sea? Look for me on a small peninsula where the river meets the Atlantic. I'll point in the direction of the rock island. You'll be able to see it from there with your binoculars."

Monique and Misty locked eyes one more time before Monique turned and walked away without saying good-bye. As she passed Mikey, she snapped her fingers and he followed her.

Misty turned to Captain Kev. "Nice gal you got there, Captain."

"Hey, hey. She's definitely on the rag today, but don't worry." He raised his infamous prosthetic right forearm and grinned. "She loves my attachments. I'll calm her down tonight."

Misty thought back to the night in Alaska that she had spent in Captain Kev's quarters while training him. Shaking her head she said teasingly, "You are just too much."

Misty motioned to Thor, and they headed out. The captain pulled up the fake eye patch he wore to get a good look at Misty as she walked down the plank. She was still as gorgeous as ever. He wished she and Monique could find common ground and get along, but deep down, he knew they had about as much chance of being friends as did two feral cats.

When she was out of sight, he yelled, "Get up here, Mikey! Time to shove off!"

* * *

When *Dirty Pirates* came into view, Misty pointed to the small rock island that lay a quarter mile off the rocky cliffs of Gabriella's estate. Now it was time to get back and apologize to Tom and Rosie for leaving their wedding in such a hurry.

Once on the road again, Misty said to Thor, "You're pretty quiet up there. Whatcha thinking about?"

"What? Oh, just what a crazy day this has been, I guess."

"Are you sure you weren't thinking about Monique?"

Thor blushed, "She is beautiful." He looked in the rearview mirror at Misty and added, "Almost as beautiful as you."

"Oh, buttering me up so I'll agree to take you on my next trip."

Thor grinned. "Did it work?"

"Compliments never hurt. So what else did you think about Monique?"

"That she is very, how would you say it in English, forward?"

Misty looked out her window. "I'd say that's putting it mildly." Misty thought about how long Captain Kev and Miniature Mike would be in Buenos Aires and how much exposure she would have to Monique. The thought was somewhat unsettling.

Upon arrival, Thor dropped Misty off and parked the limo. Misty raced to Tom and Rosie's cottage and then bounded up the stairs to the second-floor porch. She was relieved to find the wedding guests still there. The long strings of low-wattage light bulbs gave the porch a relaxed ambiance. She could hear the sound of waves crashing on the nearby shore and felt the soft ocean breeze sweep over her face. *What a perfect venue for a small wedding*, Misty thought.

"Misty! Where have you been?" Gabriella said as she walked up.

"I'm sorry. I know running off was very rude of me."

"What would cause you to do such a thing?"

"Remember when I was in Alaska training the sea captain?" Misty pointed out to the Atlantic Ocean. "Well, I was relatively certain I spotted them heading for the mouth of Rio de la Plata. Had I not followed when I did, I might never have found them."

Miguel tapped Misty on the shoulder from behind. "Was it really them?" he asked.

Misty laughed. "In all their glory. Captain Kev and Mikey haven't changed."

"When will I get to see them?"

"I imagine in the morning. They are going to moor *Dirty Pirates* to the outcropping of rocks just offshore. I bet they will wait until morning before coming ashore in their dinghy."

"We have plenty of room in the main house," Gabriella said. "I insist they stay with us."

As much as Misty would have loved to have them stay at the house, she thought about Monique and cringed. "I'm sure they are very comfortable on their boat, Gabriella, but you can always ask. You might want to get to know them better before you make up your mind."

Misty spent the next few hours visiting with Tom and Rosie before the newlyweds left for the private airport. Gabriella's Gulfstream was waiting to whisk them off to Isla de Margarita. The island lay just off the coast of Venezuela, a perfect getaway for their honeymoon. Once they had left, Misty settled into a chair next to Miguel, and the two reminisced about their trip to Alaska. During their conversation Misty noticed a face staring at her between the porch-railing slats. The mischievous grin was unmistakable. Misty poked Miguel with her elbow. "Well, I'll be damned," Miguel said.

Mikey sprang over the railing and looked around. Miguel walked over and rubbed the little guy's head the way he used to do in Alaska.

"It's good to see you, my little friend."

Mikey frowned.

"Okay, no more *little* jokes. It's good to see you, my good friend."

Mikey returned a big smile and gave Miguel a hug.

"So where's Captain Kev?" Misty asked.

Mikey pointed to the captain arriving through the door behind them. "Ahoy there! Permission to come aboard!" Captain Kev said as he walked through the main door to the porch.

"Permission granted!" Miguel yelled back.

Monique walked out from behind Captain Kev and surveyed everyone on the porch. Spotting Thor, she walked in his direction. Thor gave Misty a look as if to say, what now? Misty simply shrugged her shoulders and walked toward Captain Kev.

Reaching the captain at the same time as Misty, Gabriella said, "So this must be the infamous Captain Kev from Alaska?"

Gabriella reached out to offer her hand, only to pull it back when she realized he had a prosthetic forearm with an attachment on the end. The captain let out a loud laugh and gave Gabriella a hug.

"You must be the beautiful Gabriella," he said. "I'd say that was an understatement." Releasing her, he looked around. "This is quite the house you have, Madam."

"This is nothing, Captain. Wait until you see the main house," Misty said. "It's fit for a pirate!"

Using the apparatuses on the end of his forearm to scratch the side of his head, the captain replied, "Sounds like a castle."

Gabriella said to Misty, "Why don't you take our guests over there now?" Turning to Captain Kev she added, "Are you hungry? I can have my chef prepare some food."

"Some grub sounds mighty nice, ma'am. That row to shore left me starving."

"You rowed to shore? I assumed your dinghy would have a motor."

He held up his arm, showing Gabriella the attachment he slid the oar through. "Motor? No, ma'am. That's for sissies."

When the captain walked off to greet Miguel, Gabriella looked at Misty. "Mikey makes attachments for the captain's arm?"

Misty rolled her eyes. "Mikey makes the captain all sorts of attachments. I'll leave it at that."

Miguel noticed the stunning woman talking with Thor and joined them. "Are you going to introduce me to your friend?" he asked Thor.

Before Thor could answer, Monique introduced herself. She looked Miguel over as she asked, "And who are you?"

"Miguel. I'm Misty's bodyguard."

"Why on earth would Misty need a bodyguard?" she asked.

"Misty's the Black Widow Trainer," Thor volunteered.

"So, just what does that mean?" she asked.

"It's a long story," Miguel said. He made eye contact with Thor and frowned.

Monique smiled. "The captain says we will be around for a while. Maybe you can fill me in tomorrow."

"Maybe," Miguel replied.

* * *

After the wedding guests had gone, they all went over to Gabriella's mansion, where they sat poolside, getting to know each other over a meal of fish stew.

Gabriella studied Monique and then said, "You look Italian, honey."

"I'm half Italian, a quarter French, and a quarter Irish," Monique said.

Misty bristled. "I'm sure there is a story there. Why don't you tell us about your family tree?"

Monique gave Misty a curt look. "There's nothing exciting to tell on my Italian and Irish side, however my great-great-great-great-grand-father was a French pirate. They referred to them as buccaneers, to be exact."

Miguel and Thor perked up and moved their chairs closer to Monique. Emboldened, she boastfully began her story. "In 1720, Black Bart captured a fifty-two-gun warship that happened to be carrying the governor of Martinique. They hung the governor from the yardarm and then proceeded to throw the French buccaneers overboard." Monique paused for effect. "But one buccaneer caught Black Bart's attention with his wit and steady nerve. Pirating was a lonely business, so Black Bart kept the young Frenchman around to entertain him. It didn't take long for their captive to win over the entire crew with his jokes and tall tales. The pirates taught the young Frenchman everything they knew about pirating before eventually dropping him off on a tiny, uncharted island. They said it would be his initiation, and if he was still alive when they returned, he could become one of them. But the young man had other ideas. He worked night and day to build a small, seaworthy craft. When he finished, he set out in search of civilization. After making it to the island of St. John, he put his humor and wit to good use in the local bars, recruiting his own crew of pirates. After commandeering a frigate, he returned to the tiny island with his men and preyed on unsuspecting ships that wandered too far from the shipping lanes on their routes to the Americas from Europe. My grandfather, Jerry Le Boucher, was not particularly ruthless, so he agreed to release the sailors they took captive if they promised to tell horrendous tales of their time in captivity. He became infamously known as Jerry Le Butcher!"

Monique stopped to survey the group. Gabriella and Misty seemed skeptical, but Thor and Miguel hung on her every word.

"This is where the story gets interesting," Captain Kev said. "Tell them about the treasure map."

Miniature Mike placed an old, weathered scroll on a small table and everyone gathered around. Upon close inspection, the map seemed to be authentic. "Does it say where the treasure is buried?" Thor asked.

"We're working on that," the captain said. "It's written in riddles, and eighteenth-century French, so it may take us some time to figure it out."

"Are you going to live on that tiny island while searching for the gold?" Thor asked.

"We need a home base, so we're in the process of purchasing a bar on the island of St. Thomas. That way we can go on weekly excursions from time to time and not draw any attention."

Gabriella looked at Monique wearily and asked, "So why isn't your grandfather mentioned in the history books? I studied Caribbean pirates while working on an assignment in college, and I can't remember reading about a Jerry Le Butcher."

Monique spun around and looked directly at Gabriella. "Who knows?" she said. "Maybe he wasn't a pirate long enough."

"Finish your story, Monique," Thor said.

"The rumor is that he captured a Spanish ship heavily laden with gold bullion. He split a portion of it with his crew and buried the rest. Their plan was to go back to France and live off what they had until it was gone and then return for the rest. Unfortunately, some of his crew couldn't keep their mouths shut while drinking in the local pubs, and the story got out. When Jerry Le Butcher found out, he hid the map in his son's house and fled France, never to return. To this day, no one knows what became of him."

Mikey vigorously nodded his head.

Noticing how skeptical Misty looked, Monique asked, "So, Misty, I hear you are referred to as the Black Widow Trainer?"

Not wanting Thor to know the full meaning of her profession, Misty replied, "I'm a personal trainer, and I have clients all over the world. It's only a nickname."

"That's intriguing," Monique said. "Tell me more."

"It's a long story. Maybe some other time."

"When do you go on another assignment?" Monique prodded.

"Hopefully not for a while," Gabriella said.

"I just got home from an assignment, so it won't be for several months," Misty said.

"But how do you stay in such good shape when you are not working?" Monique asked.

"I keep it varied. In a few days I will start studying Brazilian jujitsu."

"I've always wanted to learn a martial art," Monique said, excitedly. "Would you mind if I attend the classes with you?"

Mikey, who was sitting next to Misty, tugged on her shirtsleeve and asked, "Can I come too? Can I? Can I?"

Misty patted him on the head and replied, "Sure, Mikey. You can attend." She looked to Monique. "It's a free country. You can come if you want."

"What about you, Miguel?" Monique asked.

Miguel shook his head. "Sorry. I'm still healing from my knife wound."

"Knife wound?" Monique asked and pulled up a chair next to Miguel. "Tell me all about how you got wounded."

Misty walked over to Gabriella and whispered in her ear, "I've had enough of her for tonight. I think I'll retire to my bedroom."

"I understand, dear," Gabriella said. "I'll see you in the morning."

2

JUJITSU MAMAS

Misty, Monique, and Mikey stood near the entrance to the modest gym in the Puerto Madro barrio, waiting for the jujitsu instructor to show up. Mikey's workout attire made him look as if he were wearing oversized pajamas. He teased the girls, maneuvering himself around them in what he thought was classic martial arts manner. Misty looked at Monique and rolled her eyes.

When Mikey wandered off, Monique asked, "Where does Mikey get his energy?"

"Not sure," Misty said. "He's one hyper dude."

Taking advantage of her time alone with Misty, Monique asked, "When are you going on your next training assignment?"

"It's looking like sometime in July. I'm working it out with my client right now."

"Who are you going to train?" Monique asked enthusiastically.

Before Misty had a chance to answer, Mikey crashed into Misty's legs and drove her to the mat. Misty placed her hands over her eyes and shook her head. *I should have known better than to take my eyes off him!* she thought.

While chasing Mikey around the gym, Misty heard a loud voice: "You are full of energy today. Excelente!"

The three gathered around their instructor, and he said, "My name is Carlos." Carlos gave a short bow to Misty, Monique, and Mikey as he said each of their names out loud. "Welcome, my American friends. As you know, the Brazilian form of jujitsu is a martial art, combat sport, and self-defense system. Misty, I believe you said you would like to concentrate more on the self-defense system. Is this correct?"

"That is correct."

"Self-defense?" Monique said. "Do you have to fight off your clients?"

Carlos turned to Misty, "What line of work are you in?"

Misty said, "How about I tell you at the end of our training sessions?"

"*Muy bien*. Let's get down to business, then. The moves I will teach you allow a smaller, weaker person to successfully defend against a bigger, stronger assailant by using leverage and proper technique. You will gain the upper hand with a series of joint-locks and chokeholds."

Carlos stopped to look across the room. When the girls turned around, they saw Mikey climbing a rope that hung from the rafters. Carlos gave Misty a queer look. She laughed. "Don't worry about Mikey. He's pretty much along for the ride."

"Then I will continue," Carlos said. "Stronger opponents' strengths come from their superior reach and powerful strikes. This is why our objective is to level the playing field by taking them down and grappling on the ground. From there you will learn how to gain the upper hand."

The girls nodded their approval, so Carlos said, "We have a lot of drilling to do over the next several weeks. Shall we begin?"

"Let's do," Misty said.

At dinner that night, Misty and Monique were the center of attention as they explained what they had learned. After they finished eating, the girls got up and gave some demonstrations. Miguel teased them while Thor sat back and imagined what it would be like on the road with Misty. Later that night Misty excused herself and headed for her bedroom. Monique caught up to her and asked, "Where are you going next, and who will you be training?"

Against her better judgment, Misty said, "I'm going to Las Vegas to train a casino owner."

Monique moved a little closer to Misty and asked, "So you're taking me with you, right?"

Misty frowned. "Take *you* with me? Why on earth would I do that?"

"Because Miguel says you have hundreds of potential clients that you will never have time to train. Teach me what to do, and I can train men you don't have time to train."

Misty vehemently shook her head, "Oh, no! I work alone. I can't risk someone screwing up and ruining my reputation."

"Ruin your reputation! I'm sure I could do just as good a job as you once I've been trained."

"What do you know about being a personal trainer?" Misty asked.

"I was a trainer in the Virgin Islands."

"Oh, yeah, what was the name of the club you worked at?"

Monique said sarcastically, "You think I'm lying, don't you?"

"Are you?"

Monique blurted out, "The Virgin Islands Health Club." She then quickly added, "But that was years ago, and the club is no longer open."

Misty was certain it was bullshit. "Sorry. I work alone."

Monique grabbed Misty by her arm as she started to walk away. Misty looked at Monique's hand on her arm and then stared into her eyes. Monique released her arm and said confidently, "I'll bet you'll change your mind in due time."

Misty watched Monique as she walked away and thought, *Apparently she doesn't understand who she is dealing with.*

3

WEEKS LATER

Mikey emerged from a small cave halfway up the cliff that Gabriella's mansion was built on. The climb was steep, but Mikey was up to the task. He inspected several small crevasses along the way until he found the perfect hiding place. Looking down at Captain Kev, he gave a thumbs-up.

The captain mumbled, "It's about time."

Mikey hammered metal rods into the rock wall above the cave entrance to anchor his block and tackle. He threaded the rope he had been carrying over his shoulder through the groves of the pulley. Without warning, he let the rope fall to the ground below, hitting the captain on his head.

"Damn it, Mikey. Give me some warning next time!" the captain yelled up as he rubbed his head.

Mikey shrugged his shoulders and grinned. The captain tied the rope to a heavy wooden chest while Mikey made his way back down the cliff. They both began hoisting the chest skyward. Once they had hoisted the chest up to the opening, the captain tied the rope to a jagged rock while Mikey made his way back up the cliff. Mikey swung the chest toward the cave entrance and motioned for Captain Kev to give him some slack until the chest of gold sat squarely on the ground. It took awhile for Mikey to scoot the treasure chest as deep into the cave as possible. After covering the entrance the best he could with brush, loose rocks, and debris, he made his way back down. Captain Kev patted Mikey on the back, and they rowed back to the *Dirty Pirates*.

* * *

It was the final day of training, and time for their long-awaited sparring session. Misty was impressed with the progress Monique had made and was concerned Monique might win. Monique moved into Misty's space until their faces were inches apart. Her face glistened with sweat from a fifteen-minute warm-up.

"You know I'm going to take you down," Monique said.

Misty laughed, "That will be the day."

Monique smiled, "We need to come up with a bet to make things interesting."

"We could bet ten thousand dollars, but I doubt you have that kind of money," Misty said.

"No, but I will after you teach me how to become a Black Widow Trainer. Here's my offer. If you win, I will never ask you to teach me how to become your protégé again. But if I win, you have to take me with you to Vegas and teach me the ropes."

Misty stared into Monique's eyes as she contemplated the proposal. Not wanting to show concern, she eventually replied, "You're on!"

"Senoritas, are you ready to spar?" Carlos asked as he walked into the gym. Feeling the tension in the room, he continued without delay. "Okay then, here are the rules. The first one with two takedowns wins. There is no time limit, so take your time and do your best. On the count of three, we will begin."

Carlos counted down, and Misty and Monique began circling each other, each looking for an opening. Monique made the first move, lunging at Misty, but Misty gracefully sidestepped, causing her to miss. Monique was frustrated, but she was too proud to show it. When Misty made her move, Monique deftly maneuvered behind her, wrapped her arms around Misty, and fell backward onto the ground. Misty found herself lying on her back on top of Monique. She tried to grapple, but Monique hooked her heels around Misty's thighs. Monique placed her in a chokehold and constricted her windpipe. Misty was on the verge of passing out when Carlos pulled Monique's arms from Misty's neck.

"Monique!" Carlos yelled. "You were using an air choke. That is a dangerous move. You could have damaged Misty's trachea!"

Monique pushed Misty aside and rose to her feet. "You never said anything about not using air chokes in the rules."

Carlos was too busy attending to Misty to immediately answer, but once he realized she was all right, he said, "Yes, you are technically correct. I will award you the takedown, but no more air chokes."

Monique shrugged her shoulders and replied, "Duly noted."

Misty stood up and looked Monique over. She had obviously underestimated her opponent's skill level, but she was determined not to let that happen again. Misty felt a calmness sweep over her, and it showed in her face. Sensing Misty's renewed strength, Monique took a step back.

"On the count of three," Carlos yelled.

The girls circled again in an effort to look for an opening. After several failed attempts, Misty grabbed Monique's legs, causing her to lose balance and fall to the floor. Misty placed her firmly in a side hold. She dug her right elbow into Monique's chest as she moved atop her. Misty stared into Monique's eyes as she moved her elbow to Monique's opposite shoulder and shifted her weight. She could see the pain in Monique's eyes as muscle ground against bone. Soon, Monique mouthed the word "surrender." Carlos pulled Misty up from behind so he could attend to Monique, but Monique pushed him aside and staggered to her feet, attempting to walk it off while rotating her shoulder in circles. After the pain subsided, she looked at Carlos and gave him a nod.

"Again, on the count of three," Carlos said.

Determined not to let Monique accompany her to Vegas, Misty rotated her neck to increase blood flow to her brain. Misty sensed apprehension in her opponent and decided to use it to her advantage. With lightning speed, Misty dove down, wrapped her arms around the back of Monique's ankles, and yanked Monique's feet into the air. Monique crashed backward onto the mat, causing the air to release from her lungs.

When she finally caught her breath, Misty was sitting on top of her with knees wedged firmly into her armpits. Misty had Monique immobilized, and Monique knew it. In no hurry for the kill, Misty sat atop Monique enjoying the moment.

After her futile attempts to struggle out of the hold, Monique snarled, "Go ahead, choke me and get it over with!"

Misty laughed, "Carlos said no more choking, so I guess I'll just have to be creative."

With a mischievous grin, Misty slid her hands beneath Monique's sports bra. She squeezed Monique's nipples hard between her thumbs and forefingers until Monique screamed out in pain. Misty released the pressure and said, "Had enough?"

Monique scrunched her nose and glared back at Misty.

Misty did not let up the second time until Monique slammed her hands into the mat several times, indicating submission. When Misty got off her and stood up, Monique rolled onto her side and began rubbing her breasts. Carlos stood there, dumbfounded.

Misty walked over and patted Carlos on the back and said, "Bet you've never seen that submission hold before," and walked away. Carlos reached down in an effort to help Monique up from the floor, but she pushed his hand away and rose to her feet on her own. Their eyes met briefly before she stormed out of the gym.

* * *

At dinner that night, Monique ate her meal in silence. Miguel inquired several times about how the match went, but neither girl gave a willing answer, so he changed the subject.

"I wish I could go with you to Vegas tomorrow, Misty." Miguel reached out and grabbed Thor playfully by his arm. "I think Thor is up for the task, though. He's learned everything Tom and I have thrown his way."

Tom and Thor were beaming with pride, making Misty feel good about her decision to take Thor with her. "I'm sure Thor will do just fine until you are well enough to relieve him, Miguel."

Monique pushed away from the table and said, "I'm going to retire to my room." When everyone at the table looked at Misty, she shrugged them off.

As dinner was wrapping up, Misty followed Gabriella into the kitchen and whispered into her ear, "How about a late-night swim?"

Gabriella gave her a big smile. "I'll let everyone know we're all going to bed early tonight because you are leaving in the morning. Shall we meet at eleven?"

Misty placed her hands on Gabriella's butt, pulled her close, and planted a long, slow kiss.

Gabriella was waiting for Misty in the pool when she got there. When she saw Gabriella's naked silhouette dancing in the light of the pool, Misty reached behind her head and tugged off her full-length cotton nightgown. She dropped it to her feet and stood there, giving Gabriella a full-frontal shot of her magnificent, naked body. Misty ran her hands through her long blonde hair and shook her head.

"Stop teasing and come to me, dear," Gabriella said in a serious tone.

Still in a playful mood, Misty cupped her plentiful breasts with her hands and bounced them gently up and down. "Is this what you desire?" she asked.

"Yes, damn it! Come to me, now!" Gabriella replied with a heavy voice.

Misty laughed and dove into the pool. Within seconds she was in Gabriella's arms. The women embraced, pressing their naked bodies together until they felt as one. Gabriella said softly as she stroked Misty's hair, "I'm having a hard time letting you go."

Up until now their relationship had been one of mutual respect, deep friendship, and an occasional night of sex. Misty wondered if Gabriella was hinting that she wanted more. She placed a hand on the side of Gabriella's face, looked into her eyes, and asked, "What are you saying?"

Gabriella looked back into Misty's eyes as she summoned her courage. "I'm so sorry, Misty. I know our agreement is for you to come and go as you please, with no strings attached. It's just that ... well ... I must have fallen in love with you."

Misty's heart swelled with emotions. Knowing how independent Gabriella was, she knew how difficult it must be for a woman so proud to be so forthcoming with her feelings. Misty found herself conflicted between her love for Gabriella and her love for her profession. Being the Black Widow Trainer protected Misty from having to commit to one person. Plus, she got to travel the world and experience all it had to offer.

Giving Gabriella a big hug, Misty said, "You know I love you, don't you? But living as your full-time partner could cause difficulties in the long run. You know we both love being with men."

Gabriella gave Misty a kiss and said, "I'm sorry if you thought I was asking you to give up what you love to stay with me. That was not my intention, dear. I just couldn't fight the urge to let you know how much I care for you is all." Gabriella laughed. "Yes, I still desire men and their penises and will use them to entertain myself while you are away."

"Then that is settled," Misty said, smiling.

Misty gazed at the woman she so admired, taking in her dark brown eyes, full lips, and her cute little button nose. She ran her hands over Gabriella's smooth, olive skin, stroking her arms and placing her hands delicately on her bosoms. Gabriella leaned her head on Misty's shoulder and kissed the nape of her neck. Misty moved her hands down Gabriella's backside, placing her ass firmly in her grip, digging her fingers into her firm buttocks with each kiss. Misty's breath grew heavy and her loins ached. Reflection of the water from the pool danced all around them, as the moonlit sky gave the night a sense of tranquility. The women's lips met, kissing softly at first but soon intensifying until they became ravenous. When Gabriella's hand found its way to Misty's vagina, she laid her head on Gabriella's shoulder and spread her legs apart, allowing Gabriella's fingers to penetrate her deeply. Craving more, Misty wrapped her arms around the back of Gabriella's neck and locked her ankles around the back of Gabriella's waist. Gabriella placed one hand on the small of Misty's back while circling Misty's swollen clitoris with the thumb of her other. As her pleasure intensified, Misty held Gabriella tight, moving her pelvis up and down in rhythm with Gabriella's hand movements.

"Oh, God!" Misty moaned. "Rub me harder, my love. I'm so close."

Gabriella's arm was tiring, so she switched hands and quickened her movements. Misty grabbed the back of Gabriella's neck and threw her head backward, looking to the sky as she exploded. When her body went limp, they released each other, and Misty sunk to the bottom of the pool.

When Misty surfaced, she found Gabriella sitting on the edge of the pool with her legs dangling in the water. Misty paddled over and positioned herself between Gabriella's legs, which Gabriella draped over her shoulders. Misty had mastered the art of the tongue since knowing Gabriella and had come to enjoy pleasuring her friend as much as being pleasured. As she worked dutifully, Misty reveled in the sound of her friend's soft moans to a backdrop of waves from the Atlantic crashing to the shore. As Gabriella came closer to orgasm, Misty moved her hands over Gabriella's breasts to lightly pinch her nipples.

After Gabriella came, the girls switched positions. Misty was intensely aroused from the excitement of pleasuring her friend. She leaned back on her elbows, breathing in the sweet smell of ocean air as a soft breeze swept sensuously over her body. It was then that Misty realized someone was watching them make love from a bedroom balcony. As the moon came out from behind a cloud, she could see Monique slumped in a chair with her feet on the railing in front of her.

A plethora of emotions swept over her. She wondered if she should stop, but she decided not to do anything that would ruin Gabriella's last night with her. Besides, she was close to coming, and why spoil a good orgasm? Misty found herself even more turned on. She mashed Gabriella's face deeper into her swollen clit. She then forcefully moved Gabriella's head up and down. Misty watched as Monique rolled her head from side to side. Watching Monique triggered her own powerful orgasm, and Misty grabbed Gabriella by the hair and wrapped her legs around the back of Gabriella's neck, while flailing her own head around like a rag doll. When the moment passed, Misty fell backward onto the surface surrounding the pool. Lying there, she watched Monique bring herself to a powerful climax. She realized Monique's body was every bit as beautiful as hers. She also admitted that Monique would be a very successful apprentice. Had Monique not been such a bitch, she might have seriously considered teaching her the tricks of the trade.

A loud boom broke the silence. *What was that? Some kind of aftershock?* Misty wondered. She turned her head in the direction of the Atlantic Ocean. The once dark sky was illuminated as brilliantly as a morning sunrise. Misty and Gabriella leaped to their feet and ran to the railing. A second explosion sent a fireball high into the night sky.

Misty looked at Gabriella in horror. "That was Captain Kev's boat!"

Gabriella pulled Misty to her and held her tight. "Go get some clothes on while I call the authorities."

Misty looked to the balcony as she was leaving and saw Monique holding her hands over her mouth, horrified. She realized that for once they shared something in common. Why did it have to be the horror of witnessing their good friend's boat going up in flames?

* * *

The next morning, everyone stood on the shoreline watching the armada of small boats scour the water for signs of survivors. It was obvious that they would have already found the captain and his little buddy if they were still alive.

"Damn," Miguel said. "I can't believe they are gone. I'm really going to miss those two."

Misty walked over and gave Miguel a hug. "I will too."

Misty noticed Monique walking away with her head down, and for the first time she felt compassion for her.

4

TIME TO MOVE ON

In reverence to their lost friends, Gabriella rented a boat, and they held the funeral at sea, close to where the *Dirty Pirates* had gone down. The girls had placed two large reefs of flowers in the water and watched them float away as the preacher said some kind things. Misty had postponed her departure several days, but now it was time to go. She stood on the driveway waiting for Tom and Thor to load their luggage into the limo.

Gabriella wrapped her arms around Misty and said, "I'm so sorry you have to leave with such a heavy heart, but getting away is the best thing for you right now. I'm certain Captain Kev and Mikey would expect you to move on with your life."

"I suppose you're right," Misty said with a heavy heart.

As Misty loaded her last bag into the car, she glanced up and saw that Monique was watching. She decided to go over and give her a hug, but before she could reach her, Miguel shouted, "Who the hell is that?"

A rusty old truck came zooming through the gates and screeched to a halt next to the limo. An older man with short grey hair sat in the middle with men wearing large sombreros on either side of him.

The two sombrero-wearing men exited the vehicle. They each had also wrapped blankets around themselves. "It's been awhile since I've seen someone wearing a serape."

"There's something familiar about these guys," Misty said.

Miniature Mike tipped the brim of his sombrero up enough for Misty to recognize him. His grin was wide as the fake handlebar mustache he was wearing. A prosthetic right forearm confirmed that the other man was Captain Kev. They had shoe polished their faces brown. Everyone ran over to give them hugs.

"You scared the hell out of us!" Misty said. "Do you realize we had a funeral for you?"

Captain Kev looked around suspiciously to ensure no one he didn't know was there and then said, "Yes, and we appreciated the effort. Mikey was touched by the two reefs of flowers."

"We'll be happy to pay for the funeral," Mikey said and tossed a gold coin to Gabriella.

"You found Sam!" Monique said and then ran over to talk to the man in the cab of the pickup truck.

"Who the hell is Sam?" Misty asked.

The captain rubbed the back of his neck and said, "You know, the guy we told you we were here to locate. The one that's going to cover for us by putting the bar in his name. When we finally located him, he said there were men asking around town about our whereabouts. We decided it would be best to blow up the *Dirty Pirates* and fake our deaths. Sorry about all the grief we put you through, but it was necessary."

"So what's up with the old pickup and the costumes?" Miguel said.

"Don't want anyone to recognize us on our way to the Virgin Islands," the captain said.

Miguel laughed, "You can't drive to the islands."

"Hell, I know that. We're going overland to a small fishing village in Venezuela. From there we'll buy an old fishing boat and make our way to St. Thomas."

Monique walked back over to the captain and said, "But what about me? There's not enough room for the four of us in that truck."

"I thought you wanted to go to Vegas with Misty," the captain said.

Monique lowered her head and said, "I can't ask Misty to take me along. That issue kind of got settled."

Mikey said in his high, squeaky voice, "Please, Misty. Please take Monique with you to Vegas. There's no room in our truck."

"You could probably use an extra hand since I won't be going with you. Maybe taking Monique isn't a bad idea," Miguel said.

Misty swung around and gave Miguel a sharp look. She then turned to Gabriella and said, "You're not going to suggest I take her too, are you?"

Gabriella walked over to Misty and said softly, "With the authorities looking for them, it's probably best if Monique leaves the country in my private jet versus trying to fly commercial, dear."

Misty stood silent for a moment. The sight of Mikey's pitiful little face looking up at her from underneath a sombrero twice the size of his head and a handlebar mustache so curled on the ends they hid his ears caused Misty to break out laughing. She decided that if everyone else thought Monique should go, then maybe she was being a little hard on her.

"Okay, Monique can come," Misty said. Turning to Monique she added, "Hurry up and get your things. I don't want to be late for my first meeting."

Monique hurried off.

5

LEAVING ON A JET PLANE

Monique and Thor waited inside the Gulfstream while Misty and Gabriella said their good-byes.

Gabriella fixed the collar of Misty's blouse. "Your outfit is adorable."

"Thank you, Gabby! I wanted to give you something to remember me by."

"Honey, you gave me plenty to remember you by a few nights ago," Gabriella said with a twinkle in her eye.

"I better get going," Misty said.

"Okay, dear, but please promise me one thing before you leave."

"Sure, anything."

"Try not to let Monique get under your skin. There is usually a good reason why people act the way they do. We have no idea what she has endured growing up."

Misty thought about her friend's comments for a moment before saying, "I'll try my best, but no promises."

"Fair enough," Gabriella replied.

Misty gave Gabriella a long kiss and then turned to climb up the airstair. She stepped into the plane and poked her head inside the cock-pit. "We're all aboard, boys. Next stop, Las Vegas!"

The pilots looked back and gave her two thumbs-up. As Misty passed between Monique and Thor on her way to the back of the plane, she patted Thor on his shoulder. Three months was a long time, so there was no way she could keep Thor sequestered from Monique, but that didn't mean she wouldn't keep a close eye on Monique. She had every reason to believe Monique was hot for Thor, and she felt a responsibility to Tom and Rosie to look after him. After takeoff, Misty closed her eyes, relived her night with Gabriella, and then fell sound asleep.

Misty woke hours later to the sound of laughter. Monique was tell-ing Thor stories. It was obvious he was hanging onto her every word. Monique's animated movements seemed free and easy, almost as if she were a different person. Misty wondered why Monique never acted that way around her. After dinner, Thor went into the cockpit to visit with the pilots, so Misty got up and took Thor's old seat.

"Look, I'm sorry I've been tough on you," Misty said. "I want you to understand that this is my livelihood, and I take it very seriously. My reputation with my clients is everything, and screwing up is not an option."

"Are you insinuating I'm a screwup?" Monique asked.

Once again, Monique managed to strike a nerve. Misty shot back without thinking, "I don't know, are you?"

Monique crossed her arms and stared straight ahead.

Misty, now totally pissed, said, "This might be a good time to go over the ground rules." Monique continued staring at the cockpit door.

"Rule number one. When we are in the presence of my client, I am in complete control. Do you understand?"

Monique shrugged her shoulders. "Whatever."

"Okay, rule two. I will give you a daily allowance. When we are free from our training commitments, you are free to do as you please. Go sightseeing, gamble, attend some shows, do whatever turns you on."

"So you want me out of your sight," Monique said. "That won't be a problem. Is that it?"

"There's one more thing. It's obvious you are interested in Thor."

Monique turned and made eye contact. Misty furled her brow and said, "I don't want you to go cougar on him! *Comprenda?*"

Monique shot back, "You can't be serious. Any man that is as hot looking as Thor has slept with plenty of women. Don't make him out to be some naive little kid."

Misty looked at Thor, who was standing in the doorway of the cockpit. There was no doubt he was one of the more handsome men she had ever seen, with his long curly blonde hair, baby blue eyes, and muscular frame. There was little doubt women swooned over him. Yet, he was such a nice guy that it was hard to think about him as a woman chaser. Maybe Monique was right, but Misty still felt she owed it to his parents to keep someone like Monique away from him.

Misty said, "I wouldn't doubt that Thor has experienced plenty of women, but just the same, I feel a responsibility to his mother to look after him." Misty softened her demeanor: "If we were back in Argentina, I would leave things up to Thor, but we're not. In a sense we are a team out here, and if you sleep with him, things could get complicated." Misty thought about her recent relationship with her cowboy friend, Travis, and how he was several years younger than she. "So this is not about you being older than Thor. It's about us remaining professional. You say you want to learn how I do things. Well, this is one area where I do not cross the line. I would never think of sleeping with Miguel, and I forbid you to sleep with Thor."

Monique wasn't happy about Misty's edict, but she assumed there would be a price to pay if she didn't obey her, so she said, "There's no need to discuss this any longer. I understand Thor is off-limits." She then said sarcastically, "As far as you not sleeping with Miguel, I didn't think you were into men."

Misty decided to set the record straight. "Yes, Gabriella and I are lovers, but I'm not gay. I'm bisexual, and you may be as well."

Monique looked puzzled.

"I saw you getting off watching Gabriella and me making love in the swimming pool."

Monique blushed.

"Don't tell me you didn't want to join us." Monique didn't answer.

"Maybe now's a good time for you to know what being the Black Widow Trainer means. I command so much money because in my contract, in addition to being my client's personal trainer, I agree to sleep with my clients *once*. If they can't hold out for the contracted time, I get paid for the entire three months and get to go home."

Monique perked up and asked, "So what is the shortest time that has happened?"

Misty said with pride, "I had a client a few years ago who only made it one week."

"That's totally awesome!" Monique replied.

"Get some sleep," Misty said. "We meet my new client tonight at 10:00 p.m. Vegas time, which will be 2:00 a.m. Buenos Aires time. I need you sharp when we meet Salvatore." Misty returned to her seat at the back of the plane.

* * *

Thor's face was glued to the window as they approached McCarran International Airport. It was not only his first time in Las Vegas, it was also his first time to travel anywhere outside of South America.

"Is that the Eiffel Tower?" he asked, confused.

"Didn't you hear? The rent was too high so they moved it from France to the United States," Monique said with a hint of sarcasm. Thor was so engrossed with the view outside his window, he didn't even hear Monique's attempt at humor.

Excited for Thor, Misty moved into the seat next to him and pointed out the different hotels. "The one that looks like New York is called New York, New York. And the one directly across the Strip is the MGM Grand."

"The Strip?"

"The Las Vegas Strip is where most of the biggest hotels are located," Misty explained.

Monique slid into the seat behind Thor. "If you follow the Strip north, you'll run into older casinos like the Golden Nugget and Binion's Horseshoe."

"You've been to Vegas?" Misty asked.

"My dad brought me here once when I was a teenager. He was a professional gambler."

"You don't sound very thrilled about it."

"I'm not thrilled about a lot of things my dad did," Monique said.

A limo was waiting for them when they arrived at the private hangar. "Nice ride!" Monique said as she ran her finger along the side of the vehicle. "I'm liking this gig already."

Little was said as the limo driver sped away from the airport. The trio gazed at billboards advertising the different shows playing in Vegas and admired the massive casino resorts. It had been years since Misty visited Vegas, and she noticed that many of the casinos were new. She marveled at the lengths that were being gone to in an effort to attract customers. Crowds gathered to watch the streams of choreographed water dance high into the air in front of the Bellagio. Life-size pirate ships battled in the moats surrounding Treasure Island.

"Hey, Monique! I'll bet that was Jerry Le Butcher's ship," Thor said, laughing.

"Cute," Monique replied.

Their limo driver pulled into the most impressive hotel of all. "Welcome to the Amicus Resort and Casino. This is Mr. Salvatore's private entrance." He handed them each a room key that resembled a black credit card. "Just present this card wherever you go. There is no need to tip as everything has been taken care of."

Misty stepped out of the limo and looked up at the massive, curved glass building. It was stunning. Once inside, the attendant whisked them off to their rooms. Thor's mouth fell open as he walked around the spacious suite. Misty motioned for the luggage carrier to place her things in the far bedroom and then said, "Thor, you can take the other bedroom."

"What about me?" Monique said.

Misty walked over to the large sectional couch, patted on the seat cushions, and said, "Just be sure to put your sheets away in the morning. I'm sure you'll find an extra pillow around somewhere." Monique gave Misty an unpleasant stare.

After unpacking their luggage, they walked through the main floor of the casino on their way to meet Misty's new client. They admired the massive stone columns and sheets of metal riveted to the walls. A massive escalator carried them to the second floor, where they found the night-club Salvatore's. Misty prepared herself for a man with a healthy ego. A large floor poster depicting a middle-aged man trying to look cool stood to the left of the entrance. A throwback to the seventies, he had left his shirt unbuttoned almost down to his navel. A massive gold chain hung around his neck, resting comfortably atop a carpet of thick, black chest hair. His index finger and thumb pointed at you as if mimicking a gun. The line "I'm The Guy. Who are you?" ran along the bottom edge of the poster.

The club had a seventies disco theme, complete with a large, spinning silver ball that peppered the walls, table, and floor with squares of light. It was late on a Wednesday night, so there were very few people in the club. Misty noticed eight men at a large table in the back and led Thor and Monique in the men's direction. A large man walked up to intercept them.

"Are you here on business?" he asked Misty.

"Yes, I'm Salvatore's new personal trainer, and he had requested we meet him here. I'm assuming he's one of the gentlemen around the table?"

"Wait here," he replied and then walked over to the table and whispered into a man's ear. Misty had no idea if the man was Salvatore because one of his stipulations was that they not exchange pictures. He was an attractive man with thick, dark hair; a smooth, rich complexion; and dark brown eyes. After saying something to the man on his left, Salvatore got up from the table and walked in their direction.

Misty extended her hand to greet him, but she quickly dropped it when she realized he was looking past her. He brushed past Misty on his way to Monique. He took Monique by the hands and kissed each side of her cheeks, bringing a smile to her face.

"Magnificent!" he said. "It's obvious why they refer to you as the Black Widow Trainer."

Monique said nothing as she turned to Misty with a big smile. The man also turned to Misty; she approached him. Being careful not to reveal how upset she was, Misty feigned a smile and said, "Now you know why I wanted to share pictures. I am Misty, your trainer."

"You? But you're a blonde!" He looked back at Monique and said, "I just assumed."

His remark made it harder for Misty to retain her composure. "I can see that," she replied. She placed her hand in Monique's jet-black hair and held it up. "Yes, I can see how you could have thought she was your trainer."

"So you are Salvatore?" Monique asked flirtatiously.

"Indeed I am," he said. "And who might you be, my darling?"

"I'm Monique."

"I must say your name is as beautiful as you are. I trust your accommodations are suitable?"

Before Misty could assure him they were, Monique said, "The room is nice, but we are a bit cramped. I'm afraid I will be sleeping on the couch."

He looked at Misty and said, "Misty did not notify my staff you were coming."

Snapping his fingers, he summoned one of his men. "Move them to one of my private villas."

"You will find a master bedroom on the first floor and several bedrooms on the second," Salvatore said. He looked at Monique as he added, "I insist Monique take the master suite to make up for our little misunderstanding." Misty gritted her teeth and nodded her approval.

As Thor watched the ordeal unfold with great interest, a man moved up next to him. Thor did a double take and asked, "Are you The Guy? The guy on the poster?"

The man beamed proudly, "Yep, I'm The Guy. Who are you?"

"I'm Thor. I'm with the women talking to Salvatore."

"I see. Will you be staying at the hotel?"

"Yes, possibly for three months while my boss trains Salvatore."

"Well, then I will be seeing you around the casino."

As the man was walking off, Thor asked, "So what's your real name?"

The Guy turned back and said, "Benny. I'm Salvatore's cousin Benny."

After setting up a time to train Salvatore, the three followed one of Salvatore's men back to their room. During the walk, Misty asked Thor, "So who was the guy you were talking to?"

"The Guy."

"Yes, the guy you were talking to."

Realizing Misty didn't understand what he was saying, Thor glanced around the room until he spotted another stand-up poster. He pointed it out. "You know, The Guy."

"Oh, that guy!" she said.

"His real name is Benny. He's Salvatore's cousin."

"Interesting."

After gathering up their things, the man escorted them to their new home. The three walked to the middle of the room and looked around in amazement.

"The villa is over three thousand square feet," Salvatore's man said.

He picked up a remote control and pushed a button. Massive motorized curtains rose up to the ceiling, revealing a panoramic view of the mountain ranges far off in the distance northwest of town. Lights twinkled along the base of one of the mountains. Monique stood at the window and looked down at the Vegas Strip, watching the hordes of people moving around like ants. Thor climbed a massive stairway that curved up to the second level. Salvatore's man clicked another button and the 220-inch, high-def TV came to life. He set the remote on the table and said, "The remote controls everything in the villa, even the temperature. There are two bedrooms upstairs, a full kitchen through the door to your right, and a master bedroom on the other side of the kitchen."

Monique picked up her things and headed directly for the master bedroom. Misty thanked the man and climbed the stairway with her belongings in tow. After putting her stuff away, she told Thor goodnight. She took a long, hot shower and then crawled into bed. After pondering her predicament, she decided the best thing to do would be to get a good night's sleep and rethink things in the morning when she was rested.

Misty got anything but a good night's sleep. She remained in a dreamlike state as the events of the day ran through her head. It was so surreal, she had difficulty knowing whether she was actually asleep or just daydreaming. Still on Buenos Aires time, she rose promptly at 4:00 a.m., pulled a chair up to the enormous window, and gazed onto the Las Vegas Strip below. She couldn't help but wonder what a typical light bill might cost the larger casinos. She put together a laundry list of all the issues agitating her. First, her constant companion, Miguel, was not by her side. Thor was a neat kid and she enjoyed having him around, but it was just not the same. Then she thought about the long list of things that bothered her about Monique. Was she just jealous of all the attention Monique garnered, or was she jealous because Monique was every bit as gorgeous as she was? The fact that Monique better resembled a black widow trainer than she did with her blonde hair didn't help. She thought about whether she should dye her hair black but decided it was not an option. When the aroma of freshly brewed coffee reached Misty's upstairs bedroom, she breathed in deeply and thought *Coffee, just the thing I need to get my motor running.* She wound her way down the circular stairway and into the kitchen where she found Monique looking out the window, a cup of coffee in hand. Monique wore a lightweight silky black jacket and black polyester Capri training pants that were so tight that they formed to the shape of her powerful lower body.

"Reminiscing the old times you had with your father in Vegas?" Misty asked.

Without turning around, Monique replied, "No, they are not memories I am fond of." Her voice was subdued; she suddenly seemed like a different person. She then changed the subject. "I made a fresh pot of coffee."

"That's why I came down," Misty said. "I could smell it from my bedroom." She poured a cup of coffee and said, "Nice outfit. Are you excited about this morning's workout session with Salvatore?"

Monique shrugged her shoulders. "I guess so."

Monique's indifference upset Misty. After all she had done to finagle her way onto the trip, Misty thought Monique would be more excited. She realized Monique was a much more complicated person than she ever imagined.

Misty heard a loud yawn and turned toward the doorway of the kitchen, where Thor stood with his arms stretched above his head.

"Well, look what the cat dragged in," Misty teased. "How did you sleep?"

"I slept great! I'm really looking forward to watching you train Salvatore and then getting to tour Las Vegas." He looked at Monique. "So how did you sleep last night, Monique?"

She spun around. "Like a baby."

He looked at Misty and said, "And you?"

"Just swell," Misty said sarcastically and then went back upstairs.

6

THEIR CLIENT

Misty and Monique were limbering up in the hotel workout facility
when Salvatore arrived with a four-man entourage. As he walked briskly
toward them, Salvatore sensed the girls seemed slightly intimidated by
the large group. "No need for alarm, ladies. These are my associates. You
will be seeing a lot of them over the next several months." He turned to
the men and said, "Please introduce yourselves to the ladies."

They looked at each other hesitantly, and then a moderately built
man with a serious expression stepped forward. "I am Antonio. If Sal is
away, I will be your main contact."

Antonio gave Misty the creeps. He seemed too cocky and self-assured.
She noticed that he looked Monique up and down, and she made a mental note to stay as far away from him as possible.

The next man stepped forward. His broad shoulders and thick frame
indicated that he was a man you didn't want to cross. He said, "My name
is Santo," and then stepped back as quickly as he had appeared.

"Tomasso," the next man said. "My buddies refer to me as Slick
Masso. What lovely ladies you are. Welcome to Las Vegas, and I wish
you a wonderful stay." The girls both had experience with men like

Tomasso, and they were very aware how he might have come by his nickname.

As the entourage turned to leave, a pudgy man with a baby face said, "Hey, what about me?"

The other men appeared put out as he lumbered up to the women. He looked at them nervously and said, "I'm Diego and, well, uh . . ." before turning back to Antonio for help.

Antonio shook his head, "Just tell them you're glad to meet them, Allocco."

"Oh, yeah. I'm really glad to meet you."

Diego seemed somewhat endearing to Misty, so she said, "Nice to meet you too, big guy." Diego grinned.

"Let's go, Allocco," Antonio said.

After they had gone, Misty asked Salvatore, "So, what does Allocco mean?"

Monique answered for him: "It means stupid."

"That's not very nice of them," Misty said. She looked at Salvatore. "Let's get you warmed up so you don't pull a muscle."

Misty noticed Salvatore wasn't particularly muscular, but she knew that would change by the time she was through with him. It wasn't hard to envision how attractive he might be once he bulked up. Misty caught Salvatore glancing at her as she stripped down to her workout outfit. The outfit was more colorful than sexy, but she still looked hot.

Wanting to catch Salvatore's attention, Monique reached under her light jacket and pulled down a zipper in the middle of her sports bra to enhance her considerable cleavage. She bent over to take her top off, making her breasts look even larger. Salvatore was quick to notice and approached Monique. Taking her hands into his, he gazed at her body and said, "*Magnifico la mia bellezza*!" Monique's smile made Misty want to puke.

"May I ask how you keep your body so fit?" Salvatore said.

"I use an exercise system called P90X. It stands for 'Power 90 Extreme' because it improves your physical fitness in ninety days." Monique flashed her beautiful set of white teeth and added, "That's exactly how long we are scheduled to be here."

Misty had heard about the exercise regimen from some of her trainer friends in Malibu. It was all the rage, and they were losing clients because of its simplicity, lack of equipment, and the fact it could easily be done at home. *Surely he isn't contemplating using P90X*, she thought. After a moment of careful consideration, he turned to address Misty.

"Why don't we do the P90 thing? Look how good it made Monique look."

"That's an interesting idea," she said. "Do you mind if I speak with my associate in private for a moment? You start warming up on the treadmill."

"Sure. Take your time."

Once Salvatore was out of earshot, Misty placed her hands on her hips and looked squarely into Monique's eyes. Monique seemed unfazed.

"Monique! That was a stupid move. If my clients figure out they can use P90X, they will soon realize they don't need to pay me $5,000 a session."

Monique laughed, "So you think they pay you $5,000 a session for your skills as a trainer? I think they pay it for your companionship and the chance to fuck you."

Misty realized Monique had a point and her argument wouldn't hold. Everything seemed to be crumbling all around her, and she was uncertain what to do next. Knowing the last thing she wanted to do was make a scene in front of a client, she said, "All right, Monique. I have no idea how to instruct P90X, so you will need to take charge. I'll pick it up as we go."

"I'd love to," Monique replied.

When Misty informed Salvatore that Monique would lead the P90X training, his mood seemed to brighten, and he quickened his pace on the treadmill. Misty walked off feeling like a third wheel.

Over the next two sessions, Misty learned the various techniques of P90X from strength training (mostly lightweight dumbbells and elastic resistance bands) to cardio, plyometrics, and even yoga, which she was already an expert at.

At the end of the third session, Salvatore wanted to spend more time alone with Monique, so he said to Misty, "I forgot to tell you that one of your amenities is unlimited visits with my personal masseuse. May I suggest you visit him now? Esteban has no clients today, and it would give him something to do."

Slightly sore from her new workout routine and anxious to get away herself, she said, "That sounds wonderful, Salvatore. Where do I go?"

"The front desk will give you directions. I'll call him while you take a shower and freshen up. You'll find that Esteban has some very special talents. Feel free to have him work on you as long as you wish." He gave Misty a wink and added, "I'm sure you will find the massage very stimulating."

Whatever, Misty thought as she walked away. *I've experienced the best masseuses all over the world.*

As she walked past Thor, she noticed he was staring into space. It was obvious what he was staring at. "So you like Monique's big butt?"

He gave Misty a sheepish grin and said, "It's not that big! Miguel says that she has 'junk in her trunk.' That's a good thing, right?"

Misty walked away without answering. In the empty elevator she stuck her butt out and took a good look in the mirror. *I think I'll start hitting the glut machines a little harder*, she thought.

7

THE HANDYMAN

Misty lay facedown on the massage table, bare except for the sheet that covered her from the waist down. Two scented oil lamps and several candles provided a soft light. New age music played from the speakers mounted in the ceiling. The fully stocked bar built into the wall made her realize this was no ordinary massage room. Misty lapsed into a tranquil state while waiting for her masseuse to show. A short while later, Esteban knocked lightly on the door. When he did not get a response, he quietly made his way to a chair in the corner of the room and remained seated until she awoke.

When Misty next opened her eyes, she saw him sitting quietly in the corner and asked, "How long have you been in here?"

"About fifteen minutes. You were resting so peacefully I didn't want to wake you. Besides, you're my only client today, so there was no reason to wake you."

Esteban rose gently and prepared his hands by coating them with an oily substance. Misty gazed at his sturdy hands with their perfectly manicured nails as he rubbed them together with a slow and deliberate manner. They had the look of a professional model's hands. Misty found herself stimulated and said without thinking, "So what's your name, lover boy?"

"Lover boy. That's an interesting American expression."

"So where are you from?"

"I am from Cuba, and my name is Esteban."

"Esteban. That's beautiful."

"Thank you. It's a family name used for many generations. One day I hope to pass it down to a son of my own."

"So you're not married?"

"Not yet. I have a beautiful woman back in Cuba, but . . ." After a few seconds, he said, "Hopefully we will find a way to be together again, someday."

"Now, that's a sad story," Misty said.

He patted her on the back and said, "Enough about me. Let's get to work on you."

Misty nestled her face snuggly into the headrest. Esteban placed the palms of his hands flat on each side of her spine, just above the hips, and moved them firmly up the middle of her back and then over her shoulder blades. He then pressed his hands firmly onto each of her sides and dragged them down over her rib cage until he reached the place he had started. He tirelessly retraced his movements, over and over, until every muscle in Misty's back had completely relaxed. When he began massaging her more gently, Misty said, "Now don't go sissy on me, Romeo. You've got wonderfully strong hands. Use them."

"Oh, now I'm Romeo. Did I just get promoted?"

"Absolutely!"

Without hesitation, he grabbed two handfuls of flesh, and began kneading every square inch of her back and neck. Misty's soft moans of pleasure let Esteban know he was not squeezing too hard. When Misty's moans turned into groans he stepped away, giving her a moment of rest. She was so zoned out that she did not notice him remove the sheet. Esteban took her left foot in his left hand and used his right to locate her pleasure points. He then moved on to her right foot. Misty felt as if she were having an out-of-body experience as he moved onto her muscular calves and then onto the base of her thighs, working on her hamstrings with strong powerful digs. Again she drifted into a semiconscious state.

When she awoke, she could feel his hands digging into her firm buttocks. With one quick move, she rose onto her left forearm and twisted her head around. That's when she realized she was totally exposed. Outraged, Misty sat up and grabbed a startled Esteban by the front of his shirt. She pulled him to her until they were intimately face-to-face.

"Tell me why I shouldn't report you to Salvatore and have you fired!" she demanded.

"Salvatore didn't inform you?" he said, surprised. "This is Vegas. Being in Salvatore's hotel is like being in another country. Anything goes here."

Esteban gingerly slipped his hands up until they were in front of Misty's face. "Salvatore leases these hands for $150,000 a year. For all practical matters, my hands belong to Salvatore and his guests." He smiled and gave her a slight nod. "Only women guests, of course."

Amazed at what she had just been told, Misty released his shirt and placed her hands on his. She explored every detail of these magnificently strong and exquisitely manicured tools. They had just wonderfully restored her sore muscles to their pre-P90X condition.

She leaned in until she could feel his warm breath on her face. She said, "So while I'm in here I own your hands?"

Esteban smiled softly and nodded. "They are yours to command."

Looking his face over carefully to make sure he wasn't pulling her leg, she noticed how exquisitely handsome he was. He had beautiful brown eyes framed by thick eyebrows, a cute little nose, and perfectly formed ears. His dark brown, silky hair was cut short, giving him a fresh, wholesome look. His thick whiskers left a dark shadow atop his smooth, unblemished skin. Misty looked into his eyes as she placed his hands onto her fully exposed breasts. Without a trace of embarrassment from his boyishly handsome face, he skillfully massaged the soft mounds of flesh that had been offered to him. The pleasure was so immense it took all of her willpower to remove them. As she did, he unashamedly lowered his eyes to inspect his handy work. Misty placed her hands on the side of his face and pulled it up until their eyes met. Grinning, she said, "I was just testing you to see if you were telling the truth. Now I would like you to leave the room so I can get dressed."

Esteban nodded obediently and did as he was asked.

8

HIT ME

Over the next month, Misty felt more and more like a participant in their training sessions than an instructor. Monique and Sal had grown close. Monique had masterfully played hard to get at first only to have Sal do what he did so well—shower her with gifts to lure her closer to him. Sal opened up accounts for Monique with merchants like Louis Vuitton, Gucci, and Prada so he could show her off on their nights out on the town. Night after night Misty watched Monique leave their apartment dressed to kill only to return a few hours before morning to catch some sleep and then clean up and prepare for the day ahead. Very little was said between the two, which suited Misty just fine. She began to realize Monique had what it took to become a Black Widow Trainer and, had they gotten along better, she might have considered taking her on as an apprentice.

One evening, Monique passed Misty on her way to the front door. "Going out with Sal?" Misty asked.

Monique gave her a sly smile. "You know I am. Why ask?"

Misty frowned. "Are you sleeping with him on a regular basis?"

Monique thought a moment before replying. "There's nothing in your contract that prohibits me sleeping with your client."

"Guess I need to add a 'slut' clause in my contract," Misty shot back.

Taken aback, Monique countered with, "I just hope Sal isn't underwhelmed when he sleeps with you after having slept with me first."

"Enjoy it while it lasts, because you will never have the opportunity to sleep with one of my clients again," Misty said angrily. Monique shrugged her shoulders and headed out.

Misty had had about enough of Monique's surly attitude, but she realized Monique was too entrenched with her client to do anything about it. She decided to try and think of something fun to do in an effort to take her mind off of Monique. Going out to dinner and a show was wearing thin.

When Thor came down the stairs on his way to the kitchen, Misty said, "Let's do something fun tonight, Thor!"

"Sure, what do you have in mind?"

"I don't know. Why don't you think of something this time? And don't say go to a show."

Returning from the kitchen with a soda in his hand, he said, "Let's go gambling."

"Gambling! I don't know the first thing about gambling, do you?"

"No, but it can't be that hard. I've watched people play blackjack How complicated can it be? All you've got to be able to do is count to twenty-one."

Misty said teasingly, "Math was never my strong suit, so I'm not so sure."

"You'll do fine, Misty. Your fingers and toes get you to twenty."

Misty laughed, thinking that was the type of crack Miguel might have made had he been here. Thor was beginning to loosen up, and it eased the pain of not having Miguel by her side—at least for now.

"Get dressed, Thor. Wear something casual. I feel like slumming it tonight."

* * *

Thor and Misty walked the downstairs casino floor in search of a table.

Slightly intimidated, they hoped to find a few friendly faces. Misty felt that an elderly grandmother would be the ideal mentor, but grandmothers seemed to be in short supply. As they walked past one of the many bars spread around the casino, they heard a familiar laugh. It was Monique. She was sitting surrounded by Antonio, Tomasso, and the boys, and it was obvious she was enjoying being the center of attention. Monique caught Misty looking and gave her a big grin.

Misty tugged Thor's arm. "Let's go find someplace else to gamble. This place isn't doing it for me."

They made their way to the front of the casino and exited onto the Vegas Strip. Even though it was early evening, a stifling108-degree temperature greeted them.

"Do you really want to walk around in this heat?" Thor asked.

Determined to find anyplace new, Misty said, "Let's head up the street, and we will go into the first place we run across."

They didn't have to journey far before coming across an old building that seemed out of place. As if seeing a mirage, Misty stepped back toward the Strip to get a better look at the establishment. Devil's Cove was situated on a tiny corner of Salvatore's property. Amicus was considered the elite casino and resort not only on the strip but also in all of Las Vegas, and Devil's Cove was a major blemish.

"What do you think, Thor? Do you want to give it a shot?"

Wiping the sweat from his brow, he said, "As long as it's got air-conditioning, I'm good."

They found Devil's Cove teeming with excitement. The clientele seemed much more rowdy than where they were staying, and the place reminded Misty of the bars she frequented while on her Alaskan adventure. Thor fixed his gaze on one of the cocktail waitresses walking past. Misty could understand why. She was a gorgeous woman, and she was showing major cleavage. Her outfit was equipped with a full devil's tail that curled upward. Thor's eyes lit up as if he were a kid in a candy store, and he scanned the casino looking for more devilish women. Misty found the girls' naughty looks intriguing. She had to remind herself that she was there to gamble.

A ruckus broke out at a nearby craps table, so Misty and Thor went to check it out. A man who looked totally blitzed was throwing dice.

Before each throw, he would blow on his cupped hand and then bounce the dice off the wall at the far end of the table. Each time the dice combination added up to seven, the crowd went wild. The man held his role for over fifteen minutes. The crazier things got, the more bystanders gathered round, until close to half the people in the little casino were watching him roll the dice.

A very attractive Hispanic waitress walked up to Thor and handed him a double shot of tequila, unsolicited. Thor looked at her, puzzled, and said, "*Por qué?*"

Running her hand lightly across the side of his face she replied seductively, "*Porque es magnifico.*"

Thor smiled broadly and said, "Gracias!"

"I don't have to understand Spanish to know she likes you," Misty said.

Thor shrugged his shoulders and threw back the tequila. "You made a good choice selecting this place," he said.

All of a sudden they heard a loud groan and saw the man in charge of the chips raking all the chips on the table his way. The crowd dispersed.

Misty and Thor moved on to the roulette table and watched the large wheel spin around and around. The ball landed on the number six. Misty noticed there weren't any chips on the number six. The board was then swept of chips, which were then added to the enormous stack under management control. Misty was beginning to wonder why anyone would ever play this game when the ball landed on the number eight. A young woman screamed hysterically and then hugged the man next to her as an enormous stack of chips were pushed her way.

A man standing behind Misty said, "Aren't you going to place a bet?"

Misty looked him over. He seemed to be in his fifties, around six foot tall and 180 pounds. She was attracted to his semi-long, dusty-blonde hair and boyish good looks.

Before she could think of something witty to say, one of the pit bosses interrupted, "Boss, we have a situation at table nine."

"Excuse me," he said to Misty graciously and left.

Misty drifted halfway over to table nine. She watched him place a calming hand on the drunk man's shoulder. After talking to the man politely, he offered him a hand. When the man took it in his, Misty noticed how gently the man in charge patted his patron on the shoulder as they shook hands. Misty was impressed at how masterfully he diffused a volatile situation and wished she had been able to get to know him better.

Misty decided that it was time to give blackjack a try. She scanned the room for a few minutes and then led Thor over to a table where she plopped down between two men. After paying some men and taking chips away from others, the dealer looked at Misty inquisitively. She nervously looked around the table until the gentleman on her right said, "You need to place a bet."

Slightly embarrassed, she replied, "Oh, sure. I knew that," and looked at Thor. He reached into his pocket, took out a roll of hundreds Misty had given him for safekeeping, and handed her five.

She placed the Benjamins on the table, and the dealer yelled out, "Five black coming out." Misty thought, *Coming out? What the hell does that mean?*

She noticed the other players putting chips in the square on the table in front of them, so she did the same. The dealer said, "This is a one-hundred-dollar-minimum bet table."

"Oh, how much did I put down?"

"Twenty-five dollars. You need to either put down three more of those green chips or replace that green one with a black chip. Misty chose to place three more greenies down.

She looked down at the hand she had been dealt and discovered a jack of spades staring up at her. She turned to Thor and shrugged her shoulders. Thor shrugged back. She began to panic but fought the urge to get up from the table. *How hard can this be?* she asked herself. *I only need to count to twenty-one.*

Sitting fifth in line at a table of six gave her time to monitor the other four players' moves before it was her turn. The first man waived an open hand over the ten of hearts in front of him, so the dealer moved on to the next man. That man turned over the card that had been face down. The dealer took his cards and pushed seven black chips and two green chips his way while leaving his five black chips on the table in front of him. Everyone at the table congratulated him except Misty, who just smiled.

She leaned over and whispered to the large man sitting on the other side of her, "What just happened?"

He raised his eyebrows and said, "He hit a blackjack." Recognizing she was still confused, he added, "The king is worth ten points and the ace is worth eleven."

Misty added the two together and thought, *"Twenty-one! No wonder."*

The next man moved his middle finger toward himself in three quick motions, and the dealer placed a two of hearts on the table next to the man's five of spades. He calmly took a peek at his down card and made the same motion again. This time the dealer threw down a ten of diamonds, and the man passed his hands over his cards. The dealer moved to the next man. When it was Misty's turn, she began to perspire. She took a peek at her down card. It was a six to go with her jack of spades. *Hmmm, that's easy. Six and ten equal sixteen. But now what do I do?*

As the dealer looked at her impatiently, the scrawny guy smoking a cigarette on her left said in a sarcastic tone, "Do you want to take a hit or not?"

The dealer said, "If you would like another card, pull your fingers several times quickly toward yourself. If not, wave your hand over your cards one time."

Misty motioned for another card. The dealer threw down a six of spades, and Misty counted. *Twenty-two!*

Turning to the large man on her right, she said excitedly, "I've got twenty two. That's very close to twenty one, so I'm doing pretty good, right?"

Overhearing her, the dealer said, "Please turn up your hole card." Misty looked at him funny, and the dealer pointed to the card facing down. "Your hole card," he repeated.

Misty laughed to herself. *Geez, like he expected me to only turn up half a card. How dumb does he think I am?*

The second she turned her card face up, the dealer swept away her chips and put them with his.

Turning to the big guy again, she said, "Hey, what's he doing? I thought twenty-two was pretty good."

He rolled his eyes. "If you go over twenty-one, you bust. That means you lose."

Misty sheepishly replied, "Oh."

The man on her left became belligerent. As the dealer swept away his four black chips, he turned to Misty, "You caused me to lose with your stupid play. The dealer had a four showing and you had sixteen. You never take a hit when the dealer has a four showing."

"Why not?"

"Because he has a good chance of busting, that's why!"

"You mean going over twenty-one?"

With a grimace of disbelief, he said, "What planet are you from, lady?"

Misty sat up in a huff, "So what's it to you if I lose my own money?"

"Because you changed the rotation of the cards and caused me to bust!" he said rudely. Thor positioned himself directly behind the man in case the situation turned nasty. But the man pushed back his chair and grabbed his chips. "I'm going to another table where they know how to play blackjack," he said. He turned quickly to leave and bounced off Thor. It was obvious the man wanted to lash out, but seeing how big Thor was, he chose to walk away.

Misty looked back to the man on her right. "I don't understand. What just happened?"

"He was upset because you were not supposed to take a hit, but you did. He was sitting on fifteen, and your six would have given him twenty-one. Instead, you took the six and the next card was an eight, causing him to bust."

"Having a tough go of it?" she heard a man say and turned back to her left.

The good-looking, blonde-haired man she had run into earlier was sitting in the seat that had just been vacated.

"Oh, it's you! I guess there is more to blackjack than meets the eye."

He patted her on the back and said, "Come on. Let's open up a private table, and I'll teach you how to play correctly."

"They'll do that for you?"

He stood up and extended his hand. When Misty took it, he said, "My name is Gary, and I happen to own Devil's Cove."

Well, I guess all casino owners aren't creeps, Misty thought.

"My name is Misty, and this is my friend Thor," she said.

Gary shook Thor's hand and said, "Terrific! The more the merrier."

* * *

Gary rose from the table and thanked his dealer for working over his dinner break. He then asked Misty, "So do you think you can handle yourself around a blackjack table now?"

"I sure do! Thanks so much for taking time out of your busy schedule to teach me."

"How about you, Thor?"

"Yes, sir. I can't believe how easy you made it seem. Now I have something to do with my free time."

Misty gave Thor a little shove. "You better not lose all the money I'm paying you. You're supposed to be saving up for college."

Gary said, "So, Thor, what are you doing in Vegas if you are a college student?"

Misty placed her hand on Thor's bicep and gave it a squeeze. "He's my bodyguard."

"Are you someone famous I should have recognized?" Gary asked.

Thor said enthusiastically, "Misty is a renowned physical fitness trainer. She trains rich and powerful men all over the world. She's in very high demand." Thor grinned proudly. "I'm here in case any of them get out of hand."

Gary looked at Misty inquisitively, "So, who are you training in Vegas?"

"She's here to train the owner of Amicus," Thor said proudly.

Gary's demeanor became somber, "I see. How well do you know Salvatore?"

"Not well," Misty said. "You seem concerned."

"Sorry, just curious."

Gary placed his hands on her shoulders and said, "Be careful, Misty."

He then shook Thor's hand. "It was a pleasure meeting you, Thor. I hope to see both of you again sometime."

"Gary seems like a really nice guy," Thor said on their way back to their room.

Deep in thought, Misty hesitated before answering, "What? Oh yes, he sure seems to be."

Salvatore's men were drinking at the hotel bar as Misty and Thor passed by. Tomasso got a glimpse of them and said to the others, "Hey, there goes Misty and her bodyguard."

Antonio looked over the top of his drink and said, "Now that's a prime piece of ass going to waste. The boss spends all his time with Monique. He might as well send Misty home."

"Not sure which one I would rather have," Tomasso said. "It's a tough call."

"Monique is off-limits, but maybe we can get somewhere with Misty," Antonio said. "Come on, boys. Let's pay ol' Misty a little visit." Antonio raised his glass in the air, and the rest of the boys clanked their glasses against Antonio's.

Diego walked back from the restroom as the men were leaving. "Hey, wait for me!" he said and lumbered after them.

Misty and Thor were halfway down the passageway that led to their elevator when they spotted Antonio and his men leaning against the wall. As Misty and Thor approached, Antonio stepped into the middle of the hall to block them from passing.

"Isn't it a little past your bedtime?" Antonio said.

Turned off by his tone and the alcohol on his breath, Misty said calmly, "I'm really tired, Antonio. Please move out of my way."

The rest of the men moved off the wall and took a position behind Antonio. Thor stepped between Misty and Antonio.

"Look what we have here," Antonio said in a degrading tone.

Misty admired Thor's courage, but she didn't like the odds, so she stepped up next to Thor and poked Antonio in his shoulder. "If you don't step aside, I'm going to report you to Salvatore!"

Antonio looked back at the boys and laughed. "Hear that, men? She's going to tell Salvatore on us."

Antonio pulled a package of gum from his pocket and slowly unwrapped a piece before placing it into his mouth. He gave it a good chewing before saying, "Salvatore doesn't give a shit about you. He's getting all the pussy he wants from Monique. As a matter of fact, she's up there with him right now. It's a shame to let yours go to waste. What do you say you and me go join them?"

Thor reacted without thinking, shoving Antonio so hard he went flying across the floor on his back. Santo caught Thor in the side of his face with his clinched fist. Thor shook it off as he squared up to Santo. Tomasso and Diego began moving forward, but Santo waved them off.

Misty attempted to move in between the two, and Santo grabbed her by the arm and flung her to the side. Thor didn't hesitate, landing a crushing blow to the side of Santo's face. Santo dropped to one knee and looked up at Thor while rubbing his jaw. Misty returned to Thor's side.

Tomasso and Diego looked at each other and then made a move in Thor's direction, but before a confrontation could ensue, someone yelled at them from down the hall.

"Hey! Hey! What's going on here?"

"It's fucking Benny," Antonio said, as he pulled himself up off the floor.

"What's going on here, Antonio?" Benny asked as he approached the group. "You know my cousin Sal doesn't allow violence in the casino."

Santo's pride was hurt, so Benny or no Benny, he staggered to his feet and reached out to grab Thor. Benny latched onto Santo's arm and held on tight while yelling, "I'm The Guy here, I'm The Guy. You know Salvatore made me The Guy, Santo."

Santo slowly backed away, but his eyes remained fixed on Thor. He smiled and said, "Sure, Benny. You're The Guy."

"We're just having a little fun," Antonio said. "Right, guys?"

"Yeah, Benny. Antonio's right," Tomasso said. "We're just having a little fun."

Benny puffed out his chest. "Okay, then. I'm going back to greeting the casino guests. I want everyone to behave." Benny looked at Antonio. "Don't make me have to come back here."

Antonio grinned and said, "Sure thing, Benny. You're The Guy."

After Benny left, Antonio turned to Thor. "You're lucky Benny showed up." Antonio motioned for the boys to follow him. Santo stopped and looked into Thor's eyes. Thor glared back. "We've got unfinished business," Santo said and then walked off.

Misty wrapped her arm around Thor when the men were gone. "That was a close call. Are you okay?"

"I'm fine," he said. "I might have gotten my ass kicked, but I would have left them with a few things to remember us by."

Later that night, Misty was too wound up to fall asleep, so she picked up the hotel phone and dialed.

"Who is it?" the voice on the other end of the phone asked.

"Did you really mean it when you said you are at my service 24/7?"

"Yes, I'm at your service, Misty. When would you like to meet?"

"In about twenty minutes?"

"Sure, that's fine."

"Thanks, Esteban."

* * *

Esteban rubbed the sleep from his eyes and checked the time. Misty wasn't his first client to call him into work after one o'clock in the morning, but she was the first client who made him want to get up. Esteban had few friends in Vegas and had enjoyed his conversations with Misty. Being from a foreign country, it was difficult to know who to trust. Over the past several weeks, Misty had earned his trust through her interest in his well-being, always making it a point to ask him how he was doing and if there was anything she could do for him. They were on their way to becoming friends.

To Esteban's surprise, when he opened the massage room door, he found Misty not only in her normal facedown position on the table but butt naked as well. Before him lay the most spectacular specimen of a woman he had ever seen, and from the look of things, tonight she would be his to please. He could feel his heart pounding in his throat. He made no attempt at conversation, nor did she. Realizing how special this night could be, he uncorked his favorite bottle of scented massage oil and proceeded to drip it evenly over her back. When he placed his hands on her upper back, he found her skin hot to the touch. He knew from experience that she was there to let off some steam. He was not prepared for his own body's response. He slowly and methodically applied the oil onto every square inch of her body, the way a proud owner of an expensive sports car might apply wax to his prized hot rod. Esteban stopped to rearrange his own hot rod to give it room to grow.

Esteban moved on to her inner thighs, starting just above her knees, then he gently worked his way up. Misty's legs gradually separated along the way as if summoning him to her. He surprised Misty, bypassing her opening invitation to sink his hands into the two wonderful mounds of firm flesh. After six weeks of strenuous glute exercises, Misty's ass was now the equal of Monique's. It would pass Miguel's junk-in-the-trunk test with ease. Esteban dug in deep, kneading her buttocks as if they were dough. Misty moaned with pleasure until any stiffness from her last workout had subsided. When she felt totally relaxed, she drew herself up onto her knees and supported herself with her forearms, raising her butt high into the air, making her intended target impossible to miss.

Lost in the moment, Esteban followed his instinct. He lightly spanked her bottom, ready to back off at the slightest sign of being out of line. When Misty did not protest, he gradually increased the intensity. Over time the slaps became so audible they echoed through the room, helping to muffle her groans of pleasure. She turned her head around and gave him a crazed look. It was time to make his move. Esteban climbed onto the table, next to Misty. He wrapped his left arm around her side to hold her snuggly. With his right hand he located her mound and used his three middle fingers to delicately spank in rapid succession. Misty moved her hips rhythmically to his pats. He slid his middle finger gently between the hood of her outer labia of her vagina deep enough to reach her wet inner labia, working his finger in and out until she had loosened.

Misty moaned. His fingers probed along her lower vaginal wall, several inches up the canal, until finding the egg-shaped G-spot he was in search of. He placed his split fingers on the outer perimeter of the tiny mound, rubbing up and down gently. As she filled up with natural lubricant, he targeted the mound directly, rubbing on it until it felt like a small, inflated balloon. Misty rocked back and forth to enhance the sensation. Each time he sensed she was close to coming, he backed off and let the area cool down. This drove her crazy. He located her clitoris, which was now as erect and swollen as a miniature penis, and stimulated it between his thumb and forefinger. Misty's moans turned to groans. Esteban located one of her nipples with his left hand and found it firm and hard. He stroked the back of Misty's shoulder-length blonde hair, letting her know the time was near. She nodded knowingly.

He relocated her G-spot, finding it the size of a small grape. He rubbed on it vigorously. Her breaths became short, rapid, and irregular. He could feel her vulva and vagina contracting and relaxing involuntarily. She was fighting to hold back, so he whispered, "Do you feel a peeing sensation?"

"Uh, huh," she said frantically. He patted her on the back and said, "It's not pee, let it flow."

When she did, her body and legs stiffened and then began shaking uncontrollably as the mind-blowing waves of pleasure crashed through her body. When they subsided, she collapsed onto the table, her chest heaving in and out in its quest to refill with oxygen. Esteban lifted his fingers to his face nonchalantly and inspected the clear ejaculation on his fingertips—not that he needed evidence she had just come. With her breathing back to normal, he washed her off with cool wet towels from a small refrigerator, scrubbing her like a surgeon's nurse. After wiping her down with a towel, he gave her a small slap on the rear. "All done," he said.

Esteban took a seat and watched her dress. Before leaving, Misty bent down and kissed his forehead. She grinned at him before leaving the room without saying a word.

When the door shut behind her, Esteban placed his head in his hands. He had remained professional throughout the ordeal, but it had taken its toll. He walked over and wedged a chair under the doorknob, disrobed, and climbed onto the table. Esteban lay on his back and reached for the massage oil. The wait had been almost torturous, but finally relief was at hand.

* * *

Monique was sitting on the sofa when Misty got home.

"My, what happened to you?" she blurted out.

"Why? What do you mean?"

Monique laughed, "You look like you just had the heck screwed out of you. Where have you been?"

Misty grinned, "Just getting a late-night massage."

"With Esteban?"

"Who else!"

Hmmm. Looks like I need to schedule an appointment with Esteban, Monique thought, and she made her way to the bedroom.

* * *

Misty had a glow about her during Monday morning's training session, putting an extra X or two into their P90X routine. Monique caught Salvatore eyeing Misty, so she countered by sliding the zipper of her workout top down until exposing more of her ample breasts. Her quickened tempo caused them to jiggle. *Black Widow Trainer, indeed. I'm every bit the trainer Misty is. Maybe I should start up my own business and call it The Real Black Widow Trainer.* Monique glanced over to Salvatore to make sure she had caught his attention. The expression on his face was not what she expected, nor was the expression on Misty's face. Looking down, she noticed one of her breasts had escaped from captivity, revealing her large brown nipple. She quickly turned around, but her reflection from the full-length mirror broadcast her every movement. When she turned back around, every man in the club was staring at her with cantaloupe-sized eyes while the women looked on in horror.

Thoroughly embarrassed and not sure what to do, Monique said, "I'll be right back," and hurried off to the women's locker room. Misty stepped forward to lead the exercise.

When Monique returned, she was wearing a large T-shirt over her training top. Misty said, "I guess the show is over?" As Monique gave Misty a dirty look, a voice called out from across the room.

It was Antonio walking toward them with Tomasso by his side. She resisted the temptation to hurl a few choice epithets his way. She stepped back to put some distance between them instead. Thor dismounted his stationary bike and placed his hands on Misty's shoulders to indicate he had her back. Antonio looked Misty up and down as if she were a piece of meat.

Tomasso broke the tension. "Boss, we heard you are leaving today. Anything you need us to do before you go?"

Salvatore shook his head. "I've got everything under control. The syndicate—ah, I mean the company—has taken care of all my arrangements."

Noticing the puzzled look on Misty's and Monique's faces, Salvatore said, "I received an unexpected call last night requesting my presence in Sicily. I'll be leaving after Friday morning's workout session and might miss up to three training sessions."

Monique placed her hand on his arm and said, "If you would like some companionship on your trip . . ." Salvatore patted her hand. "I'm afraid this is a business trip, honey. Maybe next trip." He pointed to Antonio. "You're in capable hands. Antonio is at your disposal."

"Night or day, ladies," Antonio said smugly.

While toweling off, Salvatore said, "That's enough for me today." He left the room. Not wanting to be in the same room as Antonio without Salvatore around, Misty and Thor left right behind him. When Monique attempted to do the same, Antonio grabbed her by the arm. "Where you going, girl?"

Monique attempted to jerk her arm away, causing Antonio to intensify his grip. She stared him down until he let her go. Monique went storming out of the room in a huff.

"That one's a pistol," Tomasso said.

"Just the way I like them," Antonio said with a large grin. "Come on, let's get a drink."

* * *

Gary was in his office looking over paperwork when Bobbie, his longtime friend and associate, walked in. "Hey, boss. You might want to come take a look. The hot-looking woman you taught blackjack to is on a roll."

Misty had a large stack of chips in front of her when Gary arrived. Standing directly behind Misty, without her knowledge, he caught a glimpse of her hole card as she snuck a peek. He then looked at the seven of hearts she had up, matched against the dealer's three of spades, and waited to see if she made the right move. Misty pushed ten black chips next to the ten black chips she had already bet.

"Doubling down. Good luck," the man next to her said.

When the dealer got to Misty, he turned over her hole card. It revealed the four of spades, giving her eleven.

The dealer dealt Misty a king of clubs, and the man next to her yelled, "Sweet! She's still smoking hot!"

"Still not as hot as she looks!" another man at the table said.

The dealer turned over a nine to go with his three.

"Face card, baby!" Misty said. "Deal yourself a face card, my friend, and I'll give you a big ol' tip!" And that's what he did.

"Busted!" Misty yelled. "You're so nice to me, Charlie. I'm going to put in a good word to Gary for ya, buddy."

Misty was rearranging the twenty black chips when she heard a voice from behind. "So you were paying attention to my lessons."

Without turning around, Misty said, "I'm sure you've got plenty of money, Gary. You won't miss a few chips."

Gary laughed. "You're pretty cocky tonight. I hope your luck doesn't run out."

Misty doubled her bet this time and the dealer dealt her blackjack. "You go, girl!" the man next to her said. "I wish I was as lucky as you."

"I had a good teacher," she said, as the dealer pushed thirty blacks her way.

Gary placed his hands on her shoulders, leaned in, and whispered into her ear, "Come with me to the mountains this weekend."

Misty turned around and said, "That was random."

"Not if it's an attempt to entice you away from the tables before you own my casino."

"I'll sit this one out," she said to the dealer and then stood up to address Gary. "How do I know I can trust you?"

"How do I know I can trust you?" he shot back.

When Gary could tell she was giving it some serious thought, he said, "I know some excellent hiking trails that lead to an incredible mountain-top view, and I cook a mean steak."

The thought of getting away from Monique, Antonio, and his boys for the weekend sounded good to Misty. "How long would we be gone?" she asked.

"I'll pick you up in front of your hotel at 4:00 p.m. Friday and have you back Sunday morning."

"And just where will we stay?"

"I have a cabin that's been in the family for three generations. It's old and rustic, but it's comfortable. You'll love the view from my deck."

"Then I'll see you Friday," she said with a smile.

9

HIGH ALTITUDE

Friday afternoon, Misty packed some belongings into a small duffel bag before provisioning her new Osprey backpack with water bottles, sunscreen, a first-aid kit, and energy bars for the hike. When that was done, she sat on her bed and gazed out her window at the Spring mountain range in the distance. The view conjured up memories of hiking in the Sierra Nevada Mountains with her ex-husband, Rob, and she wondered how Rob and his new wife, Amelia, were getting along. She made a mental note to give him a call to catch up. The ringing of her cell phone broke her concentration.

She looked at her caller ID before answering. "Gabriella! What a nice surprise."

"Hello, dear. How have you been?"

"Okay, I guess."

"What's the matter? You don't sound that convincing."

Misty sighed. "To be honest with you, Gabriella, I'm not sure what's going on. Things just aren't the same this time around. Some good, but I guess mostly bad."

Misty gave Gabriella a blow-by-blow account of everything that had happened since they took off from Buenos Aires. She decided to save the part about having a personal masseuse for when she returned to Buenos Aires and was back in Gabriella's arms. It would prove an excellent aphrodisiac over a bottle of wine. She ended with, "I guess that's it."

"That's a lot to digest, my friend. Let's see if I can summarize things. Monique hijacked your client, Salvatore. Your client has four creeps working for him who are causing trouble. And you are bored to tears? Does that sum it up?"

"You forgot the part about Monique driving me crazy."

"I'm sorry I suggested she should accompany you. It seemed like a good idea at the time."

"Well, there is some good news," Misty said in an attempt to keep Gabriella from feeling bad about making her bring Monique with her. "I met the nicest man, and he's taking me hiking in the mountains. I think getting out of here for the weekend is just what I need right now."

"How well do you know this man, Misty?"

"Well enough."

"You're taking Thor with you, aren't you?"

When Misty remained silent, Gabriella said, "You're not taking Thor with you."

"I think Thor could use some time alone as well. I know this might sound crazy, but even though I just met Gary, I'm comfortable around him. I know a decent guy when I meet one."

Misty changed the subject before Gabriella had a chance to talk her out of it. "So how is Miguel?"

"Miguel claims he's fully recovered and can't wait to get back to work. I caught him sparring with Tom yesterday and watched him take several blows to the abdomen without favoring his side. I have no reason to doubt him at this juncture."

"Not many men can absorb body punches from Tom even if they aren't injured."

"And how is Thor?"

"He's a stud!" Misty replied without thinking. "Thor knocked one of Salvatore's men to the ground with one punch. Tom would have been proud of him."

"Thor did what? You're not telling me everything, are you?"

Not in a mood to get lectured, Misty said, "I'm late, Gabriella. Can't keep Gary waiting. I gotta run. It was great catching up. Give everyone my love." She then abruptly ended the conversation and put away her cell phone.

Having remorse for hanging up before Gabriella had a chance to say good-bye, she was contemplating calling her back when Thor walked in. Seeing her two bags, he said, "Are you going somewhere?"

Misty grinned and said, "To the mountains with Gary for the weekend." After letting out a nervous chuckle, she added, "Looks like it's you and Monique this weekend, buddy."

"You're not taking me with you?"

"Not to worry. Gary's a really great guy, don't you think?"

Thor didn't answer immediately as he tried to decide whether trying to talk Misty out of it would do any good. After coming to a conclusion, he said, "You've got me on your speed-dial. Keep your phone handy at all times."

Misty patted his chest. "You know I will. Well, I've got to go." She grabbed her bags and then set them back down and pulled out a credit card. She handed it to Thor. "Have a good time this weekend on me. You've done a good job and deserve a break."

"Thanks, Misty. Maybe I'll take one of those helicopter tours of the Grand Canyon."

"Cool! Take a camera so you can show everyone when we get home."

Misty left, leaving Thor to wonder if he had done the right thing.

* * *

Gabriella was sitting on her living room sofa looking over some papers when Tom and Miguel arrived.

"So, what's up?" Miguel asked.

Knowing her well, Tom said, "Trouble, boss?"

Gabriella took off her reading glasses and laid them on the end table next to her. "I just got off the phone with Misty, and she said some things that were troubling."

"If Thor isn't doing his job . . ." Tom said.

"Oh, no, Tom. I'm sorry I gave you that impression," Gabriella said. "Misty was glowing about Thor decking a guy with one blow."

Miguel bobbed and weaved as he threw some short punches. "He's a chip off the old block," he said and threw several more phantom punches.

Tom grinned and asked Gabriella, "Would you like me to go check things out?"

"I like that idea!" Miguel said. "Gas up the jet and fly us out there for round two."

When they noticed Gabriella giving it some serious thought, Miguel began shadow boxing again. But it wasn't to be.

"Sorry," she said. "I lent my plane out to the mayor next week so he can campaign for the president. They're old school buddies." Gabriella patted Tom on the knee. "We're probably all overreacting. Let's talk about it when I get the plane back."

"We'll be ready," Tom said. He looked at Miguel. "What do you say we get in a little more sparring?"

"Let's do it, my friend!"

* * *

Misty woke Saturday morning to the sound of birds chirping outside her window. It took her a moment to remember she was at Gary's house in the mountains. She closed her eyes and reminisced about her trip there late yesterday afternoon. They had stopped at the base of the mountains and had a wonderful dinner at a quaint little inn. Gary was so easy to talk to. Spending time with him provided the transition she needed to unwind and readjust her attitude. While riding up the dark, narrow, winding mountain road to Gary's remote cabin, Misty promised she would leave her troubles in the flatlands and throw herself whole-heartedly into what appeared to be shaping up as a wonderful weekend. When they arrived, he had given her a tour of the cabin and a short history of when and how it was built. She loved Gary's stories about his great grandfather, who was the original owner. She was surprised to find out his ancestors were real mountain men who had lived off the land. When it got late, he escorted her to a small bedroom on the far side of the house. After making sure she had towels and an extra blanket, he wished her a peaceful sleep and retired to the other end of the house, like the true gentleman he appeared to be.

Oh my-gosh, that smells wonderful! Stomach rumbling, she jumped from bed, put on a robe, and sniffed her way all the way to the kitchen. Gary whistled away while flipping flapjacks. Eggs were frying on the stove. Gary noticed Misty watching him when he turned toward the kitchen table with a plate of bacon in his hands. "You're up?"

"There's no way I could sleep through the aroma of cooking bacon. I'm famished!"

"Excellent!" he said and held out the plate of bacon. Misty took a piece and placed it in her mouth. "Yummy. This is the best bacon I have ever had." She licked her lips. "You're either a good cook or things just taste better in high altitudes."

"It's probably the altitude." Gary held his hand out. "Please take a seat, and I'll bring you a cup of coffee. How do you take it?"

"Black."

"Then black it is."

Misty savored every bite. The scrambled eggs were moist, yet not runny, just the way she liked them. Even though the thick pieces of bacon had the sweet flavor of maple wood, she drenched them in hot maple syrup. When finished, she leaned her chair back and sipped on her second cup of coffee, noticing how rugged yet warm the kitchen was. She was pretty certain his ancestors had sat around the same table and ate the same food. Gary was busy polishing off the food on his plate, so she placed her napkin on the table and walked over to the old windows to admire the magnificent view. Finally, she walked out past the stone fire pit onto the small deck and gazed over the rail to the canyon floor below.

When Gary joined her, she said, "It's beautiful!"

"We're supposed to have clear skies and a pretty-full moon tonight. Maybe I'll grill some steaks on that hundred-year-old pit you passed by. There's a little butcher shop at the base of the mountain. We'll stop on the way back from our afternoon climb, and you can pick out your own steak."

"That sounds wonderful. So, when do we head out?"

"Not for a few more hours. Why don't you go take a nice hot shower and relax? I'll come get you when it's time."

Misty wrapped her arms around Gary's chest and gave him a gentle squeeze. "Thank you so much for inviting me. Things have been a little crazy lately, and the cool fresh air is just what I need to clear my head."

"I'm glad you came as well," Gary said as he returned the hug.

* * *

It was early afternoon and Thor was famished. Deep in thought as he walked through a passageway, he didn't notice Santo and Tomasso until he was upon them. Santo stood with his arms crossed, blocking Thor's way.

"Hey, it must be Groundhog Day. Look who's here," Tomasso said.

"It looks more like round two, to me," Santo said.

Thor ignored Tomasso as he looked coldly into Santo's eyes and said, "Why don't we make it the final round." Thor's calmness made Tomasso a little uneasy, so he said to Santo, "Are you sure Benny isn't nearby? You know what he told us."

"Fuck Cousin Benny and his polyester pants!" Santo replied angrily. "I couldn't give a shit about what he said."

"Fuck who?" Monique asked as she joined them.

"Hi, Monique," Tomasso said. "Is Salvatore around?"

"I just had coffee with him. He said you guys were running an errand for him before he catches his flight."

Tomasso patted Santo on his shoulder. "Let's go, buddy. You know how Salvatore hates for us to be late."

Santo poked Thor in the chest and said, "Must be your lucky day."

Thor eased his posture just enough to allow Santo to leave without losing face. When they were gone, Monique placed her hand on the side of Thor's face and asked, "Are you okay?"

"Yes, but I wish you would have let me get this over with while there were only two of them. I kind of liked my odds."

Monique gave Thor a funny look. "You're serious, aren't you?"

Thor's face softened. "Yes, but thank you for diffusing the situation just the same."

"Well, I couldn't let you beat up Salvatore's men, now could I? He's the client, you know."

"He seems to be more your client than Misty's these days."

Monique ran a hand through her jet-black hair. "That's because I look more like a real Black Widow Trainer, don't you think?"

"I'm not touching that one," Thor said, shaking his head. "I'd much rather take on two men than get in the middle of a catfight between you and Misty."

Monique laughed. "That's probably a smart move. Where is Misty anyway?"

"In the mountains with a friend."

"And she left you here all alone?" Monique asked with a puzzled look.

"Maybe she's more worried about you being with Salvatore than she is about being alone with her friend."

"I doubt she gives a shit about what Salvatore might do to me after the way I've treated her."

"I can't argue with that. How come you and Misty can't get along any better?"

"Maybe we are too much alike," Monique said.

"Maybe you need to give her a little more respect."

"I'll give it some thought," Monique said with a smile and then left.

* * *

Misty stood waiting at the trailhead of the Cathedral Rock picnic area.

"We better get a move on. We've got fifteen hundred feet to climb," Gary said as he walked past her.

"Let's do it!" she said.

When they came upon the mixed pine-fir forest, Misty said, "Hang on a minute."

She threw her head back, closed her eyes, and inhaled the sweet, scented air. The pungent pine-fir fragrance shot through her nostrils to her oxygen-starved brain. Misty was so lightheaded that she almost felt a little tipsy. She stretched out her arms and spun around and around until she was so dizzy she fell to the forest floor. She looked up at Gary, who stood over her. "If I had known you weren't twenty-one yet, I never would have let you gamble in my casino," he said.

"That was a blast, Mr. Serious. You should try it sometime," she said.

He offered his hand and helped her to her feet. When he was confident the dizziness had abated, he headed back up the trail.

Misty picked up a pinecone and threw it at the back of his head. He turned around and gave her a curious look. "You really should lighten up, you know," she said.

"You're not the first person to tell me that," he said and smiled. "I guess I'm just not the silly type."

"I'm usually not either. Guess I'm just so fricken glad to get away from Monique and Salvatore."

"I don't know much about Monique, but you should be glad you're away from Salvatore."

"Why, what do you know about Salvatore?" Misty asked in a more solemn tone.

Sorry he had said something to spoil her mood, Gary picked up a few pinecones and began pelting her with them. She immediately began to fire back. After a few minutes, he said, "I surrender. You are the pinecone champion of the forest. Let's continue to the top, shall we?"

"To the top!" she replied.

Gary led her up an avalanche chute that had been cleared of brush and thicket by the winter snow until limestone cliffs forced them back to the center of the canyon. They followed a steep slope on the west side of the canyon for forty-five minutes until reaching the Echo Overlook at the top of Echo Cliffs. Working their way through the ponderosa pine and white fir, they came to the edge of Echo Cliff. Gary took a seat on the ground and pulled Misty down beside him.

The view took Misty's breath away. After giving her enough time to take it all in he said, "That's Kyle Canyon below us and the desert to the east."

She patted his hand without prying her eyes away from the majestic view. "I had no idea what was in store. This is fantastic! Thank you so much for inviting me." She could tell from the look on Gary's face that he was pleased she appreciated his efforts.

* * *

Esteban had just settled in to read a few chapters of his new book when he got a call from the spa receptionist. "Sorry, Esteban, but there's a lady friend of the boss here requesting your services."

"That's strange. Salvatore didn't mention anything about a new guest. Okay, give me time to get into uniform, and I'll be right down."

When Esteban arrived, he pushed the door open slowly, peering into the room to see if he recognized his new guest. The woman was already lying on his massage table with a sheet draped over half of her buttocks. Her body was magnificent, and if not for the long jet-black hair, he would have mistaken her for Misty. Without saying a word, he walked over to his table. While coating his hands with massage oil, he noticed the liquor cabinet was open. He heard heavy breathing coming from the woman and noticed a bottle of Grey Goose Vodka on the floor in front of her.

"I take it you are a friend of Salvatore's," he said.

She rolled over onto her side and peered up at him, fully exposing her breasts. "I am. I work with Misty, so whatever you do for her, you should do for me."

"So you're Monique."

"See, you do know who I am," she said and placed her head face down again. "Shall we get started?"

He placed his strong hands on her back and for the next ten minutes demonstrated why Salvatore paid him so well. When she was thoroughly relaxed, she lifted up on one arm and flung the sheet onto the floor with her other. Looking up, she said, "Do you mind me being naked?"

He calmly replied, "If that's what makes you comfortable. What would you like me to work on next?"

"My buttocks, sweetie. They're sore from my workout."

Esteban sunk his fingers deep enough into the two beautiful mounds of firm flesh to cause her to flinch.

"Was that too hard?" he asked.

"Not even close. Dig deeper, I can take it."

Monique rotated her hips in sync with the movement of his hands. Her breathing became heavy as she moaned softly. He could tell she was interested in more than a massage. Without warning, she rolled over onto her back, leaving her soft mound fully exposed.

She waited until she caught him looking and then said, "Not down there, honey, up here."

He raised his eyes to her massive, gravity-laden breasts that spread over her chest. She cupped her breasts with her hands and said, "Put some more lotion on your hands, but be more gentle with these."

Esteban dripped the oily substance directly onto her breasts and delicately rubbed it in with his hands. She watched for a while and then rested her head back on the table and closed her eyes. He was no stranger to giving breast massages, working the tender mounds just firm enough not to give her discomfort. Her demand had been more of a dare, and she was surprised when he dove right in. She was also surprised at how invigorating it was. At times she prepared to yell out but never once did he cause her pain. To heighten her pleasure, she gazed upon him unashamedly, hoping to draw eye contact. He ignored her overt attention and placed her erect and heavily lubricated nipples between his index fingers and thumbs and began rubbing them delicately. She watched him stretch her nipples as far out as they could comfortably go, only to let them slip through his grasp over and over again. On the sixth try, she let out a loud moan and her eyes rolled back in her head. Not able to stand it any longer, she braced herself on her elbows and forearms and stared into his eyes. When he finally looked up at her, she grabbed him behind the neck with one arm and pulled him to her until their lips embraced. Unexpectedly, he removed her hand from his neck and backed away.

She looked at him, confused. "What's wrong? Don't you find me attractive?"

"That's not it."

"Well then what, for crying out loud!"

"I don't want to be unfaithful to my girlfriend."

"Unfaithful! You weren't being unfaithful when you were massaging my tits?"

"That's different. I'm paid to massage you."

"And if I tell on you? Are you sure she would be fine with it?"

Esteban grinned. "She lives in Cuba."

"Cuba? When's the last time you were with her?"

"Eighteen months."

Monique shook her head and sat all the way up. She untucked his shirt and ran her hands over his bare chest. He showed no emotion, so she attempted to unbutton his shirt, but he backed away.

"So you'd rather do it with your shirt on?" she asked.

"Do what?"

"Fuck me, of course. That's what you do for Misty, right?"

"I'm afraid you are mistaken."

"Come on, now. I can tell she's been fucked every time she comes back from her visits to you."

Placing his hands in front of her face, he said, "Salvatore pays me handsomely for my hands. They are yours to instruct, but the rest of my body is off limits."

"Salvatore just left for Sicily. He would never know," Monique said and then grabbed him by the crotch. "Oh my. You're a big one. You can't tell me you don't want to fuck me."

He grabbed her by the wrist and pulled her hand away. "It's not a matter of want. It's a matter of won't."

Furious about not getting her way, Monique rolled over and got down from the table. She took her time getting dressed, acting as if she didn't have a care in the world, and then strolled to the door.

She paused before leaving and said without turning around. "You have no idea what you are passing up."

When Esteban did not reply, Monique walked briskly past the receptionist and into the elevator. When the door closed, she blew air inside the front of her shirt and shook it vigorously. Esteban's marvelous hands left her wanting. She pushed the button to the elevator and thought, *I wonder what Thor's up to tonight.*

10

WHILE THE BOSS IS AWAY

Misty enjoyed the fresh air of the late evening as she watched Gary attending to the steaks on the grill. The two huge bone-in rib eyes sizzled over the open coals. A day of strenuous hiking in high altitude had left her famished. She took a sip of the single barrel bourbon Gary had poured her, holding it in her mouth for a moment to savor before enjoying the burn it made on its way down her throat.

She meandered over, placed her hand under Gary's arm and said, "Those look delicious. Maybe you should own a fancy restaurant instead of a casino."

He smiled softly and then excused himself. He returned holding two massive ears of corn. "How's your drink holding up?" he asked.

"It's holding up fine, but I reserve the right to have another one after I devour your delicious-looking steaks."

When everything was done, Gary ushered Misty to the table and asked her to sit down. "Dig in, Misty. There are no rules of etiquette in the mountains. You can even throw your bones over the deck railing when you're finished if you like. Some lucky creature will find them and have a midnight snack."

Misty picked up the large protruding portion of the bone, brought it to her mouth, and said, "Is this how mountain people eat?" She opened her mouth wide and ripped off a large chunk of meat, smiling mischievously as she chewed like a wild woman.

With a slight grin, he shrugged his shoulders and said, "Works for me."

She pointed the steak at him with her right hand and said, "You cook one fine steak, mountain man."

Before she knew what was happening, he leaned forward and latched the steak out of her hands with his mouth. She grabbed the bone and tugged on it until a piece of meat came off in his mouth.

"Now this is quite the culinary experience," she said, laughing. Gary laughed with her.

When Gary finished the last of his steak, Misty reached across, grabbed the bone, and threw it out the open door onto the deck.

"Hey, I thought I told you to throw it over the railing so some lucky creature could eat it."

"Well, I thought it would be easier for you if you didn't have to climb all the way down the side of the mountain for your midnight snack," Misty said playfully.

Gary grabbed the bone off her plate and slung it over his shoulder. The bone flew over the railing. "That's how you do it," he said.

Misty helped Gary clean the few dishes after dinner and then followed him into a small, interior den. He struck a match, lit some kindling, and then expertly waived a magazine back and forth until the fire was raging. He then sat next to Misty in the oversized armchair. Once settled in, he locked his eyes onto hers and said, "I apologize for the intrusion into your personal affairs, but there's something we need to talk about."

She placed her bourbon glass on the small table between them and sat back. "And that would be?"

"How well do you know Salvatore?"

"I vet my clients pretty good. I know enough."

"Then you know the FBI is investigating Salvatore for murder."

Misty drummed her fingers rapidly on the arms of her chair and then said, "No, I have to admit that was not in the background check.

But then I assume the FBI isn't in the habit of sharing about an ongoing investigation with a common security firm. How do you know he's being investigated?"

"I can't tell you anything beyond that. In fact, I shouldn't have told you he was under investigation, but I would feel bad if anything happened to you."

"Happened to me? What are you talking about?"

"Forget about the murder rap. Salvatore has wanted my casino ever since he built his. He tried to strong-arm me into selling to him, but he backed off when the FBI started to investigate."

"And just how did you find out the FBI was investigating Salvatore?" Misty asked.

"I can't tell you. I wish I could, but I'm not at liberty to discuss it. I hope you understand."

"Sure, I guess," she said and then drummed her fingers again while she thought for a few seconds. "What do you suggest I do now?"

"Go home!"

"It's not that easy, Gary."

"Why not?"

Misty began to squirm. "Look, just like you can't tell me about the FBI investigation, I'm not at liberty to discuss the contract with my clients."

Gary frowned. "I'm sorry. Maybe I shouldn't have brought this up. It's none of my business anyway."

Misty looked noticeably shaken, so Gary held out his hand. When she willingly took it, he pulled her up onto his lap.

Holding her in his arms, he said, "I'm really sorry I've upset you. It's a crappy way to end the day."

Sitting in his lap had a calming effect, so she snuggled closer. She pushed the thought of Salvatore out of her mind and concentrated on the man holding her. Gary was kindhearted, easygoing, and fun to be around. Feeling the moment was right, she lifted her head up, hoping he would take the hint and kiss her. Instead, he tapped her on the nose with his index finger.

"I'm sorry you've misunderstood my intentions," Gary said softly.

"So, you have a steady girlfriend?" Misty asked to clear the air. "Or you don't find me attractive?"

"Girlfriend, check. Find you attractive, check. Believe me, it's not because I don't have the urge to kiss you." Gary said it in a way that kept her from feeling uncomfortable about making a move on him.

As the two continued to cuddle, Misty asked, "What's her name and where is she now?"

"Her name is Guinevere, and she's back home in England visiting her parents." He stopped short of mentioning he sent Guinevere out of harm's way while he was helping the FBI probe Salvatore.

"How long has she been there?"

"Going on six months now."

"Six months!" Misty said. "What did you do? Banish her to her castle?"

Gary laughed. "No, she's visiting family and, well, let's not talk about it, okay?"

She gave his nose a little pinch. "If it's been six months, I'd say you have some mighty strong willpower."

Gary nodded. "Yes, having a beautiful woman sitting in my lap is definitely putting me to the test."

They nestled together and talked for another hour until Gary patted Misty on her arm and said, "It's getting late. I have an important meeting tomorrow morning, so we will need to leave early. We should get some sleep."

She patted him on his chest. "Okay, I'm getting a little sleepy anyway."

Misty gave him a kiss on the forehead, got out of the chair, and walked to the doorway. She stopped, looked back at him, and said, "So King Arthur, if you didn't have your precious Guinevere, would tonight have ended any differently?"

Gary smiled and said, "If I didn't have a girlfriend, I might have tied you to one of those fir trees this afternoon and had my way with you!"

"Damn, Gary! You are a mountain man," she said with a twinkle in her eye. She then blew him a kiss and retired to her room.

* * *

Returning from a night of blackjack, Thor unlocked the door and turned on the lights. He was in a good mood, having won twelve hundred dollars, but he wished he had someone to share the moment with. He headed to the kitchen where he planned on drinking plenty of water to flush the alcohol from his system and rehydrate his body.

"Whatcha doing there, Thor?"

Thor spun around. "Oh, Monique! How come you're home so early?"

She got up from the sofa, sauntered over to him, and patted him on his chest. "I want you to be my bodyguard tonight."

"I'm pretty sure you're fully capable of taking care of yourself. I was about to head to bed."

"That's what you think," Monique said as she grabbed his hand and led him to the door.

"And where are you taking me?"

"You'll see."

"I won twelve hundred dollars playing blackjack tonight!" he boasted.

"Perfect! You can pay for the taxi ride and cover charge."

"That sounds more like I'm your date than a bodyguard," he said.

Monique slid her arm under Thor's and held on tight. "Maybe you should be my bodyguard *and* my date."

Thor started to worry about what he might be getting himself into.

Their cabby pulled up in front of a famous downtown Vegas strip joint. After Thor paid the driver, they got out of the cab.

Thor stared at the neon sign of a woman taking her top off. "Looks like trouble to me. I can see why you wanted a bodyguard."

She pushed him toward the door and said, "Don't be silly. I'm sure there are plenty of bouncers on call here. Chill out, and let's have some fun. Concentrate on being my boyfriend tonight."

"Boyfriend? You said date."

"You just got promoted," she said in a commanding tone.

"But Misty doesn't—" Monique placed her hand over his mouth and said, "Misty's not here, and she will never know unless you tell her." Thor knew he was on his way to trouble and that he needed to summon up all the willpower he could muster.

The receptionist did a double take when she saw Monique and asked, "Don't I know you?" Monique shrugged her off. "Hmmm, you look familiar. I guess I'm mistaken. Sandra, please escort them to a table."

Paying no attention to Sandra, Monique grabbed Thor by the hand and led him to seats at the end of a long runway. The waitress caught up to them. "We have a two drink minimum. What are you having?" she asked with a sour look on her face.

The waitress took their drink order and turned to walk away. Monique slapped her on her bottom and said, "We are going to need a big stack of ones."

Monique held her hand out to Thor, and he begrudgingly gave her a twenty. She grabbed his money clip and peeled off two more twenties and then handed over sixty dollars to the waitress. "Fifty ones, sugar. The rest is a tip."

"You got it, sweetie," the waitress said and disappeared into the crowded bar.

After a couple drinks, Thor zeroed in on a hot redhead working the pole closest to them. Her milky-white tits swirled round and round as she gyrated to the music. After catching Thor staring, she put on a delicious smile and moved in his direction.

She pulled up in front of him with her hands on her hips and said, "You're a cutie. Why don't I take you to the back so we can get to know each other better?"

"Get your pasty ass over here, girl," Monique said in a commanding voice. "I'm the one with the stack of ones."

The dancer frowned but knew she needed to please all customers. Not wanting Thor to get away, she blew him a kiss before positioning herself in front of Monique. She put on quite a show, but it was obvious her attention was still on Thor. Monique motioned for the girl to come closer. When she squatted, Monique stood up and tucked five dollar-bills under her G-string. Monique stared into her eyes and leaned in until their faces were only inches apart. She grabbed the top of the little patch of fabric covering the dancer's crotch and with both hands yanked it up. The dancer cringed when the fabric wedged deep into her mound.

"Damn you! That hurts."

Monique laughed. "That's because you paid more attention to him than to me. Don't let it happen again." The dancer gave her a dirty look and walked away. She stopped and whispered something into the ears of the other dancers as she passed them. "Now why did you go and do that?" Thor asked.

She patted him on the face and, with a twinkle in her eye, said, "Stay here for a moment. There's something I need to do."

Thor caught her arm as she rose from the table. "Leave me some ones!" She placed the entire stack of bills on the runway in front of him, knowing there wasn't a girl on the runway who would dare come his way while she was gone.

As Monique attempted to enter a doorway that led to the back of the club, a burly man stepped in front of her. She gave him a sideways glance and grinned. "You don't remember me, do you, Slim?"

He looked her over good and then said with a smile, "Well, I'll be damned. Miss Monique, is it really you?"

"Yes, Slim. It's me."

"How long's it been, fifteen years? You sure have grown up!"

"It's been twenty years. I was only sixteen years old at the time!"

"Oh, no, Monique. Why that would have been illegal."

With a stone-cold look, she said, "Very illegal, but I had little choice. Now can you let me back so I can say hi to Mr. Montoya?"

"Now you're just going to say hi, right?" Slim asked as he looked around nervously. "I don't want to get in no trouble, you know."

Monique held her hands out wide. "Go ahead if you need to frisk me."

"Oh, no, ma'am. That won't be necessary," he said, blushing. "Go on back, but remember to behave yourself!"

"Don't worry, Slim. Is his office still the third door on the right?"

"Yes, ma'am."

Monique stood quietly outside the open door watching Mr. Montoya busily doing paperwork. His grey hair made him look a bit older, but his facial features were the same. She had worked under him in servitude for two long years, but she had no ill feelings toward him; she knew he had no choice but to obey his bosses' orders. He had never mistreated her while she worked for him, and she gave him credit for that. But that was all the credit she would give him.

"Who are you?" he demanded when he noticed her standing in the doorway. "What do you want?"

Monique walked confidently toward him, placed her hands in the middle of his desk, and leaned in until their faces were only inches apart. "I was your personal property for two long years and you don't recognize me!"

He sat back and diligently studied her, eyebrows furled. Monique stepped back with her hands on her hips.

His eyes came alive as he said with trepidation, "Monique, honey. How have you been, how is your—"

"How's my father? Is that what you were going to ask me? How's my father?"

"Yes, I can see you still harbor ill feelings toward him."

"Why wouldn't I? He sold me into servitude. I assume to pay his gambling debts. How much was a little slave girl worth back then?"

Mr. Montoya stood to his feet in reverence. "I had little choice, honey. You know I don't own this joint. I just run it for some real unsavory men. Your dad owed them a lot of money, and had we not worked out a deal, they most likely would have killed him." With a nervous smile, he added, "You wouldn't have wanted your poor father dead, would you?"

"Wanted him dead? Hell, I probably would have pulled the trigger. So how much, Montoya? How much was a sixteen-year-old virgin pole dancer worth?"

Mr. Montoya lowered his head and said in a soft voice, "Two hundred thousand dollars."

"Two hundred thousand dollars?"

"One hundred and fifty thousand to settle his debts, but then he borrowed and lost another fifty thousand, so we kept you another six months," Mr. Montoya smiled feebly.

"I showed off my tits and ass to those filthy men for an extra six months just so my father could blow another fifty thousand dollars gambling!"

"Before you get too down on your father, you should know he borrowed the extra fifty to try and win your freedom sooner."

"Ha! What a moron he was. So how long did it take him to lose the extra fifty?"

"Not long, dear. You know he was a lousy gambler."

Feeling weak in her stomach, Monique settled into a chair in the corner. She had effectively suppressed these memories over the last ten years, but the wounds had been reopened, and they felt as raw as the day she was told her fate. Had she known where her father was at this moment, she would have pleaded with Slim to bash his face in. Hell, she would have done it herself. Mr. Montoya poured her a generous glass of bourbon. "Here, honey. Drink up. It will calm your nerves."

She knew he was right. She took a big gulp and started to cough. He stepped toward her, but she waived him off. A few minutes later she threw back the last of the bourbon, wiped her mouth, and handed him the empty glass.

She stood up with her head held high, acting as if she didn't have a care in the world. "Mr. Montoya, I need you to do me a favor."

"If I can."

She stripped off her blouse and then stepped out of her jeans. When she stood back up straight, she was wearing only a low-cut black bra and skimpy black panties. Mr. Montoya remembered Monique as a hottie, but now that she had matured, she was a knockout.

She could see the dollar signs in his eyes. "No, I'm not coming back to work, so don't get so excited."

"But you could make a fortune! Your body is magnificent. Far better than any girl on my staff."

"I want to use your runway one more time, for old time's sake?"

"By all means. I'll even let you keep all the tips that come your way."

Monique laughed, "That's nice of you, but it's not my intention."

Thor was on his fourth drink and still trying to figure out why the dancers were treating him like he had the plague. The redhead wouldn't even look his way. He sat back and looked the room over. A few women were scattered here and there, but the clientele was mainly men. He couldn't understand what attracted the women to this place, but he decided it wasn't any of his business. He noticed a crowd was gathering around a dark-haired woman at the far end of the runway. Men were lining up excitedly along the runway trying to get her attention. The noise level grew louder as she toyed with them, never coming close enough for the men to touch her. After awhile they began to return to their tables, one at a time. When the last had left the stage, the dancer began walking toward Thor's side of the stage. As she drew closer, Thor realized it was *Monique*!

He had often gazed upon her smoking-hot body during workouts, but he was never able to see this much of her. Her magnificently full breasts almost pushed up and out of her sexy black bra. Her skimpy black panties didn't leave much to the imagination. He broke his gaze and quickly scanned the room, noticing that all eyes in the place were fixated on her every movement. Monique seemed different in an eerie way. She had always been overly confident, but tonight she was in command—of every dick in the place. Monique stopped in front of him and squatted down, her breasts inches from his face. Thor wiped the sweat from his brow and turned away. Monique gently placed her hands on his head and directed his gaze back to her. He barely resisted. She kissed him on the forehead and then stood back up and danced seductively to the music. Her moves were hot and sexy, and Thor could see that she was making the other dancers jealous. He watched intently as she slipped her bra straps off and let them hang down her arms. The crowd let out a collective gasp as she reached behind her back with both hands and unlatched her bra. Monique gave Thor a sultry look as she slowly pulled off her bra and then threw it into the crowd. A fight ensued as several patrons clamored for the souvenir, but Thor remained fixated on her voluptuous breasts. She got on her hands and knees in front of Thor and gently jostled her plump mounds of mother's flesh to and fro only inches from his eyes.

Monique whispered into his ear, "I thought you might like to know what you were protecting tonight." Completely out of character and to her amazement, Thor cupped her breasts in his large hands and bounced them up and down. He leaned forward and whispered in her ear, "Your breasts are magnificent."

She pulled back abruptly and uttered, "Why, Thor! That's a naughty thing to say. You surprise me."

He said in a calm, confident demeanor, "Do you think just because I'm a nice guy I'm not an experienced lover?"

She studied him diligently and realized she had underestimated him. His directness fired her up as much as her visit with Esteban had.

Not wanting the moment to dissipate, she jumped off the stage, grabbed Thor's jacket from the back of his chair, and put it on. Taking him by the hand she said, "Let's get you home so we can see how experienced you really are."

Snuggled up to Thor in the backseat of the taxi, Monique placed his hand beneath her coat, on her left breast. She then leaned over and began kissing him. Thor was slightly hesitant at first, but soon the two were passionately making out, his hands groping her nakedness.

Fishing for compliments, Monique whispered into his ear, "How do I match up to your little Brazilian girlfriends?"

Instead of taking the bait, Thor located the moist entrance to Monique's vagina and worked his middle finger until fully penetrated. Monique laid her head back and spread her legs to welcome him. She was becoming a combustible ball of hot flesh. It started with the touch of Esteban's skilled hands, moved onto her dominance over the men in the strip club, and was now culminating with the seduction of a much younger boy. She unzipped his pants with her right hand and reached inside his trousers. To her delight, she found a massive, throbbing cylinder of flesh. Thor was more man than she realized, and she couldn't wait to get him home so she could bring him inside her. If Thor decided to pull an Esteban, she would probably have to rape him.

Thor flipped a switch as they entered their suite, and the room lit up bright. Monique picked up the universal remote and backed the lights down low. After turning on some light jazz, she took him by the hand and led him to the couch. She smiled at him and said, "Here, let me help you out of your clothes."

Monique pulled Thor's shirt over his head and dropped it to the floor. The soft neon light from the Strip illuminated his well-developed upper torso. His dark brown skin had a creamy texture and was void of blemishes. Monique explored his body with her hands, marveling at how muscular he was. She unzipped his trousers and let them drop to the floor. She ran her hands up and down his solidly built thighs, which reminded her of tree trunks. She looked into his eyes and began rubbing his penis, which bulged beneath his underwear. "The cougar's on the prowl tonight," she whispered into his ear.

Thor grabbed the lapel of her jacket and pulled it open, exposing the trophies that lurked inside.

"Do you like?" Monique asked. "Tonight they are just for you."

He placed his strong hands under each breast and lifted them up until they rested in his palms.

"They are truly magnificent to look at, Monique. The best I have ever seen."

Excitement that only an older woman could understand welled up inside of her.

"Take your panties off," Thor said confidently.

"You first," she replied.

Until now, Monique had been the temptress, but once she got a look at how well-hung Thor was, she immediately pulled her panties off and pushed him to the couch. She had never seen a penis that large, and she quickly became enamored. She dropped to her knees as if under a spell. Pushing his legs apart, she placed both hands around the base of his dick and slid it into her mouth. The massive head was all she could comfortably take in. After getting her fill, she held out her hands and pulled him from the couch. It was truly a primal moment. Two genetically superior bodies stood before each other representing the best the homo sapien species had to offer. A real testament to the species' evolutionary progress.

"I'm all yours. Take me as you wish, but take me now," she said in a submissive voice.

Thor placed his hands under her armpits and effortlessly lifted Monique into the air. Her eyes opened wide. He backed her into the large plate glass window and slowly let her slide down onto his penis. His thickness spread her vagina walls so far apart that her clitoris rode snugly against his penis. The sensation was most pleasant. Sex was exciting to her again for the first time in many years. It may have been the most exciting ever.

The glass began to shake, and she became alarmed. "Thor! We might crash through the window!"

But when he kept driving into her and the hot flashes of her impending orgasm grew near, she stopped thinking about the danger. "Oh, God! Fuck me, Thor. Fuck me, fuck me, fuck me!" she screamed.

By now she couldn't have given a shit whether she fell twenty stories or not, as long as she could reach climax first. To her dismay, Thor climaxed first with a massive grunt.

"Oh, goddamn it, no! You can't come yet!"

Thor let out a sigh of relief and his penis softened.

Shit! That's what I get for screwing a guy ten years younger than me. They are so full of testosterone; they come at the drop of a hat.

Thor grinned. "Oops!"

"Oops! That's all you can say?"

"Don't worry; I'll make it up to you."

Thor carried Monique over to the couch and placed her in a sitting position. He kneeled before her and spread her legs apart. She found his tongue thick and hot, just like his penis, only better as she no longer worried about what was inside of her going limp.

Completely satiated after multiple orgasms, Monique coaxed Thor to her and held him tight. She found his body warm and comforting. There was more to this young man than met the eye. He was a perfect gentleman in public and a total animal in bed. What more could a woman want?

"Thor, you're going to make some young woman very happy some day."

"And you. Why haven't you met someone and settled down?" he asked. "I would think you could have anyone you wanted."

"I'm not the marrying type."

"Sure you are. You just haven't found the right guy yet."

"I'm damaged goods. It's too late for me."

Thor wouldn't let it go, pressing the issue until she broke down. "If I share my secret with you, do you promise never to tell anyone?"

"I promise," he said.

After a short pause to gather her thoughts, Monique began. "My mother died when I was young, leaving my father, a professional gambler, to raise me. He was such a lousy gambler we were always on the run. I can't remember all the times he pulled me out of class in the middle of the school year. As a result, I only have an eighth-grade education."

"But you're a smart woman. No one would ever guess if you never told."

"Yeah, right," she said. "Anyway, we moved to Las Vegas when I was only fifteen. I was mature looking, even at a young age." Monique laughed. "Big tits, you know. No one caught on when he bought me a fake ID. That's when he taught me how to count cards so I could help him cheat. I still remember the day he was on a roll. He had chips stacked everywhere. Like a fool, he started drinking heavily and quadrupled his bets. You know, betting with house money and all that stupid stuff. When the losing streak came, it only took a fourth the time to lose what he had won. He didn't stop there, talking the casino into giving him credit, thinking it was only a matter of time before he won all his money back. I can remember him surrounded by tough-looking men, pointing my way. The men came over to inspect me, touching me in private places, and laughing. I was his collateral for his loans. Without the ability to pay up, he had no choice but to force me into servitude.

"What did they make you do?" Thor was horrified. "What happened to your dad?"

Looking more through him than at him, she said, "You saw tonight what they had me do."

"So that's why you were so skilled on the runway. But you were underage."

"I'm sure it's not the first time the law has looked the other way in Las Vegas," she said.

"So how have you managed to get by the last twenty years?"

"I traveled from town to town, taking odd jobs and using my anger for motivation. I did a lot of things I'm not proud of, Thor, and I've had a lot of things done to me. I'll spare you the gory details."

Thor sat there in a daze. Monique leaned over and lay down, pulling him with her. She couldn't believe she had just told someone something she had held in for so long. It felt good, like the warmth of his body over her. Tonight Thor would be her security blanket, making her feel as safe and secure as she could be.

* * *

The next morning, Misty kissed Gary on the cheek as he dropped her off at her hotel. "I really had a wonderful weekend, Gary. Thank you so much!"

"I did as well. Thanks for helping to fill the void of not having Guinevere here. I get lonely at times, and you make for great company."

Misty dashed onto the elevator. First she would share her weekend with Thor and then, of course, she would call Gabriella to fill her in with a more detailed version. She unlocked the door and hurried toward the kitchen, hoping to find Thor. She caught something stirring as she passed the sofa and turned to the sight of Thor lying over Monique. A blanket covered the lower half of their bodies, leaving everything else exposed. Monique's bosom protruded from under Thor's chest. Misty exploded in a fit of rage.

"Get up, Monique!" Misty screamed.

"Misty, you're home early," Thor said as he rubbed the sleep from his eyes.

Monique pushed Thor off her and stood to her feet. Misty grabbed Monique by her shoulders and shook her vigorously.

Thor yelled, "Misty! I can explain."

Misty looked Thor in the eyes as he stumbled to come up with an explanation. She turned back to Monique and yelled, "What the hell were you doing with Thor?"

Monique decided she didn't like Misty's tone, so she answered matter-of-factly, "Why, fucking the boy. What did it look like?"

Misty slapped her hard across the face with an open hand. Monique stumbled back a step, shook it off, and moved back into Misty's face, defiantly.

"I warned you about going cougar on Thor," Misty said.

The two stood silently staring into each other's eyes, as Thor remained frozen. Misty grabbed Monique by her hair and jerked her head to the side. "Go get your things out of my master suite and get the hell out of here."

"Misty! You don't understand!" Thor yelled as he rose, holding the blanket around his waist.

"That's all right, Thor," Monique said. "I'll gladly pack my things and leave. That's one thing life has taught me how to do well."

Monique walked to her bedroom and slammed the door behind her. Misty took a deep breath trying to calm down.

"Misty," Thor said softly. "It's not what you think."

"Not now, Thor. I'm going up to my room to lie down and hopefully calm down. Please stay here to make sure Monique gets her stuff out. I'll move into her vacated room tonight."

Thor was waiting on the sofa when Monique reappeared from the bedroom. She walked quickly past him toward the door, a suitcase in each hand.

Thor yelled after her, "I am really sorry, Monique. I'll explain things to Misty when she's in a better mood, and we'll get this all worked out."

Monique stopped but did not turn around. "No, Thor. Leave it be. I'll land on my feet. I always do."

Thor was left all alone with his thoughts. He was torn between a deep loyalty to Misty and his newfound appreciation of Monique and how she had somehow endured the shitty hand life had dealt her. He was too nauseous to think about it, so he lay down, placed his arm over his eyes, and tried to fall back to sleep.

11

TIME TO SORT THINGS OUT

Antonio located Monique sitting in a chair in the main hotel lobby with her bags at her feet. She was obviously distraught, and he reveled in her misery. Antonio had been hot for Monique from the moment he laid eyes on her. She belonged to Salvatore now, but like all the others, Antonio knew that Salvatore would soon tire of Monique and pass her down to him. If like the others, she would be broken down and stripped of her self-confidence by then, making it that much easier for him to dominate. But he sensed Monique might be different than the others. She was head-strong and proud, and he prayed there would still be some fight left in her. He anticipated how much fun it would be to strip Monique of her remaining dignity. Running his tongue over his lips, he strode toward her.

"So, you want access to the boss's apartment, do you?" he asked.

Without looking up, Monique said, "Yes, Misty is cramping my style, so I thought I would make the change. She's been pissed ever since Sal-vatore gave me the master bedroom, and I'm tired of her complaining."

"So Misty can be a real bitch?"

Not wanting to overdo it, she replied, "Well, we get along other than that, I suppose." She rose from her chair and stood confidently before him. "Are you going to get me a key, or will I have to track Salvatore down in Sicily?"

He resisted the urge to slap her. There would be plenty of time for that later, so he toyed with her, "I have plenty of room at my place. Why don't you stay with me until Salvatore returns?"

She bit her lip and replied, "Nice try. Come on, go get the key."

He laughed. "Follow me. I'll take you up there now."

Monique waited for Antonio to call a porter or offer to grab at least one of her bags, but he simply turned and walked away. She cursed under her breath as she followed after him with bags in tow.

When they arrived at Salvatore's apartment, Antonio slung the door open and walked in ahead of her. Monique headed straight for the master bedroom she knew so well. The room brought back memories of what a lousy, selfish lover Salvatore was, and she cherished the thought of sleeping in his bed alone until his return. She set one bag on the floor and the other on the bed and then began unpacking clothes.

"What do you think you are doing?" Antonio asked as he walked into the room.

"I'm putting my things away," she replied while thinking to herself, *You big dork.*

Antonio laughed. "Pick up your bags and follow me. Salvatore has a separate room for his dames."

"But I've been in this bed many times before with Salvatore," she said, surprised.

He turned back and said, "You must be confusing sleeping with getting fucked. He might let you move into his bedroom when he gets back, but that will be his call."

She put her things back in, zipped her bag, and trudged to the far side of the suite. She found the bedroom feminine and frilly, everything she disdained. *Oh well,* she thought. *It's a place to sleep.*

Setting her bags on the floor, she turned to Antonio and held out her hand. "My key!"

Antonio grabbed Monique by the wrist, placed the key in the palm of her hand, and rolled her fingers over it with his other hand. She cringed at his touch. When he continued to hold onto her hand, she said, "Don't you have something more productive to do?"

When his eyes hardened, she regretted her remarks, but then he quickly loosened his grip and gave her a patronizing smile. "Like Salvatore said before he left, if you need anything, give me a call." He turned and walked out the door.

Monique waited for the front door to close and then sat on the bed, bent over, and placed her face in her hands. *What have I gotten myself into?*

* * *

Misty stirred in her bed the next morning as she replayed the previous day's events. She wasn't proud of the way she had treated Monique, but she felt justified. Sorry she hadn't taken the time to set things right with Thor, she put on a robe and went downstairs to check on him. She found him sitting at the kitchen table with his back to her, drinking a cup of coffee. Placing her hands on his broad shoulders, she said, "Thor, I'm sorry I ignored you. I'm ready to talk things out now."

Replying softly and without turning around, Thor said, "What I did last night with Monique was not professional. You had every right to be upset."

"Yes, you're right about that. Miguel would have never mixed business with pleasure. But hey, you are learning, right? Just think of it as on-the-job training."

He patted her hand. "Thank you, Misty."

His contriteness and humility reminded her of what a wonderful boy he was. She bent over him, wrapped her arms around his shoulders, and gave him a big hug. Afterwards, she poured herself a cup of black coffee and sat at the table. She took a few sips before looking at him with caring eyes. "Thor, is there something still bothering you?"

With his head hung low he said, "I'm still embarrassed you found me like you did."

"Oh, Thor. Why are you embarrassed? Because you were sleeping with a woman?"

Misty reached over and placed her hand on his. "You're a grown man, and you have needs. I understand that."

Thor shrugged his shoulders.

Misty laughed. "Your dad told Miguel some of his adventures while in the navy. You're just a chip off the old block, as they say."

Thor looked at her funny. "Chip off what?"

She laughed. "It means you are just like your father. Do you have a problem with that?"

Thor shook his head, smiling. "No, I guess not."

"Good," Misty replied. Then she became more serious. "Thor, I think now might be a good time to tell you the reason I get paid so much." Now it was Misty doing the squirming. "They call me the Black Widow Trainer because I permit my clients to sleep with me." Misty gave Thor time for her words to settle in before adding, "But once they sleep with me, the training sessions are over and we go home."

"That means you haven't slept with Salvatore yet?" he asked.

"No," Misty said as she frowned. "Nor do I want to."

"So why don't we just go home?"

"We can't. I have a reputation to maintain. If I ever break a contract, I won't be able to charge what I do."

"How much do you charge?"

"Five thousand dollars a session."

"Holy shit! That's a lot of money."

Misty tried to read his thoughts before continuing. She was slightly embarrassed and Thor could sense it. He grinned and said, "I think it's great! I know the older generation has hang-ups about sex, but I can assure you, I don't. I often wonder why people don't think twice about watching violence on TV or in movies, but when it comes to sex they get offended. Seems like watching someone get their head chopped off would be worse. Amazed and relieved at Thor's maturity, Misty blurted out, "Yeah, how fucked up is that?"

With the nervous tension in the room broken, Misty said, "Don't ever be ashamed about bowing to your natural instincts. Humans, like animals, were given strong sexual drives to ensure they propagate the species. Yes, it's for reproductive purposes, but since we were never given a shut-off valve, well, you know, the urge keeps urging us on. I guarantee you that if you were a mind reader and could read all the thoughts people had, you'd be blown away by how many of them are about sex." Misty paused before adding, "Are we cool with everything?"

"You mean you're okay with me sleeping with Monique last night?" he said.

Misty's face went sour as she realized it was more complicated than that. "I guess I'm okay with you sleeping with Monique, but not Monique sleeping with you, if you know what I mean."

From the look on Thor's face, she had managed to undo all the progress she had just made. Not wanting to go back through things again, she said, "Oh, just forget it. I'm fine. Let's not discuss it anymore."

"Okay, so what do you want to do?" he asked.

"Get a massage."

As she rose from the table, Thor reached out, grabbing her gently by her wrist. He said, "I really need to tell you what I found out about Monique last night."

"Not now, Thor. I'll let you know when I'm ready."

Thor nodded and released her wrist.

* * *

Esteban's skilled hands discovered knots under Misty's skin. "Rough weekend?" he asked.

Misty sighed, "No, my weekend was great. I just . . . well, stumbled into something when I got back that irritated me."

"Why don't we stick to your wonderful weekend so you can relax? It will make it easier for me to work these knots out of your back."

Misty cringed from the pressure he applied. "Good idea."

Esteban dug in deep. After some progress was made, she said, "Went to the mountains for the weekend."

"Salvatore is out of the country. Did you go by yourself?"

"No, I went with the nicest man. He owns that little casino attached to the hotel."

When Esteban's hands stopped working on her neck, she asked, "What's up?"

"You mean Gary?" he asked.

"So you know Gary?"

"Not really, but I know of Gary."

"How so?"

When Esteban stopped again, she turned over and sat up. Misty's breasts were fully exposed, but she paid it no mind as the two had become quite intimate over the last several sessions.

"Okay, you are obviously concerned about something, so let's hear it."

Esteban looked nervously around the room and then leaned in to whisper in her ear, "There's a feud between Salvatore and Gary. It would be best if you didn't get involved."

"But Gary's such a nice guy," she whispered back.

"He is, but Salvatore's not a nice man."

Misty got as close to his ear as possible this time and whispered in an even lower volume, "So how bad is Salvatore?"

"Trust me. As bad as it gets."

"How do you know?"

"You forget I've been giving massages to all Salvatore's girlfriends for the past few years."

"All? How many is all?"

"I don't know, quite a few. Maybe nine?"

"Nine, in only two years," she said. "Why so many?"

He shook his head. "You don't want to know."

"But my associate, Monique, is his girlfriend now."

"And a pretty one."

"How do you know how pretty she is?" Misty asked.

"She came for a massage yesterday afternoon."

"How did that go?"

"Everything was going fine until she demanded I have sex with her."

Misty responded like a jealous lover, "You didn't!"

He placed his hands in front of Misty's face and said, "I told her these hands were the only thing she could command. No other part of me is under contract."

Misty chuckled, "I assume *that* didn't go over well."

"She acted as if it didn't bother her, but I know better. I can sense how sexually charged a woman is with the touch of my hands. The heat of their skin reveals all."

"Oh, really," she said. "So what's my skin tell you?"

Esteban shook his head. "You, my friend, are not ready yet. Too much talking."

Misty lay face down on the table. "Well, get back to work then."

Not even Esteban's magnificent hands could free her mind. She began putting the pieces together from the night before. She reasoned that Monique got horny and since Salvatore was out of the country, Monique seduced Thor. Misty knew firsthand that a massage session with Esteban that didn't end with a happy ending could make any woman passionately insane. Thor just happened to be in the wrong place at the wrong time. But then she came to realize how fortunate she was to have Monique buffering her from someone like Salvatore, and for the first time she was glad she had been forced to bring Monique with her to Vegas.

"So, Esteban. If Salvatore is such a monster, why haven't you left?"

His hands stopped again and she thought, *Crap, if I don't quit asking him questions, he'll never finish my massage or raise my temperature.*

"What is it this time?" she asked.

When he didn't respond, she rose up on an arm, turned her head, and saw that he was staring into space.

"Esteban?"

He leaned in and whispered into Misty's ear, "To do so I would have to break my contract with Salvatore, and no one breaks their contract with Salvatore!"

The reality of her predicament hit home. *Oh my God! If I don't sleep with Salvatore at some point, I will be breaking my contract.* Not wanting to think about the horrible things a man like Salvatore might do to her in bed, Misty slowly pulled her knees up and tucked them under her belly. Esteban pulled the sheet off of Misty as he had done so many times before and dropped it onto the floor. After coating his fingers with lotion, he proceeded to fill her mind with pleasurable thoughts.

12

SALVATORE'S RETURN

Monique unlocked the door to Salvatore's apartment Thursday evening and walked to her bedroom. Antonio had notified her of Salvatore's return and told her that Salvatore requested that she wait for him in the suite wearing something comfortable. She settled into the sofa to await Salvatore's impending arrival, wondering how he would react to her moving in without first consulting him. Anxious from worry, she closed her eyes and drifted off. At two in the morning, she awoke to the sound of a key turning the front lock. The door opened, and she caught her first glimpse of Salvatore. He placed a few things on the table, and one of his employees carried his luggage to the bedroom. He noticed her on the sofa, but he took a seat in the large chair across the room. He motioned for Monique to join him. She sat in his lap and nervously wrapped her arms around Salvatore and gave him a hug.

"I missed you. How was your trip?" she asked.

"Excellent! The family was very pleased about how things are going here in the States."

"Family? I didn't know your family lived in Sicily. So you were with your mother and dad?"

He laughed. "No, you can consider them my extended family."

"But you do have family?"

"No," he answered without a hint of remorse.

"But what about the guy who says he's related to you?"

"Cousin Benny?"

"Yes, he's The Guy," she said and then chuckled. "Well, at least he keeps saying he's The Guy."

Salvatore rolled his eyes. "Benny's an imbecile. If my mother hadn't made me promise on her dying bed to look after him, he would be out on his own. Her damn sister came down with breast cancer a month after my mother passed away and died a few months later."

"You mean, your aunt?"

"What the fuck? Yeah, my aunt."

"I didn't mean anything by it. I just thought—"

"Don't think. I like you better when you listen."

"I'm sorry," Monique said and began rubbing his shoulders. "I didn't mean to upset you."

"Get undressed, and wait for me in bed," he demanded. "I'll be there in a minute."

She had seen that look in men's eyes all too often, and she didn't want to face the consequences if she refused to do as she was told.

Salvatore called after her, "Put on some red lipstick. All my women wear red lipstick."

Not owning any lipstick, she walked into his bathroom and looked around. As she rummaged through the bathroom cabinets, she wondered why he had never made her put on red lipstick when she slept with him before. When she found four full tubes, it hit her. She took one out, pulled off the top, and stared into the mirror, knowing full well if she applied it to her lips, she was branding herself just another one of Salvatore's bimbos. The face looking back at her was listless and void of emotion. She had been down this road many times before, and it always ended badly. She flashed back to her first night as a stripper. The silver-haired lady who managed the dancers had two of the girls hold her down as she applied a generous portion of lipstick around Monique's lips. Monique traced the lipstick over her lips aimlessly, giving no thought to whether it was on straight or not. She looked past herself in the mirror as if not in her body. She made her way to the bed and looked out the high-rise window. When she disrobed, Monique caught a glimpse of her voluptuous curvy body in the plate-glass window and wondered how much easier life would have been if she had been born ugly.

She moved around the room like a zombie, turning off lights. She slipped into bed, pulled the sheets to her neck, retraced the events leading up to her current predicament, and realized her jealousy of Misty had brought her here. How many times had Captain Kev and Miniature Mike mentioned how much she reminded them of Misty? It was Misty this and Misty that, causing her to resent this woman who could do no wrong. How foolish she had been. She realized taking Salvatore away from Misty did not make her a better person. It only protected Misty from a vile man. Monique's envy turned to admiration, and she suddenly began wishing she were more like Misty. She told herself that if given the chance, she would make sure things would be different between her and Misty going forward. But who was she kidding? The die was cast, and she had no one to blame but herself.

Salvatore readied himself for bed in the bathroom. He came out in nothing but his birthday suit and slid in under the sheets. He climbed over her as if she were an object, never giving any thought to foreplay, only wanting to get his rocks off and go to sleep. She lifted her knees like a robot, opening herself up to him like she had done many times before. He worked its way inside her, and, still dry, she dutifully endured the pain as punishment for her stupidity. When her natural juices flowed enough for the pain to subside, she drifted off to a place far away, completely detaching herself from the here and now. She had become a master at disconnecting her mind from her body during the unpleasantness of being abused by men. In a sadistic way, the familiarity of her predicament made her feel like she was home.

* * *

Misty greeted Salvatore at their workout session as if he were a long lost friend. "How was your trip? Things went well, I hope."

Monique walked out of his shadow, passing Misty without a word.

She gave it little thought, chalking it up to the spat they'd had when she threw Monique out of the apartment.

"Why don't we just get on with the workout, Misty? I've got things to catch up on."

"Sure," Misty said with a frown on her face.

Misty began to realize something wasn't right. Salvatore treated Monique as if she were a piece of property, and Monique did as he said without any resistance. It was becoming obvious that the way Monique was acting had nothing to do with her throwing Monique out of the apartment, and for some reason Misty could not understand, she almost wished Monique would revert to her old diva ways.

As they gathered their things to leave, Misty said to Monique, "Look, I'm sorry for throwing you out of the apartment like that. Why don't you move back in with Thor and me?"

"She's not going anywhere!" Salvatore interjected with a coldness that caught Misty by surprise. Looking Misty's body over he added, "But I'm considering having you move in with us one of these nights." Misty pulled back, creating space between them. *He has changed since his trip*, she thought. *I wonder what went on over there.*

"I assumed that since you have been seeing Monique that you would consider relations with my assistant more than enough compensation," Misty said in a hopeful tone.

Salvatore closed the distance and placed his finger under Misty's chin and said, "No, you are contractually bound, and no one breaks a contract with Salvatore."

Now I know he's full of it, referring to himself in the first person, she thought.

"Maybe we'll have a threesome. I'll bet you girls would like that, wouldn't you?" Salvatore said as he walked past Misty and motioned for Monique to follow.

Once they left, Misty gathered her things and stormed into the elevator. Wrapping her workout jacket around her hand, she slammed her balled fist into the elevator mirror, shattering it to pieces. As she propped herself against the back wall, she sensed someone else and turned her head to the sight of an elderly lady backing up into the far corner.

Misty took a deep, cleansing breath, flashed a smile, and said, "Sorry."

* * *

After taking a hot bath in her apartment, Misty still found herself steamed over the way Salvatore was acting. Needing someone calm, cool, and collected to help her reason things out, she headed off to find Gary. If nothing else, she knew Gary was a good listener.

After arriving at Devil's Cove, Misty asked the pit boss, "Jake, have you seen Gary?" He pointed to a hallway. Misty walked until she came to a lone door at the end of the hallway with Gary's name on it. When she knocked, Gary yelled out, "Come in. It's not locked."

Without looking up, he said, "How can I help you?"

Misty didn't respond, so he looked up. He dropped his pen, sat back in his chair, and placed his hands behind his head. "Why the long face? Is something troubling you?"

Her eyes became moist, so she turned her back to him to wipe them dry. *What's come over me? Is Salvatore really getting to me this bad?* She turned back around, slightly embarrassed.

"I'm sorry. It's not that big of a deal. I don't know why I reacted like that."

Gary said jokingly, "It's not that time of the month, is it?"

She laughed, "I wish that is all it was."

He got up from his desk, walked over to her, and lifted her chin with his finger. He looked into her eyes and said, "Please tell me what's troubling you."

The concerned look on his face let Misty know she had come to the right person. Although she had only known Gary for a short time, it felt as if they were lifelong friends. Thor was a great kid, but in the absence of Miguel, she needed someone more mature.

Misty stepped into his arms and said, "Oh, Gary. You have been trying to warn me about Salvatore." She added defiantly, "If I was a man, I'd straighten him out!"

"Maybe," he said, "and maybe not. He's not some bully you can beat up in the schoolyard. Salvatore is a very dangerous man." Misty let out a big sigh and held on tighter. "There are other ways you can get back at Salvatore if it would make you feel better."

"Are you serious?" she said as she leaned back to look at him.

Gary smiled and said, "Are you willing to put the twenty thousand dollars you won from my casino in blackjack at risk?"

"Hey, I won that money fair and square. I'm not giving it back to you."

"That's not what I'm implying. Are you willing to place a bet at Salvatore's sportsbook that, if you won, would pay out two hundred thousand dollars?"

"I can win that much by placing a twenty thousand dollar bet?"

"Yes, if you place it on a four-team parlay during the NFL football games tomorrow."

"Four team what-ee? I don't know anything about betting on football games."

"You don't need to. I know a guy that is so good he is banned from every major sportsbook in Vegas. He's sitting in my sportsbook right now crunching numbers."

"Crunching numbers? What the hell are you talking about?"

Gary laughed, "Come with me." He took her hand and hurried her out the door. When they entered Devil's Cove's tiny sportsbook, he pointed to a skinny man with thick, black glasses hunched over a computer, muttering to himself. He was so engrossed in what he was doing that he didn't even notice Gary and Misty standing next to him. She thought he was the strangest man she had seen since training Chester Naples, a former client who lived in San Antonio. Gary gently laid a hand on his shoulder, and he jumped.

"Damn it, Gary. Why did you break my concentration? I just about had the Cowboys/Giants game figured out."

"Misty, meet Two Team Tommy. Smartest football handicapper on the planet."

Tommy bent down to crunch more numbers as if they weren't there.

Gary whispered in Misty's ear, "As you can see, Tommy's love affair is with handicapping, not socializing with people."

"Why do they call him Two Team Tommy?"

"Because any time he comes up with a two-team parlay, you can take it to the bank."

"But you said we were going to bet on a four-team parlay."

Gary smiled. "That just means we need to get two, two-team parlays out of Tommy and place all four games in the same bet."

Misty groaned, "Oh, whatever. I don't know what you're talking about."

Gary placed his hand on Tommy's shoulder and he jumped again. "Jeepers! What now, Gary?"

"Do you like me letting you use my sportsbook and allowing you to place small bets on Sunday?" Gary said in a more serious tone. Tommy sighed and sat back attentively. "Okay, then. I need a small favor."

"Anything, Gary. Just don't throw me out," he whimpered.

"Tommy, give me your two best two-team parlays for this weekend's games."

Tommy's eyes caught fire. "Oh, Gary. I've got some great games." He froze. "You're not going to ban me from placing small bets on those games, are you?"

"I'll stop you if you don't tell me."

Tommy smiled. "Okay, get a pencil."

* * *

At 9:45 a.m. Vegas time, Misty left Gary in the middle of the crowd and walked up to the betting window and handed the man a punched parlay card. As Gary had instructed, she said, "I would like to place a bet on a four-team parlay, please."

The man behind the counter snickered as he read aloud, "Baltimore minus 2, Pittsburg minus 3, Miami plus 7, Minnesota minus 10." He said, "And just how much would you like to place on this bet?"

Misty slid twenty thousand-dollar chips his way.

He looked at her with his mouth held open and then said, "Do you realize how much money that is?"

Misty smiled back, "Do you realize how much money you're going to owe me when I win?"

He motioned for his boss to come over and then whispered something into his ear.

His boss barked out orders to another man. "Open up another

window and have everyone in line behind this lady move over." He looked back at Misty. "Ma'am, I'll be right back."

Misty couldn't understand why her bet was causing such a stir. She nervously glanced back at Gary, but he turned his head and moved deeper into the crowd. *Great! He throws me to the sharks and then disappears.*

With only a couple minutes left to place the bet before kickoff, the man returned with Antonio at his side. When Antonio realized it was Misty, he motioned for her to come closer. "What the hell are you doing? You can't bet that much on a four-team parlay. At ten to one, you would win two hundred thousand dollars from the casino."

Misty smiled, "So you're afraid of my betting prowess, are you?"

When Antonio laughed out loud, she leaned in closer and said at point-blank range, "Obviously you think this is all a big joke, so why don't you just take my money? It will be the easiest twenty thousand dollars this casino has ever made if you are right."

Antonio pulled back and snapped at the employee, "Take her fucking money."

On her way back to Gary, ticket stub in hand, she jumped when the crowd let out a roar to celebrate the 10:00 a.m. kick-offs of the opening games. Misty walked to a booth in the far corner that faced away from the betting windows as Gary had instructed her to. He joined her shortly after she arrived.

"So what do we do now?" she asked Gary.

He smiled as he summoned the waitress over. When she returned with a bottle of the casino's finest champagne, Gary uncorked the bottle and poured them each a glass. Holding his glass high, he said, "Drink up. Let's enjoy the day."

After banging glasses with Gary and taking a drink of the bubbly liquid, she surveyed the room. Games were playing on more than twenty TV screens. She couldn't understand how all these men could process the information necessary to keep up with each game. Just looking at the big screens made her dizzy. *This is retarded. I should be up in the mountains hiking or something!*

By the time they finished off their first bottle of champagne, most of the games had reached halftime. A little tipsy, she looked at Gary and asked, "So how are we doing?"

Gary smiled back smugly. "We are winning all three of our early games by ten points or more. Things are looking up!"

Misty felt a wave of pleasure shoot through her body as the thought of actually winning all four games and the two hundred thousand dollars sank in. She found the better's high she was experiencing remarkably similar to the endorphin high she always felt after running a marathon!

"Hell, yes! Fucking A!" she yelled out.

Gary chuckled as Misty stood up and waived her hands at one of the big screens and said, "Win baby, win!"

When the waitress came by the booth, Misty ordered another bottle of champagne. Gary wisely ordered some sandwiches so she wouldn't get too wasted. After a couple more glasses of her sweet nectar, she was back at it, waving her arms and yelling. Gary thought it hilarious that she wasn't even watching any of the games that they had their bets on, but he decided not to say anything since she was having a grand old time. When the last of their three games wrapped up, he said, "Three down and one to go. Win that game, and you'll be bathing in Salvatore's money."

Misty jumped into Gary's arms and gave him a big kiss before heading off to the restroom. He placed his fingers to his lips as she bounded off. Misty passed Antonio on the way to the restroom and stopped to pat him on his cheek. She had just won the first three games, and he did not find her little gesture humorous in the least. As the afternoon game moved into the fourth quarter, Antonio was well aware her final team, Minnesota, was ahead of the spread. He nervously moved among the other gamblers so he could get a better view of the game. He refused to look her way out of pride, but when Arizona scored an unexpected touchdown by intercepting a pass and running it all the way back, he smugly glanced in her direction. Infuriated at the sight of Gary sitting next to Misty, he hurried over to their booth.

"What the hell are *you* doing here, Gary?"

"It's a free country, my friend."

"You know Salvatore would be very upset if he knew you were placing bets in our casino."

Gary shrugged his comment off and replied, "But I'm not."

"Don't fuck with me, Gary. This dame doesn't know shit about football, and you and I both know it!"

"For someone who doesn't know shit about football, she seems to be doing pretty good to me. Maybe you should just chalk it up to beginner's luck."

"We'll see. For now she's losing the fourth game," Antonio said.

Misty turned to Gary and said, "We are? I mean, I am?"

"The game's not over. There's plenty of time left," Gary said.

Antonio walked back to watch the game in solitude. He became more on edge with each passing minute. Minnesota scored another touchdown. Antonio grabbed a waitress by the arm and demanded, "Bring me a shot of whiskey."

With two minutes left in the game, Misty asked Gary, "So we are going to win?" She noticed Gary seemed a bit nervous. "We are going to win, right?"

"Here's the deal," Gary said. Arizona has the ball on their own twenty-yard line with only two minutes left in the game. Minnesota is winning by fourteen points, so you are covering the spread, but if Arizona scores a last-minute touchdown, we lose. You see, we could lose the bet even if Minnesota wins the game. Do you understand?"

Misty looked at Gary as if he were speaking Mandarin. "I don't understand a word you are saying. This is crazy!"

Arizona completed a pass to their own thirty-two-yard line, and the crowd rooting for Arizona erupted.

She turned to Gary. "So that was bad, right?"

He nodded, "Yes, that was bad. The problem is, Minnesota will win the game even if Arizona scores another touchdown, so they are in what we call a prevent defense. This means the defenders back off and let them have all the short passes they want, as they try to run out the clock."

Misty's face turned beet red. She looked at Antonio who was showing some optimism and then said to Gary, "So what you are saying is that Minnesota doesn't give a shit whether I win my bet or not?"

Gary tried to keep from grinning at her naivety and replied, "No, Misty. All they care about is having more total points than Arizona at the end of the game."

Misty scowled, "Well, those inconsiderate bastards!"

She gulped down some more champagne after Arizona completed a pass and the crowd roared. Arizona's quarterback completed another fifteen-yard pass so they were now on Minnesota's side of the field with a minute left in the game. Misty placed her hand on her forehead and contemplated losing the two hundred thousand dollar bet that she had already imagined winning. What was worse, she realized she could also lose the twenty thousand dollars she placed on the bet. When Arizona easily completed another short pass, she thought, *Prevent defense, my ass. The only thing they are doing is preventing me from winning my bet!* Her hands were sweating, and she felt nauseous. She looked at Antonio who was looking back at her and grinning. Misty walked into the women's bathroom, entered a stall, lowered the toilet seat, sat down, and placed her head in her hands. Her head was spinning from all the alcohol, and her knees were shaking nervously. She swore then and there she would never bet on another professional football game as long as she lived.

A somewhat muffled roar came from the crowd outside the rest-room. Figuring Arizona had just scored, she decided to go back out and face the consequences. Walking up to Gary, she said dejectedly, "Did we just lose?"

Gary pointed to the screen, "No! There are only twenty seconds left; Arizona is on Minnesota's twenty yard line and its fourth down."

She placed her hands on his shoulders, looked him directly in his eyes, and said, "English, man. You've got to talk to me in plain English. What does that all mean?"

Gary pushed her aside and said, "I'll tell you after this play."

Arizona's quarterback barked out the signals. "Hup one, hup two," and the center hiked the ball. The quarterback ran around the aggressive pass rush from the Minnesota defensive line. In desperation he threw the ball wildly at the running back standing near the sideline. The ball landed behind the running back and rolled pathetically out of bounds. The crowd let out a groan, and Misty looked at Gary.

"Tell me, damn it! Tell me what just happened!"

"All you need to know is we just won the game," he said calmly.

Misty watched the Minnesota quarterback snap the ball and place a knee on the field. The clock ticked down to zero, and the players from both teams walked onto the field. She noticed Antonio was looking her way, and she flipped him the bird. He snarled back and then left the sportsbook in a hurry. No doubt he was on his way to tell Salvatore.

"Let's go get our money!" she said.

Gary looked at the long line of betters lining up at the window to get paid and said, "I've got a better idea. Your winning ticket is good for months, so let's go get a nice dinner and a bottle of wine and savor your victory while we wait for the line to thin out.

Passing a lobster tank on their way to the table, Misty stopped and pointed to a massive seven-pounder and said, "I might not get all of him down, but I'm sure going to give it a try."

An hour later, Misty walked up to the cashier and slid her ticket to the attendant. Her grin was so big her teeth were showing. The older man got a good look at the ticket and gulped.

13

RETALIATION

Antonio stood just outside the bar, contemplating his next move. Tomasso studied him intently from inside. Santo was preoccupied with a cute waitress, and Diego was oblivious to anything but the mountainous pastrami sandwich he was devouring. Antonio finally decided to join them at their table.

"Hey, why the long face, boss?" Tomasso asked.

Antonio made eye contact with everyone around the table, one at a time, until he had their attention.

"We need to all go up to Salvatore's suite."

"But this is Sunday, boss," Tomasso said in a weary tone. "You know he doesn't like to be disturbed on Sundays. That's his girlfriend time."

"I'm well aware of that, but what we need to tell Salvatore can't wait until tomorrow."

"We, boss?" Tomasso looked at Santo. "We don't even know what we need to tell him."

"We need to tell him that Misty and her guardian angel, Gary, just took the house for two hundred thousand."

Diego said with a mouthful of pastrami, "She got the house in the settlement? I didn't even know they were married."

"Shut the fuck up, Diego!" Antonio snapped. He looked at Santo. "Get Diego out of here before I hurt him."

Santo got up, grabbed Diego by the arm, and led him out of the bar.

"How the fuck did they do that? Blackjack?" Tomasso asked.

"Misty placed a twenty thousand dollar bet on a four-team parlay."

"I never took her for a football fan, boss."

"She's not. Use your brain! I told you Gary was with her."

Tomasso scratched his chin. "Oh, I get it. But who let them bet that much? Don't we have limits on the size of four-team parlay bets?"

Antonio didn't reply.

"Oh man, don't tell me you approved it."

Antonio placed his head in his hands and said, "Who would have thought Misty was smart enough to pick four games?" He looked up at the ceiling. "Shit, Salvatore is going to explode."

"If we have to go up there, let's send his cousin Benny ahead of us so we are not the ones to interrupt him first."

"Best idea you've had in a while, Slick."

First they arranged to have a cocktail waitress convince Benny that Salvatore wanted to see him in his suite. Then they had the waitress's manager fire the waitress so Salvatore would never find out. They walked with Benny toward the elevator.

"What do you think is up, Benny?" Tomasso asked.

"I just know that Salvatore needs me," Benny said with the look of importance plastered on his face.

"You're The Man!" Tomasso said, and they watched the elevator doors close.

When the elevator returned from dropping Benny off on the top floor, they all piled in, rode it to the top floor, and then hung around until Benny came trudging down the hall toward them.

"Why the long face, Benny?" Santo asked.

"I wouldn't go down there if I was you. He's in a pretty foul mood. I'm going to fire me a waitress when I get back to the ground floor."

"Well, you're The Man," Tomasso said as he slapped him on his shoulder. "Listen, thanks for the advice about Salvatore, Benny. We owe you one. Say, how about you and me get a drink sometime?"

"That would be swell!" Benny replied.

After Benny's elevator door closed, Tomasso walked briskly down the hall to catch up with Antonio and Santo.

The door was still open, so they walked in, finding Salvatore standing in the foyer in his robe.

"Now what? Is there a sign downstairs that says I'm throwing a party for dumbasses?" Salvatore said.

"Boss, there's something the boys and I need to tell you," Antonio said. "I'm sorry, but it couldn't wait." Looking at the others he added, "Right, boys?"

As they walked past Salvatore into the living room, they found Monique pulling the top of her robe together and tying it tightly about her. After Salvatore nodded at her, she left for the bedroom and closed the door behind her.

"This better be good, fellas," Salvatore said.

Antonio cleared his throat before saying, "Misty took the house for two hundred K."

"Get outta here! I'm in no mood for jokes." When Salvatore looked from Tomasso to Santo and then back to Antonio, he realized they were not joking.

"What did she do, drop a dollar in the slot machine and hit the lucky jackpot? That's the only way a blonde bimbo could take us for that kind of jack."

"Four-team parlay, boss," Antonio said. "I thought she was alone and figured it would be easy money. She placed the bet right before kick-off. I followed her back to her table, and you'll never guess who I saw waiting for her."

Salvatore's eyes narrowed. "Gary. It had to be Gary."

"He was sitting with her all afternoon drinking champagne," Antonio quickly replied. "You should have seen the shit-eating grin he had on his face."

Salvatore yanked a lamp out of the electrical socket and threw it into the wall, causing an expensive painting to crash to the floor. Monique opened the bedroom door but closed it when she realized it was just Salvatore in one of his rages. Prone to outbursts, he wouldn't have made it this far in the mafia without being able to quickly get in control of his emotions. He walked over to the sofa, sat down, and placed his hands over his head as he contemplated. Several moments later, he addressed the men calmly.

"Gary has gone too far this time. He must pay. Bribe one of his employees and find out when he plans on leaving that little piece of shit casino he runs. When we catch him alone, we're going to fuck him up good."

"We're on it, boss. Sorry for the intrusion," Antonio said and then quickly headed out the front door with Tomasso and Santo right behind him.

Salvatore's thoughts turned to his next training session with Misty. *I'm going to make life miserable for that little bitch.*

* * *

Shortly after midnight, the doorbell rang to Misty's suite. Thor put on a robe and went downstairs to check it out.

"So, are you going to step back and let us in, or what?" one of the two men standing outside the door asked.

Thor gave Tom a big hug. "Pops! Why didn't you tell me you and Miguel were coming? I could have picked you up at the airport."

Miguel slapped Thor on his shoulder as he walked by. "We caught a cab. Your dad wanted to surprise you."

"That you did," Thor said as he turned loose of Tom.

"Where's Misty?" Miguel asked.

Thor walked them over to her bedroom door. When they got there, Miguel pushed Thor aside, cupped his hands over his mouth, and said in a muffled tone, "Attention! Attention! You must evacuate the building. The hotel is on fire."

Misty sat up with her back against the headboard. The room was dark, and all she could make out was a silhouette in her doorway. She quickly pulled the covers over her see-through nightgown. Then she noticed something familiar about the silhouette.

"Migs! Is that you?"

Miguel felt along the wall until his fingers found the light switch. The glow of the soft light paled in comparison to the glow emanating from Misty's enraptured smile.

After drinking each other in for a spell, she said, "My, don't we look fit. I'd say you've recovered from your wound."

Miguel sat next to her on the bed, and Misty wrapped her arms around him.

"Yes, I am completely healed and in the best shape of my life. Actually, Tom and I both are. We've been trying to outdo each other as usual."

Tom appeared in the doorway. "Not trying. I *did* outdo you."

"Yeah, right, old man!" Miguel replied.

Misty enjoyed the same banter that would have ordinarily annoyed her. She marveled at how good both Miguel and Tom looked. When Thor stepped up next to his dad, the sight of three able-bodied men by her side made her feel safe and secure for the first time in more than a month. They were her knights in shining armor.

"Tell them about the money you won today, Misty," Thor said.

Misty grinned. "Oh, it was nothing. A measly little two hundred thousand."

"Dollars!?" Miguel asked.

Misty shrugged. "Yeah, I wish it were euros, but dollars will do."

Tom said, "Seriously. You won two hundred K?"

She nodded. "Yes, Tom. Seriously."

She insisted they all get comfortable on her big bed because it was going to be a long story. She spent the next hour catching them up with everything that had transpired since her arrival. Tom was concerned about Thor's run-in with Santo. Thor held his breath throughout Misty's entire monologue, anxious that she would say something about his insane night with Monique. Miguel basked in the presence of his close friend as he listened intently to everything Misty said. He soaked up her energy and enthusiasm like a man released from solitary confinement soaks up the sun. They had seldom been apart over the last few years, and he had missed her dearly. Now he was back at her side where he felt most comfortable.

"So, that's my story, and I'm sticking to it," she said as she wrapped up.

As if imitating *Le Penseur*, the bronze and marble sculpture by Auguste Rodin, Tom sat in the "thinker's pose" as he pondered the seriousness of Misty's situation. His experience told him she might be in serious danger, but his maturity kept him from sharing his concern with the others, at least for now.

"We better let Misty get some sleep," Miguel said. "She might have some training scheduled in the morning."

"Get a good night sleep, Misty," Tom said confidently. "Everything is going to be just fine."

* * *

The next morning, after a hearty breakfast and lots of laughs, they all headed to the gym. The guys began their workout while Misty got the equipment ready for her training session. At 10:00 a.m. sharp, Salvatore, Monique, and the boys walked through the door. As the entourage made their way over to Misty, Miguel stopped his workout to look at Monique. Their eyes locked for a good four counts. Miguel couldn't help but notice how distant she appeared, a shell of the vibrant and confident woman he had gotten to know in Argentina. Sensing his friend's concern, Tom placed his large hand on Miguel's shoulder.

Salvatore wasted no time. "They tell me you robbed me blind yesterday," he said sharply.

In the presence of her posse, she replied, "If you don't like to lose money, you shouldn't own a casino."

Her curtness caught Salvatore by surprise. Not knowing whether to be angry or prideful, he eventually chose prideful. "Honey, your money was only a dent in my overall winnings yesterday!"

"Good to hear it," she shot back. "Now that that's settled, why don't we get started?"

Misty and Monique did their best not to bring attention to Tom, Miguel, and Thor during the workout, always keeping eyes focused on Salvatore. Things were flowing fine until the end of the session when Salvatore started ordering Monique around. When it was time to leave, he grabbed Monique by her arm and began to pull her after him. Miguel darted toward Salvatore, but Antonio, Tomasso, and Santo cut him off.

Diego lay back, not quite sure what to do. Thor made a move to join Miguel, but Tom held him back. Tom moved slowly forward with Thor by his side.

"Take your hands off her!" Miguel demanded.

"Take one more step, and you will regret it," Antonio said to Miguel.

Miguel inched closer to Antonio until their faces were inches apart, but Monique quickly yelled out before anything could happen. "Stop it, Miguel! Go away! I'm fine." She latched onto Salvatore's arm. "I'm where I want to be. Don't interfere."

Misty slid in between Miguel and Antonio. "Don't you have something better to do?" She stared into Antonio's eyes.

"So, who's your friend?" Antonio asked.

She stepped back, wrapped an arm around Miguel, and replied, "Miguel. There's nothing in my contract about not having visitors."

"Knock it off, Antonio. We've got business to attend to," Salvatore said.

Salvatore turned and headed toward the door, pulling Monique after him. Monique glanced at Miguel as she trailed behind.

"You heard your boss, Antonio," Misty said. Antonio glanced at Miguel before turning and escorting his boys off with him. Diego gave Misty an apologetic grin on the way out.

"That was not called for," Tom said.

"That was total bullshit is what that was!" Miguel said.

"That is what I have been dealing with alone," Thor said.

Misty turned to them. "And that is why I'm glad there are now three of you to protect me."

"So what's the deal with Monique and Salvatore?" Miguel asked. "How could she let him order her around like that?"

"It's a long, sad story," Thor answered. "I'll fill you guys in on what I know later."

"Let's go shower and discuss this over dinner," Misty suggested.

14

WHO'S TRACKING WHO?

Antonio was beaming Friday morning as he slid past Salvatore into the room. "What's gotten into you?" Salvatore asked with a furled brow.

"Gary's going to his cabin in the mountains alone this weekend, and from what we hear, no one lives within five miles of it."

Salvatore slapped him on the back. "Excellent! This was the break I was hoping for." He looked over to Monique to see if she would react to the news. When she made no indication that she had heard, he escorted her to his bedroom. He said, "Give us a second," and closed the door.

Turning back to Antonio, he said, "Round up the boys and get there ahead of Gary. Find a place to hide the car and hike the rest of the way in. We don't want any fresh tire tracks leading up to his cabin."

With a twinkle in his eye, Antonio asked, "So how bad do you want us to mess Gary up?" Salvatore pondered the question with the excitement of a child trying to decide whether he wanted chocolate or butterscotch on his ice cream sundae. "Let me savor the thought all day, and I'll let you know this evening."

"Sure thing, boss," Antonio said excitedly before heading out.

Monique removed her ear from the drinking glass that she had placed against the door and retreated to the bathroom. She stared at herself in the mirror, trying to get a handle on the emotions she was feeling. Her self-reflection was interrupted by a call from Salvatore, who was now in a good mood. He requested that she join him in bed, giving her a different set of emotions to deal with.

* * *

Gary sat behind the wheel of his maroon Jaguar as he wound his way up the narrow, winding mountain road. He regretted his decision to coax Misty into winning money from Salvatore's casino and now worried that there might be ramifications. He thought about all the pressure Salvatore had put on him to sell his casino, the tiny blight attached to Salvatore's magnificent structure. Now Misty was in danger, and it was all because of his crazy idea to get revenge for the both of them. He was also beginning to regret not sleeping with Misty when she offered herself to him the weekend before. He needed a day of solitude to get his mind straight and sort everything out.

* * *

Antonio called Salvatore from the deck of Gary's cabin. There was no phone reception on the way up the mountain, but not finding a landline in the cabin, he felt certain Gary had some type of receiver to boost the signal from the nearest cell tower. He was relieved when the phone on the other end began to ring.

"Salvatore's not here. Do you want me to take a message?" Monique asked on the other end.

"Well, isn't that nice. The boss has a new phone receptionist."

"Fuck off, Antonio. I'll make you call back later if you don't cut it out."

"Testy! I like it. Just tell him the eagle has landed."

"That's it, the eagle has landed?"

"He'll know what I'm referring to."

"No problem," she replied and then hung up. She was sure it had to do with the conversation she had overheard earlier.

She paced the room as if a caged lioness. Her hands were clammy and her stomach was upset. It was no longer possible for her to stay in the middle. She knew it was time to choose sides and wondered if she had the courage to do what was right.

* * *

Diego searched through the refrigerator looking for something to eat. He pulled out some sausage and looked at the big cooking pit outside on the porch. Antonio walked up from behind, took the sausage out of his hand, and put it back.

"The last thing we need is for Gary to smell smoke before he gets here," Antonio said. "Eat those protein bars I brought."

Tomasso meandered into the kitchen and said, "Gary's really got a nice place here. I could dig coming up here on the weekends."

Antonio picked up a baseball bat from the bag of goodies they brought, patted the inside of his left hand with the barrel of the bat, and said, "Well, after we get finished with Gary, this place might be on the market. "

Antonio looked at his watch. "It's four o'clock. Tell Santo to take his position. Not another word until Gary arrives, and then we'll let our bats do the talking."

* * *

When Salvatore showed up, Monique picked up her coat and said, "I've got to get some fresh air. I've been cooped up too long."

He grabbed her by the arm when she passed by. Looking at her through squinty eyes, he said, "Don't do anything stupid."

Monique jerked her arm away and shot back as she walked out, "I told you I need some fresh air." As soon as she got into the elevator, she began rapidly pressing the Close button. *Come on, come on! Damn it, close!* When the doors finally shut, she breathed a sigh of relief. Her hands shook as she hurried through the casino on her way to find Gary. She had not been out of Salvatore's custody in weeks, and it felt great, even under these circumstances. It was the first time she had stepped into

Devil's Cove since they had arrived, yet it felt familiar to her. No time to reminisce, she told herself. She grabbed a pit boss by the arm and asked, "Where's your boss?"

"Which boss?" he replied.

"The big boss, Gary."

"His office is down that hallway," he said and pointed. "But I'm not sure if he's here or not."

The pit boss tried to break away to talk to security, but an older woman from Iowa kept bending his ear about how much money she had lost in the slot machines and accused the casino of rigging the machines.

Monique pushed open the door at the end of the corridor and walked in. She looked the office over only to find a young man cleaning up paperwork on Gary's desk.

"Who are you?" Monique demanded. "Where's Gary?"

The frail young man stuttered, "I, I, I'm Johnny, one of Gary's clerks."

Monique moved toward him aggressively, so Johnny backed away until he was pinned against the wall.

At point-blank range, she stared at him and demanded again, "Where is Gary?"

"I, uh, I don't really know. He left several hours ago and told me to clean up his desk. I've been bugging him for some receipts, and he thought they might be in the items on his desk."

"What's Gary's cell number?"

Johnny adjusted his glasses until they sat perfectly on the rim of his nose and said wide-eyed, "Oh, no, ma'am! I could never give you his cell number. That's against company policy."

Monique gave him a look so resolute he cringed, sure she was going to hit him. Not getting anywhere, she changed her strategy. Johnny gulped as he watched her pull her blouse free from her pants, reach behind her back, and unlatch her bra. After sliding the straps off expertly beneath her blouse, she pulled the black beauty out from under her shirt and wrapped it around his head, a cup covering his face all the way up to his eyes. He got hard as he inhaled the sweet aroma.

She removed the cup from his face and demanded again, "Gary's phone number, damn it! Give it to me, now!"

Johnny trembled, but he held his silence in fear of losing his job. Monique was out of patience. *Damn you, boy. You leave me no choice.*

Monique planted a massive kiss on his thin little lips, slipping her tongue halfway down the poor boy's throat. She grabbed his hands and guided them up under her blouse, planting them firmly on her voluptuous mounds of soft flesh. Johnny moaned with pleasure. She decided even this was taking too long, so she reached down and grabbed his tiny package firmly in her right hand. She repeated her request again. Johnny's brain short-circuited, and he gave her what she was after. When Monique patted him on the side of his face and left, Johnny scurried down the hall in search of the first bathroom stall he could find before he came in his pants.

Monique rushed out of Devil's Cove and hurried down the Vegas strip. She darted into a hotel and hid in the ladies' room, where she was certain neither Salvatore nor his men could see her using the phone. She dialed Gary's cell number, but her call went directly to his voice mail. She left a detailed message and then kept dialing until her cell battery died.

* * *

When the paved road turned to dirt, Gary noticed fresh vehicle tracks. He assumed the propane man had made them while making his weekly rounds. But when the tracks disappeared before reaching the cabin, he stopped the car in the middle of the road. Just as he reached for the door handle, his cell phone beeped, and the messages he had missed while out of cell service began to flow in. He raised his eyebrows when he saw that he had missed eight calls. Most of the messages were updates from his different casino department heads, but one was from a number he didn't recognize. He sat dumbfounded as he listened to the woman's warning.

His mind raced as he thought about his plan of action. Should he go back down the mountain and check on Misty? Or should he deal with the issue at hand? Gary's ancestors were tough and rugged pioneers who had to endure all types of hardships. Up until now he had lived the good life—that is, until Salvatore showed up. Down deep he had known this day was coming. It was the day of reckoning, and he had two choices. Turn and run, or face it head-on the way his great-grandfather would have.

He thought of the only other time he had felt this way. It was during high school, he had come upon his best friend getting beaten. The rest was pretty much just a blur, but when it ended, everyone was hauled off to the principal's office dirty, bloody, and bruised. It was the last time they bothered his friend.

As Gary traversed the old hunting trail on the side of the mountain, dusk closed in around him. In the dimming light he could barely make out the initials carved into the mountain cedar. *JD* stood for Janet Dewey, his junior high sweetheart. He came upon his childhood fort. The fallen tree branches stacked together, protecting the entrance to a tiny cave. He had spent many afternoons crouched behind the earthy wall, BB gun at the ready, shots flying at anything that rustled, such as approaching Indians. Whooping and hollering they came, like, well, wild Indians. His heart pounded with every attack. Maybe it was the ghosts of imaginary Indians he now heard in the windswept valley below. He made a mental note that his fort might be a good place to hide out if things went astray. The trail soon leveled out, allowing him to quicken his pace. He sat only yards from the house, contemplating his next move. A barn owl hooted, and he remembered the old passageway under the house that his great grandfather had built in the event of a real Indian attack. He ground his teeth and moved on.

The passageway that led him underneath the master bedroom closet was narrower than he remembered. One by one he quietly removed the rough-edged floorboard planks until the opening was wide enough for him to pull himself up into the tiny closet. He tiptoed across the bedroom and cracked open the door, thankful he was a stickler about keeping the door hinges well lubricated. His eyes focused on a familiar figure at the end of the hallway. Santo, the one who had roughed him up the first time he told Salvatore he would never sell out. Santo's fist had felt like an anvil every time he buried it deep into Gary's gut. His thoughts turned to sweet vengeance. It was time for payback.

The closet was dark, but the blackness didn't stop Gary from locating the leather case he was looking for on the top shelf. It was as heavy as he remembered. He had thought about locking the bedroom door earlier, but he couldn't risk making a noise and giving his position away. Any false move and Santo would barrel through the door and give him another beat down. From the look of the club Santo had been holding, it would be far worse than the last time. He meticulously worked the zipper until the case was open. He smiled as he felt the contents inside. The last time it had been opened was five years ago when his now-deceased father had taught him how to fire the prized possession, his great-grandfather's 1875 model Sharps Buffalo rifle. He found the box of ammunition on the middle shelf. There was no mistaking the two-and-a-half-inch 64-millimeter casings he held in his hand. The box was full; there were plenty of rounds for the task ahead. It was time!

* * *

Gary had a bounce in his step as he strolled off down the main road to his car. He convinced himself this was for Misty as much as it was for him. There was a slight chill in the air, which only made him feel alive, and he wondered if this was how his ancestors felt when they faced up to their many challenges. He was proud to be carrying their DNA. When he reached the car, he placed the weapon in the backseat and casually got in. He rolled down the windows to enjoy the cool evening air while he listened to the sound of the tires grinding on the gravel road as the Jag rolled back down the mountain. When he came upon the tire tracks he had noticed earlier, Gary turned off the road. He found his target on the other side of a brush thicket and brought the car to a halt. He got out of the car, opened the back door, and pulled out the instrument his ancestors used to bring down charging buffalo. A single bullet to the beast's onrushing skull and it would crumple to the ground, or so the old stories told. They used black powder ammunition in those days. The smokeless powder ammunition he held in his hand gave the gun over a thousand more foot-pounds of force. He loaded a round in the chamber, cocked the gun, and aimed it at the object in front of him. Antonio's prize possession, a two hundred thousand dollar gold-colored Maybach shone like a massive gold nugget from the illumination of the Jag's halogen headlights. When the front windshield was in his sight, he let out a chuckle and squeezed off a round. The car was so airtight, not only did the front and rear windows blow but the side windows as well. The roar of his gun subsided in time to hear the tinkling of broken glass falling all about.

Diego was choking on his Power Bar as Santo leaped up and ran to the window. Antonio and Tomasso followed close behind. "What the fuck was that?" Tomasso asked. Antonio raised his hand up so the boys would be quiet as he trained his ears on a potential subsequent blast.

Gary chambered a second round, curious what sound a 550-grain bullet would make when striking the engine block head-on. The front grill exploded high into the air as the sound echoed through the valley. The loud thud of the grill falling to the ground was accompanied by the sound of grinding metal, while the car rocked back and forth as if broadsided by a charging buffalo. Gary thought, *Two down and ten to go.* He threw round after round into his target, as fast as he could discharge one round and slam another one into the chamber. He squatted down and took both front tires out with a single round and did the same to the back tires. He climbed a small hill and aimed at the middle of the undamaged trunk. Gary lay prone on his back as he looked up at the fireball cascading into the sky. The Maybach's rear end lifted high in the air and slammed back to the ground. As he watched flames engulf the car, he laughed and thought, *Oops, I guess I hit the gas tank.*

Salvatore's boys bolted outside the cabin and stared at the fireball in the sky. And then Antonio figured it out. "Mother fucker! That's coming from where we parked my car!"

There wasn't much left of the Maybach when they arrived. Antonio went on a rampage while the others stood gawking at the car.

"What do we do now?" Diego said.

Tomasso replied, "We call for someone to pick us up."

Gary thought of how he had disconnected his cell phone amplifier at the cabin before heading out and smiled. It would be a long, cold walk down the mountain for Antonio and his boys. Unfortunately, Antonio's expletives would scare away any mountain lions in the vicinity.

15

WHAT NOW?

The bright lights of Vegas brought Gary back to reality. It felt good being the hunter instead of the hunted for a change, but he knew it came with consequences. There was something he needed to attend to, and it was no small matter.

On his way to Misty's room, Gary noticed someone waving at him from one of the classy bars.

"Are you lost?" Thor asked as Gary approached his table.

"Do you know if Misty's in her room? I have something important I need to tell her."

"You can find her in the gym getting in a late-night workout."

"But isn't it closed?"

"It is, but I've got the code. Follow me! I was headed back anyway."

When the door opened, Gary asked Thor, "Do you mind if I go in alone? It's kind of confidential."

Thor thought for a moment and then said, "Lock the door behind you, and if you leave before Misty, come get me."

"Fair enough."

Gary stood quietly by Misty's side as she finished her set of bench presses. He grabbed the middle of the bar after her last rep and helped her place it back onto the rack while also gazing at her rack, which was wedged against her skimpy black tank top. Had her hair not hung down off the bench like that of a fairy-tale princess, her bulging biceps and powerful thighs would have belied her femininity. He never realized muscle tone could make a woman look so hot.

Misty looked up at Gary from the bench and asked through a mischievous smile, "Who let you in?"

"Thor. I talked him into letting me take his shift."

"Will you throw me my towel?" she asked, still lying on the bench. She wiped her face dry and said, "Make yourself useful. I feel strong tonight. Put a couple twenties on each side and lower the bar. I think I'll go for my personal best."

When he had locked both sides in place, she scooted up into position, measured her hands along the bar until perfectly spaced, and then wrapped her fingers tightly around the bar.

"How much are you lifting?" he asked.

"One hundred and ninety-five pounds."

Gary had lifted a little over two hundred pounds in his younger days, and he was rather shocked that Misty, a middle-aged woman, could lift so much. Misty positioned her feet firmly on the floor, gave her butt a little wiggle, arched her back slightly, and grunted. Her arms strained under the weight of the bar. She lowered it slowly until it almost touched her nipples and then strained to bring it up. Gary instinctively reached his hands under the bar in the event Misty's arms gave out. But he was careful not to interfere in any way. Struggling, she regrouped, let out a loud grunt, and slowly inched the bar skyward. With arms fully extended, she held the bar at its apex for a count of three before attempting a second rep. But this time the bar only hovered over her breasts.

"Okay!" she yelled. Gary assisted with the rep and then guided it to its resting place when finished.

Her magnificent chest heaved up and down as she attempted to catch her breath. She placed her right hand behind her left elbow and gave it a stretch before repeating the process on the right side. Gary offered his hand, which she took, and then he assisted her up from the bench. Misty placed her hands on her hips and said, "That was my personal best. Thanks."

Gary didn't say anything. Misty watched him looking her over. She said, "Get an eyeful of what you passed up that night in the mountains. Any regrets?"

"What?" he said, snapping out of his daze. "I'm sorry, what did you just say?" She lightly brushed the side of his face with her hand. "I think I've done enough damage for one night."

"Listen, Misty. There's something I really need to tell you."

She turned and walked away. "Tell me while I'm wrapping up."

Gary followed her halfway until she walked through the women's locker-room door. She popped her head back out of the door and said, "Come on. I don't bite."

Gary stopped at the door, gave it a push, and looked inside, tentatively. He saw three shower stalls, a row of sinks, and a couple toilet stalls, but there was no sign of Misty. Once inside the room, her shorts appeared on the top of the stall door, soon followed by her tank top. She emerged from the stall with a towel wrapped around her body, revealing ample cleavage and bare legs from the top of her thighs down.

She motioned to him to follow as she headed to a shower stall. "Come talk to me while I shower off. Talk loud so I can hear you over the water."

Gary stood silently watching as Misty opened the shower door and worked the knobs, her right leg off the floor revealing the base of her buttock as she reached forward. When finished, she placed her hands on the top of the towel in a way that indicated her next move would be to remove it.

"Please turn around, Gary."

He heard the shower door shut as his eyes looked back at the entrance door. "Okay, what was it you wanted to tell me?" she asked loudly over the rush of water.

He turned back around to the sight of her naked silhouette, clouded by the steamy glass shower door. It still left little to the imagination.

"I need to tell you about my trip to the mountains," he yelled.

"What! I can't hear you. You need to come closer."

It had been months since Gary last slept with his girlfriend, longer than he had ever gone before. His penis was swollen, and his juices were flowing. Overcome with passion, he couldn't resist attempting to look through the shower door; he felt like a teenage boy attempting to get his first glimpse of hot flesh. He noticed Misty drop her soap and bend over slowly to pick it up off the shower floor. Her boobs hung low, stretched to their fullness, her nipples pointing to the slippery bar of soap. He wiped his brow. Steam from the shower mixed with his perspiration. He wondered if she had dropped the soap on purpose to test his resolve or to punish him for not accepting her invitation the night they were alone in the mountains.

"Can you hear me better now?" he asked, lowering his voice even more than before.

When Misty requested he move even closer, he answered her in a whisper. Misty shut the water off. "You seem to have lost your voice, Gary." She cracked the shower stall. "Maybe I could hear you better if you were in here."

After Misty turned the shower back on, Gary stood staring at the steam exiting the crack she had left in the shower door. His girlfriend crossed his mind for a fleeting moment in his futile attempt to clear the image of Misty's naked body out of his head, but it was no use. Within moments he found himself shedding clothing as if his clothes were on fire.

Misty heard the shower door close and turned around. She looked his body over unashamedly, from his chest hair to his baby love handles.

She exaggerated his love handles by pinching the skin and stretching it out. "So what do we have here? Maybe you're not getting enough exercise."

Misty found her little joke wasted as his mind was elsewhere. She offered him the bar of soap.

"Do you mind?" she asked with a mischievous grin.

Gary took the soap out of her hands without losing eye contact. Misty turned to face the showerhead and dipped her head under the flowing hot water. When her hair was waterlogged, she whipped her head back and ran her hands through her damp hair. It afforded Gary a tantalizing view of the sides of her breasts peeking out from behind her rib cage. He lathered her back with his warm, soapy hands before sliding them over her firm buttocks. Leaning into her firmly, he moved his soapy hands along her front midsection, up until his masculine hands soaped and fondled her breasts. She noticed his fingernails were well manicured, worthy of a magazine cover. Her loins ached, reminding her how much she had wanted him that night. It was more about her yearning to be taken by a man she truly admired and respected than payback. What better way to let him know how much she cared?

Gary forced her legs apart and began soaping her inner thighs. She grabbed onto the showerhead for support and opened wider, beckoning his hands ever closer. He answered the call by splitting her moist lips with two thick, soapy fingers before exploring every inch of her outer mound. He used circular motions, teasing her clitoris until she couldn't stand it any longer.

"Please, Gary," she whispered. He answered her plea by applying direct pressure to her swollen clit with two fingers, pressing and releasing over and over again in a pleasurable fashion. She threw her head back and thrashed it about in a circular motion.

Gary leaned in and said, "Hang onto the showerhead tight."

He took a firm grip of her inner thighs with each hand and in one swift motion lifted Misty off her feet, holding them in the air as he placed his throbbing penis deep inside her. His thrusts were deep and powerful, exactly what you would expect from a mountain man. She hung on tight while the water cascaded over her jiggling breasts on its journey to the drain below.

"God, Gary! You're a beast. Harder, harder."

Had Gary still been in his twenties he would have already come by now, but nature has a way of giving older men staying power. He rocked her world until she finally gripped the showerhead, raised her chest upward, and came explosively. He kept it up, bringing her to another orgasm before finally delivering a payload of his own. When it was over, the two lay together at the bottom of the shower, totally exhausted, as the warm water washed over them. Misty placed her arms around his neck and gave him a kiss. They stared into each other's eyes and then dressed and headed out the front door without conversation. Once outside, Misty reached around his neck and gave him one last hug.

As they walked down the corridor, she squeezed his hand and said, "I'll come visit you tomorrow."

* * *

The next morning, Misty spotted Gary sitting on a counter stool, look-ing over some papers. She stood behind him, trying to think of an ice-breaker and wondering how he would react to their little escapade the night before. Gary noticed her in the bar mirror and spun around. He stared at her until she broke out grinning.

"What?" Misty asked. "You should know better than to walk into a shower with a naked woman." She placed her hand gently on the side of his face and asked, "Are you okay?"

"Why wouldn't I be?" he answered.

"I guess that's settled," she said

Misty sat down next to him, grabbed his glass of orange juice, and took a sip.

"No vodka?"

"I don't drink when I'm on duty."

"Good boy. Hey, barkeep. I'll have what Gary's drinking."

Misty downed half her glass with a couple of swigs. She fanned her face with her hand. "Oh, that went down really well. I wonder why I'm so thirsty," she teased.

Gary raised his glass and took another drink before saying, "Me too. This is my third glass."

After finishing the rest of her juice, Misty clunked her glass on the bar and said, "You didn't ask me down here to drink orange juice. What's up?"

Gary finished his juice, wiped his mouth, and said, "How much time do you have left with Salvatore?"

"Two weeks. Why?"

He repositioned himself and placed his hands on her knees. "You have to leave now."

Misty frowned, "You're serious, aren't you?"

"Yes, I am." He motioned for the bartender to come over. "Bring me a bottle of A.H. Hirsch Reserve Bourbon from my private stock, with a couple glasses."

"Yes, sir."

Gary poured several ounces into each glass. She raised her glass to her nose and sniffed the sweet fragrance before taking a sip, "Oh, this is really good. You're not trying to get me drunk, are you?"

Gary threw back his bourbon and let it slowly burn its way down his throat before turning back to Misty. "Sorry, I'm not in my thirties anymore. Last night will hold me for a while."

He refreshed his glass, threw back another one, and said, "I thought I was going to be spending tonight at my cabin, looking up at the stars."

"Really, so why don't we drive up there now?" she said with a wink.

He gathered his thoughts. "I was on my way up to the cabin yesterday afternoon. Fortunately for me, I stopped to check my phone messages just before I arrived at the cabin."

He reached in his pocket, took out his phone, and found the voice message he was looking for. After he activated it, he placed the phone to Misty's ear, and she listened intently. Misty recognized Monique's voice immediately: "Gary, we have never met, but I'm a friend . . . well, I'm an acquaintance of Misty's. You've got to trust me when I tell you that Antonio and the boys are waiting for you in your cabin right now. They intend to do you harm. You must believe me." The message ended.

Misty looked up at Gary soberly. "That was Monique! If Salvatore ever found out she warned you he might have her—"

"Killed?"

"I wasn't thinking of anything that harsh, but apparently you know the man better than I do." She placed her hand on his arm. "So what happened? Do you suppose they are still waiting for you up there?"

"That's the last place I saw them."

"You were in the cabin with them?"

"There was something I needed to get. I stole my way in through an old passageway under the cabin, found what I was looking for, and left."

"What was it? What could possibly cause you to risk your life?"

He shrugged his shoulders. "A buffalo gun."

She sat back to ponder. *Oh my. He didn't shoot them, did he? No, not mild-mannered Gary. At least I don't think so. Of course, he said they were still there last he saw them. Are they lying on the floor dead?*

She looked into his eyes and said, "And?"

He laughed. "And, I went back to where Antonio parked his Maybach and put twelve rounds into it."

She covered her open mouth with her hand, staring at him wide-eyed. She then burst out laughing. "Oh shit. You blew up his expensive car?"

"I guess you could say that. The last round mistakenly hit the gas tank, causing it to explode. The car was engulfed in flames when I left."

She bent over and laughed uncontrollably. Looking back up with tears in her eyes, she said, "That is the most awesome thing I've heard in a long time. I would have loved to be there when Antonio arrived at his car."

But their laughter was short lived when her thoughts returned to Monique and what Salvatore might do to her. She now realized Gary was right. She needed to leave town as quickly as possible. But if she did, she would be breaking all the rules. Before making a final decision, it was critical she make one phone call.

She said, "Can we go to your office? I need someplace quiet so I can track someone down."

"Sure, follow me."

When they arrived, Gary pointed to his desk chair. Misty sat down and dialed the number. It rang and rang and rang.

"Hello! Who's calling?"

"Eddie, it's me, Misty!"

"Misty? Hmmm. Hot-looking blonde with the body of a brick shit house?"

"Brick what?"

Eddie laughed. "Sorry, Misty. I couldn't resist. It's been a few years. How have you been?"

"I'm afraid I've gotten myself into a mess, Eddie. I need your masterly advice. Is this a good time to talk?"

"Wait a second, dear."

A little time passed before Eddie returned to the line.

"Sorry, just got off the Schwarzsee cable car, and we were preparing to hike up to Hörnli Hut. You remember that hike, don't you, Misty?"

"You're in Switzerland. How wonderful!" Her tone softened. "Yes, how could I forget our night in Hörnli Hut. I was so—" Misty noticed Gary frowning and changed the subject. "I mean what a nice view of the mountains. The Swiss Alps are so beautiful from that altitude."

"Yes, they are, and so were you that night."

Misty blushed. "So what's the occasion?" she asked.

"You won't believe this. I'm getting up at 3:00 a.m. tomorrow to scale the Matterhorn!"

"But aren't you a tad too—"

Eddie laughed, "Too old?"

"Well, I'm just saying. That's a dangerous climb."

"Don't worry about me. I hired professionals to come along with me. If things get dicey, we will turn around and come back. I've got too many things I still want to do in life to risk it. Enough about me! Why are you calling?"

"Do you remember helping me get started as the Black Widow Trainer?"

"Of course I do. That was one of my most gratifying achievements!"

"Well, I've been working by the principles you taught me ever since and they have, for the most part, served me well. I remember you telling me never to back out on a written contract. You said that if I did, it would ruin my reputation, resulting in me never being able to charge big money again."

"You have a good memory."

"Well, I'm in a little predicament. My client, one of the large casino owners in Las Vegas, turned out to be a really nasty man." She looked at Gary when she said, "He may even be tied up with the mafia. I'm scared, Eddie."

When Eddie finally responded, he did so without his normal levity. "Is his name Salvatore?"

Misty looked at Gary, shocked, before replying, "Yes, how did you know?"

"I didn't. I just tried to think of the meanest son of a bitch in Vegas. Misty, he's not a man to be associated with. He's also not a man you want to sleep with."

"And why, exactly?"

"Let's just say he has a reputation for . . . Never mind. Break your contract and leave town!"

"But what about my reputation?"

"Don't worry about your reputation, dear. You know how well connected I am. Believe me. Bailing on Salvatore will only help your reputation. If you stay with him, everyone will wonder about you."

"But Salvatore told me, in no uncertain terms, that no one breaks a contract with him and gets away with it."

"You are in a tough spot, Misty, a real catch twenty-two. Damned if you do, and damned if you don't."

Misty sat back, dejected. Sensing her angst, Gary began rubbing her neck and shoulders.

Eddie waited patiently as Misty thought things over. Soon she said, "I have no choice. I will leave and deal with the consequences later."

"Misty, don't just leave Las Vegas. Go back to Argentina to give this time to blow over. I can send you to some clients who live far away from the States, clients who can offer you protection. How do you feel about two midget brothers living in the Ukraine?"

"Eddie, how could you suggest such a thing?"

Eddie laughed heartily. "I thought a little levity was in order. A very wise man once told me, you need a clear head to make good decisions, and there is no better way to clear your head than to laugh."

"Knowing you, it was probably the Dalai Lama."

"No, but you are warm. Is Miguel with you on this trip?"

"He is, and so are two friends of ours from Argentina."

"Are they capable men?"

"Very capable, Eddie. And strong, too."

"That makes me feel better. Now hurry, dear, leave Vegas as quick as you can."

"I will. Thank you so much, Eddie."

"Misty?"

"Yes?"

"Please let me know when you are out of harm's way so that I can stop worrying."

"I will. You be careful climbing that rock."

"Yes, it will be a big day for both of us tomorrow. Keep your chin up."

When she hung up, she concentrated on the gentle massage Gary was still administering to her neck and realized that laughter wasn't the only way to clear one's head. After a few moments, she placed her hands on his and said, "I've got an idea."

"I hope it's a good one."

Over the next hour, the two worked through her idea. Gary was good when it came to the small details. When the plan was finalized, she paid Esteban a visit and then headed back to her room.

"It's kind of late," Gabriella said on the other end of the line. "Is everything all right?"

"Gabriella, I need you to pull some strings for me."

"Strings?"

"Figure of speech. Okay, here's the deal."

* * *

Antonio and the boys were eating breakfast at a small diner at the base of the mountain, waiting for their ride. The long walk down the mountain at night left them grumpy and famished. Antonio watched as Diego emptied half a jar of syrup onto his pancakes, wondering why they kept Diego around. Every time Antonio wanted to get rid of him, Tomasso would talk him out of it. At least with a mouth full of pancakes, Antonio figured Diego couldn't say anything stupid.

When the driver Salvatore sent from town arrived, Antonio took his last gulp of coffee and said, "Let's go. We don't want to keep the boss waiting. He's pissed enough already."

Diego was the last to rise, stuffing his coat pocket with biscuits before following the others to the door. Their waitress patted him on the back as he passed and said, "You're still a growing boy, aren't you?"

Back in Vegas, Tomasso kept his head down as they made their way through the lobby toward the private elevator. He had a reputation to keep and didn't want any of the cute cocktail waitresses seeing him looking this shabby. Salvatore's door was cracked open when they arrived, so they went right in. They found him sitting at the kitchen table drinking a cup of coffee Monique had just poured. Monique glanced at the men, put the coffee pot back on the warmer, and left the kitchen. As she passed Antonio, she held her nose, letting him know he smelled. Antonio hardly noticed.

Salvatore looked at Antonio and said, "This better be good."

"He never showed, boss. We were waiting for him, but he never showed. At around 7:00 p.m. we all heard what sounded like cannon shots. There were at least ten of them. At first we just thought it was some hunter, so we held our positions." Antonio paused to look at Tomasso and Santo for assurance and then continued, "Then we heard a loud explosion and looked out of the window."

"What did you see?"

"A fireball shooting high into the night sky. When I realized it came from the direction where my car was parked, we hurried to check it out."

"A fireball?" Salvatore yelled.

"It was magnificent!" Diego said. Santo kicked him under the table.

"That son of a bitch blew up my Maybach," Antonio said with disgust.

"How do you know it was Gary?" Salvatore challenged.

"Because he never showed up at the cabin," Antonio said.

"We never passed him, even on our walk down the mountain last night," Tomasso said.

Salvatore got up and left the room, causing the boys to give each other inquisitive glances. When he returned, he had Monique in tow. Salvatore slung her toward the boys and then held out his hand. "Give me your cell phone!"

Monique seemed despondent, detached from the moment. She reached into her pocket as if she were a robot and then placed the phone in his hand. Salvatore then handed the phone over to Tomasso, who hurriedly scrolled through her call log.

Looking up at Salvatore, Tomasso said, "The only thing on her phone over the past four days are six phone calls, late yesterday afternoon. All to the same number."

Salvatore thought back to Monique leaving the room in a hurry the day before, brushing past him like someone on a mission. He glared at her. "Who did you call, Monique?"

She remained silent, knowing nothing she could say would help her.

Salvatore grabbed the phone from Tomasso and pressed the call button.

"Who's calling?" Gary answered.

Salvatore said sarcastically, "I would like to report a missing car. It's a gold Maybach, last seen not far from your cabin."

Gary had been expecting to hear from Salvatore but not this early and not on his private cell phone number. It didn't take him long to surmise how Salvatore got his number. Kickoff had come early, and the game was afoot. Gary was thankful he had game-planned with Misty the night before.

"I'm really sorry to hear that, Salvatore. I know how much Antonio loved that car."

"So you know it's Antonio's car?"

His first pass fell incomplete so he threw another. "I know he was trespassing on my property. Maybe if it was parked in front of my cabin instead of hidden in the brush, he'd still have it. You sent them to rough me up, didn't you Sal?"

"You didn't think you could take my casino for two hundred K and not pay a price, did you?"

"I'm not that naive."

"Then why did you fuck with me in the first place?"

The conversation wasn't going in the direction Gary wanted, so he went on the offensive. It was time to throw a Hail Mary. "Would it change things if I told you I was ready to negotiate a deal for Devil's Cove?"

"Don't be jacking with me if you don't mean it, Gary."

"Why don't you come by my office and we can continue our conversation? You can find out firsthand how serious I am."

"Why don't you come to my suite?" Salvatore said.

"I would if we were negotiating to buy your casino."

Salvatore placed his finger under Monique's chin and lifted her face up until their eyes met. "Sure, I'll come pay you a visit. Be down in fifteen minutes." He hung up without saying good-bye.

"So Gary wants to sell out?" Antonio asked.

Salvatore frowned. "We'll see." He took his finger out from under Monique's chin, letting her head sink back down until it rested on her chest. He glanced at Antonio and said, "She's all yours. Do with her as you like. I'm done with the bitch!"

Antonio grabbed her by the arm and pulled her into her bedroom, slamming the door behind them.

Squaring up in front of Monique, Antonio said, "Look at me when I'm talking to you!"

HANGING BY A THREAD

She looked at him with disdain. He slapped her in return. Monique held the side of her face, but she refused to give him the pleasure of knowing how much pain he had dealt.

"Damn it, woman. I've had enough of your insolence. You heard Salvatore. You belong to me now, and you better start showing me some respect."

Without thinking or caring, she dug up a loogie from deep in her throat and plastered it over his face. After wiping his face with his left hand, Antonio slammed the full force of his right fist into Monique's face, sending her reeling across the room. She attempted to get up but crumpled back to the floor. The left side of her face went numb and her left ear began to ring. She bit her tongue and rolled onto her side so he could not see her tear-filled eyes.

Grabbing a pillow and blanket from off the bed, Antonio walked over and threw them on top of her.

"You're probably going to be there for a while, so you might as well get comfortable," he said, half laughing. "See, I can be a nice guy when I want to. When you learn to show me respect, I'll play nice."

He left the room and locked the door behind him. Monique was paying a hefty price, but for the first time in a long, long time, she felt the satisfaction of helping someone.

* * *

Misty put her cell phone back into her pocket, looked up at the boys, who were in the process of packing, and said, "That was Gary, and things are moving quicker than anticipated. Salvatore is on his way to Gary's office, so we need to make our move now!"

"Just about done," Miguel replied.

Tom and Thor held up their bags, indicating they were ready to roll.

"Okay," Misty replied. "I'll head down to Salvatore's private elevator to secure it while you load up the limo."

"I would guess that elevator is pretty secure," Miguel said. "How are we going to get to Salvatore's private floor?"

"Esteban gave me the code," she beamed.

"Sweet!" Thor said.

Esteban was sitting behind the wheel of a sleek, black limo when

Miguel, Tom, and Thor arrived. He exited the limo and helped them stash their bags.

Misty stood with her back to the elevator as she waited for them to join her. Deep in thought, she didn't notice the elevator door opening behind her, and she was caught off guard when a strong arm reached around from behind her while another hand covered her mouth. She fought to keep from being dragged into the elevator, but her assailant was too strong. Salvatore stepped out of the elevator then pushed the button to send it back to his private floor. He smiled at her as the doors closed between them. She caught a glimpse in the mirror of Santo holding her from behind.

"Where's Misty?" Thor said when they arrived at the elevator.

"Tom, check the bar," Miguel said. "I'll check the women's room."

When Tom gave him a queer look, Miguel said, "Don't worry, I learned my way around the ladies' room during our stay in Alaska."

Miguel crossed himself outside the door and then barged in, causing a lady at the sink to shriek.

"I'm a bodyguard, ma'am!" he said as he started checking each stall. He banged on the only one locked while the lady at the sink ran out of the restroom. "Misty, are you in there?"

When a lady yelled at him from within, he thought, *Guess not.*

When they all met back at the elevator, Thor said, "Looks like she must have gone up without us."

"It's all we have to go on," Miguel said.

"Either way, we need to free Monique, so we might as well get it done whether she's up there or not."

"But doesn't Misty have the code?" Thor asked.

Miguel thought a moment and said, "Misty got the code from Esteban. I'll be right back!"

* * *

Salvatore entered Gary's office without knocking. After looking around, he said to Gary, "This office's going to look a lot better once you sell."

Gary rocked back in his chair, putting his feet on the desk. "You mean, if I sell out. We still have some negotiating to do."

Salvatore placed a chair backward on the opposite side of Gary's desk, hung his arms over the back of the chair, and said, "Don't worry. I'll be fair. What's your asking price?"

Gary replied, "What's the rush? Let's get to know each other a little better first. How about a drink?"

Gary opened a desk drawer and pulled out the bottle of A.H. Hirsh Reserve Bourbon he had shared with Misty the night before, placed a glass in front of Salvatore, poured him a generous portion, and then did the same for himself. Salvatore took a sip, swished it in his mouth, and nodded his approval.

*　*　*

When Tomasso opened the door, Santo dragged Misty through it and flung her to the floor. Santo sucked on the soft tissue between his thumb and index finger.

"The bitch bit me!" he wailed.

Misty rose to her feet calmly and brushed herself off. "You should be more careful where you put your hand." Looking around the room, she demanded, "Where's Monique?"

Antonio walked up to Misty and eyed her from top to bottom.

"Take your eyes off me or I'll—"

"Or you'll what?" Antonio shot back.

She wanted to say "Have Miguel kick your ass," but instead she chose not to respond.

Antonio sneered at her, "Come to your senses, have you?"

Misty began to assess just what kind of trouble she was really in. *I'm not scared of these buffoons . . . or should I be?* she thought. *I wonder if Miguel and the guys will figure out where I've gone. I wouldn't mind seeing them come through that door right now!*

She softened her tone and smiled at Antonio. "All you needed to do was ask me to come up nicely, and I would have graciously accepted."

"You would have gladly come if you knew Salvatore was ready to consummate your deal?" Antonio said. "I doubt it. Salvatore sent Santo to fetch you because he wanted to make sure you didn't do something stupid, like run away."

"And she fell right into my arms," Santo boasted.

Misty sauntered over to the sofa and took a seat. She crossed her right leg over her left knee and picked at her nails.

"No big deal," she said. "Where did Salvatore go anyway?"

"He had business to attend to," Diego proudly blurted out. Antonio glared and added in a condescending way, "Gary's going to sell out."

"Imagine that," Misty said. "Who would have ever thought?" She fluffed up the sofa pillows and stretched out. "I had a rough night. Will you boys wake me when he returns?"

Lying there with her eyes closed gave Misty some time to think. *Damn, if I had only gone with the guys I wouldn't be in this predicament.* The thought about sleeping with Salvatore made her ill. It wasn't his looks. It was what he might do to her if she didn't cooperate with his every wish. She calculated her odds of bolting out the front door and making it to the elevator without getting caught. Figuring her chances were ten percent at best, she put the idea out of her head and tried to think of something more pleasant.

* * *

Gary was proud of himself for convincing Salvatore to talk about how he had come up with the grand design for the most talked-about casino in Vegas and how he had finagled the land it was built on. Gary refreshed his glass of bourbon when it got low and kept a close eye on the time while anxiously awaiting a call from Misty that would indicate she had completed her mission. His phone lay concealed in an open drawer, with the ringer off. Only he would be able to see the caller ID.

Eventually, Salvatore tired of talking about himself and said, "Okay, enough about me. Now let's get down to business."

"Why, Sal. Don't you want to know why I've resisted selling out for so long?"

Salvatore was growing impatient but decided he could wait another half hour if it got him what he had so desperately wanted for the last five years. Besides, he reveled in the fact Misty was securely in his apartment, and there was no risk of her going anywhere. He pretended to be listening to Gary while filling the void with thoughts of things he planned to do to Misty. If Gary kept his word and agreed to a deal, he would go easier on her, but if this was all a ruse and Gary backed out, she would pay dearly for Gary's bad behavior. He knew Gary had a soft spot for Misty, so what better way to get back at him than to make Misty his sex slave for the next forty-eight hours? The thought made Salvatore almost hope Gary backed out.

* * *

Miguel peered out of the elevator and looked down the long corridor. "There seems to be only one door on this floor, and it's at the end of the hallway," he said to the others. "No one is standing guard."

"Why would they?" Tom asked. "They don't know we are coming. Let's move before they figure it out."

When Misty's phone rang, Santo moved in and ripped it from her hand before she could answer. "It's your precious Miguel calling you. Too bad he doesn't know where you are."

Santo took the battery out and placed it in his back pocket. He handed her the phone and grinned.

There was a knock at the door. "That was quick," Tomasso said. "Gary must have caved fast. If not, boss is going to be in a foul mood." He took a deep breath and opened the door.

The moment the door cracked open, Tom shouldered his way through, knocking Tomasso back a few steps. Before Antonio and the boys figured things out, Miguel stood in the middle of the room, flanked by Tom and Thor. Miguel looked around the room and said, "So this is where you ran off to, Misty. I don't blame you, nice digs."

Misty was on her way to join her comrades when Santo stepped into her path. Tomasso and Antonio moved next to Santo, forming a wall. Diego eventually figured it out and joined them.

"Misty's not going anywhere," Antonio said. "She has a contract to fulfill, and that's exactly what she's going to do."

Tom turned a bag upside down, and two hundred thousand dollars worth of casino chips spilled out onto the floor.

Tom said, "Consider her contract null and void. She's returning your boss's cash. Plus, there's an extra twenty thousand. Keep the change."

Antonio snickered. "That's the money she won at our sportsbook. We'll gladly accept all of it, but that money has nothing to do with the obligations of her contract. Nice try."

"Salvatore broke our contract by choosing to have Monique lead the training sessions instead of me, and she filled any bedroom obligations many times over," Misty said from behind them. "I'd say Salvatore got his money's worth."

Scratching his head, Diego said, "I think she's got a point, boss."

"Remind me to shoot him when we're done," Antonio said.

A voice rang out from the front door: "Salvatore."

Cousin Benny brushed past Miguel and took a position between the two groups and said, "What's going on here, Antonio?"

"It's none of your business, Benny. Now go back down to the casino floor and be an ambassador to the customers."

"You better take a hike, funny little man," Miguel said. "This is none of your concern."

Benny stuck out his chest and replied, "I'm The Guy! You will do as I wish if you know what's good for you."

Antonio thought about hitting Benny upside the head, but he knew he would get reprimanded by Salvatore.

Not knowing the true pecking order, Tom stepped in front of Benny and asked him, "So you're The Guy?"

Benny answered proudly, "Yep, I'm The Guy!"

Tom replied, "Then you are just the guy I've been looking for!"

Benny turned his head and gave Antonio a smug look. He turned back just in time to be greeted by Tom's seven-inch balled-up fist slamming into the side of his face. The powerful blow snapped Benny's head to the right as the crack of Benny's jawbone echoed through the room. Both groups cringed. As if they were watching a Saturday morning cartoon, time slowed to a halt. Benny stood there motionless for a full count before gravity kicked in. In an instant, his body crumpled to the floor in a pile.

Tom pointed across the room.

"Now who wants to be The Guy?" Tom bellowed.

Antonio took a step back, using Tomasso, Santo, and Diego as cover.

Sizing up Santo as the toughest, Tom started to move in his direction before Thor grabbed him by the arm.

"He's mine," Thor whispered. "We have unfinished business."

Tom moved on Diego, causing him to nervously backpedal around the room. True to his name, Slick Masso tried talking some sense into Miguel until Miguel's fist crashed into his jaw, sending him to the floor. Antonio pulled Tomasso up by the arm and pushed him toward Miguel. When his glancing blow to the side of Miguel's face didn't faze Miguel, Tomasso took a step back. Miguel stepped in quickly, feinted a right hook, and delivered a thunderous straight left jab to Tomasso's face. Although Tomasso's knees buckled, he kept his balance until Miguel followed up with a right cross. Tomasso never knew what hit him.

All it took Tom was one right hand to Diego's solar plexus to crumple him to his knees. The gentle giant fell forward, gasping for air. Tom noticed Thor kneeling on one knee, with blood dripping from his mouth. Tom made a move in Santo's direction, but Thor yelled out for him to stop. After getting to his feet, Thor said, "I told you he was mine."

Thor drove into Santo's midsection with his shoulder, driving him over the sofa and onto the floor. If Misty had not dived out of the way, she would have gone over with them. Thor rolled over and quickly got to his feet, ahead of Santo. Thor's right hand crashed across Santo's temple as he attempted to rise. Quickly reloading, Thor hit him again. When Tom noticed Santo was disoriented, he stepped between the two. Santo attempted to rise, only to stumble to his knees. Santo regrouped, willed himself to his feet, and let out a blood-curdling scream. Tom moved out of the way as Santo lunged at Thor, only to be met with another crushing blow to the head. Santo lay on the floor, knocked out cold. Tom patted Thor on his shoulder and said, "Well done, son." Misty walked over and removed her cell phone battery from his back pocket.

Across the room, Antonio backed away from Miguel until he was up against the back wall.

With nowhere to go, Antonio said to Miguel in a threatening voice, "You don't know what you are getting yourself into. If I were you, I'd turn around and walk out that door."

"He must think he's The Guy," Tom yelled out to Miguel in a sarcastic tone.

Antonio pointed a finger at Tom and repeated his threat. Miguel slammed a thundering fist into Antonio's right shoulder. Antonio's right arm dangled limply by his side as he slid down the wall onto his butt. He sat there, holding his shoulder with his left hand.

Looking up at Miguel, Antonio said, "Take Misty and get the hell out of here, but remember, there will be a heavy price to pay."

Tom motioned to Misty to follow him toward the door, but Miguel and Thor did not budge. Tom looked back with a puzzled look. "Aren't you forgetting why we came up here?" Thor asked. "Where's Monique?"

Thor walked over to the bedroom door. It was locked. Antonio yelled out, "You better not go in there."

Thor threw his shoulder into the door. The top hinge cracked. Tom motioned for Thor to step back and then rammed into the door, knocking it completely off the hinges. Miguel pushed passed them and kneeled by Monique's side. She looked up at him and attempted a grin, but it quickly turned into a grimace. Miguel delicately stroked her long, beautiful black hair. He leaned down and whispered into her ear, "Let me help you up. It's time to go home."

Thor walked to her other side and helped Miguel lift her gently off the floor. Almost to the front door, Monique heard Antonio say, "Go ahead and run off, but know this, I'll eventually catch you and make you pay."

Monique's brows furled. She removed her arms from the boys, pushing them aside and walked gingerly over to Antonio. With a look of disdain, she said, "Say that again."

"I said—"

Monique's foot crashed into his scrotum before he could finish his sentence. Antonio rolled onto the floor and lay there on top of his bad shoulder in agony. He moaned loudly as Monique made her way to the bedroom. When she returned, she threw a pillow and blanket on top of Antonio.

"You're probably going to be there for a while, so you might as well be comfortable." Monique placed her arms around the boys again and said, "Okay, now I'm ready to go home."

As the group approached the limo, Esteban got out and greeted them. Esteban stopped when he noticed that Monique's left eye was almost shut and her cheekbone swollen. Although he and Monique had gotten off on the wrong foot the night she came to him for a massage, he was upset. He figured no woman deserved to be punched in the face. Esteban placed his hand on her arm as she steadied herself to get into the limo. Monique paused to look into Esteban's eyes, acknowledging his concern.

Once they were all squared away inside the limo, Misty put her battery back into her phone and called Gary. He didn't answer, so she left a voice mail: "Mission accomplished. Please be careful, my dear friend. Hopefully I'll see you in Buenos Aires someday."

* * *

When Misty's name appeared on his phone, Gary held back a smile. He slowly wound down the story he was telling Salvatore. "And that is why I could never sell Devil's Cove," Gary said. "To you or anyone else."

Salvatore's mind was still focused on the salacious details of his impending rendezvous with Misty, so it took him a moment to realize Gary had finished talking. He then sorted through his vague memory of Gary's last sentence.

Salvatore looked at Gary puzzled, "Would you mind repeating that last sentence? I think I misunderstood you."

After Gary repeated, word for word, Salvatore said, "Are you playing with me? Have you lost your mind?"

Gary pushed his chair back from his desk and walked over to the door. "It's no game. I asked you here so I could fully explain why I could never sell out to you or anyone else. There are just too many personal memories here for me to leave behind. I figured the only way to get you to listen to me was to pretend I would sell out."

Salvatore stood, resisting the urge to sling his chair across the room, if not at Gary. When his flash of anger passed, he regained his composure.

He walked up to Gary calmly and said, "You have just made the biggest mistake of your life."

Gary leaned in close to Salvatore and said confidently, yet void of anger, "If you ever come back to the Cove, I will have you escorted out."

"So this is how it's going to be," Salvatore said, and walked out. Salvatore was livid as he walked briskly back to his casino. But then his anger succumbed to a smile. *Misty is going to pay dearly for Gary's insolence.*

Two FBI agents emerged from Gary's office closet. It was small and much too cozy, but it had served its purpose.

After rearranging their suits, the senior agent said, "Things will probably escalate." Patting the other agent on the shoulder, he added. "Bill is going undercover for a while to keep an eye on you. Let your pit bosses know to let him gamble at will and track his losses."

"Hey," Bill said, "who said I'm going to lose?"

The senior agent shook his head and continued, "Track his play, and we will make sure it all balances out at the end."

Gary nodded. "Thanks, I appreciate your offer."

* * *

When Salvatore entered his suite, he immediately noticed the bedroom door was off its hinge. He scanned the apartment, surveying the damage in disbelief. Diego was on his knees, held up only by his head leaning on the floor. Santo was out cold, and Tomasso was only beginning to stir. Antonio lay on his side, moaning. Salvatore then noticed his cousin Benny crumpled at his feet. He walked briskly into the bedroom and found it empty. He stormed back out into the main room and yelled, "Where are the girls?"

Tomasso replied meekly, "They're gone, boss. I'll be happy to explain."

"Explain! Hell, you don't need to explain. It's plain to see you guys got your butts kicked!" Salvatore looked down at Benny and yelled out for someone to call for a medic.

When the medics arrived, they quickly looked over the group and attended to Benny first. Salvatore looked down at the sight of Benny strapped onto a stretcher. The left side of Benny's face was so swollen Salvatore could barely recognize him. Salvatore noticed Benny motioning with his finger for him to come closer, so Salvatore got down on his knees. Benny was having difficulty speaking, so Salvatore leaned in until his ear was only inches away from Benny's mouth.

Benny whispered into Salvatore's ear, "I don't want to be 'The Guy' anymore."

Salvatore patted Benny on the top of his head as he stared into space, "Okay, Benny. You don't have to be The Guy anymore."

A relieved Benny closed his eyes and drifted off. Salvatore walked over to the plate-glass window and peered out to the mountain range in the distance. After some time to think, he took out his cell phone and called a contact he had at the airport. "I need you to e-mail me every flight plan from now until midnight, Charlie. Particularly flight plans with Buenos Aires, Argentina, as their final destination."

16

Into the Wild Blue Yonder

Gabriella's jet stood ready as the group pulled up to the private hanger. The captain was waiting at the bottom of the ramp as they hurried to the plane. "I understand this is some type of emergency," he said to Misty as she approached.

She patted him on his arm and said, "I'll explain it to you once we're airborne." She then handed the cocaptain two hundred-dollar bills along with the keys to the limo and said, "Find someone in the hangar who will agree to drive the limo someplace on the other side of town and leave it, but hurry."

"You got it. Two bills should get the job done."

The cabin was eerily quiet as the plane screamed down the runway. There was a collective sigh of relief once airborne. Esteban looked out the window at the Las Vegas skyline, knowing it would be the last time he would ever see what had been his home for the last several years. He prayed it would be the last he ever saw of Salvatore and his men. When it was safe to move about, Misty rose from her seat and looked to the back of the plane. Monique's head was resting comfortably on Miguel's shoulder. Misty made her way back and kneeled in the aisle next to Miguel.

"How's she doing?" Misty whispered.

Before he could answer, Monique opened her eyes, so Miguel asked her directly, "How are you doing?"

Monique looked past Miguel and addressed Misty, "I'll be fine. Thanks for asking," and then closed her eyes. Miguel stroked the side of Monique's head.

Misty went back to her seat to contemplate. Even though Monique had been a major pain in the butt over the last several months, no woman deserved to be abused the way Salvatore and his men had abused Monique. Misty began to imagine what they might have put Monique through if they had not gotten her out of there but found the thought too disturbing, so she tried to get a little shut-eye.

* * *

Salvatore was sitting on the sofa in his suite, drinking whiskey and gazing upon the mountain range to the west of the city, when his contact from McCarran International airport called him back. "I have only one flight plan heading for Miami International airport and then on to Buenos Aires."

"Excellent," Salvatore said with a smile. He nodded to Antonio who lay sprawled out in an easy chair with an ice pack on his crotch and a drink in his hand. After writing a few things down, Salvatore hung up the phone, walked over to Antonio, and handed him a piece of paper. "Pack your bags. You and the boys are headed to Buenos Aires."

Antonio set the ice pack down, sat up, and downed the rest of his drink. "Okay, boss. I'll call the hangar and give the pilot our plans."

Before Antonio could struggle to his feet, the phone rang again. "What the fuck!" Salvatore yelled and hung up the phone.

"What's the story, boss?"

"They changed their flight plan to Antonio Maceo Airport, Santiago de Cuba!" Salvatore replied.

"Cuba! How in the hell did they get permission to land in Cuba?"

"Their plane is registered in Argentina, not the United States," Salvatore said. "They must have connections high up in the government."

"So how are we going to follow them to Cuba?" Antonio asked.

Salvatore gulped down the remainder of the whiskey from his glass and slung the empty glass across the room, shouting, "You're not!"

"So we'll just wait until they file a flight plan from Cuba and then follow them, right?" Antonio asked.

Salvatore gave Antonio a look of disgust. "And what, you're best buds with Fidel? That's a communist country, how the hell are we going to secure a flight plan leaving Cuba?"

Antonio scratched the back of his head. "I see your point. So what are we going to do?"

Salvatore paced the room deep in thought before saying, "There's only one thing we can do. Send someone to Buenos Aires to keep an eye on the airport. That plane has got to show up there sooner or later."

* * *

Night had fallen as the Gulfstream approached Antonio Maceo Airport. Tom stared out of the window at the magnificent fluffy cumulus clouds that were brilliantly illuminated by the moon. He anxiously worried his service record would not serve him well if detained.

Misty sensed tension among the group and stood up. "I owe you an explanation as to why we are landing in Cuba." She looked at Esteban and said, "Esteban took great risk helping us rescue Monique. I felt it too dangerous to leave him behind." She turned to Esteban, "I'm very sorry you must now abandon your dream about earning enough money to help your girlfriend escape and come to live with you in the United States. You gave all that up when you chose to help us."

"And I would do it again, if given the choice," Esteban said. "Salvatore is an evil man. I never should have sold my soul to work for him in the first place." Esteban looked down at his feet and then back up. "I have come to realize that as much as I hate the government, Cuba is my home. I am at peace with this decision."

"Gabriella pulled some strings to get us into Cuba. We are landing in Santiago de Cuba, not Havana, so hopefully there will be less curiosity surrounding our arrival," Misty replied.

"Tell us about your girlfriend," Miguel said to Esteban.

Esteban's mood brightened. "Her name is Catalina. She lives with her father on a small rural tobacco plantation that is situated along a river basin."

"But how will you explain your absence if the authorities question you?" Tom asked.

"The plantation is secluded and officials seldom venture into the area. If they come, I can pose as one of the hired hands," Esteban smiled. "At least it is a place Salvatore will never be able to find me."

"Aren't you the lucky one! You got room for one more hired hand?" Miguel asked and laughed.

Tom said, in an effort to ease any tension surrounding the afterthought of Miguel's remarks, especially his son's, "I'm sure Salvatore has more important things to do than go on a worldwide manhunt."

"And what about a woman hunt?" Monique said sarcastically.

The pilot came out of the cockpit and said, "Buckle up and place your heads in your hands when we land. I hear this airport is better suited for turbo props. Not really sure how long the runway is or what shape it's in, so best we prepare for the worst."

The landing was a bit bumpy, but the runway proved to be adequately long. As they taxied toward the airport, a vehicle followed after, with twirling red lights.

"I didn't expect Gabriella to send a welcoming party," Miguel joked. "She really outdid herself this time."

Tom was more than a little concerned, but he kept it to himself.

Two men in military fatigues boarded the plane and quietly looked everyone over. The skinny guy with greasy hair smirked at the sight of Misty. When he headed in her direction, Misty took in a deep breath and then slowly let it out. She reminded herself that this was no time to be her usual smart ass. As they stood face-to-face, Miguel, against his better judgment, made a move in their direction. The man at the front of the plane immediately drew his revolver from his holster and pointed it at Miguel. The tension was palpable until a third man entered the plane and said in a commanding, yet pleasant, voice, "*Excelente. Le veo ha encontrado todo. Edwardo, tengo todos sus papeles conmigo. La son invitados por Fidel él mismo.*"

The man was of medium build, wore a freshly pressed black suit, and carried himself with dignity. The military men were obviously perturbed, yet they were respectful of the man's position. After the skinny one returned to the front of the plane, a lengthy discussion ensued.

"What are they saying?" Misty whispered to Tom.

"He's explaining to the two men that we are guests of Fidel's, and he is on a diplomatic mission to welcome us to Cuba. It's obvious from their tone that they wish he had not arrived."

The men reluctantly exited the plane, giving Misty a long glare before debarking.

The diplomat smiled congenially as he greeted them, "Balboa Ignacio at your service."

Misty squeezed past Tom and walked up to offer her hand. Balboa raised her hand to his lips and kissed it. Misty smiled back graciously and asked, "Did Gabriella send you?"

"It was someone very high up in the Argentina government. Perhaps someone your Gabriella knows."

"We are extremely grateful you showed up when you did. Things were getting rather tense."

Balboa surveyed the group before his eyes fixed on Esteban. He said to Esteban in the local dialect, "Are you my package?" Esteban nodded.

Balboa turned back to Misty. "I would prefer not to know his name. It's best we make the drop as quickly as possible. The longer you stay, the more quickly things could become, how do you say it in America, quite sticky?"

"But you are an important man. Those two men did as you said," Misty said, somewhat confused.

Balboa straightened his suit and smiled. "Yes, yes, I am. But in Cuba, dignitaries, as everyone else in this country, do what the military demands. These men were of a very low rank. Had I been addressing an officer, things may have turned out quite differently."

"I couldn't help but overhear you discussing with the men something about a tobacco farm," Tom said.

"Yes, I persuaded them that a tobacco farmer was worried his crop had a rare form of disease and that you were here to instruct the farmer how to keep the disease from spreading to the other crops in the area. I said if it did so, the local economy would take years to recover."

"And they bought it?" Tom asked.

"For now," Balboa replied.

"So what's the next move?" Miguel asked.

"I will take the package to his destination and then return here to ensure you get on your way safely."

"You're coming back here?" Misty asked.

"You're not going with them, Misty!" Miguel said intuitively. "Don't even think about it."

Misty paid him no heed, turning to Balboa and saying, "We better get going then."

Knowing how headstrong Misty was when she made her mind up, Miguel said firmly, "You're not going without your bodyguard."

"My vehicle can only hold four people, so everyone else will have to stay here," Balboa said before moving past Misty and leading the way.

Tom yelled out, "I don't have a good feeling about this, Migs."

Miguel turned back around and shrugged his shoulders.

Tom shook his head and said, "Drop Esteban off, and get Misty back here as fast as you can." Miguel rolled his eyes and nodded his head in the affirmative and then ran to catch up with Misty, Esteban, and Balboa.

Misty recognized the look on Miguel's face as he approached them. "Bodyguard, my ass!" she said. "You just wanted a ride in this boss car." She pointed to the emblem and mouthed the letters G-T-O.

"Not just any GTO," Miguel said. "A 1969 Goat with a Hurst, three speed on the floor, and 350 horses under the hood!"

"Goat?"

"That's their nickname, Misty. My older brother had a Chevy Super Sport when I was growing up in LA, and he was always pissed he never won a street race with a GTO."

He poked Misty and then whispered in her ear so Esteban could not hear him "You're not fooling me. You only came along because you want to see how hot-looking Catalina is." Misty made no effort to deny it.

When Balboa turned the key, the engine rumbled. Miguel closed his eyes and pretended he was about to hit the streets of LA with his brother. His bubble slightly burst when Balboa eased the clutch out and drove down the road at a controlled speed.

Misty picked up on how disappointed Miguel was and said, "Okay, Mario Andretti. Just leave it alone."

Miguel slumped down in the back seat and covered his face with his hands.

Fifteen minutes out, they pulled off the highway and wound their way along a riverbed. The narrow dirt road was smoother than one would have expected. By now the brilliant moon had faded away, leaving them in total darkness. The Goat's headlights were dim, having probably not been replaced in a decade. The car wasn't air-conditioned, so they drove with windows down. Had it not been for the rumble from the engine, they would have been able to hear the sounds of the birds, animals, and insects that resided along the banks of the river.

The thought of Salvatore and his men was a distant memory to Misty at this moment. This communist country was fully capable of suppressing its own citizens without the help of Italian mobsters. Misty was older and wiser now, not the naive girl who had plunged headlong into her Black Widow Trainer gig a few years back. Risk and danger had become a common occurrence, and she was adept at managing fear. Aware the next several hours could bring her harm, she refused to let it drag her down, choosing instead to revel in *how alive* she felt at this very moment.

Balboa turned off the road and headed up a narrow drive. Esteban stuck his head out the window and breathed in the aroma from the rows of coffee beans. Misty was living vicariously through him, feeling what he felt and anticipating what was to come. Just because she had trouble with commitment didn't mean she couldn't share in his. She fully expected Esteban's upcoming reunion with his beloved Catalina would bring with it all the romance and drama of Bogart and Bacall.

Balboa pulled up in front of a large wooden building. Misty guessed it had been built several hundred years ago. The exterior walls were dark and dull, void of color, yet the structure seemed sound. She assumed money was scarce and supplies hard to come by. Colorful paint was a luxury, not a necessity.

As the others got out of the car, Esteban grabbed Balboa's hand, indicating he wanted him to remain in the car. Balboa watched curiously as Esteban reached into his back sack and pulled out a fat envelope. Esteban opened it up and fanned the thick stack of hundred dollar bills before placing the envelope in the glove box.

"Forty thousand American dollars so that no one knows I'm here," Esteban said.

Balboa flashed a row of white teeth. "You are a generous man. You can rest assured, my friend."

The porch boards squeaked under their feet as they approached the front door. Esteban knocked lightly for quite some time before the front door cracked open and a man peeked out. He appeared to be in his early sixties and had a weathered face and graying hair. His eyes were clear and alert. They became more alert when he recognized Esteban. When the man's face softened, he looked over the others quickly and then opened the door wide. Esteban embraced the man heartily, and then they rambled on in Spanish. The man clasped the side of Esteban's face and looked him over once more as if still not believing it was truly him. He smiled broadly, placing his index finger to his mouth, before disappearing back into the house. Esteban shifted back and forth while tapping his fingers nervously on his thighs. A soft yellow light came on inside the house, revealing a warm and cozy living room on the other side of the doorway. Esteban motioned for the others to follow him inside. The old furniture gave the room great character. Misty wished they could stay for a week.

Two figures approached through a doorway. The woman rubbed her eyes as she was led by her other arm into the room. Once directly in front of Esteban, she removed her hand and squinted at him through sleep-filled eyes. An instant later, she let out a loud shriek, wrapped her arms around Esteban, and buried her face into his chest. The older man took a couple steps back to observe the reunion. She looked back up at Esteban with tears streaming down her cheeks. Esteban gently wiped them from her face. They inched closer and closer until their mouths met, kissing for what seemed like an eternity. When a tear rolled down the side of Misty's face, she quickly used her sleeve to remove the evidence. But it was too late. Miguel had noticed and was mimicking her. Misty stuck her tongue out at him and gave him a little shove.

When their commotion caught Catalina's attention, Esteban said, "Where are my manners?"

Catalina's eyes locked onto Misty, sizing her up as Esteban made the introductions. Misty could sense a heavy dose of curiosity with a touch of jealousy. Worried about misconceptions, she stepped forward and gave Catalina a warm hug. As she pulled back, she noticed how naturally beautiful Catalina was. She had dark hair and smooth, dark brown skin. Her soft eyes were set wide apart and nestled atop high cheekbones. Her face narrowed down to her chin, showcasing deliciously full lips. But it was the innocence she portrayed that made her so endearing.

Misty placed her hand on the side of Catalina's face and said, "You are so beautiful!"

Catalina blushed but did not respond.

"She does not understand English," Esteban offered, "but I have little doubt she understands your meaning."

Catalina reached out and touched the side of Misty's face in return, saying, "Muy bonita!"

"Looks like the two of you have a mutual admiration for each other," Esteban said and smiled.

Still not completely comfortable, Catalina narrowed her eyes and looked at Esteban. He smiled warmly and said, "Amiga."

"I hate to break this up, but we need to get back to the plane," Miguel interjected.

Balboa nodded, "Miguel is right. This is taking more time than I had allotted."

"Okay, then," Misty said. "You guys get the car started while I say good-bye to Esteban."

Miguel gave Esteban a fist bump and then headed to the car with Balboa. Miguel got there ahead of Balboa and rested his butt against the driver's door. He held out his hand.

"The keys, my friend," Miguel said in a firm but unthreatening way.

"Why?" Balboa asked.

"Because we need to make up some time, and you are too cautious of a driver."

Balboa handed over the keys. "I can't argue with your logic. Just don't strip the gears."

Miguel jumped in and cranked the engine. He gripped the steering wheel firmly with both hands as he revved the engine. Memories of street races in his early days danced through his head. He backed off the accelerator and rested the back of his head on the seat. With eyes closed, he let the vibration of the Goat's powerful engine permeate his body and recharge his soul.

Misty gave Esteban a hug. "I'm so happy for you, Este. You are home where you belong."

"I will always think of you as the angel that led me back to where I belong."

Moved by his kind words, Misty bit her bottom lip to keep from shedding another tear. She thanked him one more time with her eyes and left. The night air was crisp as she walked to the GTO. She took one last look around the little tobacco plantation, committing it to memory. When she slid into the backseat, she remembered one of her and Esteban's massage encounters and cracked a smile.

Miguel looked back at her through his rearview mirror and said, "Buckle up, boss. We've got some time to make up."

Misty noticed Balboa was strapped into the shotgun seat tight and uncommonly silent. She was about to say something when Miguel eased off the clutch and moved out. Misty quickly located her seat belt and strapped it tightly around her midsection, wondering how people got by for years without shoulder harnesses.

"You get us killed, Miguel, and you're not getting a bonus this year, dude," Misty yelled above the engine. Miguel grinned.

Esteban and Catalina followed her father into the kitchen. It was warm and cozy, a place where Esteban had enjoyed many discussions over the years and a fitting place to share his secret with his true love and her father. Esteban placed his backpack on the kitchen table and motioned for the two to join him. They gathered around, wide-eyed, wondering what he might have brought them. Esteban unzipped the backpack and dumped the contents onto the table. Catalina gasped, and her father's knees almost buckled. It was the rest of the money Esteban had saved to get Catalina out of the country. Money that could now be used to put food on the table, hire more hands to take the burden off an aging old man, and to make much-needed repairs to the home. The more than a hundred thousand dollars would last them a lifetime in Cuba. Her father placed his hands on the side of Esteban's face and gave him a big kiss on the forehead before taking the money to a safe hiding place. Catalina took Esteban by the hand, leading him into her bedroom and closing the door behind them. She unbuttoned Esteban's shirt and kissed his chest and then guided him into bed. The reunion they had been dreaming about for almost two years had finally arrived.

* * *

Misty watched Miguel intently as he guided the car along a windy road, negotiating the ruts and speeding up where he could. He felt confident and in control. Misty noted that he was more focused than she had ever seen him. As they approached the highway, Misty realized Miguel was not slowing down, so she screamed out, "Miguel!" as she closed her eyes and held on tight. Miguel hit the brakes and turned the steering wheel hard to the left. The GTO went into a controlled slide, coming to rest in the middle of the highway with the front of the car pointing down the road in the direction of the airport. Miguel threw the car into first gear and let out the clutch. Misty smelled the stench of burning rubber and opened her eyes to the sight of white smoke from the tires on either side, but once the GTO caught traction, the car exploded forward. The smoke instantly vanished into thin air. Centrifugal force penned Misty back against her seat, where she remained captive. She heard Balboa let out a blood-curdling scream as he held onto the armrest with both hands. Misty became mesmerized at the site of the speedometer as it leaped into the air. Miguel slammed the clutch to the floor with his left leg and power-shifted into second gear, causing the speedometer to dip for an instant before resuming its upward track. At ninety miles an hour he power-shifted once more, and they were off to the races. At a hundred and twenty miles an hour, Misty looked out her window. Telephone poles passed by so fast they resembled a picket fence. Glancing back at the speedometer, she noticed the needle was buried back at zero. A police car with blaring red lights pulled onto the highway. She looked out the rear window and watched the lights get smaller and smaller until they completely disappeared. Ten long minutes passed before the speedometer worked its way down, ever so slowly. Misty and Balboa relaxed their grips as the car approached seventy. Miguel exercised his fingers to allow the blood to flow through them once again. Turning around and looking at Misty, he said, "Pretty cool, right?" Misty was *not* smiling.

In an attempt at regaining his manhood, Balboa said, "Very well done, Miguel. I had no idea my car was capable of going so fast."

"Well, now you know," Miguel replied.

Balboa pointed up the road. "Turn right at the next intersection. The airport isn't far."

The calm was broken with the sound of Miguel's voice, "What the . . ."

Misty looked out the front window at the sight of their plane surrounded by a dozen or more military vehicles. Tom, Thor, Monique, and the pilots all stood on the tarmac with their hands raised over their heads.

"Shit!" Misty yelled out. "What I would give to be back in Vegas right now."

Misty raced to their companions' side ahead of Miguel, but she was snatched by a group of men before she could get to them. They weren't as gentle with Miguel. As she struggled, Misty looked at Balboa who was straightening his finely pressed suit.

"Miguel!" Tom shouted. "Be smart, my amigo."

The military men escorted Misty and Miguel to their companions and walked away.

"Did you drop off the package successfully?" Tom asked Misty.

"Yeah. It looks like that was the easy part," she answered.

Misty looked over a group of men wearing dull-green fatigues. One man in particular seemed to move with authority. When he got a look at Misty and Monique, he began moving in their direction with the rest of his men on his heels.

"Here comes a fricken alpha male with his pack," Monique said with disdain. "Looks like I went from the frying pan into the fire."

"Keep your head up, Monique," Thor said. "We're not going to let anything happen to you."

The commander's pitted face and handlebar mustache gave him a much more menacing look than Salvatore. He gave little attention to the men, concentrating on Misty first and then on Monique. Tom, Thor, and Miguel felt helpless. A man walked up to the commander and handed him a document, which he began to read.

"This document indicates six passengers arrived. I only count five. Where is the missing person?" he demanded.

When they all remained quiet, he stepped up closer and said in a much tougher tone, "Is my English not good enough for you? Where is the sixth person?"

Misty thought back to how fairytale happy Esteban was when they had left him. She had heard stories about how they treated dissidents in Cuban prisons and shuddered at the thought of Esteban being held in one. But if that weren't depressing enough, it dawned on her that they all could wind up in prison for helping him back into the country. She doubted even Gabriella could help if that happened.

"Coronal! Balboa Ignacio, a su disposición," Balboa said as he walked up. He stood tall and confident, but Misty could tell he was scared as well. She remembered Balboa telling them earlier that he had limited power and how fortunate there wasn't a high-ranking officer around when they had landed.

As Balboa exchanged words with the full-blown coronal, Misty whispered, "Who wants to translate what they are saying?"

Miguel spoke softly: "They started out with pleasantries, but now the coronal is turning up the heat. He wants to know what Balboa is doing here and if he knows us. Our buddy is doing some serious tap dancing. I'm not so sure he's going to back us up this time. The stakes are probably too high for him."

Misty frowned. "Sorry I asked."

The coronal turned sideways, showing he no longer addressed Balboa as an equal. When his men began to laugh, Misty knew things were not going well. She couldn't understand how Balboa was staying so remarkably calm under such intense scrutiny. Just when it looked like the coronal was tiring of this little escapade, Balboa moved dangerously close and whispered something into the coronal's ear. The coronal's demeanor softened as he gave Balboa's words time to sink in. No one made a sound until he broke out in a smile and addressed Balboa by placing his hands on each side of his arms and giving him a friendly shake before leading Balboa away. When the men began to follow, the coronal raised his right hand for them not to follow. Their walk took them to Balboa's GTO, where the coronal got into the front passenger's seat while Balboa remained on the tarmac.

"What the hell do you think they are doing?" Misty asked.

"Maybe the coronal likes boss cars," Miguel said.

Misty glared back and said, "Seriously. You can make jokes at a time like this?"

"He's getting out of the car," Thor said.

The coronal slapped Balboa on the back as if they were old friends on their walk back to the group. Before long, the coronal's men were laughing and carrying on. After the two embraced, the coronal patted his front left breast pocket, gave Balboa a quick nod, and walked to his awaiting vehicle. Balboa waited for them to leave before wiping sweat from his brow and walking over to the group.

"You are all free to go, my friends, but I suggest you leave quickly."

The pilot motioned to his copilot and quickly climbed up the ramp to start up the plane. Everyone thanked Balboa and climbed aboard, leaving only Misty. After giving him a big hug, she said, "Please tell me what just happened so I don't wonder about it the rest of my life."

Balboa smiled genteelly and said, "Let's just say the coronal had forty thousand reasons to let you go."

Misty smiled back. "Let's just say we all owe you a debt of gratitude. If you ever flee this country, look me up in Buenos Aires, and I'll help you start a new life."

"You are too kind, but I have many family members in Cuba. I could never leave them."

Misty hugged Balboa long and hard this time before walking up the ramp to the doorway. She turned and blew him a kiss. After Balboa pretended to catch the kiss in his hand, Misty laughed and waved good-bye.

* * *

Uneasiness persisted until the pilot notified them they had officially left Cuban airspace and would be landing on St. Thomas Virgin Island shortly before sunrise.

The bump of the tires striking the runway woke Misty from her short catnap. As they taxied up to a tiny private hangar, she looked out her window at a mountainside that was sprinkled with sparkling white lights. On her way down the ramp, a soft breeze kissed her cheeks, giving a subtle hint of the wonderful weather in store. A tall local man greeted them. "Please climb in, and I will drive you to your destination across the island."

The sun began to rise as they wound their way through town. The driver pointed out Blackbeard's castle partway up the mountainside. At the top of the mountain, Misty looked out over the harbor and noticed a large cruise ship coming in from sea. She thought, *This is so my speed right now.*

As they drove along the crest of the hilltop, the driver pointed to a U-shaped bay on the other side of the mountain and said, "That is Magens Bay. We will be there in the next twenty minutes."

"It's looks awesome!" Miguel said.

Monique placed her head on Miguel's shoulder and whispered, "I'm almost home."

17

THE ISLAND

Misty thrashed about in bed while still half asleep. As she came to, she realized someone, or something, was making a loud screeching sound. She peered out the small slit in her right eye and discovered a multicolored parrot staring back at her.

"So you're the culprit," she said.

"Ark, pretty bird," the parrot squawked back.

"Pretty bird, my ass," she shot back. "You're going to be a featherless bird if you don't let me get some sleep."

Realizing her threats were pointless, Misty sat up and scooted back against the wall to better take in her surroundings. Her next sight was that of a seabird diving into the water and coming up with a small fish.

Where the hell am I? she thought, and then it all came back. A driver had dropped them off just as the sun was coming up. They had all walked down a long pier to a really cool bar that stood on pilings over the bay. Tom had knocked on the front door until a man let them in. She was pretty sure he had said his name was Sam. The man led them across a narrow wooden bridge to the living quarters twenty yards east of the bar. He said something about Captain Kev and Mikey being away on an island and guessed they would most likely return the next day. He said it was hard to tell because the island was uninhabited and had no cell service. The last thing she remembered was crashing on the first empty bed she came across.

Further inspection revealed twin beds on either side of her. One was made up and one was not. She seemed to be sleeping on a porch, with a wall at her back, a wall on her left, and a ceiling above her. A thin railing in front of her and on her right was the only thing separating her from Magens Bay. She got up out of bed and stretched her arms high into the air. She was wearing a beige cotton tank top and a pair of tight cotton shorts, not her usual birthday suit. Misty strolled to the far end of the room and peeked around the corner. She saw a large living area with a sofa and four chairs. Behind the sofa was a long bar and on the other side of the bar was a kitchen. The living room was open to the bay as well. Hungry, she walked over to the refrigerator and opened the door. It was fully stocked with wonderful native fruits and vegetables, plenty of eggs, and many types of fresh-squeezed juices. Misty chose an orange. She peeled and then ate it leaning over the sink, gazing at the bay. The orange slices were cold, sweet, and juicy, and just what she needed to get her day started. As she took her last bite, she noticed a hand depositing snorkeling gear onto the wooden floor, just under the railing. Soon two hands gripped the railing and in one swift move, a man sprang up and over into the living room. He was about six-feet tall and all lean muscle, a body built for both strength and endurance. His razor-sharp eyes gave her a once over before going back to what he was doing without a word.

Misty walked toward him, arms crossed, and said, "So, how was the snorkeling?"

Looking up from a kneeling position, he shrugged and returned to attending to his things.

"You're the guy in the old pickup truck sitting between Captain and Mikey in Buenos Aires, aren't you?"

He nodded without looking up.

"Are you upset with me for some reason?" she asked.

He stood up with gear in hand and said, "Nope." Looking down at her braless chest and swollen nipples, he added, "You might want to put on some clothes."

"So who do you think you are, my dad?"

"I'm old enough."

Once he left, Misty took a tour of the rest of the cottage. The guys' sleeping quarters, located on the opposite side of the girls', had four beds and two hammocks. A large bathroom connected the sleeping areas. The separate toilet areas were sealed off by sliding doors, but in the middle stood two shower stalls on either side of a beautiful, old-fashioned porcelain tub. Misty took a quick shower, dressed even quicker, and then towel dried her hair until it was only slightly damp. She walked back across the small bridge to the bar. A sign above the door read: Sam's Island Hideaway.

Misty found Sam behind the bar, restocking liquor bottles.

"So *you* own this bar?"

Sam spoke to her reflection in the mirror, "I'm Sam, we're on an island, and Captain and Mikey are hideaways. The sign over the door pretty much sums it up."

"How much did they give you to use your name as cover?"

"Captain Kev, Mikey, Monique, and I each own twenty-five percent."

Misty said, "Hey!" Sam turned to look at her. She held out her arms and spun around. "Am I dressed conservatively enough for you now?" she asked. "I buttoned my shirt all the way up to the tippy top."

"I bet you are hungry," Sam said dryly. "How about something to eat?"

"I'm starved," Misty said. "What have you got in mind?"

"Follow me," he replied.

The kitchen had one large grill, a four-basket fryer, and a large cooler. A young woman with long, curly hair, a cute face, and a slender body was slicing tomatoes on a chopping block.

"This is Sally," Sam said. "She came to the islands for a change of scenery. Great little worker."

"Nice to meet you," Sally said with a big smile.

Sam reached into the cooler and pulled out a quarter-pound hamburger patty. "One or two?" he asked.

"Better make it two, Sam. And some fries if you've got 'em," Misty said.

As the patties sizzled on the hot grill, Sam took out a box from the cooler and loaded one of the baskets with a handful of crinkle-cut fries. The ice-cold fries let out a crackle and pop when he submerged them in hot peanut oil. When the time was right, Sam flipped over the meat patties and sprinkled them with seasoning. He placed a thick piece of cheese on each meat patty before setting the bottom of the bun on top of one of them.

He removed the top of the bun, which had been coated with butter and toasting on the grill, and began coating it with mustard. Next came ample portions of lettuce, plenty of ripe tomatoes, and pickles. After centering sweet rings of onions on top, Misty said, "I guess this means you're not going to make a pass at me."

Sam raised his eyebrows, "And I thought I was protecting you from vampires."

"That's garlic, not onions."

Sam handed Misty the tray of food, and she took a seat at the bar. He went back to stocking bottles behind the bar. She savored the first bite and said, "Damn! You should be on the cooking channel."

The heat from the meat had melted the cheese, gluing the steam-soaked bun to the hamburger patty.

"You make one mean hamburger, Sammy boy."

"Sam, not Sammy boy," he said in a deep voice that resembled the actor Sam Sheppard.

With her mouth still half full, she mumbled, "Whatever you say . . . Sammy boy." He shook his head and resumed his duties.

Misty took him in as she ate her burger and fries. He was clean shaven and had cropped grey hair. His face was tan and chiseled, giving him the look of someone you didn't want to mess with. Yet she sensed he was an honorable man, a man who would not seek out trouble, only respond to it.

A loud voice echoed from the front of the bar. "Well, I declare. You got tired of leading your client around by the nose and decided to visit the ol' Captain."

Misty jumped down from her stool, ran across the floor, and gave Captain Kev a powerful embrace. Mikey wrapped his arms around her waist from behind. Looking over her shoulder at Mikey, she asked, "What have you guys been up to?"

Mikey released Misty, grabbed his shovel, and raised it into the air. He looked around the bar suspiciously before saying, "Digging for gold, of course!"

He reached into his pocket and pulled out two Portuguese gold coins. He held them up close to Misty's face and rubbed them together. Her eyes opened wide.

She snatched them away and bounced them in her hand. When she was done, they lay heavy in her palms. "Yeah, these are fake, right?"

Mikey confidently shook his head no.

Tom, Thor, Miguel, and Monique walked through the door. Misty looked at Monique and she said to Captain Kev, "So Monique wasn't bullshitting about the gold?"

Captain Kev took a coin from her hand, placed it between his teeth, and said in a boisterous voice, "Doesn't taste like bullshit to me!" He laughed heartily.

Misty looked at the new arrivals and said, "So where have you guys been?"

"Taking a tour of the island while you slept the day away, boss," Miguel replied.

"Yeah, I can't believe I slept so long. You should have woken me up before you left."

"I tried," Monique said, "but you wouldn't come around."

After Captain Kev, Miniature Mike, and the others all hugged and exchanged pleasantries, Captain Kev said, "Better let Sam get you something to eat. We've got a band showing up in a few hours and things are going to get wild and crazy. You don't want to be drinking on an empty stomach."

"You are in for a treat," Misty offered. "Sam makes the best hamburgers in the world." She winked at Sam, and he fought back a grin.

"I'm starving," Miguel said.

"Me too," said Thor.

The group gathered on the large outdoor back porch that ran the entire length of the bar. Misty leaned back in her chair to sun her face and listen to the lighthearted banter from her dear friends. Only twenty-four hours ago they were rescuing Monique from Salvatore and his goons. She cracked one eye and noticed Miguel and Thor flanking Monique,

acting like two school boys. Monique seemed to be enjoying the attention. Misty felt like she deserved it after all she had been through. With
a closer inspection, Misty noticed Monique's makeup didn't totally hide
the bruise on the left side of her face. She hoped the disfiguration and
swelling would go away soon so they could all try to put Vegas out of
their minds.

When they had finished the mounds of food Sam brought them,
Monique looked around the table and said, "You're in the islands now.
You need the proper clothes to get in the mood. Why don't I take every-
one shopping downtown before tonight's get-together?"

Monique's suggestion to buy clothes reminded her of something
Gabriella would have suggested. It also reminded her of how long it had
been since she and Gabriella had last been together. "I think that's a great
idea," she said. She reached into her pocket, took out her credit card, and
handed it to Monique. "It's on me."

"That's very nice of you, Misty!" Thor said.

"No problem, Thor. You guys did a heck of a job taking care of
us girls in Vegas. I'd like to show my appreciation." Misty turned to
Monique. "I'll write down my sizes and you can pick something out for
me too, okay?"

"You trust my taste in clothes?"

Misty nodded. "I do."

Misty looked at Sam as she whispered into Monique's ear. Monique
looked at Sam and smiled before giving Misty a wink.

"Misty, are you sure you don't want to come with us?" Tom said.

"No, I want to hang back and call your boss."

Tom grinned. "Tell Gabriella hello for me, but don't tell her I'm
slacking off." Misty laughed.

After everyone left, Misty asked Sam, "Where's a comfortable place
to make a long phone call?"

"With your cell phone?"

"Yes."

"Follow me."

Sam led her out the side door and pointed to a hammock on the side
deck of the bar.

"Wonderful!" Misty said. "This is perfect."

Gabriella was in the middle of reviewing a contract when her receptionist's voice came across the intercom. "Misty's on the line for you. Can you take her call?"

"Absolutely. Please hold all calls until I am done."

Gabriella sat back in her chair, propped her feet up on the desk, and then picked up her phone. "My pilots tell me you are in the Virgin Islands. How's the weather?"

"Oh, Gabby. You wouldn't believe this place. It's paradise. I'm lying on a hammock and a soft breeze is blowing over me. I feel like I've died and gone to heaven."

"Sounds wonderful! Speaking of dying, what did you just get yourself into?"

"You had to bring that up, didn't you! I'll admit things have been a little nerve-racking over the last forty-eight hours. It's a good thing Tom and Miguel showed up when they did. Thank you for sending them."

"What are friends for?" Gabriella said, less than joyful.

"I've become high maintenance, haven't I?" Misty said with a nervous laugh.

Wanting to keep the conversation on the serious side until she could discern whether Misty was still in danger, Gabriella asked, "Are you sure your client won't send someone looking for you? From what you told me, Salvatore is a pretty ruthless guy."

"Miguel checked with the pilots, and they said that although Salvatore could have uncovered our flight plan out of Vegas, there is no way he could have tracked us out of Cuba. That's why I was thinking about hanging out in the Virgin Islands for a month or so." Feeling her life was beginning to resemble an action movie, Misty added, "You know, lie low for a while."

"I think you may be taking this a little too lightly, dear."

"Cheer up, Gabriella. It'll blow over. You'll see."

After an uncomfortable pause, Gabriella said, "All right. Let's talk about something a little less precarious. How did your stop in Cuba go?"

Misty rolled her eyes. "Umm, I think I'll just let Tom tell you the story when he gets back, if that's all right."

There was another long pause, and then Gabriella said, "You didn't start an international incident, did you? I thought all you needed to do was drop Esteban off and leave?"

"Oh, we did. That's exactly what we did, Gabby. His girlfriend was so happy to see him. It was a touching scene. I wish you could have been there." Wanting to change the subject, Misty said, "There is something that happened in Vegas that I really feel bad about."

"Hold on, dear. I need to do something before you start. It won't take long."

"Sure."

Gabriella walked over and opened a small cabinet. It was stocked with all types of liquor that she kept for special occasions, like closing a big real estate deal. She pulled down a single malt scotch and walked back to her desk. After pouring herself a generous portion, she took a healthy drink and placed the phone back to her ear. "Please continue."

"While I was away in the mountains one weekend, Monique went cougar on Thor," Misty said.

"Cougar? Did she scratch him or something? I don't understand 'cougar.'"

"I'm sorry. In the states, older women who prey on younger men are referred to as cougars."

"Prey? You don't mean—"

"I mean they had sex."

"Does Tom know?"

"No, I'm hesitant to tell him."

"It's not Tom I'm worried about. It's Rosie. We all helped talk her into letting Thor go with you."

"I know, but Thor isn't as polite and innocent as his mother thinks. He's not as naive as he pretends."

"Well, he is a man, I guess. Do you think he's fallen for Monique?"

"I think both Miguel and Thor have fallen for Monique."

"That's trouble waiting to happen. I'll call Tom and have him come back to Buenos Aires with Thor. That should resolve the issue."

"It will to Miguel's liking," Misty said.

"I'm afraid to ask, but is there anything else I need to know?" Gabriella said.

"Oh, just that I think there really is something to the treasure map Monique told us about. I'm kind of excited about it, to tell you the truth. Maybe I'll tag along next time they go digging for gold. It apparently is on a tiny island, far off the trade routes, that isn't even charted. No cell phone service either. At least I can't get into anymore trouble way out there."

Gabriella took another drink of her scotch, resisting the urge to answer. "I better run. Don't worry! I'll come home to you nice and rested, in great shape from digging, and with a terrific tan. How would you like my boobies, white or tan?"

Gabriella took another gulp of scotch before saying, "The white contrast would be nice."

"They refer to them as 'white pointers' in Australia," Misty teased.

"You are being so naughty. Are you sure you don't want to come home sooner?"

"Absence makes the heart grow fonder. Just think how wonderful it will be after waiting another month," Misty teased seductively.

"That's okay. I have a male friend I met recently who can entertain me until you get back."

"Good for you. Have fun, and I'll see you soon."

* * *

The guys showered and then congregated in the bar. "I'll never understand why it takes girls so long to get ready," Miguel said to Tom.

"I've got a ten-spot that says it's over half an hour."

"Ha, I wouldn't touch that bet," Miguel said. "Let's get some drinks at the bar."

When the girls joined them an hour later, the boys touched their beer bottles together to celebrate how right-on they had been. They rose from their chairs to greet the women. Monique was wearing a white, floor-length, crinkled cotton dress that dangled above a pair of white flip-flops, which were decorated with gold pineapple embellishments. Her silky black hair was a magnificent contrast.

Misty wore a black halter dress with matching black tiger-stoned sandals. Her golden blonde hair also contrasted with her outfit. Each dress was cut low in the front, drawing attention to the women's ample and wondrous cleavages.

As they drew closer, Misty poked Monique and whispered, "I'd say they love your selection of outfits." The women exchanged warm smiles.

Monique walked up to Miguel and lightly stroked his silk shirt as if smoothing out wrinkles.

"I thought your legs would be tanner, Papi," Monique said to Miguel. He stepped away and looked down at his muscular legs. "I haven't worn shorts in a while, I guess."

"We can remedy that," she said. "I know just the spot."

"Sounds like a plan," he said.

Misty took special notice of Monique's decision to sit between Miguel and Thor. She was pretty certain it was a calculated move on Monique's part. Not being able to think of a way to split them up without causing waves, Misty walked over to the bar and set a bag down on the counter in front of Sam.

"What's this?" Sam asked with a puzzled look on his face.

"Open it and see, old man."

Sam slowly peeked into the bag as if something might jump out at him. "What do you want me to do with these?" he asked.

Misty placed her hands on her hips and said, "Wear them, of course."

"What's wrong with what I have on?"

"That's pretty obvious," she said as she looked over his V-neck T-shirt and holey shorts. "You are a handsome man. Life is short. You should live a little."

"Maybe I've already lived enough for two lifetimes," he said.

Misty stared at him, not realizing her crossed arms were almost causing her breasts to pop out of her dress. Sam reached across the counter and used both hands to pull up the little material he had to work with. "You shouldn't advertise," he said. "We get some tough characters in this bar."

"Now you're going gramps on me," she said, laughingly. "I think I liked you better when you were just my father."

Misty placed her fingers on her dress and contemplated pulling her front back down. They stared at each other for a moment until she removed her hands and said, "Whatever. Don't wear your new clothes then." She spun around and walked off, leaving Sam at a loss for words. He watched her all the way back to her table and then looked into the bag one more time. Turning to the bartender next to him, Sam said, "Hold down the fort, I'll be right back."

Noticing Misty's mood change when she returned, Captain Kev pushed back from the table, stood up, and said, "What do you say we do some shots to get things going. Come on, Mikey. I'll get some bottles of tequila, and you keep the pitchers of beer coming."

"Would you like some help?" Tom said.

"Just sit there," the captain shot back. "We got you covered."

It wasn't long before the band members came walking through the door in typical, loose-fitting island clothes and sandals. One had his hair tucked underneath a colorful beanie hat, but the others let their dread-locks flow.

"You gonna play some reggae tonight?" Miguel yelled out to the guy setting up steel drums.

"Ya, mon. You be jammin to roots reggae tonight," he replied.

Tom threw back a shot of tequila and said sarcastically, "Can't wait, mon."

Miguel's new buddy, the drummer, introduced everyone to the key-board player, bass player, and percussionist. As the sun set, everyone enjoyed the calm for a few moments before the band kicked in. Misty looked around the room as she moved to the beat of the music. The place had already filled up without her noticing. Tourists mingled with the islanders and asked them all sorts of questions. They consorted with one another as if they were all long-lost friends. As they did, the noise level grew until the music and customers seemed to become one. Miniature Mike walked through the crowd high-fiving islanders and tourists alike.

"Mikey, my mon," one of the locals yelled out, "dance for us on da table."

Mikey jumped up onto a chair and then onto the tabletop in quick succession. He danced island-style, grinning and staring at all of the women in close proximity. Marveling at Mikey's smooth, rhythmic moves, Misty grabbed Captain Kev by the arm as he passed by.

Pointing to Mikey, she said, "Does he do that every night?"

"Oh, yeah. He's a real crowd pleaser, he is!" Captain Kev shouted over the noise of the crowd. He reached over and pinched Monique's nose and added, "She taught Mikey how to shake a leg, didn't you Monique?"

Monique pried his finger away and said, "I tried to teach the one-armed bandit here, but it turns out he's got two left feet."

He raised his prosthetic arm in the air and said, "At least I got two feet!"

Captain Kev took a seat next to Misty and waited for everyone else to get back to their conversations before saying to Misty, "Don't take this the wrong way, but you sure seem different than when we spent all that time in Alaska. I think you've got it together a little more now."

Misty patted Captain Kev on his leg. "I was going through a little self-discovery while I was still married. I've been through a lot since then, some of it pretty scary. I know myself better now. Can't say I've got my shit together yet, but I'm getting there."

"Atta girl," Captain Kev said. "Life's a journey, so just sit back and enjoy the ride. Hell, God knows I do!" He scratched his chin with his good hand and said, "Doubt many people ride the wild side the way you and me do, Misters."

"Ain't that the truth," she said before throwing back another shot.

Monique pulled Miguel out onto the dance floor. The two made a spectacular-looking couple, well built, good-looking, and the same jet-black hair. Monique moved smooth and seductive as Miguel worked on converting his salsa moves into something more tropical. Misty took her eyes off of the pair and noticed the look on Thor's face. It was obvious he was hurt. She sprang to her feet and grabbed him by the hand in an effort to coax him from the table. "Come on, Thor," she said. "Show me what you got."

For the next thirty minutes they be jammin like the drummer said they would. Misty soaked up the scene, reveling in the great music, beloved friends, and the soft sea breeze blowing through the bar. Misty caught a glimpse of Sam heading into the back room. At the end of the song, Thor asked Misty, "Were you looking at Sam?"

"Yeah, I feel bad he has to work while we're all having so much fun."

"Sam doesn't look like the having-fun type to me," Thor said.

"Oh, sure he is. He just doesn't know it yet." She turned back to Thor and added, "Come on. Let's go sit on the porch to cool off. I thought we could enjoy one more visit before you leave."

"Leave? Who said anything about leaving?"

"Gabriella is going to call your dad later tonight to let him know that she needs both of you and her plane back in Buenos Aires."

Thor stumbled along behind Misty as she searched out the perfect table on the porch. After they settled in, she set her elbows on the table and rested her chin in her hands. Thor resembled a schoolboy who had just been dumped as he stared out across the bay.

"But why do I have to go back?" he said.

"Why, school, of course. You promised your parents you would go back next semester if they let you come with me to Vegas. They upheld their end of the bargain, now you need to uphold your end."

Thor continued to stare out into space, so Misty said, "Oh, Thor. We had a wonderful adventure. Can you believe you stood up to true mafiosi without backing down? Just think of the stories you can tell back home."

When Misty detected the hint of a grin, she said, "You have a thing for Monique, don't you?"

Thor's grin became more detectable. "It's understandable," she said. "Monique is a gorgeous woman. The night you guys spent together must have been magnificent." Thor was now grinning broadly. "Not many men your age get to bed a thoroughbred like Monique. No one can ever take that away."

"I suppose you're right," he lamented.

"Thor, you came to Vegas a boy, and you are leaving a man. I'm really privileged to have witnessed your growth."

"And I'm glad I got a chance to take care of you for the time we were there. I'm sorry if I seem anything but grateful you brought me along." Misty reached out and mussed up his hair to show her appreciation.

Thor glanced over to Monique and said, "She seems so different, Misty. Remember when we first met her on Captain Kev's boat? She was so full of, how do you say it in the states, piss and vinegar?"

Misty laughed. "I would just leave it at . . . full of something."

Thor said in a somber tone, "Whatever happened to Monique in Vegas must have been horrific, because she's just not the same person now."

"You are mature beyond your age. I wouldn't worry too much if I were you. Monique is one tough woman. Don't worry, Miguel and I will take good care of her when you are gone."

Misty wished she could have taken back her words when she noticed how mentioning Miguel's name affected him. Regrouping quickly, she said, "Go cut in on Miguel and dance with Monique. Say you're leaving tomorrow and just wanted to spend a little time with her before you left. When you tap Miguel on his shoulder, tell him I need to visit with him about a few things. That will give you the cover you need."

Misty was so intently watching Thor as he headed to the dance floor that she was oblivious to the fact that Sam was now standing by her side. When she felt a hand on her shoulder, she turned to see who it was. She rose to her feet with her mouth wide open. "Oh my word!" she said as she rubbed one of his silk shirtsleeves between her fingers. "Look at you."

Sam's ginger-red shirt hung down over a pair of breeze linen shorts. "Well, I'll be damned, Sam. You clean up really nice. So what made you change your mind, Mr. Serious?"

"Do I need a reason?" Sam said. His generous smile exposed the baby crow's feet around his eyes.

"You don't," Misty said glibly. "So who's minding the store?"

Sam pointed to a sharp-dressed local attending bar. "Myron likes to come over and tend bar from time to time as a hobby. He's fluent in many languages, and our multinational tourist base gives him the chance to practice. He came in tonight, so I just figured—" Misty placed her fingers to Sam's lips.

"You don't need a reason, remember?"

She took Sam by the hand and pulled him toward the dance floor. "Let's see what you've got, Daddy-O."

Miguel intercepted them on their way there. "What's up, Misty? Thor said you wanted to talk to me."

Misty whispered in his ear, "Thor is leaving tomorrow morning and wants to spend a little time with Monique. I just thought it might be nice if you gave him some room."

"So, Thor's leaving tomorrow?" Miguel said with a grin.

"I know that look," Misty said.

"What?" Miguel replied.

It took some doing, but Misty helped Sam find a few repetitive dance moves, allowing him to become semi-comfortable on the dance floor. When Sam noticed Mikey standing next to him, staring, he said, "What's your problem, little man?"

Mikey mimicked Sam's moves for a few seconds. He cracked up laughing as he headed off to do another table dance.

"Don't pay any attention to Mikey," Misty said. "You're doing just fine."

18

BLACKBEARD'S CASTLE

After saying their good-byes to Tom and Thor the next morning, Miguel and Misty decided to tour the Charlotte Amalie shopping district. They found the area bustling with tourists from the cruise ships that had made port that morning. After a nice lunch at a restaurant on the dock, they headed out to meet up with Captain Kev and Miniature Mike. Racing up the famed ninety-nine steps on their way up to Blackbeard's Castle left them short of breath.

"I think I counted a hundred and three," Miguel said, gasping for air.

"Impossible," Misty teased. "You should walk back down and count them again."

"No thanks."

When they made it to the entrance of the castle, Captain Kev was waiting for them with tickets in hand.

"You could pass as one of the pirate statues with that eye patch, Captain," Misty said. Miguel added, "Don't stand in one place too long or the birds will shit on your head."

Before Captain Kev could come back with a witty reply, a commotion ensued. When they turned to look, Mikey was perched on the shoulders of the gargantuan statue of Blackbeard in the plaza. Mikey slid down Blackbeard's outstretched arm. Groundskeepers escorted him out the front gate.

"Don't worry about Mikey," Captain Kev bellowed. "He's made the tour before." He scratched the side of his face and said in a more subdued voice, "He's also been thrown out before."

Blackbeard's castle turned out to be nothing more than a circular tower about four stories high. When it was their turn, they wound their way up a narrow metal stairwell. Since the stairwell was not part of the original structure, Miguel studied the remnants of the wooden frame inside. Noticing a pattern of small openings in the stone wall every ten feet led Miguel to think the original castle had a series of floors. There was little doubt the holes were made for muskets to fit through. Their enemies would have to have been pretty brave to traverse the hill he and Misty had run up with musket shot zinging all around them.

"What a beautiful view!" Misty said, once out on the rooftop.

"Yes. Quite the watchtower in its day," Captain Kev said.

"So did Blackbeard really hide out here?" she asked.

"So the story goes, but most people think it's just that, a story. Some say the Danish authorities used it to keep a sharp lookout for Edward Teach and his brethren of pirates who frequented the duty-free port."

"I find it hard to believe that ruthless pirates like Blackbeard and his crew would be disciplined enough to build something like this," Miguel said.

Captain Kev raised an eyebrow.

"What was that look?" Misty asked.

"Oh, nothing," he said.

"What a great lookout," Miguel said. "There are two ways in and out of the harbor. If a ship approached from one side, a signal could be given, and their ship moored in the harbor could slip out the other side."

"But how would the people in the tower get away if there were too many enemies?" Misty asked.

Miguel looked up at the ridge that split the island in half. "Hike up and over the top of the mountain and make their way down the other side to Magens Bay, where their ship that just left the harbor could sail around and pick them up."

"You should have been a pirate," Captain Kev said.

Misty pointed down below. "Look at Mikey."

With his shirt off, his small but powerful upper torso glistened with sweat as he ran up the ninety-nine steps. Captain Kev waved, and Mikey waved back.

"You know Mikey. He can never sit still." He turned to Misty. "How about you? Are you ready to go?"

"Yep, seen enough."

They found Monique sitting on a bar stool visiting with Sam when they returned to the bar. Catching them talking before they knew she was back, Misty noticed they seemed to be very comfortable with one another.

"How well do they know each other?" she discreetly asked the captain.

"I guess you could say Sam is, or has been, Monique's guardian angel over the years. The way I hear it, she might not be alive today if it were not for Sam."

"Really?" Misty said. "So what's the story?"

"Wish I knew, but those two don't give up too much personal info."

When Sam got up and went into the back room, Miguel walked over and took a seat at the bar next to Monique. "So what's your story, Monique?"

"Got all day?" she asked.

Miguel thought for a moment. "As a matter of fact, I do. Let's go spend the day on St. John's Island tomorrow. I hear they have a wonderful snorkeling beach."

"You're referring to Trunk Bay."

"Yeah, that's it," Miguel said.

"I don't know. That Trunk Bay can be somewhat secluded this time of year," she said provocatively. "How can I be sure I can trust you?"

"You can't," Miguel shot back with a twinkle in his eye.

Monique stood up from the table and said, "Pack some gear tonight. We can catch the ferry at ten tomorrow morning."

When she left, Misty sat down in Monique's vacated seat. "What was that all about?"

Miguel shrugged. "Monique and I are going to spend the day on St. John's tomorrow. That is, if it's okay with you, boss."

"Have at it, buddy. We're on vacation for the next month, so do as you please." She looked into his eyes and added, "Do you think you can handle her?"

"You forget my nickname *is* The Handle," he shot back.

Misty shook her head. "You may need more than one to handle this woman. Good luck!"

When Sam came out from the back room, Misty said, "Sam's taking me scuba diving tomorrow anyway. Right, Sammy boy?"

"You scuba dive?" Sam asked.

"Child's play," Misty said.

"Great! I'll rent you some scuba gear in the morning."

"Now that that's all set, I think I'll go hang out and read a book."

After Misty left the room, Sam asked Miguel, "Would you like to join us?"

"Sorry, I'm spending the day on St. John's with Monique."

Sam rolled his eyes then walked away, leaving Miguel wondering what he was missing.

19

ST. JOHN'S

Mikey dropped Miguel and Monique off at the ferry and sped away. Monique grabbed Miguel's backpack out of his hand and looked inside.

"You're big on protein bars, aren't you?" she asked.

Miguel pulled up a shirtsleeve and flexed. "Gotta nourish my guns," he said.

Monique handed Miguel his pack and said, "Better put those things back in their holster and follow me, or we'll miss the ferry."

Miguel found the oceangoing vessel short on amenities. Everything was built out of metal and painted a drab grey. They popped their heads into a cabin and saw that rows and rows of benches had already been taken by workers on their day's shuttle to St. John's. He followed Monique up a metal ladder to the top of the vessel where there were more rows of benches. A local scooted down on one of the benches, leaving them just enough room to sit. A well-muscled police officer strolled up and down the aisle, making his presence known. Soon the engines became louder, and the ferry pulled away from the dock. It was a beautiful, cloudless day with a light breeze and calm waters. Seabirds darted in and out of the water, and a toddler played with blocks on his mother's lap. Once out to sea, Miguel looked over at a somber Monique and said, "Are you okay?"

She smiled genteelly. "Why? Because I'm not carrying the conversation?"

"Well, yes, I mean no. It's okay if you don't want to talk. It's just . . . well . . . I just assumed you had something heavy weighing on your mind." Miguel shook his head. "Oh, never mind."

When he sensed Monique was still staring at him, he turned back to her and asked, "What?"

She broke into a big smile and said, "You sure give up easily."

"Maybe I'm not sure you are worth the effort?" he said, smartly.

She leaned over and kissed his cheek. "Oh, I'm worth it."

Monique laid her head back, closed her eyes, and basked in the sun. Miguel took his time looking over every inch of her body and came to the same conclusion—she was worth it.

As the ferry eased its way into Cruz Bay, Miguel fixed his eyes on a row of lively colored wooden structures. So far, St John's was everything he had hoped it would be. The two were in no hurry, so they laid back and let the other passengers disembark. Once everyone was off the ship, Monique sprang to her feet, grabbed Miguel by the hand, and led him along the way. He sensed something had changed and that he was seeing a side of her he didn't know existed. "I'm starving. What about you?" she asked as they approached a small restaurant.

"Are you sure this place is safe to eat?"

"Don't be silly," she said.

Once inside, she pointed to a small table in the front of the restaurant and said, "Take a seat. I'll be right back."

Miguel sat down and looked around. Although sparse, the place was clean and colorful. It reminded him of the little Mexican cafés he frequented as a kid. He took interest in the array of hot sauces on the table, reading the labels to ensure he knew what he was getting into. Before he could get to all of them, Monique returned, arm in arm, with a very large black woman who was smiling broadly.

The lady let go of Monique and held out her arms to Miguel. He gave Monique an inquisitive look and then got up and moved tentatively toward the woman. He had only taken a step when she pulled him to her big bosom and held him tightly. "You brought my baby home to Big Mama! I can never thank you enough."

Barely able to move in the throes of her death grip, he turned his head to Monique and raised his eyebrows. Monique put her hand over her mouth and laughed.

Big Mama gave him another squeeze and then released him. She said, "Sit down, young man. Relax! Big Mama's gonna fix you a mighty nice lunch." She hustled off to the kitchen.

Miguel mouthed, "Big Mama?"

"Yep, that's my Big Mama. She took me in around five years ago when things were not going so well."

"So, are there times when things do go well for you?" Miguel teased.

"I had been living in Georgia and owed money to some very unsavory characters. More money than I could ever hope to come up with. "

"Georgia is a long way from Big Mama's. How'd you wind up here?"

"Sam brought me to her."

"You knew Sam in Georgia?"

"Not really. I was coming out of my apartment complex one afternoon when two men jumped me. They said I was out of time and that if I didn't give them the money right then and there, that they were going to rape me first and then cut up my face so bad I would never look in a mirror again."

"How much money did you owe them?"

"Twenty large," she said.

"Twenty thousand dollars? Why so much?"

"You don't know loan sharks very well, do you? It starts out at a thousand, and before you know it, the absurd interest rate compounds so fast you lose control."

He slid his hand across her smooth face and said, "I think there's more to this story."

"Thank God Sam had been sitting on his porch just above us, overhearing the whole thing. Before I knew it, he jumped down and took the first guy out at the knees with a blow from his foot. The man dropped his switchblade to grab his injured knees, and Sam picked it up from the ground and squared off with the other guy. When the second man thrust his knife at him and missed, Sam pinned the man's arm under his armpit and gave him a compound fracture in two places. Sam never did use the switchblade."

"Go on," Miguel said, wide-eyed.

"Sam said it wasn't safe for either of us to return to our apartments, so he asked me how I'd like to accompany him to the Virgin Islands. Not in the habit of trusting a man's attention, I told him I didn't think it was a good idea. Sam said, 'Suit yourself,' and basically told me that I was a dead woman walking. I realized he was right and that his offer was the best choice I had if I wanted to stay alive."

Monique's mood softened when she said, "Sam turned out to be a perfect gentleman."

"Yes, my intuition told me that Sam is a man of principle," Miguel said. "It's good to get confirmation."

Monique smiled at him and said, "Sam took me on the same ferry we were on today. Once we got to St. Thomas, he introduced me to Big Mama, and she agreed to look after me. He gave her a big wad of money and left."

"So that's why you were so quiet on the ferry," Miguel said.

Monique grinned. "Maybe. Maybe not."

Before Miguel could prod further, Big Mama came back with a trayful of food. Miguel loaded his plate with fresh fish, fried okra, sweet potatoes and plenty of fried plantains. It wasn't Mexican food, but it was tasty home cooking just the same. Big Mama took a seat at the table, enjoying watching them eat. When Miguel couldn't eat another bite, he pushed away from the table and patted his belly.

"Oh, don't quit on me now, honey," Big Mama said to Miguel. She loaded up a serving spoon full of sweet potatoes. "Have some more."

"That was delicious. Really, it was," he said. "But we've got some snorkeling to do, and I have enough trouble keeping from sinking to the bottom without being stuffed."

Mama looked at Monique. "Are you taking him to Trunk Bay?" she asked with a smile.

"It was his idea, not mine," Monique answered.

"Well, hold onto your trunks, Miguel. That beach got its name for a reason," Mama said. She pinched him on his cheek and added, "Oh, honey. If I were younger, I'd be taken you to dat beach myself."

Miguel stood up and gave Big Mama a big hug. "It's a good thing you aren't, or I'd have to dump Monique for you."

"You got dat straight, lover boy."

Monique said to Miguel, "Why don't you tour the plaza and walk off your lunch while I talk with my Mama for a bit."

"Sure thing," he said, waving bye as he walked out of the restaurant.

"Dat boy's a keeper, honey. I knows you ain't much for relationships, but listen to your Mama, girl." She placed her hand under Monique's chin and raised her head until Monique had no choice but to look into her eyes. "Yous got to find a good man someday, baby child. You can't run from your past forever. I can tell from your eyes you've been in some more trouble. Am I right?"

Monique gave her a big hug. "It gives me comfort just knowing you are here for me. Thanks so much for caring." Monique held Mama by the hands and said, "Someday, Mama. Someday I will settle down, I promise."

"I believe you, honey. Now you go run off and catch up to dat boy. I hope you has a wonderful time today."

"Thanks! I'll do my best."

Monique walked briskly past Miguel and headed down the sidewalk. Miguel was certain she had tears in her eyes, but by the time he caught up, her eyes were dry. Trying to lighten the mood, he said, "Well if dat's your mama, you better watch what you eat or—"

Monique gave him a shove. "You're bad." She broke out laughing. Miguel sensed the laugh was sincerely carefree and hoped it was the first chip in breaking down her armor.

The taxies on St. John's were truck cabs with benches in the truck beds and a roof over top. The second they climbed into the back of one, a man came running over and slid into the driver's seat. He looked at them through a small window and asked, "Trunk Bay?"

The narrow, windy road ran along a hillside that hugged the coast. The open-aired truck bed gave them a wonderful view of St. Thomas and other small islands in the area. Miguel realized how lucky he was to be in the Virgin Islands with a beautiful woman all to himself. He resisted the urge to reach out and take her by the hand, not wanting to risk ruining the mood.

The driver pulled over to the side of the road and pointed down to Trunk Bay, which was several hundred feet below them. After scanning the small beach, Miguel said, "Where is everyone?"

"We're in between seasons," the driver said. "Tourists come during summer and winter, not so much October."

Miguel thought, *Lucky me!*

The trail down the side of the hill took them through the empty park facilities before winding through rows of trees and then out onto the beach. The shoreline was slightly bowl-shaped, with trees behind them and a panoramic view of the islands in front of them. A tiny parcel of land jutted up from the bay just several hundred feet from shore. Miguel spotted only a handful of visitors and a lone lifeguard sitting atop his perch.

Monique peeled off her oversized T-shirt, revealing a skimpy, navy-blue two-piece made from very thin material. She caught Miguel gawking and gave him a smile. She walked over and patted him on his bare chest. "Nice, Miguel! If your arms are guns, what do you call these awesome pecs?"

"My IEDs, 'cause they are packed with explosives."

"You gym rats are something else," she teased. "I suppose you have a name for every part of your anatomy."

"Only the dangerous parts," he shot back. "You know, parts that get women into trouble."

"So, have a lot of women gotten into trouble?"

"There's been a few," he said coyly.

"I see," she said. "And Misty?"

Miguel gave her a puzzled look and said, "And Misty, what?" It hit him before Monique could respond. "Oh! Ha, ha. No way. Misty and I are just friends. We think of each other more as brother and sister."

"So when you told me she taught you the ropes the other day, you didn't mean—"

Miguel stepped in closer and rubbed the side of her muscled arms with his hands and said, "Maybe you'd like me to teach you the ropes."

Monique shoved Miguel away as she let out a laugh. She reached down and grabbed the snorkel gear from her backpack and ran toward the beach. She sat down in the water and grinned at him as she put on one of her flippers. "Come on!" she yelled back. "I've got a few things I can teach you."

Miguel quickly pulled out his gear and followed.

Trailing Monique, Miguel snorkeled from behind, his face mask trained on her every graceful movement. Well-defined thighs and powerful buttocks helped her effortlessly move through the water. When they had gone out far enough, she turned her head back to him and pointed out the beautiful underwater garden below. Brilliantly colored fish darted in and out of the crevices in the coral bed. As Miguel marveled at the underwater wonders, unbeknownst to him, Monique was marveling at him. After he had time to get a good feel for his underwater surroundings, Monique poked Miguel on the arm and motioned for him to follow her. She led him to the tiny island he had noticed offshore earlier. She expertly guided him up the side of a twenty-foot rock wall, showing him what to grab ahold of and where to place his feet.

When they reached the top, he said, "I can tell you've been here before."

"A hundred times, at least," she said, with a gleam in her eyes. "But never with someone else."

She set out, and he followed her all the way to the other side of the miniature island, where they escaped the view of the beachgoers. Once they reached a tiny patch of grass that was shaded by a large tree, she plopped down, pulled her knees to her chest, and secured them with her arms. Miguel did the same. He gazed upon the Caribbean, which glittered from the bright midday sun. The magnificent picture was framed by distant islands on the horizon.

"This is spectacular, Monique. Thank you for bringing me here."

"I'm glad you like it," she said, looking pleased.

"I can see why you have come here often."

Monique gazed out to sea. "After Sam brought me to stay with Big Mama, I had a lot to sort out. This plot of grass was my refuge from my past. I prayed my life would change, but look at me," she said, a hint of shame on her face.

Miguel reached out and patted her on the knee. "Don't be so hard on yourself. Things can still change for the better."

"Look at you? Mister popularity, overall great guy, everyone's buddy. I find it hard to believe you have ever had a tough time."

"So you assume I was always like this?" he asked.

"People like you come from a great upbringing. I'll bet you were a football star and your dad went to all of your games. You were the home-coming king, right? You wouldn't have the foggiest idea what it was like to be sold into servitude as a stripper when you were only sixteen by your father to pay his gambling debts."

Thor had indicated that everyone should take it easy on Monique because she had had a tough upbringing, but he had never told Miguel the full details. The thought of her being forced to bare herself in front of a crowd of men at such an early age was repulsive to Miguel and made him sick to his stomach. He didn't respond immediately, choosing to take a moment and piece things together. Her past actions became so obvious to him now. He had always known her tough act was an attempt to con-struct an impenetrable outer shell, a shell he felt served unwittingly to lock in those same bitter memories to her detriment. A shell with thick walls constructed from a deep-seated sense of shame. His heart ached for her, and all he could think about was helping to set her free.

"You've got me wrong," Miguel said.

"Oh, really! Let me guess. Your first girlfriend dumped you when you were thirteen. Spare me the details."

Miguel stood up and swung one leg over her midsection. He kneeled, pinning her to the ground.

"What are you doing, Miguel?" she demanded and looked into his eyes. "Showing me how tough you had it by pushing me around?"

"Let's just say I want your full and undivided attention while I talk some sense into that thick skull of yours."

"Well, at least release my arms so I can prop my head up. Something tells me I'm in for a long sermon."

Once Monique was comfortable, he began, "I grew up in South Cen-tral Los Angeles, raised by my older brother. He worked long hours, and I had a lot of alone time. I got bored, so I became a member in a local gang. Initiation was brutal but not as brutal as the gang wars. My turf was eight city blocks, and we were instructed to defend it at all costs.

Once you're in, you lose control. They made me sell drugs on a street corner at the age of sixteen. If I refused, they would have killed me. At least you were safe inside your strip club. Of course, we protected the strip clubs. If a club didn't pay for our protection, we tore it apart."

"Protection from whom?" Monique asked.

"Protection from us. See how fucked up things were? It made no sense." He gave her time to think a moment and then continued. "I've done things I'm not proud of, Monique. Things I am so ashamed of I have never told anyone."

"Then I guess we are kindred souls," she said. "How did you escape?"

"When my brother found out the mess I had gotten myself into, he moved us to the other side of town. He had to take two jobs to make ends meet. I was furious with him, but, eventually, he convinced me to finish high school and take some nutrition and therapy classes at our local junior college. I then applied to become a trainer."

"Is that when you met Misty?"

"Yes. Misty is the one who interviewed me. She knew I was lying about my experience, but for some reason, she hired me anyway. She must have seen something in me I never saw in myself. After being under her tutelage for several years, I built up a strong clientele of successful people. At first I envied their lives, but eventually, working with successful people showed me what one could do if given the chance."

"It's all about who you hang out with, Monique. Then it's up to you to make good choices. I'll talk to Misty for you, if you like. Maybe she can take you on as an apprentice. She has more potential clients than she can possibly train. Of course, you would have to show her the respect she deserves."

"I do respect Misty," Monique quickly shot back.

"You sure have a funny way of showing it."

"I know. We just got off on the wrong foot. Of course, it was my fault. I guess I enjoyed getting all the attention from Captain Kev and Miniature Mike. I watched Misty interact with Captain Kev and Mikey from the top of the stairs and worried she would vie for their attention. Hell, I guess I was just plain jealous."

"Then you need to explain that to Misty and apologize," Miguel said.

"And if I don't, are you going to make me?" she asked with a twinkle in her eyes.

He leaned down, pinning her arms, and stared into her eyes. "If you don't, I just might have to give you a spanking."

Monique's eyes revealed her passion. They gazed into each other's eyes as if in a game of trying to make the other blink first. Miguel felt something sweep over him. He seemed powerless to control his will. He considered moving away from her before things went too far, but the moment held him captive. As if being controlled by a force greater than himself, Miguel leaned in and kissed Monique on the lips. They were little pecks at first, just to test the waters, but when she didn't resist, he took it up a notch. He found her soft, cushy lips succulent and her hot breath a turn-on.

He soon had a burning desire to touch her. Releasing her, Miguel placed his hand lightly on top of her bosom. He was ready to remove it if she made any indication that he had gone too far, but she responded with a moan. Emboldened, he strengthened his grip, kneading her breasts as if they were mounds of dough. Monique lifted her left shoulder off the ground, giving him easy access to the clips that held her top together. As he deftly unlatched it, the straps, already stretched to their fullest in their struggle to keep Monique's bountiful breasts snug and secure, sprang the cups of her top free. With one quick maneuver, he removed her bathing suit top and tossed it to the ground. Using his arms as support, he rose above Monique and gazed down upon her magnificent chest. Encircled by splendid light brown areolas, Monique's taut, elongated nipples looked like pencil erasers. Miguel only needed to supply the lead. He plotted a course to suckle her breasts, but before he could make his move, Monique pulled him into her arms. She whispered, "I'm worried you won't respect me if we go through with this."

Respect! Miguel thought. *Why is she throwing up this roadblock when I'll die if I can't have her now!* But then he realized she was saying that she respected him and that she understood that he was different than all the other men she had been with. She wanted to be sure he would give her the same respect she was offering him.

"We won't be having sex," he whispered back. "We'll be making love."

Monique's body trembled beneath him. He struggled free from her strong grip, raised up on his elbows, and peered down into her tear-filled eyes. "Hey, what's the matter?"

She said with a shaky voice, while wiping tears from her eyes, "That better not be a line." She looked into his eyes. "I feel vulnerable, and I don't like it. Please don't hurt me. I might never recover if you do."

Miguel stroked her head. "No, baby. I would never hurt you. I don't want to make promises I can't keep, but I can promise you this. I will always consider you my dear friend and respect you for who you are. More than that I cannot promise, but I won't rule out us being more than friends in the future. My offer is sincere, but if it's not good enough for you, I'll stop right now."

Monique searched his eyes to measure his sincerity. When convinced, she smiled up at him and said, "Okay, but if you hurt me, there will be hell to pay with Big Mama."

Miguel laughed out loud. "Trust me, I ain't messin' with no Big Mama. You won't have any trouble out of me." Miguel sensed Monique was still a bit nervous, so he added, "Have you ever stood on a cliff high above the water, wanting desperately to feel the rush of diving in but worried you would get hurt?"

She nodded, and he said, "Take my hand and jump with me."

Monique laughed and said, "Okay, but I have to warn you. I make a big splash."

She reached up and pulled Miguel to her, kissing him without trepidation—tongue-filled, passionate kisses. A wild animal lay beneath him now, spirited and unpredictable. He had unlocked the cage and set her free only to be pounced upon and ravaged. Miguel slipped his hand inside the bottom of her two-piece, plunging his middle finger deep inside her. Her warm insides coated his finger with nature's wonderful lubricant. He slid in a second finger and then a third, leaving his thumb to work her clitoris. Her facial expressions clued him in on what was working and what wasn't. Monique's hips gyrated to his hand movements, assisting him in their quest for *her* orgasm. As she got close, Miguel placed his other hand under the back of her neck as she thrashed her head from side to side. Her breasts heaved up and down rapidly as they lay heavy on her chest. To Miguel, she resembled an earthly goddess, worthy of being cast in bronze. She grunted and groaned before arching her back and letting out a loud cry.

When she lay there calmly and her breathing returned to normal, Monique smiled at Miguel deviously. She wrapped her hands around his massive thighs and used them as leverage, pulling herself down until she was directly underneath his throbbing penis. It was standing at attention, swelled to the max. She wrapped her hand around the base and guided it into her warm, moist mouth. Miguel bent down and braced himself with his arms. He moaned out loud as she masterfully worked the head before guiding it deep down her throat. He raised his head up just enough to look, marveling as she swallowed him in his entirety. *Make love*, he thought. *My God! This is more than making love and sex combined.*

Not wanting it to end just yet, he patted Monique on the top of the head and gingerly pulled out.

"Let's end this nice and conventional. You know, the way most people make love."

He realized from the look on Monique's face that she had little knowledge of how tame most people made love: a little kissing, a little missionary style, and then off to take a quick hot shower and go to bed.

"The way mere mortals make love," he said. "Not goddesses like you."

"Or studs like you," she said.

Miguel pushed on her legs until they bent at the knees, giving him an easy entry. He took his time as he worked himself deep inside her. His penis was on fire, as if dipping into molten lava. Monique expertly used the muscle wall of her vagina to tighten her grip on him. He worked in and out of her until he couldn't hold it any longer. He arched his back and lifted his chest skyward, depositing his massive load deep inside, and then collapsed onto her chest, gasping for air. She swallowed him up in her arms and held him tight. Miguel whispered into her ear, "You were spectacular."

Monique whispered back, "So we did it the way normal people do it?"

"I hope you never find out how normal people do it. Stick to the way Monique does it."

"So you enjoyed it?" she asked modestly.

"I don't think the word enjoy comes close to describing what I just experienced. Let me come up with a better word and get back to you."

"Speaking of getting back," Monique said when she sat up and looked at her phone. "The last taxi leaves at 4:00 p.m. Gather up your stuff. We need to get a move on."

When they stopped by to say good-bye to Big Mama, she talked them into waiting on the 10:00 p.m. ferry so she could cook them another meal. Both famished from their day of activity, it was an easy sell. Monique entered the girls' sleeping quarters just after midnight. She tried to quietly slip into bed without being noticed, but Misty woke up.

"You're home. How was your trip?" Misty asked.

"Wonderful. Thanks for asking."

"Did Miguel behave?"

"Perfectly!" Monique replied.

"Hmmm. I think I'll leave it at that."

"How did your scuba diving with Sam go?"

"Wonderful. The more I get to know Sam, the more I'm realizing what a truly great guy he is."

"Yes," Monique said. "Sam's one of a kind."

20

LAND HO!

Misty walked the length of the eighty-foot schooner, giving it a thorough inspection. The boat was old and in need of repair, but she wouldn't expect anything more from Captain Kev and Miniature Mike. All in all, it was a major improvement over the *Dirty Pirates*. Her inspection of the compartments below deck revealed extensive use of quality teak wood. She realized the schooner must have been something special in her day. Misty climbed back on deck in time to watch Mikey hoist a Greek flag. Captain Kev was only a few yards away. "Greek registry, CK?" she yelled.

"Long story," he said with a mischievous grin. "It's probably best if you don't know the details." Misty was in perfect agreement with Captain Kev.

Miguel spent the next half hour helping Sam bring aboard a week's worth of provisions. When the galley was fully stocked, Sam returned topside and announced to everyone on deck, "You're good to go. Have a good trip. I'm headed back to the bar."

Misty raced to catch up to Sam before he disembarked. "Thanks for everything, Sammy boy. Sorry you can't come with us," she said.

"You be careful out there," Sam said. Misty got up on her tiptoes and kissed him on his cheek as a token of her appreciation. "Are you kidding? I can already taste the delicious hamburger you are going to fix me when I return."

"It will be my pleasure," he said and left. Misty watched Sam walk back to his truck. She gave him a wave as he drove off, wishing he could have come along.

They relied on their powerful diesel engine to get them out of the harbor, but once at sea, Captain Kev yelled out, "Mikey and Monique, there's a nice breeze today. Prepare to set sail!"

Having done some sailing during her past life in Malibu, Misty helped attach the mainsheet to the forestay and then helped them join the boom to the mast's front.

"Free the shrouds!" Captain Kev bellowed.

When they finished, Mikey gave the thumbs-up. "Hoist the mast!" Captain Kev shouted. "Let's be on our way." A gust of wind filled the sails, causing the wooden schooner to creak and list slightly to the port side. When it righted itself, they were underway.

Misty made her way to the bow of the ship. She hung her arms over the rail and enjoyed the breeze blowing through her hair. She closed her eyes and breathed warm, salty air deep into her lungs. Las Vegas seemed like a distant memory. Now it was time to unwind and get her life back to normal.

Miguel caught Monique going down below and followed after. He reached out from behind and grabbed her by the arm as she made her way down the hall passage.

Monique jerked around to find a beaming Miguel. "Listen, about yesterday," she said. "I don't want you to feel obligated to move this relationship forward. I can handle it if what we did was just a fling."

Miguel pulled her to him and looked deep into her eyes. "Oh, no you don't. I'm not going to let you take the easy way out. All relationships come with the risk of being hurt. Step out on that ledge again with me, and we'll see where it takes us."

Miguel held her unwavering until she eventually closed her eyes and tilted her head to one side. He leaned in until their lips met, kissing her firmly to let her know how committed he was. Before it went much further, he pulled back and tapped her on the nose with his index finger and said, "You're my girlfriend now. Don't ever forget it."

"We'll see about that!" Monique said with a grin on her face. She spun around and marched down the hall. When she reached the doorway to the galley, she swung back around and blew him a kiss.

Miguel bounded back up the stairs on his way to the main deck. He joined Misty at the rail and said, "It sure is a wonderful day." Misty hooked her arm under his and placed her head on his shoulder. "Indeed it is," she said.

* * *

Half a day out, Captain Kev took out a pair of nautical binoculars and fixed his sight on a distant speck of land. "Land Ho!" he yelled and then put them on a new course. The tiny speck grew larger and larger until a small beach no more than a thousand yards wide came into view. The sand on the beach was fluffy white. A thick layer of green vegetation lay behind the beach and in front of a rocky outcrop that ran up to a ridge that split the island in half. Misty was thrilled she could call this flyspeck of paradise home for the coming days.

"Drop anchor and lower the dinghy," Captain Kev yelled.

They all climbed aboard the flat-bottomed wooden dinghy. Mikey manned one oar while the captain, with the help of a special round attachment, manned the other oar. The turquoise-colored water was so clear they could see every detail of the sea floor below. Misty stood up in the middle of the boat and reached her arms toward the sky. "Robinson Crusoe, I am," she said.

"I think you mean Robin Crusoe," Miguel replied.

"Whatever," she shot back.

"Come on, Misty," Monique said. "I'll race you to shore!"

They both jumped into the waist-deep water from opposite sides of the dinghy, and the boys cheered them on. Legs pumping and arms thrashing, they fought their way through shallow water toward the snowy-white sandy beach. Monique passed Misty, but Misty tackled her from behind. She pressed on Monique's back, using her as leverage to spring to her feet. Monique reciprocated by diving forward, catching Misty by one ankle and causing her to fall facedown into the surf. Monique and Misty scrambled to their feet and raced all the way to the beach. Monique stumbled to the ground, exhausted, and rolled onto her back. Misty dove on top of her. Monique looked up at Misty and laughed. "Ha, ha. I won."

Misty's look turned serious. Monique shook her head. "Oh, no you don't!" Monique said. "That hurt like hell last time you pinched my nipples."

Misty quickly placed her hands over Monique's breasts and held them for a few seconds, grinning. She then pushed off Monique's chest and rose to her feet. "No," Misty said. "That sounds more like a job for my bodyguard." She graciously held out her hand and helped Monique to her feet. "Let's go exploring," she said and headed off toward the vegetation.

"Hold up, Misty!" Miguel yelled as he climbed out of the dinghy. "We have no idea what kind of animals are in there."

When Miguel caught up, Misty was eyeing a trail that led into the thick foliage. "Are you thinking about going in there?" he asked.

"I don't know. It looks a little creepy," she said.

Suddenly, Mikey ran past, waving for them to follow. When Misty and Miguel caught up to Mikey, he was standing in front of a massive wooden door. It was part of a large stone structure that was covered with thick vines. Mikey put his hand on a large, round, metal door handle and braced his leg on the outside of the building for leverage. When the door moved ever so slightly, Miguel joined him. Together, they pulled the door wide open. All three walked into the middle of the room and looked around. The interior walls were built with the same stones used for the outside.

"Well, I'll be a—" Miguel said. "This looks just like the inside of Blackbeard's Castle. Except there's a floor just above us."

Mikey walked over to a rickety old ladder. The tree limbs were bound together with dead vines. Mikey climbed to the top, pushed open a wooden trap door in the ceiling, and disappeared from view.

"Come on!" Misty said. They climbed several flights of stairs to the top of the tower. Misty walked to the back of the tower and gazed out at the large opening in the wall.

"Oh, Migs. Come see!" she said.

It was a spectacular view of the Caribbean for as far as they could see. Looking down, Misty said, "Now that's quite a drop. How high up do you think we are?"

"We passed through four rooms with maybe fifteen-foot ceilings each. I'd say it's at least a sixty-foot drop," Miguel said.

Monique came up the ladder and joined them. "So what do you think of my relatives' castle?" she asked proudly.

"You're not going to tell me this was built by Jerry Le Boucher," Misty said.

Monique pointed to a large stone several feet from the window. Crudely chiseled into stone were the words, "Le Boucher."

"I'm not even believing this," Misty said. "So where's the treasure?"

"Come on, I'll show you!" Mikey said and slid down the stairs.

He led them back down the trail, following the rock wall. When they reached the place where the path from the beach had run into the rock wall, Mikey stopped. He pointed to the beach but then continued on along the wall. A few hundred paces later, Mikey began removing tree branches from the wall until he exposed the entrance to a cave. He reached inside the cave, pulled out a kerosene lantern, lit it, and led the others into the cave. The cave system wound deep inside the hill. They came upon a short stretch with chisel marks on the wall.

"This part must have been excavated," Miguel said.

Soon the tunnel opened into a large room. The ceiling was so high that they could only see darkness above. There were two small pools of water, separated by a rock dam. Miguel bent down and tasted the water from the pool nearest him. "Fresh," he said.

He looked at the dark trail running down the wall and said, "Must be a natural spillway from above."

When Misty tasted the second pool, she spit the water out. "Yuk! Saltwater."

Mikey dove past Misty, into the pool. When he did not come up, Misty asked Monique, "Where did he go?"

"To the other side. Come on," Monique said. She dove in and disappeared.

Misty looked at Miguel. "You first," she said.

Miguel raised his eyebrows and dove in. Misty followed close behind. She caught a glimpse of Miguel swimming through a large illuminated opening. Misty swam to the other side and surfaced alongside Miguel. As they tread water, they spotted Mikey and Monique sitting on a small rock ledge at the base of a cliff.

"We're on the other side of the island," Misty yelled.

"Yep," Monique yelled back.

"How deep's the water?" Miguel asked.

"Deep enough for Mikey to dive from the top of the cliff," Monique said.

Miguel floated on his back and looked toward the sky. "Damn, Mikey. You're the man!"

After they joined Monique and Mikey on the ledge, Misty asked, "So where's the gold?"

"Mikey found the two pieces of gold back in the tunnel," Monique said. "They were lying at the bottom of the freshwater pool, covered by silt. We're in the process of exploring every passageway, one by one. There are only a few left, so we feel we're getting close."

Mikey stood up and said, "Come on, it's getting late. Let's go get some dinner." He jumped back into the water.

"You don't have to ask me twice," Miguel said, and he jumped in after Mikey.

As they were leaving the area with the two pools, Mikey reached inside a small hole in the wall and pulled out a bow and some arrows. He then ran ahead at a fast pace.

"What's up with Mikey?" Misty asked Monique.

"He likes to shoot fish in the surf behind the castle. Don't get your hopes up, though. Odds are we'll be eating Sam's provisions."

They found Captain Kev whittling on a stick once they made it back to the beach. "So Mikey and Monique gave you the tour?" he asked.

"They did!" Misty said. "This is all so exciting. Thank you for bringing us along, CK."

"Hell, more people to dig, I figure," he said.

As predicted, Mikey didn't have any luck, so the captain made his specialty: hamburger meat fried up in a skillet with a can of ranch-style beans thrown in at the end. It was nothing fancy, but the pan of cornbread was something special. Miguel was so hungry he didn't care what he ate. After dinner, Misty took some of the leftover cornbread and hung her feet over the side of boat. She fed seabirds while watching the sun go down. Captain Kev pulled out a bottle of rum and joined her for a bit of conversation. When darkness set in, Monique squeezed Miguel's hand and motioned with her head for him to follow. She led him down to her cabin below deck.

21

TROUBLE BREWING!

Antonio was fast asleep when he received a call from Salvatore telling him to come up to his suite. Using a spare key, he let himself in and called out, "Salvatore!"

"I'm in the living room."

Antonio stepped into the dimly lit room. He found Salvatore sitting in his favorite chair with a drink in his hand, his face half illuminated from the soft glow of a floor lamp. "What's up, boss?" Antonio asked as he drew near.

"I have exciting news! We've located the bitch," Salvatore said.

"I'm sorry, the bitch?"

"Misty, damn it! Misty! We're pretty confident we know where she is."

Now wide awake, Antonio said, "No shit! Where is she?"

"St. Thomas, Virgin Islands."

"Is Monique with her?" Antonio asked, lust in his heart.

"Possibly. Our informant indicated there were five passengers aboard the plane when it landed and two passengers when it departed for Buenos Aires. I'm assuming the two men who flew in from Buenos Aires to help her escape." Salvatore put his glass down. "Go wake up the boys. My plane is being refueled as we speak. It's a long flight, so tell them they can sleep on the plane."

"Consider it done." Antonio turned to leave.

"Antonio, there is one more thing. I have asked Luigi to accompany you."

Antonio spun around and carefully measured his words. "But Boss, don't you think that would be overkill? Luigi has a pretty nasty reputation. I'm sure we can handle this without him."

Someone stepped out of the darkness. He had shiny black hair, slicked back with heavy gel. He glared at Antonio with deadpan eyes as he repositioned the toothpick in his mouth.

"Meet Luigi," Salvatore said. "Antonio meant no disrespect, did you, Antonio?"

"I, uh, meant none at all. You should take it as a compliment, in fact. For a hit man, nasty is good, right?"

Luigi stepped back into the darkness with no response.

Salvatore sprang to his feet. "Well, then, that's settled. Luigi and I have a few more matters to attend to, so tell the pilot not to take off until he arrives." Antonio nodded and left the room.

"Bring her back to me unharmed, Luigi. I don't want a scratch on her."

"What about the others?" Luigi asked.

"I'm paying you for Misty's safe return. You can deal with the others as you see fit."

Luigi's face softened.

"There is one more thing you should know," Salvatore said. "Your *family* has a close working relationship with some of the authorities on St. Thomas. We'll arrange for someone to meet you as you get off the plane."

"Excellent!" Luigi replied.

Antonio held off telling the boys about Luigi as long as he could. When a limo pulled up in front of the private hangar, he said, "There's something I haven't told you. Luigi is coming with us." Antonio pointed out the window.

"I hear he's a cold-blooded killer," Tomasso said as he squirmed in his seat.

"Luigi would be in the hit man hall of fame, if there was such a thing," Santo said. "I've wanted to meet him for quite some time."

Luigi boarded the plane and walked to the back without saying a word. He settled into his seat and closed his eyes. Tomasso and Diego quickly grabbed a pillow and a blanket and did the same.

22

Digging It

The group enjoyed breakfast as they sat on deck watching a beautiful sunrise.

"More coffee?" Captain Kev asked Misty.

"I'm buzzing enough already, Captain, but thanks for asking."

The dinghy rode low in the water, loaded down with picks and shovels for their dig.

"Everyone get out here and walk to shore," Captain Kev yelled out. "We don't want to ground the dinghy."

"A digging we will go, a digging we will go, high-ho the merry-o, a digging we will go," Mikey sang as they made their way to the cave entrance. The cave was still cool from the night air. "I never thought I would need a jacket in the Caribbean," Misty said.

"You'll actually be glad when you start digging," Monique said. "Enjoy the coolness while it lasts."

"We should get a lot of digging done with the four of you," Captain Kev said.

"What about you?" Misty asked.

"Someone's got to stay in the cave and hang onto the rope so you guys can find your way back. Besides, I've got some more whittling to do."

"I should have guessed," Misty said.

Monique gave Miguel her lantern to hold. She then unfolded the treasure map and gave it a good read in the light. "Just a little further up," she said and pointed.

Monique held the lantern low until she came to a small opening in the north wall. The opening was no higher than her knees. She placed the lantern inside the hole and took a good look. "There's a long passageway on the other side. It might be a perfect place to bury treasure."

Mikey pushed her aside and climbed through the hole. Monique passed the end of the climbing rope through, and he clamped it to his belt. She watched as the lantern slowly disappeared into the passage.

"What's so special about this passageway?" Misty asked.

Monique smiled. "Captain Kev and Mikey promised to wait to dig this site until I returned."

"Captain, let me have your lantern," Monique said. She unfolded the map again and pointed to something written in French. Monique translated:

Go two hundred and forty paces and look for a den to crawl in. It runs to the north but curves to the east. Don't you worry, you won't find a beast. Let your lamp lead the way until the walls turn to clay. Then dig all day. If you have come by this map in a dishonest way, 'The Butcher' will track you down and make you pay.

"You sure this dude is dead?" Miguel joked.

"You never know," Captain Kev said. "Maybe a piece of him lives on in Monique."

"He's coming back," Monique said as she watched the lantern in the passageway grow brighter.

Mikey climbed back out and brushed himself off. "Did the passage take a turn to the east?" Captain Kev asked. Mikey nodded. "Did the walls turn to clay?" Mikey stuck his hand out and unballed his fist. Captain Kev grabbed the substance from his hand, raised it to his nose, and sniffed. He pinched off a piece and placed it on his tongue. "It's clay all right!" he proclaimed.

Misty and Monique hugged each other, and Miniature Mike, Captain Kev, and Miguel gave each other high-fives. "This is so exciting, guys." Misty said. "Thanks so much for letting us come along."

The captain handed Misty a shovel. "No problem, girl. Now get in there and find us some gold!"

"Aye, aye, Cap-e-tan," Misty replied and climbed through the hole.

They found it tough going. Miguel and Mikey made holes in the wall with their picks and then Monique and Misty deepened the holes with the points of their shovels. After a few hours, Monique said, "Let's keep going one more hour and then head back and take a long lunch break. No sense killing ourselves. That treasure's been here for centuries. It can wait a little longer."

"Okay, but I don't mind working all afternoon," Miguel said. "I'm kind of getting into this."

"Feel free to do the work for both of us, Mr. Macho Man," Misty said.

"Hey, I'm just saying," he replied.

23

UNEXPECTED VISITORS

Sally was Sam's latest reclamation project. She had been abused by her father growing up and found it hard to trust men. Sam took it upon himself to find a good kid from a stable family and then persuaded Jake to ask Sally out for dinner. Sam said he would pay, but if things went well, Jake would have to take over from there. He wanted to make sure Jake didn't keep asking Sally out just because he was footing the bill. Preparing the kitchen for later that night, Sally asked Sam, "Would you mind if I took next Tuesday night off?"

"Got a hot book to read?" Sam asked coyly.

"No," she said and blushed.

"What's that look on your face?"

"Oh, nothing. Well, actually, if you have to know, I've got a date."

Sam enjoyed the moment for a while and then said, "That's wonderful! What's his name?"

"Jake. And he seems like a really nice boy."

"Well, how nice," Sam said. "I'd say Jake is a lucky boy."

"Thank you, Sam. That was nice of you."

Sam picked up the sound of the garbage truck a block away. He handed Sally a full trash bag from the kitchen and said, "Can you please take this out before the truck gets here?" He then handed her a second, smaller bag. "Wait for them to show up and then give the guys these leftover donuts. Tell them how much we appreciate what they do. You'll make their day."

"Okay, Sam."

After Sally walked out the back door, Sam carried a tray of clean glasses from the kitchen to the bar. He wondered how Misty and Monique were. His thoughts were interrupted when five men entered the bar.

Turning toward them, Sam said, "Sorry, we're closed. Come back at six tonight if it's convenient."

The men made no response. Instead, they dispersed and started to check the place out. Santo walked toward the entrance to the kitchen. Sam stepped in front of him, blocking his path. "I said we're not open."

Tomasso leaned up against the bar. "We just need some information, and we will be on our way," he said diplomatically.

As Antonio walked onto the back porch, Sam measured the distance between him and the Glock he kept under the bar. Sam stepped out of Santo's path and positioned himself in front of Tomasso to inch his way closer to the weapon without being obvious. Santo moved quickly into the kitchen and began looking around. Luigi walked behind the bar from the far end, toward Sam, unknowingly cutting Sam off from his gun.

"We'd like a little information," Luigi said.

"Sorry, the tourist and information bureau back in town can answer anything you want to know," Sam said.

"So do you think they can tell us where Misty is?" Antonio asked as he walked back from the porch. "Or are you the right person to ask?"

"Misty. Sounds like a frozen drink," Sam said. "Maybe you can tell me what's in it."

Santo walked back into the bar from the kitchen and said, "Coast is clear." He opened the door leading to the living quarters and said, "I'll go check it out." Sam worried he would run into Sally.

"We have it from a very reliable source that Misty is staying here," Antonio said.

"I hope you didn't tip the guy, because he doesn't know what the hell he's talking about."

"We're going to get it out of you one way or another," Luigi said. "Why make it hard on yourself?"

Santo came back in holding a picture frame in his hand. He held it up for all to see. "Looks like you're going to get your bitch back, Antonio," Santo said.

"What about Monique, smart guy?" Antonio asked. "Why don't you just tell us where she is? I'll bet Misty won't be far away."

Sam heard the garbage truck pull away and realized he needed to make his move now if he hoped to alert Sally. He turned to Santo who was closest to him and looked down at his expensive Italian shoes. "You like wearing sissy shoes? I'll bet a C-note you're wearing ladies panties underneath your dickless trousers."

Santo charged as Sam grabbed a full bottle of whiskey and smashed it over his head, stopping him cold in his tracks. Tomasso and Diego climbed over the bar, positioning themselves on either side of Sam. Sam drove his fist into Diego's solar plexus. Diego crumpled to the floor like a sack of flour. Tomasso grabbed Sam from behind and dragged him to the floor. Sam reached behind him and placed Tomasso in a choke hold. Sam stopped after Luigi pressed a gun barrel against his temple. Tomasso gagged a few moments after Sam released him. From the corner of his eye, Sam saw Sally standing in the doorway of the kitchen, obviously scared but unnoticed. She ducked back into the kitchen.

Santo staggered up from the floor and drew his gun. "That son of a bitch busted my skull," Santo said, studying the blood on his fingers. "Let me kill him."

Luigi pressed his gun barrel into Santo's ribs. "Not yet. He still hasn't told us where Misty is."

Santo and Tomasso each grabbed one of Sam's arms and directed him to a chair. Antonio cut the strings from a guitar that had been left on the stage and tied Sam's hands behind his back. Luigi kneeled on the floor in front of Sam. "It's obvious you are a trained combatant. Navy Seals? Ranger? Special Forces?" Luigi prodded.

When Sam didn't answer, Luigi shook his head and stood up. "Okay, work him over, Santo. If he doesn't give us what we want, kill him."

Sam withdrew into himself as Santo pummeled him with punches to the head and body. Every now and then the blows would knock Sam and the chair over, but each time Tomasso and Diego would right him again.

When Santo's hand became sore, he busted up a chair and used the leg to beat Sam around the arms, shoulders, and legs. "You think I'm a sissy now, wiseguy?" Santo yelled.

Luigi stepped between Santo and Sam when he realized Sam wasn't going to talk. One of Sam's eyes was completely swollen shut, and his face was a bloody mess.

Luigi kneeled down, placed his hand under Sam's chin, and raised his head so he could look him in the eyes. "You have one last chance to say something before I let him kill you."

Sam spit some blood on the floor and then smiled at Luigi. "Special Forces," Sam said proudly.

Luigi dropped his head and looked at the floor. "Got to hand it to you," he said, "you're one tough son of a bitch."

Luigi drew his pistol from its holster and ejected the clip to count the bullets. Suddenly, loud voices could be heard approaching the front door. Luigi quickly holstered his gun and said, "Quick, untie the guy and drag him out onto the porch."

As Santo and Tomasso did as they were told, Luigi and Antonio walked to the front door and greeted the new arrivals. The large group of tourists came in laughing and howling.

A twenty-year-old with earrings and spiked hair walked up to Antonio and said, "Hey, we're looking for a bitchin' place to hang tonight, dude. How's the jive here?"

"How the fuck do I know?" Antonio snarled back. "Do I look like some jive-ass turkey? We're closed, so beat it." One of the women began throwing insults Antonio's way, and a ruckus ensued.

Sam opened his one good eye just enough to make out Santo and Tomasso standing between him and the guests. They were trying to block the view of Sam and look natural as they closely watched what was going on. Sam grabbed the bottom of the porch railing with his right arm and used it as leverage. He dragged his feet under the rail until they hung over the water. He then pushed off and fell feet first into the bay. The water was soothing to his face and gave him the little jolt he needed. He rolled over and stretched his body and sank to the bottom, headfirst.

Tomasso looked back and tapped Santo on his arm. They took their guns out and looked over the rail. Tomasso said to Santo, "Don't shoot or we'll have a mess on our hands. We have plenty of time to look for him once the tourists are gone. He's in no shape to get far anyway."

Sam's body felt as if it had been run over by the garbage truck that had just made the rounds, but the thought of what they would do to Misty and the others if they trapped them on the island spurred him on. He prayed Sally had run off by now. He made his way directly under the middle of the bar and then came up and gasped for air. His ears were ringing from the blows he had taken to the side of his head. Soon his survival training kicked in, and he decided to keep moving. Using the bridge to the living quarters as cover, he swam underwater from pylon to pylon, only coming up for air as needed.

Once underneath the living quarters, he felt it was safe enough to bring his head above water. He dog paddled to his boat and placed one arm over the side of the small dinghy. Though in great pain, he managed to pull himself up so that he could lean into the boat. He found his mask first and put it on. He reached back in for his scuba tank, wondering if he had the strength to pull it over the side of the boat. He placed a small piece of rope in his mouth and bit down hard. On the count of three, he heaved the tank up, straining until it was over the side and in the water.

There was about half an hour's worth of air left in the tank. Sam heard someone running over the bridge and realized he didn't have time to strap the tank onto his back. He wrapped his mouth around the air hose and held tightly onto the tank. Once he let go of the side of the boat, the weight of the tank pulled him down to the sea floor. He inched his way along the bottom until he was back beneath the living quarters.

Tomasso and Diego looked through the living quarters and over the balcony, into the water. Finally they gave up and returned to the bar. With the young tourists now gone, Santo dragged his prime catch out of the kitchen by one arm. Sally tried her best to pull away from him, but it was no use. "Where's Sam?" she said. "What did you do with him?"

"Sam's not your concern right now," Antonio said. "You need to worry more about yourself. Tell us where Misty is, and we won't hurt you."

"I don't know," she said. "They went to an island, but they never told me what island. You've got to believe me. I really don't know."

Santo slapped Sally with the back of his hand, causing her to cover her face and sob. "What's with these people?" Antonio demanded. "Why can't they just tell us where Misty is?"

"Island," Tomasso said. "I'll be right back." He ran back to the living quarters and returned holding a map. He studied it and then raised one eyebrow. "Right here!" he said as he pointed to a spot on the map. "There's a circle around an ink dot on the map with the word 'treasure' written next to it."

"X marks the spot," Luigi said.

When Antonio showed the map to Sally, her eyes gave her away. Luigi latched on tightly to her arm and said to the others, "Why don't you go wait for me in the car? I won't be long."

Antonio looked at Sally and then back at Luigi. He sensed what was to come.

"Come on, guys. Let's do as Luigi says," Antonio said as he headed toward the front door.

Santo was hot on his heels, but Tomasso and Diego were reluctant to leave. "Get going," Luigi yelled. "You don't want to fuck with me right now, I can promise you."

When everyone had gone, Luigi turned to Sally and said, "Unfortunately, you happen to be in the wrong place at the wrong time."

When Sam's air ran out, he left his tank on the water's floor and swam up to the surface. He noticed an opening to a small crawl space overhead. Springing up from the water, he grabbed onto a two-by-four. With great pain, he pulled himself up and threw his right leg over the two-by-four. He held on tightly as the muscles in his arms burned. He noticed an exposed water pipe, latched ahold of it, and pulled himself up and onto a small piece of plywood flooring. Face down and exhausted, Sam passed out.

* * *

Antonio and Santo picked up their bags and headed toward the awaiting marine helicopter. They were approached by a tall man.

"Pardon me, are one of you Luigi?"

As Santo pointed to Luigi, who was still getting out of the car, Antonio said, "Who's asking?'

The man offered his hand. "Christopher is my name. I'm an officer in the Blue Lightning strike force. I have been instructed to help Luigi any way I can. Does the name 'Salvatore' mean anything to you?"

"Blue Lightning strike force?" Santo asked. "What do you guys do?"

"The marine unit was established to patrol territorial waters, conduct drug interdiction initiatives, search and rescue, and assist in the prevention of illegal entry into the United States via the United States Virgin Islands borders."

"Your business is with Luigi," Antonio said.

"Yes, I'll go talk to him now."

"Luigi," Christopher said as he approached.

"I've arranged for one of our helicopters to drop you off on the island, per your request," Christopher said. "I'm taking a great risk in doing so. I'm afraid you will need to find an alternate method of transportation home."

"No problem. We'll come back in our target's, I mean, friend's vessel." Luigi pointed to Tomasso and Diego who were standing near the vehicle. "If for some reason we don't make it back in three days, I've instructed them to charter a boat."

"May I suggest my cousin?" Christopher said. "Jacob operates a deep-sea fishing vessel. He can be trusted for the right price."

"Price will not be an issue," Luigi said. "How are we coming with the homicide investigation?"

"I have an investigator on the way to the scene now. The best money can buy," Christopher added with a gleam in his eye.

Luigi nodded in approval.

"Did you leave the murder weapon where it can easily be found?" Christopher asked.

"They will have no problem finding it. When they check the guns registry, they will find it belongs to the bar owner."

"Excellent. We will take it from here. Have a good flight."

Luigi climbed aboard the chopper and buckled in.

Antonio looked over and asked, "Can he be trusted?"

"Christopher is highly paid to ensure our drug-trafficking operation stays one step ahead of the strike force," Luigi said. "We're in good hands."

Luigi patted the pilot on the shoulder. The chopper rose into the air, tipped its nose down, and headed out to sea.

* * *

"Time's a wastin'," Captain Kev said. "Our bellies are full. Let's go find us some gold!"

Miguel looked at Misty and Monique. "Why don't you two just stay on the beach and chill out? Mikey and I can do the digging."

Misty laughed, "You know me better than that." She walked off toward the entrance to the cave. "Come on," she yelled back. "As Captain Kev said, 'Time's a wastin'!'"

* * *

Sam awoke to the sound of men talking in the living quarters above. He took a moment to recount what had happened. When he remembered that Sally had been in the bar, his adrenaline kicked in. But when he attempted to rise, the pain in his body was excruciating. Sam slowly lowered himself into the bay and maneuvered his way back to the bar. Once there, he treaded water under the main porch and listened to voices coming from the bar.

"We have searched everywhere, and there is no sign of him," one voice said.

"That's okay," a second voice said. "We have his name from the business license posted on the wall. Unfortunately, there is no picture of him. Hang around and talk to the locals to see if you can get a good description. And trace the registration of the murder weapon. If it's in the bar owner's name, as I have good reason to suspect, we've got our man."

"Yes, sir. I'll phone in the serial numbers right away."

"Poor girl," another voice said. "Shot in the back of the head, gangster-style. This guy must be one mean son of a bitch."

Sam felt ill and grabbed onto a pylon for support. His queasiness was quickly followed by a sense of rage. It took all his training to control his emotions and remain still.

"But why would he leave the murder weapon at the girl's side if he was a professional?" another voice said.

"You don't need to worry about that. Why don't you head across the island and help Marco patrol the shops and let me handle this matter?

"Yes, sir."

"Now don't go telling anyone about this. Tourists in a foreign port don't like to hear about a fresh murder."

"Yes, sir."

Faces of the men who had beaten him flashed through Sam's mind one at a time. He burned them into his memory bank. Things had become personal, and he reminded himself that personal meant sloppy and sloppy meant dead. He regained his composure the best he could and called on his special-forces training. Sally was gone, and there was nothing he could do to bring her back. His only concern now was to ensure the same thing didn't happen to Misty and Monique. The thought of what these cold-blooded killers would do to the girls if they got to them first set off a massive adrenaline surge, dulling his pain and clearing his head. He waited until the men left the living quarters to make his way back. He untied his twenty-foot Boston Whaler and gave it a push to set it adrift.

Once the boat had drifted far enough out, he swam underwater and climbed aboard. When he had drifted several hundred yards from the Hideaway, he cranked the three-hundred-horsepower outboard engine and screamed off toward a small marina on the other side of the bay.

When he pulled in, he called out to the attendant attending to bait, "Hey, Jimmy! Top off the tank."

"Yes, sir, Sam."

"Hey, how many of those six-gallon gas cans do you have?"

"Ah, let's see. I've got six."

Sam purchased all six and asked Jimmy to fill them up.

"Looks like you're going to travel some distance."

"Just fill the tanks, Jimmy."

Soon Sam was on his way to St. John's to pay a visit to Big Mama.

24

WE MEET AGAIN

The helicopter hovered over the schooner, looking for signs of life. "Nobody's home," Luigi said. He tapped the chopper pilot on his shoulder. "Circle the island before you land."

With no indication that anyone was on the island, Luigi instructed the pilot to set the helicopter down on the sandy beach. Antonio and Santo quickly jumped out to secure the perimeter.

"So, who did you say you guys were?" the pilot asked.

"We didn't," Luigi responded. "This mission is on a need-to-know basis, and you don't need to know."

"Anything you say," he replied. "But if you are after drug dealers, you are underarmed."

"It's not your problem," Luigi said, "so take a hike."

Once Luigi got out, the pilot gladly obliged.

"So where do you think they could be?" Santo asked.

Antonio looked back at the boat and then to the line of thick vegetation. "This island isn't that big. They can't be far."

"Stay here and guard their dinghy while Antonio and I check this place out," Luigi told Santo. "We don't want them getting back to the boat without us. That would make for a long three days."

Antonio and Luigi came upon footprints on the beach, which they followed until losing the trail in the underbrush. They rummaged around for a while, to no avail.

"Come on," Luigi said. "Let's go back and hide out in the vegetation close to the dinghy. They'll show up eventually."

"Great idea," Antonio said.

* * *

Misty set down her pick, leaned against the clay wall, and slid to the ground. She picked up her water bottle and tipped it upside down. "I'm pooped, guys. And out of water. Why don't we call it a day?"

"I hear ya, Misty," Miguel said. "Ready to head back, Monique?"

She raised her arm and wiped the sweat from her brow. "Sure. I think we've done enough digging for today."

Misty emerged from the passageway first and rummaged through a bag next to Captain Kev. "Do we have any more water, Captain?"

"Sure, there's another bottle in there. Just leave my rum alone."

"Trust me, alcohol is the last thing on my mind right now."

Misty downed a third of the bottle and then handed it over to Miguel. He handed it to Monique without taking a drink.

Misty heard a splash and turned in the direction of the saltwater pool. "Mikey likes to take a quick dip in the ocean when he's through digging," Captain Kev said. "He'll catch up to us in a bit."

Once out of the cave, Miguel arched his back and looked skyward. "Oh, man, am I sore. I can't wait to get back to the schooner, chill out, and get a bite to eat. What are you fixing, Captain?"

"Me? I figure it's your turn to cook, Miguel. What's your specialty?"

"Uh, hot dogs."

"At least that's quick," Misty said. "I'll eat anything right now."

The group laughed and carried on as they walked toward the dinghy. Halfway there, the captain stopped so abruptly that Monique ran into him. Captain Kev pointed to footprints and two long trenches in the sand.

"Someone landed a helicopter while we were gone," Miguel said. "We need to get to the schooner."

"What about Mikey?" Misty asked. "We can't leave him on the island."

"Mikey's probably better off on his own," Captain Kev said. "If we make it to the schooner, we can sail around to the other side and pick him up. I doubt whoever it is will stumble into the entrance to the caves."

"Don't you think you guys are being a little paranoid?" Monique asked.

"The drug runners in these parts don't take kindly to people seeing them," Captain Kev said. "I'd rather be safe than sorry."

"I'm with you," Miguel said.

As they approached, Santo sat up in the dinghy, brandishing a pistol. Luigi and Antonio came out of the brush, armed as well. "Look what we have here," Antonio said. "Did you think you could fuck over Salvatore and get away with it?" Antonio placed the barrel of his pistol under Monique's chin, forcing her head up. "I'll bet you've missed me," he said.

When Miguel made a move in their direction, Santo placed the barrel of his pistol to Miguel's head. "Go ahead," Santo said, "make my day." He laughed. "I've always wanted to say that." Miguel reluctantly stepped back.

Captain Kev scratched the side of his face with the attachment from his prosthetic. Antonio gave the captain a strange look and said, "Who the fuck is he? And what's up with the eye patch and the fucked-up arm?"

"I'm Captain Kev, if you must know, and you should have more respect for the misfortunate. Why I lost me eye and forearm fighting terrorists in Afghanistan."

"Afghanistan!" Antonio replied. "You're too old to have fought in Afghanistan, you old fart."

"I'm referring to the Russian occupation of Afghanistan. I helped the Afghans fight off the Ruskies, and we did a damn good job of it."

"Just shut up, old man, or I'll shut you up for good," Antonio said.

Monique placed her hand on Miguel's shoulder and said, "Don't be brave, Miguel. There's nothing he can do to me that would be worse than losing you."

Luigi walked over to Monique and traced her face with his gun barrel before pressing it firmly into her left breast. Misty latched ahold of Miguel's hand and squeezed it tight. Monique didn't flinch. "Nice and firm," Luigi said. "Just the way I like them."

Luigi walked up to Misty and looked her over. "Remember, Salvatore wants Misty back in one piece," Antonio said cautiously.

Luigi laughed, "Why that's all I want. Just *one piece* of this delicious dish."

"Speaking of dish," Captain Kev said, "why don't you guys stay for supper?"

Antonio turned to the captain. "I told you to shut the fuck up."

"Just trying to be sociable."

Miguel caught a glimpse of Mikey climbing into the dinghy and realized the captain was attempting to stall for time.

"I'm fixing my famous hot dogs," Miguel chimed in.

"Let me shoot one of them," Santo said. "They're really beginning to irritate me."

Misty's eyes opened wide at the sight of Mikey running from the dinghy toward the underbrush with an oar in each hand. Luigi noticed her looking and turned around in time to see Mikey just before he disappeared into the thick vegetation. Luigi fired two shots in Mikey's direction. "Go after him, Santo," Antonio said. "We need those oars."

Santo scoured the brush for the next five minutes. "He's not here," he yelled back.

Antonio noticed some movement halfway up the side of the hill. It was twilight and hard to make out whether it was Mikey or some type of animal. The bullets ricocheted off the rock, creating sparks where they hit.

"Climb up there and see if I hit something," Antonio said to Santo.

Mikey popped up from behind a rock, shoved his right fist into the air, and slammed his left hand on top of his right bicep.

"Nope, they missed!" Captain Kev bellowed.

When Santo fired indiscriminately, Luigi yelled, "Stop wasting ammunition. Go catch up to him and put a bullet between his eyes."

Santo began climbing the rocky hillside. It was so steep he slid backward from time to time. Not knowing the terrain, he constantly hit dead ends and had to redirect his climb. Santo eventually made the crest of the hill and worked his way over the top. He caught a glimpse of Mikey for a brief moment before he disappeared into thin air. Santo headed toward the spot where he had last spotted Mikey only to find a large, flat rock on the side of the cliff. Santo looked to his left and then to his right. When he was convinced Mikey may have indeed vanished into thin air, he did the only thing left he could think of. Tucking his pistol in the back of his trousers, he got on his hands and knees and inched his way to the edge. Once there, he leaned out and looked down at the inlet below. He listened to the sound of waves crashing into the rocks below. As soon as Santo asked himself, *Where did that little shit go?* Mikey popped up from under the rock and grabbed Santo around the back of his neck. Santo made an effort to pull back, causing Mikey to rise with him, but Mikey had his feet firmly planted on the side of the hill for leverage. Mikey taunted Santo with his crazed eyes and mischievous grin.

Mikey's short, stocky legs began to slowly win the battle. Santo stared at the water hundreds of feet below as his head hung over the cliff. "Fuck you, little man!" he yelled to conjure up some courage.

Santo finally realized he was going down whether he liked it or not, so his last act was to reach around and push his pistol as far inside the back of his trousers as he could. When the two were both in free fall, Mikey released the back of Santo's neck, arched his back, and straightened his arms out into a perfect dive. Santo's arms flailed wildly as he spiraled out of control. Mikey split the water crisply, and Santo crashed awkwardly into the surf behind him. Mikey made a beeline to the underwater entrance to the cave while Santo struggled to figure out which way was up. When Santo surfaced, he treaded water for a moment to get his bearings and then worked his way to the rocky shoreline. After pulling himself onto a rock ledge, he rolled over onto his back and gasped for air. He lay there too sore to move.

Antonio continued to yell out for Santo but got no response. Luigi handed Antonio one of the kerosene lanterns and said, "Go search the brush for the oars." After ten minutes, Antonio emerged with an oar in each hand. "I found them. They were stashed behind a tree."

As they walked toward the dinghy, Luigi said to Antonio, "Miguel and the old fart can row, but don't give them the oars until I have them covered. I'll take the back of the boat. You take the front."

"You mean you will take the aft and he will take the stern," Captain Kev said.

Luigi pointed his gun at the captain. "One more remark like that, and you'll be underneath the boat."

"If you don't know the stern from the aft, who's going to sail you back home?" Captain Kev replied.

Luigi looked at Antonio. "Don't look at me," Antonio said. "I don't know jack about boats."

25

MAMA'S HOUSE

Big Mama delivered a tray of food to a group of regulars and then pulled up a chair to join them for a visit, as she was known to do. But as soon as she hit the chair, another customer walked through the door, so she got back up and walked over to hand him a menu. "You are in Mama's house tonight, sugar. Take a seat anywhere you like."

The man pulled back the hood of his jacket just enough to reveal himself. "Oh, Sam," Mama said. "Wait for me in the kitchen."

Mama locked the front door and flipped off the Open sign, before informing her guests to take their time and that she would have the cook let them out when they were finished.

She then walked up to her cook, Jose, who was scraping down the grill, and said, "We're closen' early tonight. Lets tha guests out when they's all done, sugar."

Mama placed her hand on Sam's chin and turned his head from side to side. "Oh, my, my. Yous a mess, honey. Let's get you to my house so I's can fix you up."

Mama emptied the money from the till into a bag, and they were off.

Once on the road, Mama said, "Who done this to you, Sam? They musta been some bad dudes."

"There were five," he replied as he stared out the window.

"You make those men mad at you or sumthin?"

"Not *yet*."

"You means they just picked a fight witch ya for no good reason?"

"They had a reason."

"Sam. Last time I seens ya like dis was ten years ago. I's thought dat yuz gonna do somethins terrible to yous self."

"It's not me I'm going to do something terrible to. It's different this time," Sam said, still gazing out his window.

"You don't mean killin', do you, Sam? You and Jessie done enough killin' in your day, God rest his soul. It was for your country and all, but it was killin' just the same."

"If I'd killed one more, you wouldn't be a widow right now," he shot back.

"Them snipers are hard to sees. It wasn't your fault, Sam."

Mama pulled up in front of a modest, wood-frame house and got out. She made Sam take a seat at the kitchen table while she soaked a washcloth with hot water. She washed the blood from his face and then applied iodine to his cuts. "Nose might be broken," she said.

"Yeah, well so are some of my ribs, so I guess it has company."

Mama got up, filled the washcloth with ice, and then held it on his nose. "Least we can do is keeps the swellin' down." She then said softly, "Tell me what happen, sugar."

"Five men, who I have never seen before, came into the bar looking for Misty. I know bad men when I see them, so I refused to talk."

"Misty? You means the Misty Monique's been tellin me about?"

"Yeah, and Monique is with her."

Big Mama's face went flush, and she took a seat next to him. "Not my Monique, Sam. You can't let nobody hurt my baby. Dat poor woman has gone through a lifetime of misery."

"I know."

"Why just da other day she was here with the nicest boy. Miguel was his name. Dat boy's gonna do her some good."

Big Mama sat to contemplate for a moment. When she had come to a conclusion, she said, "Sam!" Some men just need killin'. How can I help you? If I ain't got it, Jessie Jr. can gets it for you."

"Do you still have the chest I left here?"

"Yes, it's up in the attic. Never touched it all dez years."

Sam rose from the chair and laid his ice pack on the table. "Perfect! Tell Jessie I need some explosives. Black powder, if that's all he can find, but C4 would be preferable. Have him go visit Mr. Blackwell. He owns a construction company and was good friends with his father and me. Have him tell Blackie it's for Sam, so he knows it will never be tracked back to him."

"Done!" Mama said.

Sam pulled down the old accordion ladder from the ceiling and climbed up into the attic. He found the chest exactly where he had left it ten years ago, right after he had turned in his resignation. He pried the lock open with his pocketknife. First out was his Glock 9-millimeter handgun. He looked down the end of the barrel and made a mental note to clean it before he headed out. A full fifteen rounds were in the first clip, but he counted only six in the other. He would have to fire it judiciously. The good news was that the Glocks fire even when wet, and he realized that could come in real handy on an island. Sam slipped the handgun into the back of his pants and took out what was his prized .357 Python revolver. He loaded six rounds into the cylinder and gave it a spin. If he couldn't shoot around it, at least he had something to shoot through it. After stuffing a box of shells into his jacket, he slid the gun into its holster and buckled the belt around his waist.

Next out was his Remington 870 shotgun. The butt was sawed off to convert it into a pistol grip, and the chamber was modified to hold five rounds instead of three. He stood up and placed the rigged parachute cord around his shoulder and let the rifle hang down across his lower back. He grabbed the gun by the pistol grip, pointed it from his hip, and then let it hang behind his back again. He placed the eight shotgun shells in a plastic bag and stuffed them into his jacket pocket. It was then time to clean his guns at the kitchen table while he waited on Jessie Jr.

* * *

When Santo awoke, he stared up into the night sky. His tailbone hurt from lying on his pistol. A pain shot through his neck and shoulder as he attempted to reach around back and secure his gun. He rolled onto his side and used the rock wall to help him get onto his feet. He was thankful there was a half moon to see by. He took in his surroundings, trying to determine the best direction to begin walking. To his left was a dead end. Climbing the sheer cliff he fell from was not an option. He turned to his right and began working his way around the rocky shoreline. Eventually the rocks gave way to flat beach, and he quickened his pace. When he reached the beach, Santo yelled out, "Hey, where is everybody?"

After several more tries with no response, Santo looked out to the schooner lights shining in the distance. His shoulder was too sore to make the long swim with certainty, so he walked into the water as far as he could go and began shouting again.

Antonio had just finished tying Captain Kev's, Miguel's, and Monique's hands behind their backs when Santo's shouts rang out from shore. "Your comrade must be afraid of the dark," Captain Kev said.

"Want me to go back and pick up Santo with the dinghy?" Antonio said to Luigi.

"Let him spend the night on shore. We can deal with him in the morning."

Antonio yelled back, "Make yourself comfortable, Santo. We'll come for you in the morning."

"Are you fucking serious!" Santo yelled back.

Luigi pulled out his pistol and fired a round into the air. "Damn it, Santo. We'll get you in the morning. If you want something to do, go find that little half-pint."

Santo walked back to shore in disgust.

Antonio had already begun tying up Misty when Luigi grabbed her by her arm and pulled her to her feet. "Get down into the kitchen and fix us some dinner," he said.

"Galley," Captain Kev said.

Luigi stared at him. "One more word out of you, and I'll take my chances sailing back without you. Do you understand?"

"I can see you are a man who is happy in his ignorance. I will refrain from futile attempts to educate you in the future, as it's clear you have no interest in becoming a true, seafaring man," Captain Kev replied.

Frustrated, Luigi gave Misty a shove in the direction of the stairs. "But you better go with her," Antonio said. "They might have a gun stashed below."

"Now wouldn't that be something," Luigi said. "I'm sure Salvatore would understand if I had to shoot her in self-defense." Misty kept walking as Luigi followed after her.

A shout rang out from the beach. "Ouch! That hurt!"

Miguel, Monique, and Captain Kev straightened their backs when they heard several shots ring out.

"I hope Mikey's okay," Monique said.

Santo yelled out again. "You little fucker. Stop throwing rocks at me! I might not be able to see you now, but you just wait until morning."

"Can't you just shoot the little bastard?" Antonio yelled.

"It's too dark. I have no idea where the little shit is."

"Give em hell, little buddy," Captain Kev whispered under his breath.

Misty walked out of the galley and said to Luigi as she passed him, "Your dinner's ready. Have at it."

Having not eaten since breakfast, Luigi hurried in. All he found was six cans of beans with lids in the air and spoons sticking out. She hadn't even warmed the beans. Luigi stormed onto deck and headed over to Misty, his arm raised as if he were going to backhand her. Antonio shouted, "Luigi! Remember what Salvatore told us. Not a mark."

Luigi held his pose for a few seconds. He knew Antonio was right, but it would feel so good to slap her. He looked at Antonio and said, "When you are finished tying her up, come down below. I would like to speak to you in private."

Once Antonio and Luigi were below deck, the captives breathed a collective sigh of relief. Trying to lighten the mood, Captain Kev said, "How 'bout that Mikey? I bet that Santo fella ain't going to get any shuteye tonight."

They spent the next half hour imagining all the things Mikey would do to Santo over the course of the night. It lifted their spirits until Antonio came back on deck with a bottle of Captain Kev's rum in one hand. It was only half full, and from the way Antonio was acting, it hadn't started out that way. Antonio staggered over to Monique and looked down on her. "Did I ever tell you how painful it was when you kicked me in the nuts on your way out of Vegas?" he asked her.

"You deserved it for the way you treated her," Miguel said.

Antonio pulled his firearm from his shoulder holster, kneeled on one knee, and stuck the gun barrel under Miguel's chin. "Don't think I haven't noticed, pretty boy. You've been tapping my girl, haven't you?"

"Please leave Miguel alone," Misty pleaded.

"And why should I?"

Misty spurted out the first thing that came into her head. "Because Miguel is my bodyguard and as such, he's part of my contract with Salvatore. If anything happens to him, it would void my contract."

Antonio's cognitive faculties were so impaired that he didn't want to think through the logic of what Misty said. Instead, he pulled his gun out from under Miguel's chin and rose to his feet. Antonio took a big swig of rum and wiped his mouth with the back of his hand. He tittered for a moment and then looked down at Monique with lust in his eyes. He kneeled in front of her and began untying her feet.

"What are you doing?" Misty asked.

"I know damn well Monique's not a part of your precious contract. For a time she was the property of Salvatore, but then he handed her down to me, as he's always done when he's finished with his bitches." Once she was untied, Antonio yanked Monique from the floor, but she pulled away. Not wanting to struggle with her in his condition, he placed his gun to Miguel's temple.

"Don't shoot him!" Monique yelled. When he didn't waiver, she said in a gentler tone. "I'll come with you willingly if you leave Miguel alone."

"Don't do it, Monique!" Miguel yelled. "You don't have to do this for me."

Monique hung her head and slowly walked away. Miguel struggled vehemently to free himself. Antonio holstered his gun. "You don't get it, do you, Miguel?" Antonio said with a smile. "Monique's my girl, and I'll do with her as I please. Get used to it if you don't want me to blow your head off."

When they had both gone down the steps to the quarters below, Miguel hung his head between his knees. Misty leaned over and laid her head on his shoulder. For the first time in her life she was at a loss for words.

Once Miguel got it out of his system, he said in a tone Misty had never heard. "I can promise you this. If I ever get free, I'll kill him." Misty had little doubt he meant what he said.

26

CALL TO DUTY

Sam padded the bottom of his backpack with folded towels before gingerly loading the four one-pound bricks of C4. He moved quickly in hopes of finishing before Big Mama returned from the errand he had sent her on. He needed the C batteries he sent her after, but he also wanted her out of the house in the event of a mishap.

Sam held out his hand to Jessie Jr. "Okay, let me have the blasting caps." The boy handed them over very carefully. "Are you sure you don't want to go help your mother do the shopping?"

"I want you to teach me about this stuff, Sam. I might want to join the Special Forces someday like you and Pops."

"They'd be lucky to have you, son." Sam took his knife out and cut off the cord from the lamp. "Don't tell your Mama," he said jokingly as he spliced the wire.

"Did Pops know how to handle explosives?" Jessie Jr. asked.

"He's the one who taught me. Finest soldier I ever knew."

"He said the same about you, Sam." Jessie Jr. watched some more and then said, "Mama says you two were like brothers. Kind of funny, you being white and all."

"You learn there is no such thing as color on the battlefield—or off, for that matter. Jessie and I were closer than brothers."

Mama walked in from her shopping trip, proudly holding the two C batteries. "Here ya go."

"Thanks, Mama." Sam turned to little Jessie. "Are all the gas cans on the boat full?"

"Yes, sir. Filled 'em to the top."

"Thanks, son. Now can you go start the car? We need to get going."

As Sam was about to leave, Big Mama placed her hands on the side of Sam's face and looked into his eyes. "Bring my baby chil' home to me, Sam. You'll do that for me, won't you?"

"You know I will," he replied. He picked up his backpack, placed his other hand on the side of her face, and said, "This might be good-bye, Mama."

"Don't talk like that, Sam. You're going to make it through this just fine."

"Remember me telling you about the young girl I was helping?"

"Yous mean Sally?"

"Yes, Sally. The men that beat me used my gun to put a bullet in the back of her head. They left it next to her body so the authorities could find it. If I make it through this alive, I'll be on the run."

"Those bastards!" Big Mama said, her cheeks flush with anger. "I'm comin' with you to shoot em myself. Jus' give me time to find one of Jessie's guns."

Sam gave her a kiss on the forehead. "Thanks for offering, but you know I can't take you with me."

"How far ya goin'?" she asked.

"It will take me most of the night to get there," Sam said as he headed for the door.

"Jou gottsa nuff gas to gets back?"

Sam kept walking.

Mama stood at the doorway and hollered after him. "I'll pray for you."

"I can think of five men that might need it more," Sam said just before he got into the car.

Once Sam and Jessie Jr. were aboard the Boston Whaler, they headed out to sea, full throttle. Jessie had talked Sam into taking him as far as a friend's house on one of the outer islands. It gave Sam a chance to get some much-needed sleep.

* * *

Misty was awake when Antonio brought Monique back. Her heart poured out to Monique. She looked over at Miguel and was relieved he was still fast asleep. Misty closed her eyes and pretended to be sleeping as well when Antonio tied Monique up again. Once Misty heard Antonio stagger off to pass out, she opened her eyes wide. Monique was sitting resolutely on the deck, staring into space. Misty wondered how she would hold up under the same circumstances.

27

A NEW DAY

Mikey placed his knife between his teeth and eased his way into the water, under the cloak of darkness. He started out with slow breaststrokes to keep Santo from hearing him. He switched to freestyle and then back to the breaststroke as he approached the schooner. At the first hint of light, Misty opened her eyes to the sight of Mikey grinning at her. She smiled back at him, grandly. She gently nudged Miguel as Mikey cut her ropes. Misty rubbed her wrists as the rest were cut free. Captain Kev whispered to the others, "Gather 'round best you can. I've got an idea."

Luigi rolled his legs over the edge of the bed and sat up. It was time to check on his precious cargo. After slipping on his clothes, he quietly opened the door to Antonio's cabin and looked in. Part of him was relieved Antonio hadn't been stupid enough to keep Monique in his quarters overnight, but the other part wouldn't have minded seeing her naked. He figured the trip back would take up to six hours. It would be enough time to persuade Antonio to let him have a go with Monique.

When he threw the door open at the top of the stairs and looked out, to his dismay, the captain was the only one on deck. Luigi pulled out his weapon and held it with two hands as he searched the deck. "Howdya sleep?" Captain Kev bellowed. "Would you mind bringing me a cup of coffee when you're done with your morning walk?"

Luigi growled at Captain Kev and yelled to Antonio, "Get up here, Antonio. Now!" Luigi resumed his search. He walked around to the other side of the cabin that covered the stairwell, finding no one. Antonio came stumbling onto deck with his shirt unbuttoned. He looked at Captain Kev and then walked over to Luigi. "Where the fuck are the prisoners?" Antonio asked.

"How should I know, dip shit. You should have been up here watching them all night instead of getting your rocks off." Antonio knew enough to hold his tongue.

Luigi walked over to Captain Kev and planted the barrel of his gun on his forehead. "Remember, Luigi," Antonio said, "he's the only one that can sail us home."

"Tomasso will come for us in a few days if we don't make it back. I'm not worried," Luigi said coldly.

Captain Kev gulped. Thinking quickly, he said, "Oh, you won't have to wait that long. A bunch of my old navy buddies are meeting us here tomorrow. They use the island for target practice."

Luigi assumed he was bluffing, but he couldn't be certain. Besides, the captain was still tied up, so what harm could he do? With his gun still on Captain Kev's forehead, he said, "Tell me where your friends went or I'll use your head for target practice."

"Oh, you know how women hate it when they don't get a chance to bathe." He nodded to the island. "They thought a nice swim might be refreshing."

Antonio walked over to the port side of the vessel and looked at the island. He caught a glimpse of Miguel and the women heading for foliage on the right side of the beach.

"Damn it! They're on the beach," Antonio said. He looked at the captain. "How do we lower the dinghy?"

"See that big lever on the first wench? Just unlatch the clip."

Antonio walked over and pointed at the lever. "This?"

Captain Kev nodded.

Antonio pulled the lever, releasing the spool of cable, and the bow of the boat plunged into the water. "You moron!" Antonio yelled.

"Don't get excited. Just release the lever on the other wench and you'll be fine," Captain Kev said.

Antonio glared back at the captain and then released the other side. The instant he did, the stern of the boat plunged into the water, causing a big splash. "There you go," Captain Kev said. "Happy rowing."

Luigi checked to make sure the captain's ropes were securely fastened before climbing down the rope ladder and joining Antonio. They each grabbed an oar and began to row. Luigi rowed harder than Antonio, causing the dinghy to move to the right. "Come on, keep up," Luigi said. "Put some muscle into it. Hell, your girlfriend could row harder than you." Captain Kev laughed to himself as the two argued all the way to shore.

Mikey, who had been lying on the roof of the cabin spread-eagle, popped his head up enough to make sure the coast was clear. Once he saw Luigi and Antonio halfway to shore in the dinghy, he rolled off the roof and onto the deck. He then walked nonchalantly over to the captain and cut him loose. Captain Kev shook the wrist on his good arm vigorously and said, "I've got to teach those boys how to tie a proper knot."

They both crept over to the port side and glanced over the railing. "Let's wait until they make it to shore and then we can sail to the other side of the island to pick up our friends." Mikey gave him a salute.

*　*　*

Miguel moved carefully through the heavy vegetation ahead of the girls to scout things out. When he spotted Santo between them and the cave entrance, he shook his fist and made his way back to the girls.

"All clear?" Misty asked.

"I'm afraid not. Santo is bunked down about a hundred yards this side of the cave opening. Mikey must have really gotten to him because he keeps looking up into the rocks and pointing his gun. Maybe we should wait it out here."

"If we double back we can make our way around the island by hugging the shoreline," Monique said. "I went that way with Mikey once before."

"Works for me," Misty said.

Miguel again took the point. They were almost back to where they had entered the vegetation when he heard Luigi's voice. He watched as Luigi and Antonio pushed the dinghy onto the beach and then headed their way. "I'm not believing this," he said under his breath. After returning to the women, he whispered, "Trouble's coming. We need to move out." They stopped when they heard Antonio yell out, "Santo! Where are you?"

"Over here!" Santo yelled back.

Penned in between Santo to the north and Santo's bosses to the south, Miguel weighed his options. He considered leading Misty and Monique up the hill Mikey had climbed the night before, but it offered no cover and seemed too risky. He could hear Luigi and Antonio getting closer, and out of good options, he pointed toward the sandy beach. "It's our only hope," he whispered. "Maybe we can make it to the castle. Fear is our ally," Miguel said to reassure them.

"Well, then we've got an army of allies, because I'm scared out of my wits," Misty said.

They could now hear Santo calling out to Antonio, and they realized he was going back to meet them. Miguel nodded his head toward the beach. He had them stop just short of the sand and take off their shoes. He raised three fingers, and they all crouched in a sprinter's stance as he waved finger one, then two, and then three. Misty's adrenaline was pumping as they raced across the sand, hoping they would not hear Salvatore's men yell out or a shot fired. Luckily, their adversaries were too busy looking through the undergrowth to notice them. When they reached the castle, the girls helped Miguel pull the massive wooden door toward them just enough to slip inside. They watched him break off a limb from a nearby tree and push the tree branch through the handle of the door from the inside, wedging it shut. They all breathed a sigh of relief. "What now?" Monique asked.

"Let's make our way to the top floor," Misty suggested. Monique led them up the first ladder and pushed open the trapdoor. Once on the second floor, they let the door fall back into place and looked for fragments of stone or splinters of old wood to wedge into the space around it. Miguel familiarized himself with his surroundings on each floor. The rooms were pretty much empty, and each had evenly spaced slits in the walls. He remembered from his trip to Blackbeard's Castle that the slots were for shooting rifles through.

After securing the hatch on the top floor, they walked over to the large, open window on the west wall and looked out at the Caribbean. "I wonder if Le Boucher ever had to fend someone off from where we are standing?" Miguel asked.

"If he did, he was better armed than we are," Monique replied.

They sat down below the window, their backs to the stone. "Get some rest, girls. You're going to need your strength."

"Maybe they won't find us," Misty said.

"We can only hope," Miguel replied. He reached out and took Monique's hand into his own. She gave him a warm smile. Miguel felt helpless to defend the girls without being armed. He swore that if they ever got out of this mess, packing heat would be in his job description.

* * *

Santo squatted down when he heard the approaching footsteps. "Luigi, Antonio, is that you?"

"Yeah, it's us," Luigi said. "What was going on last night? You were screaming like a little girl."

"That little shit nailed me five times with fist-size rocks." Santo pulled up his shirt to show his welts.

"Put your shirt back down," Antonio said. "We get the point. So you haven't seen anyone coming this way?"

"Not a soul."

Luigi looked to the hillside and then back to Santo. "We saw Miguel and the two women walk into the thicket and head your way. If you haven't seen them, and they aren't climbing the hill, then that leaves only the beach," Luigi said.

As they walked onto the sandy beach, Antonio caught a glimpse of the schooner under sail, making its way around the point. "The schooner's getting away!" Antonio yelled. The three ran as fast as they could to the water's edge, where they stood trying to make sense of the event. Luigi looked at Antonio, and Antonio said, "Hey, don't look at me. We both know Captain Kev was tied up tight. I checked him myself."

"Then there's no way he could have gotten free without help."

Luigi looked at Santo. "When's the last time you saw the little man?"

"Now that you mention it, he stopped chucking rocks at me right before dawn."

"I'll bet he swam out to the boat and cut them loose," Antonio said. "That means he's helping the captain sail the schooner."

"There goes our food supply until Tomasso gets here," Santo said, as they watched the schooner disappear from sight.

Luigi scowled. "We can't worry about that now. If we don't find the girls before they figure out how to meet up with the schooner, they will get away, and we will be stuck on this fucking island for two more days."

"They could cover a lot of ground—I mean water—with a two-day head start," Santo said.

"I'm not sure I'd want to go back and face Salvatore if that happened," Antonio said.

* * *

As the schooner approached the cove, Captain Kev pulled out his marine binoculars and searched the shoreline for their friends. What he found instead was a man with binoculars, looking back at him. "Well, I'll be damned. It's Sam!"

Mikey ran up, took the binoculars out of Captain Kev's hand, and looked himself. "Sam," he said fondly in his squeaky voice.

After dropping anchor in the cove, Captain Kev said, "Don't just stand there! Get ashore and give him a hand." Mikey dove into the water without uttering a word. *Knowing Sam, he's packing some serious heat*, the captain thought. *That levels the playing field.*

Sam held out his hand and helped Mikey ashore. "Where are the others?" he asked.

Mikey shrugged as he looked over Sam's firepower. He pointed at the water. "Follow me, Sam." He tugged on Sam's backpack in an effort to help, but Sam shook his head. "Not the backpack." Sam handed him the Remington that had been slung over his shoulder, and Mikey slipped the cord over his own shoulders.

Sam checked to made sure his .357 magnum was securely snapped into its holster and then placed the Glock into the back of his pants. "Okay, ready," Sam said to Mikey. "Lead the way, little man."

Sam dove in behind Mikey and followed him through the opening in the rock wall. Soon they were inside the cave, standing on dry land. Sam blew on his weapons to clear them of water.

Mikey handed Sam the Remington and then disappeared for a bit. He returned with a rag tied around his head and his bow and arrows in his hand.

"Hey, Rambo," Sam said. "How many of them are there?" Mikey held up three fingers. Sam returned the sawed-off shotgun to his shoulder, secured his weapons, and motioned for Mikey to take the lead.

Mikey placed the bow around his neck and waved for Sam to follow. When they passed the tunnel where the group had been digging for gold, Sam stopped. Reaching down, he picked up the rolled-up climber's rope they used to find their way out of the tunnel and slung it over his left shoulder. Sam nodded to Mikey, and they were on the move.

As they approached the cave entrance, Mikey put his fingers to his lips. Once outside, Sam followed him up the hillside, just high enough to get a good view of the island. They heard someone yell out and realized that Santo had spotted them. After the others joined him, Santo pointed to the tree line, and they all headed out with weapons drawn.

Sam and Mikey scurried down the hillside and onto the sandy beach. Looking down at the multiple sets of footprints, Sam said, "Where does this lead?"

"To the castle," Mikey said and then ran on ahead.

"Castle?" Sam muttered.

* * *

Santo, Antonio, and Luigi stood in front of the massive doors and looked skyward. "Well, I'll be damned," Santo said.

"Is this some kind of time warp?" Antonio said.

"I don't know, man. This is some crazy shit," Santo replied.

Luigi walked up and took the big metal ring in one hand and then waved them over. They all gripped the door handle with both hands and gave it a pull. The door barely budged. Santo looked through the small crack. "There's something wedged into the handle," he said.

"At least we know someone is in there," Luigi said. "Okay, let's yank hard on my command."

After the tenth try, they heard a crack. After a few more hard pulls, they heard the tree branch break. With the door half open, the branch was still an impediment. Santo drew his pistol and fired several rounds until the branch broke in half.

Misty and Monique froze at the sound of gunshots. They sat on the floor up against the back wall and huddled together. Miguel ripped off a hunk of splintered wood from a damaged piece of flooring and wedged it into the floor hatch. As they hugged each other, Monique said to Misty, "I need to tell you a few things in the event we don't make it."

"Don't talk like that, Monique. We need to stay positive," Misty replied.

"Things need to be said, Misty."

"Okay, I'm listening."

"I am so sorry for the way I treated you when we first met. I'm afraid I was a total bitch."

"And the point is?" Misty said jokingly to ease the tension.

"The point is I had a pretty good thing going with Captain Kev and Mikey. I could tell right away you were special to them, and I became jealous. And then at Gabriella's, things became worse. You were so beautiful and so sure of yourself. It was obvious everyone loved and adored you. I've never gotten that kind of attention before. I think, by now, you understand why."

"Yes, I know now how hard your life has been, and believe me when I tell you, I harbor no resentment toward the way you treated me," Misty said.

"There's more," Monique said. "When I found out what you did for a living, I couldn't believe it. How many women get a chance to get paid so much money and travel the world, while driving men crazy? I set out to prove I could be every bit as good as you, but I realize now I could never measure up to you. You really have a very special talent."

Misty looked into Monique's eyes and saw a mature woman looking back at her, not the brash young women she had met in Argentina. While embracing Monique one more time, Misty whispered into her ear, "All is forgiven, provided you do one thing for me."

"Anything," Monique said.

"Take good care of Miguel if you two should survive and I don't."

"Don't talk like that, Misty. Remember, you said that we need to stay positive."

The girls jumped when they heard something strike the wall outside the large open window. Misty rose up slowly and peeked over the bottom of the rock ledge. Mikey was waving at her with a handful of arrows in his hand.

Misty turned to Miguel. "It's Mikey."

Once Miguel stuck his head out the window, Mikey gave him a thumbs-up and ran off.

"Poor Mikey. I'm afraid a bow and arrow's no match for firearms," Miguel said. "I hope he doesn't do something foolish."

* * *

Santo climbed the rickety ladder on the ground floor and tried to push open the wooden hatch. It barely budged. "Hurry up!" Antonio demanded.

"Hey, I'm doing the best I can," Santo shot back. "It's wedged pretty tight."

Luigi peeked out of the rifle slits in the wall as he walked the curvature of the ground floor. His mind wandered, wondering what battles were like back then and how a man like him would have fared. Fond of killing, Luigi fantasized a world with so little law and order.

Mikey made it back to the front of the castle to find Sam holding a sturdy tree limb in each hand. "Miguel, Misty, and Monique are on the top floor," Mikey reported to Sam.

Sam propped the tree limbs up against the castle wall and then reached into his backpack and handed Mikey a string of firecrackers and a lighter. Mikey looked up at him, confused. "Fourth of July, Mikey. Promise you will secure the outside of the door with these once I'm inside," Sam said as he pointed to the tree limbs.

"But you will be locked in, Sam!"

Sam smiled and said, "That's my plan."

"Okay, Sam," Mikey said still a little wary. "What now?"

"I want you to go around the other side and set off those fire crackers. I need a diversion."

Mikey grinned and said, "Will do, Sam."

Sam hung the climbing rope on his left shoulder. He cracked open the main door just enough to locate Antonio and Luigi along the back wall, and then he waited for his opportunity.

"Hey, that little man just went by," Luigi said. "Shoot him when he comes your way."

Antonio placed his pistol in the gun slit, pushing it as far forward as possible. As Mikey passed the slit, Antonio opened fire. Antonio watched two puffs of sand fly up from the ground. "Damn it!" he yelled. "I missed him."

When the gunshots rang out, Sam nudged the door open and slipped through undetected. Santo was too busy trying to get the hatch to notice Sam was just beneath him. Sam closed his eyes and conjured up his Special Forces training manual. *When getting ready to engage the enemy, smooth is fast and slow is smooth. Apply surprise, speed, and violence of action.*

The instant the fireworks went off, Sam grabbed Santo by the back of his belt and yanked him from the ladder. Santo crashed onto the floor with so much force, all he could do was lay there, gasping for air. Sam grabbed the pistol grip of his sawed-off shotgun and aimed the barrel at the wooden latch above. He pulled the trigger and blew the door off its hinge. The blast caught Luigi and Antonio by surprise, causing them to duck for cover. Sam slipped through the opening with cat-like reflexes and headed for the next ladder on the other side of the second floor. Luigi and Antonio looked over at Santo. Unable to speak, he pointed up the ladder. Luigi pointed his gun at the opening in the floor, while Antonio looked after Santo. When enough air returned to his lungs to speak, he said, "It was the guy from the bar. You know, the one we worked over."

"Looks like we are going to find out just how badass Special Forces guys can be," Luigi said excitedly.

Another shotgun blast rang out. "He's on the third level," Luigi said. "No rush. He's not going anywhere."

The element of surprise his only weapon, Miguel had positioned himself behind the hinged door in the floor in the event someone came through. After they heard another blast, he said, "I wonder where those guys got a shotgun. They didn't have one last night."

Suddenly, a shotgun blast blew the door off its hinge. Miguel lost his balance and fell onto his back. The intruder leaped through the door and pointed his rifle at Miguel's head.

"Taking a nap?" Sam asked with a wink.

Misty and Monique jumped up and gave Sam a big hug.

"Thank God you're here," Misty said. "But how did you know?"

Sam pointed to his face. "Long story. Let's move away from the opening." He handed Miguel the Glock and said as he removed the climbing rope from his arm, "Cover the door while I secure the rope."

"Got it," Miguel replied as he positioned himself against the wall in order to get the best line of sight.

Sam removed his backpack and gently set it on the floor, near the window. Removing a spring-loaded camming device from the pack, he walked to the window and wedged it into a crack just beneath the rock windowsill. He next pulled out a karabiner and attached an SLDC and rope clip to each side. Sam climbed up onto the window ledge, threw the end of the rope spiraling toward the ground, and gripped the rope with both hands. He gave the rope a good jerk to make sure the SLDC was doing its job. Placing his feet on the outer edge of the rock ledge, he leaned back straight-legged, until perpendicular with the castle wall. "Good," Sam said and then climbed back into the room.

"What if they see us and come around back? Couldn't they shoot us coming down the rope?" Misty asked.

Sam shook his head. "Mikey secured the door from the outside. They are trapped in here with us."

"I'm not sure I like that any better," Misty said with a frown.

Monique placed her hand gently onto the side of Sam's face. "What happened, Sam?" Sam winced. "They got the drop on me at the bar. I was lucky to make it out alive."

"I wish I had been there to help you," Miguel called out from across the room. "I do too, amigo," Sam said and grinned.

Sam handed the rope to Monique. "You go first."

Monique looked from Sam, to Misty, to Miguel. "No, Sam. Let Misty go first."

"Go, Monique!" Misty yelled. "You can run to Captain Kev so he can ready the boat."

"I'm not going," Monique said defiantly.

"Damn it, Monique! Get out that window now, or none of us will get out alive," Misty said.

Monique stared back at Misty and said, "You know, sometimes you can be stubborn." She grinned and added, "Just like me."

Monique walked over to Miguel and gave him a hug. "I'll be waiting for you, boyfriend. You better not stand me up." He kissed her on the lips. "That's one thing you never have to worry about. Now go on and get out of here."

Sam handed Monique the rope, and she climbed up onto the base of the window. When she looked at Sam, he said, "Just lean back and don't be afraid. As long as you keep your legs straight, you can literally walk down the wall backward." Monique gritted her teeth and did as instructed. After taking a few steps down the outside of the castle wall, she looked back up and said, "I've got this, Sam. See you at the boat."

Sam turned to Misty and said, "It's your turn."

"I'm not going next," she said.

"That's crazy talk," Miguel yelled from across the room. "Now get going."

Misty crossed her arms. "I want you to go help Monique make it back to the schooner. I'll hang back and come with Sam." Miguel knew how stubborn Misty could be when she had her mind made up, so he reluctantly returned to the window.

"Damn it, Misty! I'm going to go just so we don't waste anymore time, but I'm not happy about it." After grabbing the rope and climbing onto the ledge, he looked at Sam and said, "She's in your hands now. Don't let anything happen to her."

Misty had her head out the window, watching Miguel make his way down the wall, when shots ring out. She turned around to the sight of Sam on one knee, holding his left shoulder. He motioned for Misty to stay put, but she ran over to him anyway. Splinters flew into the air all around her from another round of shots. Sam pulled the .357 magnum out of its holster and fired back. The shells penetrated the wooden floor as if it were made out of balsa wood. The holes were so big, Misty could see through to the next floor. They heard footsteps running in the other direction. Misty pulled Sam's hand away from his left shoulder. When blood seeped out, she quickly replaced his hand and helped him press it tight. "Oh, Sam. It really looks bad."

"Help me to my feet," he said. "They know our last position, so we need to move."

Sam placed his good arm around Misty's shoulders as she wrapped an arm around his waist. He guided her over to his backpack. "Set me down here."

She eased him into a sitting position with his back supported by the wall. "I can't leave you now," she said. "You could never make it down that rope in your condition. Give me one of your guns, and I'll help you hold them off."

Sam placed his good hand on the side of Misty's face. "Now, you know I can't let you do that."

Tears streamed down her face.

Sam reached into his vest pocket, took out an old picture, and handed it to Misty. The women in the picture stood arm in arm. One was an older woman, and the other one appeared to be somewhat younger than Misty. She froze when it dawned on her the younger woman could have been mistaken for her sister.

"My wife and my daughter," he said. "You remind me so much of Sandy. She would have been about your age now."

"My age now. Oh, Sam. Please don't tell me she's dead."

Sam detected noise on the floor below and fired off the remaining three shells from his .357. Miguel yelled out to Misty from below, "Hurry up, Misty!"

"Go now!" Sam said as he reloaded the remaining shells into the cylinder of the magnum.

Misty glared into his face. "I'm not leaving until you tell me what happened to your daughter."

Sam sighed. "I was coming back from a mission overseas," he said. "I decided to stay over in Hawaii an extra day. When I got home, the police informed me someone had broken into our home and brutally murdered both my wife, Ginger, and Sandy."

"Oh God, no!" Misty said. "I am so sorry."

Sam looked at her with deep sadness in his eyes. "If I had only come home when I was supposed to, they would still be alive today."

Misty burst into tears. She wrapped her arms around the back of his head and pulled him into her bosom. "You can't blame yourself, Sam. You had no idea." She pulled back, looking into his face, "You poor man. What a heavy burden you have been carrying all these years."

"You've got to go now, Misty." Sam said. "I get some solitude in knowing my burden is almost over."

Misty rubbed the tears from her eyes with one hand as she held out the picture for Sam to take with her other. "No, I want you to keep it," he said. "I have no use for it where I'm going. Just promise you will keep it in a safe place." Misty placed her hand inside her shirt, pulled open her bra, and secured it between her bra and her bosom. "It will stay close to my heart, as will you."

Sam patted her arm. "Please, honey. Go now. You haven't much time." She looked over Sam's face, memorizing his every feature. She wiped the tears from her eyes again with her shirtsleeve and then leaned over and kissed Sam on the forehead. She stood up, stepped onto the ledge, and grabbed the rope. Misty looked back to Sam one last time and said, "Give 'em hell, Sammy boy," after which she repelled down the wall toward an awaiting Miguel. Sam placed the backpack in his lap and prepared for his final showdown.

* * *

Santo was standing just above Luigi on the ladder leading to the third floor. Santo wanted to impress Luigi by charging to the other side, but Sam's cannon blasts from the .357 rounds gave him pause. Antonio, who was still on the first floor, caught a glimpse of Miguel holding the bottom of the rope. "Hey!" he yelled. "They've got a rope and are climbing out the window."

"Well, go outside and shoot the bastard," Luigi yelled back.

Antonio ran to the front door and laid his shoulder into it. The jolt sent him to the floor. "They've locked us in," he yelled. Luigi and Santo gave each other a queer look. "Why would he lock himself inside with us?" Santo asked.

"Shoot at them through the slits in the wall," Luigi yelled to Antonio.

* * *

When her right foot slipped out from under her, Misty wished she had spent more time on the rock-climbing wall at her gym in Malibu. "Just let yourself down with your arms," Miguel yelled. "You're strong enough."

Miguel heard a gunshot and ducked. The rope became slack in his hands and a section of it fell onto his head. He looked up and saw Misty hanging onto the rope with her arms and legs. The rope below her had been severed just below her feet. He could see a gun sticking out of the wall on the second floor. "Swing to the wall and see if you can get a finger hold," Miguel said. "Someone's shooting at you from one of those slits."

After looking down and contemplating jumping, she decided against the twenty-foot fall. She would do as Miguel had suggested.

Worried that their adversaries would get away leaving them locked in the castle, Luigi placed his gun in the back of Santo's head and said, "Run over to the fourth floor ladder or I'll ventilate your brain."

Santo had little doubt Luigi meant what he said, so he rose onto the third floor and tiptoed across the room. He climbed up the fourth floor ladder, stopping just below the door in the floor. He had no idea Luigi had followed him until he felt a gun pressed in his back. "You're almost there," Luigi whispered.

Santo closed his eyes, clenched his teeth, and pushed the door open. Luigi used the momentum Santo had created to push him up and through the floor from behind. Sam picked up his Glock and put three rounds into Santo's chest. The next two shots rang from Luigi's gun, one penetrating Sam's chest. Sam looked at his chest and then to where the shots came from. Luigi was on the top step with his gun pointed at him. Sam's Glock fell out of his hand and onto the floor. Luigi climbed up and strolled over with his gun fixed on Sam's head. He kicked the Glock away, and then reached into Sam's holster and removed the .357 magnum.

Luigi held the gun up and looked it over. "I've always thought about getting one of these. I'm sure you won't mind if I keep it." Realizing Sam was in desperate straits, he looked out the window. "Well, what do we have here? I guess no castle would be complete without a damsel in distress."

Luigi knew Salvatore wanted Misty alive, but he had other plans. He walked back to Sam and knelt down. "Hang on a little while longer, buddy. I wouldn't want to rob you of the opportunity of witnessing me putting a bullet in your lady friend's head." Sam looked back at Luigi with eyes of stone.

"I can then place it by your side, the way I placed your other gun by the side of that poor young girl the authorities think you killed back at the bar. I'll just tell Salvatore you went on a shooting spree before I could bring her back. You might even become infamous."

Luigi stood up and walked toward the window. Sam's arms hurt like hell, but it didn't stop him from grabbing the batteries with one hand and the bare end of the lamp cord with his other. When the wire was only inches from the battery, Sam yelled out, "Hey, wise guy!" When Luigi turned around, Sam peered into his eyes resolutely. "I'll see you in hell."

Luigi watched as Sam touched the lamp cord to the negative end of the C battery, knowing all too well what it meant. The positively charged blasting cap waited for its wake-up call deep inside one of the blocks of C4. Sam had calibrated the sequence to take several seconds, just enough time to enjoy the anguish in Luigi's cantaloupe-sized eyes.

The four blocks of C4 exploded at 22,000 foot-pounds per second, causing a bright light, followed by a massive fireball that evaporated all the oxygen in the top two floors of the tower. The jolt knocked Misty off the rock wall, sending her crashing into the waiting arms of Miguel. The force knocked him to the ground. Miguel instinctively pushed Misty up against the side of the castle and lay on top of her. Massive chunks of stone crashed into the Caribbean, causing the sea water to shoot high into the air as if depth charges had just gone off beneath the water's surface. When the sky cleared, the water fell back to the sea, and the ringing in their ears subsided. Misty began screaming hysterically. Miguel covered her mouth with his hand and said in a consoling but strong voice, "Sam is gone, Misty. Nothing can bring him back."

Misty's eyes told Miguel she understood, so he removed his hand from her mouth. He helped her to her feet. "Are you okay? Anything broken?" She shook her head no.

Miguel took Misty by her hand, and they ran around to the other side of the tower. They found Mikey standing there, still looking up into the sky. Miguel patted him on the chest and said, "Come on, buddy. We've got to get moving."

When they got to the cave opening, they stopped to get one more look. The entire top half of the tower was blown away. Antonio was walking around on the second floor, looking out over the island with a pistol in his hand. "The bastard lived," Miguel said. "I wish I had one of Sam's firearms."

"You can't think about that now, Miguel," Misty said. "Don't worry. Men like him always get what's coming to them eventually."

Miguel and Misty turned and saw Miniature Mike pulling back on his bow. The arrow launched high in the sky with a trajectory taking it toward the castle. It landed twenty feet from Antonio, causing him to duck down. When he popped back up, Miguel yelled out, "You're going to pay for what you did, asshole!"

Miguel grabbed Misty by her arms and looked into her eyes. "Go on without me. I can't let Antonio get away with what he did to Monique."

"I know how you feel," she said softly. "But I can't let you do that. He's armed and you're not."

"It doesn't matter. I'll find a way. Please, Misty! He can't go unpunished."

"Let's not resolve this here. Come back to the boat so we can get Captain Kev to weigh in. You need help thinking this through."

Miguel let out a big sigh. "Okay, but I better like what he has to say."

28

THE NEXT DAY

Miniature Mike's arrow was enough to make Antonio leery, so he chose to remain in the castle until help arrived. Much of the night was spent securing the front door that had been jarred open from the blast. Knowing his miniature nemesis was fully capable of scaling the walls to the second floor, he had gotten little sleep. He spent the last hour sitting on the wall, trying to figure out how he was going to spin this whole thing to Salvatore. His most recent version included a heavily armed group of six ex-Special Forces descending on them. How could he be expected to ward off so many? Had Luigi not overruled him, Tomasso and Diego would have been there to help and maybe, just maybe, they would have prevailed, his story would go. He was working out the part about how he single-handedly killed two of the men when his eye caught movement out at sea. A closer inspection revealed the back end of a schooner, racing off under full sail. He could faintly hear Captain Kev barking out orders to his crew.

"Misty, let 'er rip. Miguel, you're learning, buddy. Come on, Mikey, quit slacking. Good job, Monique."

Antonio waited until the schooner was a speck in the distance before hurrying down the stairs. He pulled the limb from the door handle and laid his shoulder into the massive door, pushing with all his might. He squeezed through the small opening and walked to the shore's edge. There was no sight of the schooner, so he rummaged through the trees and thick undergrowth. Hearing a monkey in the distance, he removed the clip from his handgun. With only eight bullets left, he would have to take close aim at anything he came across that looked edible.

It would be another day before Tomasso and Diego showed up to check on them. Having come up empty in his search for food, he sat on a log and dreamed about having a wonderful Italian dinner at his favorite Vegas restaurant. That only made him hungrier, so he forced himself to get up and continue looking for food. Later that day, exhausted and weak, Antonio propped his head against a fallen log and drifted off. A few minutes later he awoke to something tickling his nose. He opened his eyes to the sight of Miniature Mike squatting in front of him with a twig in hand. Antonio reached for his gun but found it wasn't there. "Is this what you're looking for?" Miguel asked as he targeted Antonio's head.

"Miguel! Uh, that's your name, right?" Antonio said. When Miguel didn't answer, he continued, "Look, buddy. Let's not get carried away. I can assure you that if you kill me, Salvatore will come looking for you."

"Who said anyone will find your body?"

Angry and scared, Antonio slapped the twig out of Mikey's hand and said, "Get away from me, you little creep."

Mikey stood up and gave him a quick kick in his balls. Antonio doubled over in pain and coughed repeatedly. Mikey squatted again with the twig in his hand and continued to tickle Antonio's nose. When Antonio knocked the twig out of Mikey's hand a second time, Miguel struck him in the head with the butt of Antonio's pistol.

* * *

Later that evening, Antonio came to, groggy and disoriented. He raised his head enough to look in the direction of a large fire burning on the beach. Captain Kev and Miniature Mike were searching through a small chest. That's when he realized he was bound to a tree with his hands tied behind his back.

"I'll give you anything you want," Antonio yelled. "I know the combination to Salvatore's safe. I can pay you handsomely if you release me." But Captain Kev kept rummaging around in the chest.

Misty emerged from the darkness, and Antonio said, "Oh, thank God. Misty, you've got to talk some sense into those two."

Misty walked straight up to Antonio and smashed her fist into the side of his jaw. His chin fell against his chest, and Misty grabbed the back of his hair and yanked his head back. "That was for Sam, you bastard!"

"Sam? Who's Sam?" he asked.

"The man you beat up at the bar. The man who died in the explosion yesterday."

"Misty, I had nothing to do with that. I was on the second floor when that happened."

"So you're the bastard who shot my rope out from under me?" she asked.

Antonio was afraid to speak, worried he would dig himself a deeper hole.

Miguel came up from behind Antonio and plowed his fist into the back of his rib cage. "Oh, fuck, that hurts," Antonio said. As the pain subsided, he looked up at Miguel with indignation. "You're a brave man hitting me while I'm tied to a tree."

Miguel leaned in until their eyes were inches apart. "Would you like me to untie you? We can have a go at it, here and now." Antonio looked away. "I didn't think so," Miguel said.

Monique was the last to appear. She stood in front of him, her steely eyes piercing his soul. "About the other night," he stammered. "That was the rum talking, not me." He grinned. "I'm not myself when I get like that, sugar."

The captain walked up to Antonio with Mikey by his side and raised his prosthetic arm high into the air and flipped a switch. The tool on the end of his arm twirled around and around as Mikey grinned mischievously.

"Bend him over!" the captain bellowed.

Antonio's eyes opened wide. Misty stepped in between them and said to the captain, "Put that thing back, Captain Kev. We're not going to stoop to their level."

The captain laughed. "I was just fooling around with him," and then walked back over to his chest.

As the group packed up to leave, Antonio said, "Where are you going? You can't just leave me on this deserted island like this."

"Ah, hell," the captain said. "Somebody brought you out here. I imagine they will come back for you eventually." He cut Antonio loose. "Now run off before I go back and get my tool."

Antonio took off and then stumbled over a log. He scurried back to his feet and bolted into the underbrush.

"Do you really think someone will come back and get him, Captain?" Miguel said.

"Oh, I imagine."

"That's too bad." Miguel wrapped an arm around Monique and asked, "How're you doing, baby?"

She leaned her head on his shoulder and replied, "A little better. Let's go home."

They were on their way back within the hour.

29

SET A COURSE FOR HOME

Captain Kev moored the schooner on the wayward side of St. John's, a spot he knew would draw little attention. Mikey, Miguel, and Monique were sitting in the dinghy waiting for Misty so they could shove off. "Go on ahead without me," Misty yelled down. "There's someone I need to contact while we have cell service."

"Okay, Misty," Miguel replied. "We'll gather the provisions for the trip back to Buenos Aires and return pronto."

Misty went down to her living quarters, propped some pillows under her head, and placed her call. She got a recording that said, "Leave a message."

"Ivan, I need you now. Please call as soon as you receive this message."

Miguel and Mikey walked the aisles of the tiny general merchandise store. They loaded their handheld baskets, dropped the merchandise off at the front counter, and went back for more. The merchant sat behind the counter and grinned, knowing he was going to make a lot of money today.

Monique sat on the front porch watching a familiar car pulling up to the front of the store. When Big Mama got out, Monique rushed to greet her. Enveloped in Mama's bosom, Monique said, "I'm so glad you made it before we shove off."

"Why ya way out here, child?"

"Getting provisions for our trip."

"Where ya going?"

"It's best you don't know. I'm sure the authorities will find their way to you at some point, and the less you know the better." Monique pulled back to look at Mama and said, "I don't want you involved in any of this."

"You don't worry about Big Mama, honey child. I can take cares of myself." Mama looked around. "Where's Sam?"

Monique's eyes filled with tears. When Mama's face went pale, Monique helped her over to the bench. Monique kneeled in front of Mama and held her hands in hers. "He blew himself up to save us," she said and then placed her face in Mama's lap and cried.

Mama rubbed the back of Monique's head with her massive hand. "There's no need to cry, honey. Sam wuz carry a boatload of demons round with him. Now his poor soul can rest in peace."

Misty's cell phone rang, snapping her out of her melancholy state. "Sorry it took me so long," Ivan said. "How have you been?"

"Oh, Ivan. I'm afraid it's really bad this time."

"I'm sorry to hear that, Misty. Please take your time and fill me in on every detail."

A half hour later, Misty finished telling Ivan everything that had occurred from when they first set down in Las Vegas to the present. "I'm scared, Ivan."

"You're smart to be scared, sweetie. This is not over yet."

"Oh, that's reassuring!" she said with a laugh.

"I just didn't want you to get careless until I figure things out." Ivan paused and then said, "Misty, I'll handle this situation for you, just like the others. Go back to Buenos Aires and hole up in Gabriella's compound. I'll arrange for some men to keep an eye on the place so you will be safe."

"Should I call and tell Gabriella?" she asked.

"No need to tell anyone. The fewer people that know the better. My guys are ghosts. No one will ever know they are there."

"I'm sorry to get you into this, Ivan."

"I'm not. Things have been a little boring around here lately. Besides, it's always good to hear your voice."

"If you get me out of trouble, I promise I will call you sometime just to chat," she said.

Ivan laughed, "That's a deal," he said with a more serious tone, "Get back to Buenos Aires as soon as you guys can. I figure you've got about a forty-eight-hour head start. That should get you well on your way."

"We will, Ivan. I expect the boys back any time with our provisions. We'll set sail soon."

"Misty?"

"Yes, Ivan."

"I wish I could have met this Sam fella. He seems like a great guy."

"I do too, Ivan. The two of you would have gotten along just swell."

* * *

Two days out to sea, Miguel approached Captain Kev, who was rolling up rope near the aft of the schooner. "How much longer before we make Buenos Aires?"

"A few more days if the wind holds out," the captain replied.

Misty and Monique were sitting on the port side of the schooner, their feet stuck through the bottom of the railing. They were doing more staring out over the ocean than visiting. After looking their way, Miguel said to Captain Kev, "I'm worried about the girls, CK. They're just not themselves."

"Give them time," Captain Kev replied. "They have a lot to sort out. Soldiers coming back from war go through the same thing."

"How long do you suppose it will take?"

The captain placed his good hand on Miguel's shoulder. "All you can do is extend your love and support. Only Father Time can take care of the rest."

"Monique does seem to be handling things a little better than Misty," Miguel said.

"It's because she's gone through so much hardship in her life."

"I suppose you're right."

* * *

They approached Buenos Aires several days later, as Captain Kev had predicted. After mooring the schooner on the same rocky island they last moored the *Dirty Pirates*, they all got in the dinghy and rowed to shore. "We had one hell of a memorial for you guys," Miguel said.

Captain Kev pointed to the cliff beneath Gabriella's mansion and said, "We know. Mikey and I were sitting in a small cave right up there. We saw the whole thing. It brought a tear to me eye," he said laughingly as he pointed to his uncovered eye.

Captain Kev and Mikey bowed their heads, and the captain said, "May the *Dirty Pirates* rest in peace. She was one fine bucket of bolts."

Misty found Gabriella in the workout room doing sit-ups. She waited for her to stop and then said, "You're still the best-looking woman in Buenos Aires."

"You're home!" Gabriella yelled. She jumped up off the floor and ran over to Misty to give her a big hug. "I was the best-looking woman until you got home."

Gabriella noticed something different in Misty's eyes, but she decided not to delve into it yet. After welcoming the rest of the party, Gabriella said, "I'll instruct my cook to prepare a great feast. Let me go clean up, and I'll meet everyone on the veranda." Gabriella walked briskly out of the room and yelled, "Manuela, come quickly, we have guests."

Tom, Rosie, and Thor joined them for drinks. The mood was somber as they filled Tom and Thor in on what happened after they had left. Of course, Tom and Thor wished they had remained to help out. Rosie was relieved they had not, but she chose to keep it to herself. They toasted to the fact they were all alive and then said a prayer for Sam. They spent the evening enjoying a splendid dinner and then everyone decide to turn in.

Misty crawled into her familiar bed, but she had trouble going to sleep. She felt a presence and looked up. Gabriella was standing at her doorway. Misty sat up against the headboard. She patted the bed next to her. Gabriella snuggled up beside Misty and ran her hand softly through her hair. "I can feel the anguish you are going through," Gabriella said. "I wish there was something I could do."

"That's kind of you, Gabriella." Unfortunately, this is something I must get through on my own." She kissed Gabriella on the top of her head. "I will try not to be too much of a burden to you."

Gabriella said, "You could never be a burden to me. Take all the time you need."

30

GETTING DOWN TO BUSINESS

Several weeks later, in a small town in Sicily, Ivan waited patiently out-side a small cafe. Soon, a heavyset man with two bodyguards by his side approached Ivan's table. Ivan's eyes remained intently on his newspa-per, while he discretely reached inside his overcoat and embraced his weapon. "May I join you?" the man asked.

Ivan lowered the newspaper and smiled, "I would be disappointed if you did not."

The bodyguards remained standing, and the rotund man settled into his chair. "So you are the one they call the Phantom?" the man asked.

"Oh, I've been called by plenty of other names in my time," Ivan said with a smile.

"Yes, I have referred to you in those terms myself," he replied with a frown. "You have killed some of my best men."

"It was all in the line of work, Mateo. Never personal," Ivan said as he raised his coffee cup to his lips and took a sip. "You have wonderful coffee in Sicily. Should I have the waiter bring you some?"

"An espresso, if you please."

"Waiter!" Ivan called out. "L'espresso, per favore."

"The CIA sending an agent all the way from the States just to visit a humble merchant is quite the compliment. I am honored."

"Merchant?" Ivan asked. "Yes, I think we both know what your merchandise is. That, however, is not why I have come to see you."

Mateo sat back and looked at each of his bodyguards and then asked, "Business of a personal nature seldom ends well, my friend."

When Ivan began removing his hand from his overcoat, the two bodyguards reached inside their coats and placed their hands on their pistols. They relaxed when they found Ivan's hand empty. After placing both hands face down on the table, Ivan said, "I'm here to talk, nothing else."

"Then we shall talk," Mateo said, as he waved off his men.

"I'm here to extend my personal condolences," Ivan said. "I had great admiration for Luigi as a professional. It's too bad he and I will never get the chance to find out who was the better man."

Mateo tried to conceal his anger, but his eyes betrayed him. "Luigi was my nephew. You need to choose your next words carefully."

"I bring no disrespect. My condolences are sincere," Ivan said as he looked to each bodyguard. "I just hated to see your nephew die over such a trivial matter, is all."

Mateo sat back to mull things over. The waiter brought out his espresso and set it front of him. Mateo took a sip and then looked at Ivan. "I was told otherwise. Please explain yourself."

"Luigi died because Salvatore sent him after a piece of ass. He hired the woman first to be his physical trainer and then to sleep with him. When she changed her mind and fled, Salvatore sent Luigi after her."

"What proof of this do you have?"

Ivan raised his hands and then slowly reached inside his satchel. He pulled out a document and placed it in front of Mateo.

Mateo became visibly upset as he read through a copy of Salvatore's contract with Misty. He looked at Ivan inquisitively and asked, "Why is this of such importance to you?"

Ivan leaned in and said in a serious tone, "The trainer is a personal friend of mine. Should anything happen to her, I will deal with Salvatore personally."

"You will have to get in line, my friend."

Ivan eased back in his chair. "Then I will leave the matter in your capable hands."

"Is that all you want in return for your information?" Mateo asked.

Ivan replied, "Well, there is one more thing."

31

The Visitors

"I'm so glad you could come. I know it will mean a lot to Misty," Gabriella said to her new guests.

"So I finally get to meet the infamous Gabriella," the man said. Looking over to his two companions, he added, "It was gracious of you to fly us here."

"Yes, I have always wanted to visit South America," the lady said.

"Come. Let me take you to Misty," Gabriella said.

"You go on alone, dear," the lady said.

Gabriella stopped just outside Misty's bedroom and whispered, "I have tried everything, but I'm afraid Misty's sinking deeper into depression. As you can see, it's three in the afternoon and she's still in bed."

"I'll see what I can do," he said.

After Gabriella left, he composed himself before knocking lightly on her door. "I'll get up soon, Gabriella. Just give me a few more minutes," Misty called out.

He pushed the door open just enough to be seen.

"Rob! What are you doing in Buenos Aires?"

She sat up as he walked across the room and sat on the edge of her bed. Reaching out, he took her hand in his and said, "Gabriella is worried about you. I'm supposed to be here to cheer you up. Can you believe that?"

"You look wonderful, Rob. How have you been?"

"We're doing fine. I'm still consulting, but I only accept projects close to home these days."

"I assume you are referring to you and Amelia."

"We missed you at our wedding," he said sincerely.

"I thought about it, but it just felt better this way." Misty placed her hand on the side of his face. "I'm so sorry things didn't work out for us, Rob. I often regret the way things ended."

Rob patted her on her thigh, "You shouldn't. Things turned out for the best in the end."

"I better get dressed," she said excitedly. "Just give me a few minutes."

"No hurry," Rob said. "We're going to be here several days."

"Amelia came with you?"

"Yes, she's waiting for you in the living room."

Misty sprang out of bed and walked toward the bathroom. She turned and said to Rob as he reached the door, "I'm really glad you came, Rob."

"Yes, it's been far too long since we've seen each other," he said and smiled.

After taking a shower, Misty decided to put on something nicer than the jeans she had been wearing for the past several weeks. She looked herself over one more time in the mirror and headed out. All eyes were on Misty as she walked into the room. "Hello, Misty," Amelia said. "It's great to see you again."

Misty eyes were drawn immediately to the baby girl clinging to her mother's neck. Amelia placed the little girl in her right arm and said, "She's nine months old."

Misty walked over and held her hands out. "May I?" she asked.

"Of course," Amelia replied and handed the little girl over. Misty's lips closed gently around the little girl's finger as she reached for Misty's nose.

"She is so adorable," Misty said. "What's her name?"

"Misty," Rob said.

Misty's face went pale. She turned tentatively toward Amelia, not understanding how Rob could do such a thing to his wife, but Amelia only smiled warmly back at her.

"It was actually Amelia's idea," Rob said.

Misty continued to stare at Amelia, dumbfounded.

"It's okay, Misty," Amelia said. "It was my way of thanking you for getting Rob and me back together and graciously exiting."

"Actually, we were wondering if you would like to be her godmother," Rob said.

Misty kissed the little girl's cheeks over and over. "How could I possibly say no?" she said. "It would be an honor."

Over the next week, Misty carried little Misty everywhere, as if they were joined at the hips. Misty bathed her, dressed her, and fed her whenever possible.

Sitting out back by the pool one day, Misty pulled the young girl into her bosom and imagined what it would be like if the child were her own. But then she remembered the day the doctor told her she was incapable of bearing children. *Maybe we should have adopted*, she thought, wondering if she and Rob would still be together if they had. But now she had the opportunity to play a small part in the child's life, and for that she was grateful.

Rob and Miguel had much to catch up on as Gabriella played tour guide to Amelia and Monique. Captain Kev and Miniature Mike spent their time making sure that their schooner, which they had renamed *Sammy Boy*, was seaworthy. Miguel was pretty certain they were making plans for some far-off adventure.

On the morning Rob and Amelia were leaving for the airport, Misty reluctantly handed little Misty over to Amelia.

"I'm afraid I haven't left you much time with your own child these last few days," Misty said apologetically.

"Nonsense," Amelia replied. "After nine months, a mother can use a break."

Misty kissed little Misty on her forehead and walked over to Rob. "I'm really glad you came, Rob, and I'm so happy for the three of you."

Rob gave her a big hug. "Goodbye, Misty. Come visit us in Malibu soon, will you?"

"I promise," she replied.

They waved good-bye to their friends as they left with Tom to the airport. Misty turned to give Gabriella a hug and said, "That was very thoughtful of you, Gabby."

"I was worried about you, dear. I had to try something."

"Well, it's a start," Misty said.

* * *

While they were all having breakfast the next morning, Misty spent her time observing Gabriella and Alex, the man Gabriella met while she was away. Alex was tall, handsome, and sophisticated. He seemed to be a genuinely nice guy, and she felt they made a darling couple. Her evaluation of Alex was interrupted when the phone rang. "It's for you, Misty," Gabriella said. "It's Gary."

Misty strode across the floor to retrieve the phone from Gabriella's hands. "Gary! What a pleasant surprise!"

"I'm so glad I found you," Gary said. "Do you know how many Gabriellas there are in Buenos Aires?"

"Why didn't you just call me on my cell phone?"

"Because it's been turned off for the last two weeks."

"Oh yeah," Misty said. "So what's the occasion? Or do you just miss me?"

"I have missed you, but that's not why I'm calling."

"So, what's the big news?"

"Are you sitting down?" Gary asked.

Misty sat on the couch and said, "I am now."

"Last night, Salvatore and Antonio were gunned down in their parking garage, execution-style."

"Oh my God!" Misty said. She looked at Miguel and Monique. "Salvatore and Antonio were murdered last night."

Miguel rose from the breakfast table and pumped his fist into the air. "There is a God after all!"

Monique covered her open mouth as she attempted to digest the news.

"Do they know who did it?" Misty asked Gary.

"My FBI contacts are treating it as a family feud. Salvatore must have pissed off someone at a very high level."

"So, how are you doing, Gary?"

"I couldn't be better. This morning a man walked in my place and said he was taking control of Salvatore's hotel/casino."

"That was fast," Misty said.

"That's what I thought. It was almost as if it had been planned before the murders. But wait until you hear this. He apologized for the way Salvatore had been treating me. He said that he respected my right to own and operate Devil's Cove and suggested we run cross promotions."

"That Ivan," Misty said.

"Ivan?" Gary asked. "Who's Ivan?"

"Oh, nothing. Never mind," Misty answered with a big grin on her face. "So when's your girlfriend, Guinevere, coming home?"

"I called her this morning and she's making arrangements now."

"That's wonderful, Gary. I'll make a point to visit you in Vegas so I can meet her next time I'm in the States."

"That would be just terrific! I know the two of you would get along well. Maybe we can all spend a weekend in the mountains."

"Ha!" Misty said. "Wouldn't that be fun! So, Gary?"

"Yes."

"Don't go shooting up things with that Buffalo rifle to celebrate."

Gary laughed out loud. "Now there's a thought. Bye, Misty. See you soon."

"See you soon, Gary. Thanks for giving me the good news."

Misty turned to the group and said, "I think I'm going to take a walk on the beach to sort things out." When Miguel picked up his jacket to accompany her, she said, "I need to be alone, Migs."

"Sure, Misty. I understand."

Misty made it to one of her favorite spots and took a seat on a large piece of driftwood that had washed up on the beach. Little Misty had stirred something deep inside. Something that caused her to be truly intro-spective for one of the few times in her life. She relived each adventure in her mind, trying to make sense of them in their totality. Finally it came to her in a flash. She had in essence been doing everything she could to escape commitment of any kind. With commitment came sacrifices. But then she realized with sacrifice came reward. If Sam could make the ultimate sacrifice, how could she not at least meet the people she loved halfway?

Misty found Gabriella and said, "I need to fly back to the States."

"How long will you be gone?"

"I'm really not sure."

Gabriella put her arm around Misty and said, "I understand, dear. If you had decided earlier, you could have flown back on my jet with Rob and Amelia."

"That's okay. I can go commercial."

"I'll have Tom take care of the arrangements. I assume two tickets will be in order?"

"No," Misty said. "I won't be taking Miguel on this trip."

"I see," she replied.

Misty found Miguel, Monique, Captain Kev, and Miniature Mike on the terrace. She walked up to Miguel and patted him on his arm. "I'm leaving for the states tomorrow," she said.

"You're leaving?" Miguel asked. "What about me?"

"Not this trip, Migs. I'm sorry."

"So, how long will you be gone?"

"I'm not sure, but it could be for a while."

"So what am I supposed to do while you are gone?"

Misty said to Captain Kev, "I've been watching you taking provisions to your schooner. Where are you guys off to?"

"I hear Tahiti's kind of nice this time of year."

"Tahiti's kind of nice year round," Misty replied.

The captain laughed, "I suppose you're right. Tahiti it is then." The captain turned to Mikey and asked, "Okay with you?"

Mikey grinned and began hula dancing.

Misty walked over to Miguel and Monique and put her arms around them. "Why don't you guys go along? You could use a vacation after all of these years, Miguel."

Monique looked at Miguel and said, "What do you think?"

"I think I've got a better idea," Miguel said. He looked at Misty. "I hear Elite Fitness is up for sale back in Malibu. I might have just saved up enough of my salary over the years to make a run at it."

"Is that what would make you happy?" Misty asked.

Miguel turned back to Monique and said, "If you'll come back to help me run it." Monique wrapped her arms around Miguel and held him tight. "You bet, lover boy," she said into his ear.

"How about I help you out by being a partner," Misty said. "Me, too," said Captain Kev, with Mikey quickly nodding in approval.

"What about me?" Gabriella asked. "I love being a silent partner."

Miguel looked around the room at his friends. "Now I know I—I mean we—can afford to buy the place. Would you mind handling the negotiations for me, Gabriella?"

"Why sure, Miguel. Consider it ours."

After everyone had gone their way, Misty spent the evening alone with Gabriella. With a few after-dinner drinks in hand, they stood arm and arm, overlooking the Atlantic Ocean.

"Are you going to be okay without me for a while?" Misty asked.

"No!" Gabriella said playfully. "But life goes on. As long as you're happy, I'm happy, dear."

"Same here, Gabby." Misty said. "Come on. Let's make this a night to remember."

Gabriella gave Misty a long, slow kiss. "Let's do it on the beach," she said.

"That's a good place to start," Misty replied with a mischievous grin.

32

FOLLOWING HER HEART

The plane touched down at the airport at four in the afternoon. She was both anxious and excited as she wondered if she was doing the right thing. She looked the crowd over as she rode down the escalator to the luggage area, slightly disappointed when she didn't see the person she was looking for. Her anxiety overpowered her excitement, and her hands shook as she grabbed her luggage from the carousel. A hand reached out and grabbed her bag, dragging it behind her. She turned around to the sight of Travis's smiling face. Her excitement returned with such intensity, she could feel her heart flutter. Misty placed her arms around his neck and they hugged. She gave his ponytail a slight tug. "Growing it back, I see."

"It's not as long as when you first met me, but it's getting there," he said. "Come on. Let's go home."

Home, she thought. *Is there really such a place?*

Misty climbed in the front seat of Travis's pickup and watched him put her luggage in the back of the truck. He still filled out his jeans better than any man she had ever known. She remembered the first time she saw him at the gym and how she had chased after him until they became an item. Travis was well educated and was in line to make partner at a prestigious investment banking firm in New York, but having grown up in Texas, he ultimately preferred ranching. Not many men had that kind of depth. Now she wondered what she could have been thinking the day she left him in New York City.

As they rode along interstate 10 on their way to the ranch, Travis looked at Misty and said, "There's something different about you."

"I've been through a lot lately," she said as she watched the countryside go by her window.

"When are you taking on your next client?"

"I'm not sure I am," she said softly.

They rode the next few miles in silence before Travis asked, "How long do you plan on staying?"

"How long can I?" Misty asked as she continued to look out her window.

"Keep paying your dues, and you'll be fine for a long time," he said with a grin.

Misty unbuckled her seat belt and moved over next to Travis, placing her head on his shoulder and patting his thigh. Travis gave her a quick kiss on her forehead.

When Travis pulled off the main highway and navigated his way down the narrow, windy ranch road, Misty rolled down the truck window and breathed in the fresh country air. The solitude of being in the middle of thousands of acres of private ranchland made her feel safe and secure.

"Seen George lately?" she asked.

"He was at the water hole last night. I'm sure you'll run into him in due time."

"Yeah, that's what I'm worried about," she said laughingly. "That hog scared the crap out of me."

"Now you know not to mess with the little piglets."

"Lesson learned!" she said with a quick laugh.

Once home, Misty put her things away and joined Travis on the back porch. "How are Brenda and Buddy doing?" she asked.

"Brenda pretty much stays on Mustang Island these days, leaving the ranching to me. They got married, you know."

"I didn't. How wonderful. Visiting Brenda and Buddy is on my list of things to do," Misty said as she held onto a post and looked out over the back property.

"That's all that's on your list?" he asked with eyebrows raised.

"Hmmm. Let's add country dancing at Texas Hall, tubing down the Guadalupe River, and spending the day on Lake Travis to that list as well."

She smiled at Travis. "Blake can tag along too if you want."

"That would make his day," Travis said and laughed. "How about a drink?"

"Absolutely! Make mine bourbon," she said.

Misty sat curled up to Travis on his back-porch bench as they watched the sun fade over the mesquite trees. After a period of silence, Misty said, "I'm still pretty messed up right now, you know."

"There's times you're not?" he asked.

"Stop it!" Misty said as she slapped his chest. "Seriously, I had a horrific experience. A man died saving my life."

"I'm sorry," Travis said. "I had no idea."

"That's okay; you had no way of knowing."

"I'm afraid that's something you're going to have to learn to live with the rest of your life."

"I know," she said. "I know."

When the sun was only a memory, she kissed Travis on his cheek and said, "How about we go get reacquainted, cowboy."

Travis stood from the bench and offered Misty his hand, which she took. She stopped at the bedroom door and looked into his eyes. "I don't want to just have sex," she said. "Make love to me tonight."

"Are you certain?" he asked

"I'm as certain as I've ever been about anything."

Travis wrapped an arm around her waist, placed his other under her knees, and lifted Misty effortlessly into the air. "Then you *have* changed," he said as he carried her across their bedroom threshold.